THE SPIRIT COLLECTION OF THORNE HALL

**Also available by J. Ann Thomas
(writing as Jamie Thomas)**

The Shining City

The Forest Kingdom

Asperfell

THE SPIRIT COLLECTION OF THORNE HALL

A Novel

J. ANN THOMAS

alcove press

This is a work of fiction. All of the names, characters, organizations, places and events portrayed in this novel are either products of the author's imagination or are used fictitiously. Any resemblance to real or actual events, locales, or persons, living or dead, is entirely coincidental.

Copyright © 2025 by Jamie Thomas

All rights reserved.

Published in the United States by Alcove Press, an imprint of The Quick Brown Fox & Company LLC.

Alcove Press and its logo are trademarks of The Quick Brown Fox & Company LLC.

Library of Congress Catalog-in-Publication data available upon request.

ISBN (hardcover): 979-8-89242-022-8
ISBN (paperback): 979-8-89242-223-9
ISBN (ebook): 979-8-89242-023-5

Cover design by Marisa Ware

Printed in the United States.

www.alcovepress.com

Alcove Press
34 West 27th St., 10th Floor
New York, NY 10001

First Edition: February 2025

10 9 8 7 6 5 4 3 2 1

For my family, and especially for Brian—let's grow
old together, and then find a nice house to
haunt somewhere in the Berkshires.
It's lovely there in the fall.

LAND ACKNOWLEDGMENT

This book was written on the traditional lands of the Wenatchi, Yakama, Puyallup, and Mohican peoples.

CHAPTER ONE

October 31, 1902

Willie Abner really ought to have listened to his grandmother.

She had that morning predicted snow by virtue of her aching hip, the patterns of the veins on her left ankle, and the droppings of the raven who had figured out how to lift the rusty latch of the kitchen window and helped himself to a bit of cake now and then. With nary a cloud in the vibrant blue of the cold autumn morning outside her doughty cottage, Willie had declared the very idea ridiculous, earning a pot thrown in the general vicinity of his head. Now, a wary glance at the swiftly gathering gray determined to blot out what little remained of the waning moon made him wish he'd worn woolens beneath his borrowed livery.

Hell, if the old bat had had her way, he would never have left his room at Bidwell House that Samhain evening, however handsomely he stood to be paid for his service, for 'twas an ill omen indeed that the last and greatest of the old sabbats fell upon a Friday that year, even if one was properly outfitted against unseasonable weather.

Blowing furiously into his cupped hands, the tall reed of a boy, all of twenty-four and made of gangling limbs and gaunt hollows, stared down the drive at the endless string of carriages waiting their turn to pass beneath the impressive porte cochere of Thorne Hall and deposit their glittering burdens. He'd never seen so many in one place; it would take an age to get them all through, particularly as they were, at present, waylaid by a regrettable taffeta skirt and an even more regrettable bustle, both belonging to Mrs. Vera Bishop. She was attempting to negotiate, rather poorly, the extradition of her person from a handsome black-and-gold carriage, while her husband scowled and sighed and was absolutely of no help at all. He was every bit as long as she was squat, and where she was of a jovial disposition, he was as dour as a churchyard angel and far less comely.

"Good evening," said Willie, once Mrs. Bishop had smoothed her skirts and slipped her pudgy fingers into the crook of Mr. Bishop's elbow. "Welcome to Thorne Hall."

"Yes, well," she tutted, thrusting her nose into the air as though it were a terrible affront indeed to have endured such deplorable conditions as languishing on a cushioned seat beneath a velvet blanket. "We've been waiting for half of an hour, what say you to that?"

"I am dreadfully sorry," he stammered, the words clumsy on his freezing lips. "There are a great many visitors to the manor tonight, as you see."

Invitations to some thirty households had been sent out, and every single one accepted. And still, the sight of them rendered him somewhat stupid, for he was, by occupation, but a footman at a country house some five miles away and the largest party he'd ever seen was a gathering of twenty very old and very slow residents of the Berkshires. That had been a quiet supper of only four courses, followed by card games in the parlor and an early dismissal. There had been very little drinking and no dancing, and he'd spent most of the evening in the kitchens flirting with the cook's assistant until, at the pathetically early hour of ten 'o clock, he was summoned to see grumbling old women and their stone-faced husbands back into their carriages.

The event this evening at Thorne Hall was so grand that the three footmen whom Mr. Jasper Thorne had brought from his Boston mansion would not suffice at all, and so Willie had been hired along with several other local youths, particularly in the kitchens, for there would be a dinner for three dozen guests prior to the promised entertainment afterward. Said entertainment, which had been kept entirely secret even from the staff, would be witnessed by an additional twenty guests, acquaintances of Mr. Thorne whom he wished to impress but in whose company he did not fancy spending the length of ten courses.

"Humph," Mrs. Bishop grunted. "Jasper had better deliver what he's promised. It's a long way to travel from the city this late in the season. Thank goodness he's a room for us, else we simply would not have come!"

The Spirit Collection of Thorne Hall

Willie thought this in poor taste indeed, for it seemed worth the journey simply to glimpse the famed Thorne Hall. The three-story Jacobean Revival manor at his back was laid in red brick and brownstone trim, with ornate spires rising from each gabled wing and banks of leaded and stained-glass windows. Why, the porte cochere beneath which Mrs. Bishop's carriage now stood was said to be the finest in the Berkshires. And he'd yet to see inside!

The Bishops' carriage moved on, and Willie met the next, out of which stepped a younger gentleman who had survived the lengthy wait by draining a flask that he now tucked into his pocket as he stumbled down the steps from his hansom cab.

On and on it went, until the last of the dinner guests were seen safely into the manor and Willie was sent to the kitchens to warm himself and eat before those who had been invited only to the entertainment began to arrive.

He found a place at the end of the long, hand-hewn table, and one of the kitchen maids, a buxom, golden young woman near his age, placed a bowl before him. "You'd best eat," she told him with a wink. "You look as though one strong gale could knock you clean over."

"I'm not *that* skinny," Willie grumbled, taking up a battered spoon and tucking in. The cook had prepared a lamb stew for those below that evening, and he shoveled it into his mouth with gusto.

The kitchen maid returned with a basket of brown bread still steaming from the oven, and Willie pressed his advantage. "What do you think he's got planned tonight after the dinner?"

"I really couldn't say," the girl hedged, her eyes darting to the kitchen doorway, where a stout woman of perhaps fifty with ruddy cheeks and steel curls beneath her white cap was glaring at them.

At the end of the table, a middle-aged man polishing a set of silver teaspoons spoke without looking up: "He's dabbling in the occult."

Willie's eyes widened, spoon frozen halfway to his mouth. "A séance?"

"Nah." The man placed a gleaming teaspoon down upon the table with a thump, then looked up with a grin. "Everyone's done those, haven't they? Jasper Thorne isn't everybody."

"What do you mean by that?"

"Word is the master's playing at raising the dead."

"You're teasing," the kitchen maid admonished, flicking the man with the end of her dish towel, but he paid her no mind. "He never is!"

"That's impossible."

Willie hadn't realized he'd spoken until he lifted his eyes from his bowl to find the man watching him with lips curled in amusement.

"Know something of it, do you?"

In fact, he did, but he wasn't about to say so in present company, and so he shook his head and concentrated on nothing but his supper until the man finished his work and left the room whistling. Willie finished the last of his stew and bolted back up the steps and into the vicious night, where a distant voice could be heard shouting his name none too kindly.

It was half past ten by the time all of the latecomers had been seen into the house and Willie was at last permitted inside to serve glasses of champagne and spirits to Mr. Thorne's guests in the great hall, and aptly named it was.

Rich, dark-wood floors and intricate paneling gleamed beneath beamed ceilings, and at its heart was an enormous marble hearth flanked with pillars, atop which sat two proud lions with diamonds at their feet. Directly opposite was the gallery, the long corridor leading to the ballroom where that evening's entertainment was to take place, roped off with cords of velvet until such a time as the master of Thorne Hall bid them enter.

To the immediate left of the front entrance stood the famous oak staircase, a towering marvel of superior craftsmanship. It was rumored to have been inspired by the staircase at Tilden House, a Jacobean manor in the English countryside outside Lincolnshire where Thorne Hall's mistress had spent a summer or two as a girl; when consulting with the pair of architects Jasper had hired from the city, she had declared she wanted a staircase not to match but to rival that of not only Tilden but all other houses in the Berkshires.

Thus, the four pillars and nine panels that bordered the twenty-five stairs from the first to the second floor were intricately carved in patterns of diamonds and peacock feathers, flowers and filigree, polished and gleaming, and crowned with soaring arches.

Some ten feet above the great hall but only midway to the second floor, a cunning landing was furnished with several brocade chairs as well as a newfangled invention known as a two-seater, meant to facilitate intimate conversation, before the marvelous stairway proceeded upward upon the right to the second and third floors. The usual furniture had been relocated for the occasion, save for a grand piano in one corner of the great hall near a bank of stained-glass windows that led to the veranda, alight with torches and, beyond, the sprawling lawn that gave way to the thick unruliness of a New England forest.

The Spirit Collection of Thorne Hall

Willie was instructed by Cartwright, the butler, to assist at the champagne table, where he wore white gloves and handed out coupes of effervescent gold alongside Jasper's first footman, a handsome man called Felix, perhaps ten years Willie's senior with perfectly coiffed black hair.

The cheerful strains of a string quartet drifted from the landing as Jasper Thorne's guests drank and laughed. And amongst them moving here and there, with a coupe of champagne in hand, was the most beautiful woman Willie had ever seen. She'd hair like flame and she wore it piled atop her head and crowned with diamonds, which also dripped from her ears and neck and gleamed at her wrists. There was not a soul who could deny that her gown of gold silk was the finest in the room, nor that her smile was the most blinding.

No one needed to tell Willie who she was, though he'd never set eyes upon her before that night.

Delilah Thorne, the mistress of Thorne Hall.

It was said that the manor stood only as testament to how much Delilah loved a party and how much her husband loved Delilah. Willie could well believe it. He was as helplessly entranced as the rest of them, basking in what little glow was to be had as she flirted and charmed and laughed, the sound purer than the crystal in his trembling fingers. But the more Willie watched her, and he could not seem to help himself, the more he noticed that her smile only lingered so long as her admirers did. In the moments between one and the next, her expression thinned.

Willie could scarcely fathom what cause someone like Delilah Thorne might have to fret. Perhaps she was simply exhausted. Events such as these, with so many guests and arrangements and accommodations, must be consuming.

At long last, Mr. Thorne's guests were invited to make their way to the ballroom.

Willie's spine straightened as the excited chatter grew to a crescendo, the crowd surging forward as though a dam had broken, and amidst the kerfuffle, he heard the sound of glass shattering upon the floor, followed by the crunch of heels treading upon it carelessly. There would be an awful mess to clean later, but Willie was too excited to worry over it.

The ballroom was anything but intimate. Twenty marble columns held aloft a gilded ceiling of intricately carved leaves and flowers that seemed a more fit canopy for an ancient Athenian temple to Chloris than a dwelling place for mortal man. Gold stanchions hung with velvet cords partitioned off the center of the magnificent room. Guests crowded the perimeter and whispered amongst themselves regarding what had been painted upon the wood floor: a white circle made of strange symbols with four cardinal points illuminated by the flickering flames of hundreds of beeswax candles.

At the center, a woman stood alone.

She was perhaps in her late twenties, with enormous gray eyes and hair the color of honey that spilled over her shoulders in a wild, tangled mess. Her lips were full and wide, and her chin pointed above the impossibly high neck of the black crepe gown she wore, long out of fashion. She was not beautiful, not in the way Delilah was beautiful, or any of the number of glittering young woman who gawked at her as though she were an exhibit at a fair, but Willie found himself unable to look away from her for long.

Behind her in a row stood four other women who bore such a startling resemblance that he thought they must be kin. They all wore the same sort of black dress with their pale hair free and falling. The oldest was close to his grandmother in age, while the youngest could not be more than ten. How very strange that she should be present when, Willie knew, Mr. Thorne's own son and daughter, older than she, had been left with their governess in the city.

A hush descended upon the crowd as a tall, sharp-featured man entered the room. Willie recognized him at once from his picture in the newssheets. He was even more striking in person, his thick black hair only just beginning to silver at the temples, and like his beguiling wife, he exuded a force so magnetic that the spines of every man in his general vicinity straightened.

'Twas said in certain circles that he'd been born with figures upon his tongue and that by the time he was but six years of age, could reliably speak on the subject of strategy and profit and investments. He'd made his first million at the age of eighteen, and by the time he was thirty, half the world was safe and secure in his pocket. For all its magnificence, Thorne Hall was only his summer cottage; he'd a mansion on Fifth Avenue whose ballroom could easily hold a thousand guests and several other properties scattered along the New England coast, as well as two in London.

"Ladies and gentlemen," he said, and although he'd not raised his voice, the room immediately fell silent. "Delilah and I welcome you all to Thorne Hall this Samhain night. Some of you have traveled quite far, and I hope you will believe me when I say it was a trip well worth taking—if not for the entertainment, then certainly for the champagne."

His roguish wink drew good-humored chuckles from his guests, and even Willie found himself smiling, though he'd not tasted a drop.

"By now I am sure you have heard rumors of what is to transpire, but before we begin, let me assure you that this is no charlatan performing a sham séance for the naïve and gullible. You will find no children scurrying beneath a shrouded table nor mechanisms meant to mimic miracles. What you will see here tonight is as real as I am."

As he spoke, Mr. Thorne walked slowly toward the woman who stood apart and, once he'd reached her, placed his hands upon her narrow shoulders. Out of the corner of his eye, Willie watched Delilah stiffen and look away.

"This woman is a true medium, and tonight she will summon the dead to stand before you."

There was no laughing now; the room was flooded with murmurs, of whispers and titters. Only Willie knew the truth: Jasper Thorne was a liar.

Oh, there was many a thing that could be done with the canny arts, or so said his mum. She ought to know, being what she was, and sometimes death was very near them, what with their tenets being the very stuff of it: blood and bone, earth and song. But a true death could not be reversed, she said; not without sacrifice, and not without a black curse upon them who'd done it.

Unease unfurled in Willie's stomach at the memory of a wailing woman at the door of their cottage in the black of night when he was just a boy, come because she'd heard a whisper that his mother could do the very thing Mr. Thorne claimed this medium capable of.

The woman had left disappointed. She'd also left with no memory of her dead lover, for when Willie's mother refused to raise him from the dead, she'd paid her two gold coins to eradicate him from her heart entirely instead. After the woman had gone and his mother had stashed the coins away in a small, hand-carved wooden box, her eyes had flickered to where he cowered at the threshold of the room, and she beckoned him forth.

"What are you doing awake at this hour?" she said as she went down upon one knee before him.

Willie worried his lower lip. "Could you have done it? Brought him back?"

"I could have."

"Why didn't you?"

His mother was silent for so long that he feared she'd gone away as she sometimes did, until at last she asked him, "Do you remember the song about the woman sitting upon her lover's final resting place?"

"'The Unquiet Grave,'" answered Willie; he hated that song.

"And do you remember why the dead man does not want her there?"

"He is sad because she's withered away."

"And why else?" his mother prompted gently.

Willie's voice fell to a whisper: "She grieves so much he cannot find rest."

"I do expect, of course, absolute discretion on the part of you all," Jasper Thorne continued. "Nay, I insist upon it."

The slant of his brows, the firm set of his jaw, the way his piercing blue eyes swept over the hushed assembly told them all well enough what would become of them should they defy him. It was nearly as frightening as the idea of the undead.

"But is it safe?" a woman's voice called. Clad in aubergine silk with a collar of diamonds at her throat, she clutched her husband's arm with wide eyes. This was a sentiment evidently shared by a great many others in the crowd, for they looked at Mr. Thorne with the same trepidation.

"You've naught to worry," Mr. Thorne replied smoothly. "You are perfectly safe within these walls."

And because Jasper Thorne's word was law, they began.

None of those gathered wished to be anywhere near the white drawings upon the ballroom floor, and so the medium and the women who accompanied her were afforded a wide berth as they each took their place. Once they had clasped their hands and dropped their heads, the medium began to sing in a clear, pleasing voice, the melody both beguiling and unsettling. Willie's flesh prickled; he'd never heard the tune before, but his bones recognized its likeness as sure as though he'd penned it himself. Anyone with even an ounce of canny in their blood could tell at once if a song could anchor craft. And this song . . .

The medium's sisters picked up the threads of her song one by one and wove them together, unison giving way to dissonance that resolved in harmony all too briefly.

The windows in the ballroom had not been opened that evening, but nevertheless a breeze began to stir, gently ruffling silk and satin, prompting uneasy glances amongst the glittering throng. Many present that night would later swear that with that strange breeze came the caress of fingertips upon the neck of this diamond-encrusted socialite here and this portly banker there, and yet none left. Willie could not be

The Spirit Collection of Thorne Hall

certain whether this was because they were still convinced that, as at other séances they'd attended, this show of Jasper Thorne's was just that: a show, however realistic. Money, they supposed, could create all manner of illusions to delight and terrify the senses.

And then there were those who believed.

They believed that the wraithlike woman standing before them, clad in black to her neck, with her pale skin and wide gray eyes, could do as their host said.

As best Willie could imagine, and imagine he did over the years and years that followed, they'd suffered a great loss, a wound that, left to fester, had grown necrotic and healed wrong, leaving a deep crevice in the skin and in the soul. These guests watched with breathless hope, their chests constricted with it, and they welcomed the wind and the fingertips. It strengthened their resolve to believe that unlike the chintzy affairs in the city they'd slunk from in embarrassment when it became clear they'd been had, this was *true* spiritualism—and to think they hadn't had to pay anything at all to see it!

Then came the knife, and their enthusiasm guttered like the flame of a candle with the onset of a sudden storm.

The medium's sisters continued their song as she drew the little blade with its bleached white hilt from the sleeve of her gown and, holding it aloft, fell to her knees at the center of the circle.

Bone, thought Willie, *that's what that is, all right.*

Horrified gasps and cries arose from the crowd at the sight of it, and as the sisters' song reached a fever pitch, the medium bared her wrist and drew the blade across the fragile skin, crimson blood welling to the surface in beads before spilling over and dripping upon the rich wood of the Thorne Hall ballroom.

Mrs. Bishop promptly fainted, her husband only just managing to catch her. Several others followed suit, and even the faces of the men paled and sweat broke out upon their brows as they pressed the backs of their hands to their mouths.

Willie had grown up on a farm and had a stomach for blood and a spine made of far sterner stuff than the elite trying not to retch upon Jasper Thorne's ballroom floor. He was less concerned with the medium's blood than what she was currently doing with it, coating her fingers and drawing symbols at the center of the circle. Her eyes were closed, and through the gasps and fluttering, Willie could still hear her song.

The bloodied runes upon the floor began to blacken and burn. It was at this point in the evening's festivities that Jasper Thorne's guests appeared to regret accepting his invitation. Toward the doors they retreated, where the footmen, young and untried, appeared quite panicked as to whether or not to admit them to the corridor.

Willie found himself drawn inexplicably forward, toward the summoning circle, as though there were a barb lodged deep within his chest and the string tied to it were woven around the medium's hands smeared with blood.

It was the same desperate pull he sometimes felt when his mother would fall into one of her trances, delicate fingertips tracing patterns in the ashes before the hearth as she hummed a melody that made his mouth run dry and the hairs on the back of his neck stand upon end.

When she returned from wherever it was she'd gone (for Willie knew that while her body might be there, his mother was not), she'd reach for ink and parchment, and whatever she wrote there was so valuable that men in fine coats came to their cottage with full purses, and it kept them in meat and grain through long winters.

It was the memory of his mother's eyes and the terrible things they must've seen that compelled Willie to reach out and wrap his hand firmly about the butler's trembling arm. "Get them out," said he, voice pitched low. "Tell them it was all a show on account of the holiday. Get them to the great hall and play music, serve champagne, whatever you must—just keep them calm and get them out."

That he'd commanded his better should have seen him ejected from the house, but instead, the butler merely nodded in relief.

"Ladies and gentlemen," he called. "I beg you calm yourselves. 'Twas a show and nothing more, and now it is over. Please make your way to the great hall—calmly, now, please do not panic. Calm! I beg you, be calm!"

At the butler's command, footmen threw open the ballroom doors. As Mr. Thorne's guests made an eager escape, Willie looked to the summoning circle, and to Jasper Thorne himself hovering upon the fringes. He no longer appeared the very picture of power and confidence. His eyes were wild and fixed upon the bleeding woman as her lips moved in song.

Instinct bid Willie to pull from his back pocket his tattered journal and the bit of charcoal he kept upon him in perpetuity, and he began in haste to record what he could of the runes and song, certain that should the worst befall Thorne Hall that night, another canny one might find it useful.

When the last guest had fled the ballroom, the butler paused and looked to Willie. If he'd any sense at all, Willie would have followed him, would have quit Thorne Hall altogether and left the whole messy

The Spirit Collection of Thorne Hall

affair in the shadows where it belonged, but his feet simply refused to carry him to the door. When it became evident Willie would remain, the butler dipped his head in a solemn nod and pulled the doors firmly shut. Beyond them, the musicians had taken up their instruments once more and the staff was doing its best to pass the bizarre, bloody tableau as a Hallowe'en jest. "Theater," Willie heard the butler say.

He turned away, back to the runes where the deathly woman knelt unmoving, Jasper Thorne hovering above her, his eyes gone positively feral.

"Sparrow," he demanded. "Sparrow! Answer me, damn you."

"She cannot, lad." This was spoken by the eldest of the medium's kinswomen, stooped and wizened with age, and yet her gray eyes were bright.

"Why the hell not?"

"She plies her craft now," answered the next, a woman very near the age Willie's own mother had been when she'd passed. "That which you asked, sir."

Jasper raked a hand through his black-and-silver hair, his jagged face contorted in rage. "I did not ask for *this*!"

The youngest of the women, not yet out of the schoolroom, put her finger to her lips.

"Shh," she whispered. "He comes now."

From the blackened hole that the medium's blood had created, a hand emerged, and then another, clutching wildly at the edge of the floor, and a man hauled his upper body from the abyss below until he was braced upon his elbows, half of him awash in the golden candlelight and the other mired in deepest, oily black. His shoulders heaved on either side of his bowed head, and then with a mighty wrench, he pulled himself the rest of the way until he lay sprawled out on the ballroom floor.

His mottled skin was gray as a photograph, and his military jacket was bleached of color as well, though Willie thought he must have been blue once.

Around his neck he bore the unmistakable bruising of a hangman's noose.

And as Sweet William Ezra Abner stared in mounting horror at the sight, his stomach threatening to vacate its contents upon Jasper Thorne's blood-smeared ballroom floor, a single thought pierced the gloaming that fear had made of his good sense:

He *really* ought to have listened to his grandmother.

The Unquiet Grave
Francis James Child ballad #78

The wind doth blow today, my love
And a few small drops of rain
I never had but one true love
In cold clay he was lain
I'll do as much for my true love as any young lady may
I'll sit and mourn all at his grave
For twelvemonth and a day
The twelvemonth and a day being gone
A voice spoke from the deep:
"Who is it sits upon my grave
And will not let me sleep?"
"'Tis I, 'tis I, thine own true love
Who sits upon your grave
For I crave one kiss from your sweet lips
And that is all I seek"
"You crave one kiss from my clay-cold lips
But my breath is earthy strong
Had you one kiss from my clay-cold lips
Your time would not be long
'Tis down in yonder garden green, love
Where we used to walk
The finest flower that e'er was seen
Is withered to a stalk
The stalk is withered dry, my love
So will our hearts decay
So make yourself content, my love
Till death calls you away"

CHAPTER TWO

October 4, Present Day

The hour was half past midnight, and Eugenia and Mabel were arguing in the drawing room.

This in and of itself was hardly remarkable. They played whist there every night, seated at the gold-inlaid mahogany table beneath the bank of stained-glass windows overlooking the Hawthorne grove, where they cackled at bawdy jokes and reminisced over false friends and jilted lovers. And every night, after one of them had collected more than seven tricks before the sixth round, she was accused of cheating by the other.

The truth of the matter was both women nearly always cheated, but neither could remember they'd done it.

Death did tend to muddle the senses, and neither had had much to begin with.

A great number of insults were hurled back and forth regarding everything from whose nose had decomposed at a faster rate (Eugenia's, unfortunately) to who had been buried in the finer gown (both were equally hideous) until they forgot why they had been arguing in the first place and began another game.

This time, however, having moved on from petty slights to upending the table and scattering playing cards all over the floor, Eugenia and Mabel had armed themselves with an eighteenth-century Chinese ormolu clock and a bronze bust of Aristotle respectively, and were presently standing at opposite ends of the room, brandishing the ersatz weapons over their heads, as if a blow would make any sort of difference to the spirits of two women who had been dead since the presidency of Ulysses S. Grant.

Standing between them, the last ballast against the destruction of priceless artifacts and the rousing of the entire house at a most unforgivable hour, was one Elegy Thorne, twenty-five years old, clad in a nightgown so ancient the lace choking her about the throat had gone yellow.

"Neither of you mean it," she said with the frayed patience of one who had spoken those very words far too many times before. "Why don't I help you set the table to rights, and we can play a game together?"

"Why?" demanded Mabel. "She'll do naught but cheat as she always does."

"Oh, that's rich, coming from you," countered Eugenia. "The only thing you've ever come by honestly are those three chins of yours."

"Name an occasion I have cheated! Go on, because I know you can't. I have never cheated in my li—"

Eugenia held up one finger, the flesh so decomposed that the tip of the bone gleamed in the moonlight. "April twenty-sixth, 1875," she said, and erected another finger, even more ghastly than the first. "And April twenty-eighth. And the thirtieth. And—"

"Lies!" Mabel shrieked, and wheeled upon Elegy, the sooty clouds of her wiry curls quivering. "Mark my words: I'll never play another game with that old hornswoggler again!"

"Old? I died before you!"

"A lot of good it did you, didn't it? You look like death's head upon a mop stick."

"At least I could fit into a corset! You were the jollock who got stuck in her own bathtub!"

"I told you that in confidence, you backbiter!"

"Blunderbuss!"

"Fussock!"

This went on and on until Elegy, a veritable tempest of a migraine brewing behind her eyes, held up both hands and commanded them to cease their infernal caterwauling. They immediately stopped shouting insults at one another and turned to Elegy with eyes wide and skeletal hands clutched in the decaying sleeves of their burial gowns.

"Well, *that* was entirely uncalled for," sniffed Mabel.

"Yes, you needn't shout," added Eugenia.

The Spirit Collection of Thorne Hall

"Honestly, Elegy, sometimes I think you have no regard for our poor nerves. After all, it is such a dreadful vexation to be dead."

"Your ancestors were possessed of far better manners, make no mistake."

"I miss Beatrix," Mabel pouted.

"Beatrix!" Eugenia swooned. "Now *there* was a lady of quality!"

"Beatrix nearly set fire to the library when she tried to light her brandy aflame with a cigar," Elegy reminded them through teeth clenched so tightly it was a great wonder they did not shatter.

"Yes, dear, but she was *fun*."

And thus, united against a common enemy, the two old bats laid down their arms and set the overturned table back upon its feet, while Elegy knelt and began to gather the cards. By the time she'd played with them three games (all of which she pretended to lose) and left the parlor, Eugenia and Mabel had quite forgotten that there had ever been an argument in the first place and were thick as thieves once more.

They'd met at church more than 150 years prior, when both were new to Lenox, and were promptly excommunicated from said church not two years later for organizing an underground gambling ring in one of the back rooms during the post-service social hour. It had not helped that they'd drunk freely of the blood of Christ pilfered from the wine cellar and served cheese atop communion crackers.

Stifling a yawn against the back of her hand, Elegy padded down the stairs and across the great hall, which was cold and dark and still, for the fire in the hearth had long since gone out and the spirit that lurked in the shadows of the grand staircase did not speak.

As far as Elegy knew, no one had ever seen what lay beneath the shroud of black lace that covered The Mourning from head to toe. She imagined that the disfiguring nature of the illness that had claimed her life—coupled by the passage of time in the Collection—had left her far too gruesome to behold. Veils rippling, she watched Elegy climb the staircase to the second floor and stumble drowsily toward the Ivy Room, where her rickety four-poster bed and lumpy mattress waited.

The Griswolds would be arriving that morning at precisely six o'clock, as they did every morning, and it simply would not do for Beryl to find Elegy still in bed, particularly when she doubted her father would be strong enough to rise from his own.

Elegy's hand was upon the glass doorknob when there came a great crash from the floor above, followed by a piercing wail. And in an instant, all thoughts of sleep vanished, for the ruckus had, unfortunately, come from the Honeysuckle Room on the third floor, situated directly above the bedchamber of her father, Thaddeus Thorne, the master of Thorne Hall.

With a sigh carved from deep within the marrow of her bones, Elegy abandoned the promise of a few hours' respite and lurched back down the corridor toward the staircase and the dreadful howling that echoed off the rich wood-paneled walls and spilled over the banisters of the third floor, spiraling into the open space and plummeting down into the great hall, where The Mourning lifted her head at the sound.

It could only be Calliope. Possessed of a fragile disposition, dear Calliope could be counted amongst the most docile of the Spirit Collection under ordinary circumstances but, when properly provoked, could be sent into fits of whirling about and pacing, toppling furniture and tearing at drapery and wallpaper.

Carefully traversing the rotting floorboards of the third-floor corridor, Elegy found her in a most dreadful state, shrieking and babbling unintelligibly whilst systematically wrenching great handfuls of feathers from a most unfortunate pillow and flinging them into the air, where they floated about like snow.

"Shh," Elegy soothed. "It's all right."

Elegy could see nothing at all within the dark and drafty ruin of what had once been a guest bedroom that might be responsible for Calliope's current state, but nonetheless she went to her knees before the wailing spirit and gently pried the ruined pillow from her moldering fingers.

A low sound reverberated in Calliope's throat as she shook her head, and it spilled from her blackened lips in a hoarse keening that made Elegy's scalp prickle. "Tell me what the matter is," Elegy said.

The spirit said nothing, but instead rose and drifted to the old piano that sagged in the corner of the room. She slid onto the bench and waited, fingering the ends of her hair. It had been golden once, a riot of bonny curls, or so the others had said, but like everything within Thorne Hall, death and time had stolen its luster, and it was as gray and limp now as the rest of her; as the rest of them all.

"One song," sighed Elegy, as she dragged her stiff and weary bones across the room and took her place beside Calliope. Her fingertips lightly grazed the chipped ivory keys, and she played a bit of "Tam Lin," humming the melody of Janet and her silken seam and roses green and red.

Calliope shook her head; she played a minor chord, then another, and as the strings rang out in the small room, Elegy recognized the song.

The Spirit Collection of Thorne Hall

"'The House Carpenter' it is, then," she murmured, her hands sliding into place. "Though you might've chosen something more cheerful."

As Calliope began to play a frenetic treble melody, Elegy pressed her fingertips down upon the keys in a rich counterpoint. When she sang, the spirit sang with her, their voices weaving together to tell the tragic tale of a terrible choice gone terribly wrong. "A Maid So Deep in Love" came next, and by the time Calliope began to play "Cruel Sister," she hardly noticed when Elegy's fingers fell away from the chipped ivory, nor when she slipped from the room, soundless as a phantom herself.

Elegy returned to her chamber door, desperate to bury herself beneath the ivy coverlet with its pattern of vines and flowers, but no sooner had she once more grasped the doorknob than she was beset by a prickling sense of unease blooming like a thorny rose behind her ribs. Eugenia and Mabel had been suitably mollified, Calliope soothed, and yet she could not rid herself of the feeling that something was still amiss within the house. Or would be the moment she sealed herself within, behind runes drawn freshly upon her bedroom door that morning. Tilting her head, she sought them each one by one in the staid, musty darkness, silent but for her own even breathing and the occasional groan of walls declaring their displeasure at the sudden chill of a ripe autumn night.

From the moldering attic to the boiler room pungent with the scent of smoke and burning flesh, the Spirit Collection of Thorne Hall languished in corners and glided down the corridors, stirring the dust motes in shafts of moonlight and picking at the faded, peeling wallpaper with delicate finger bones that over a century of decay had revealed. They rifled through the pages of books in the library and sat before hearths long cold, wrote nonsense upon yellowed parchment Elegy would happen upon tucked within a loose brick in the kitchen wall or torn to bits and strewn about inside the claw-foot tub of her en suite bathroom.

And in the ballroom, beneath chandeliers dripping with crystal, they whirled round and round in an endless waltz, dance cards forever filled with naught but each other's names.

All fifteen spirits were exactly where they ought to be, and yet . . .

She could not very well remain awake until dawn. The few staff whom Thaddeus still employed would be arriving in a mere handful of hours. And given the steady deterioration of her father's health since midsummer, so had Elegy's duties increased. She must sleep.

J. Ann Thomas

With a modicum of luck, the Collection would remain docile while she dreamed, and when she woke upon the morning, breathing and thankful for it (for she could never quite be sure that when she closed her eyes at night, she would open them again), all would be well.

Unfortunately, Elegy Thorne had always been as unlucky as it was possible for a person to be.

* * *

Precisely four hours and thirteen minutes later, the handsome mahogany clock on the mantel of the Ivy Room stirred and began its daily twenty-minute-long alarm, the patent for such a marvel awarded to its maker, one Seth Thomas of Thomaston, Connecticut, in the year nineteen hundred and eight.

Wrapping a thick shawl around her shoulders, Elegy staggered to her wardrobe, where endless racks of dresses and skirts and blouses in a variegated array of impractical silks and satins with plackets of buttons and lace trimmings awaited. She would've happily sold the lot of it for a pair of sweatpants.

Upon his deathbed, Jasper Thorne had, so many years ago, bequeathed to his second son and heir strict rules that he demanded each and every Thorne follow in perpetuity, particularly when it came to the Collection. This in and of itself was not so very peculiar, but alongside such tenets as "No member of the household shall divulge the existence of the Spirit Collection to anyone without the express permission of the master" or "Under no circumstances are fireworks permitted to be discharged upon the property lest someone be murdered in the subsequent uproar" were those rules that made absolutely no sense whatsoever but must under no circumstances be broken, like the one regarding the electric toaster.

Cook had ceased believing long ago that its glowing coils were demons that must be exorcised by a thorough dousing, but considering her attempt at ritual purification had shut off power to the manor for a week in the dead of winter, Thaddeus would not be swayed.

The worst rule of all, in Elegy's opinion, was that the manor and everything within it were to be kept as undisturbed as possible to the way they'd been when the Collection was summoned and that nothing new was to be added or changed unless absolutely necessary.

Which included clothing.

Under Delphine's watchful eye, Elegy had become a decent enough seamstress that she could repair the inevitable broken seams and small rents in a wardrobe in which the newest garment was a ballgown from 1939 and the oldest an ermine cape Delilah had inherited from her mother upon the occasion of her marriage. Floss referred to the lot of it as "Modern Adaptation of an Edith Wharton Novel Couture" (there were quite a few bustles involved on account of the family's long patronage with the House of Worth).

At least the brassieres and corselettes worn by Delilah's daughters after the First World War were not so terribly uncomfortable, provided Elegy fashioned her diet after that of a small bird.

But the drawers and their hideous ruffles were no substitute for sensible cotton underwear, and so in this small way she defied her father, even if he knew nothing about it. It was Mrs. Griswold who supplied said contraband, just as she did tampons and other things required of a young woman, and Elegy hid them under a floorboard in her chamber.

The lot of it belonged in a museum, really; a century of fashion impeccably preserved and delicately handled, to be appreciated and admired, not to be worn and torn and faded for the sake of the whims of a man long dead.

She drew from the wardrobe one of the Drecoll dinner dresses from 1912 with a classic pannier draping in black taffeta and a sheer overlay in the same color, upon which a motif of pink roses was embroidered at the bust and shoulders. At the center of the chic leather belt was a broach, but not the original. That had been stolen by Adelaide long ago, the diamonds removed and used as game pieces on a mancala board that had been in the family since 1891.

The door to her en suite bathroom had been locked from the inside, Adelaide's doing no doubt, and so Elegy ambled round through the corridor, where she waited ten minutes for the water to heat up before performing her morning ablutions and returning to her room.

She must've accidentally forgotten to close the door properly, owing perhaps to her exhaustion, for such carelessness was a very rare thing indeed, and when she returned, it was to find Vivian's hazy outline on the sunlit window seat, an old woman at the time of her death and dressed in a pink lace pelisse in perpetuity.

"You look lovely," Vivian said dreamily.

"How shall I wear my hair?" asked Elegy, as she sat down at her vanity. "Down?"

"Oh no, dear. Loose hair is for loose women."

"And what would you know about loose women, Vivian?"

The spirit smiled. "Never you mind, dear."

"Was it you? It was you, wasn't it. You were a loose woman."

"I should certainly hope not."

Elegy could not say with certainty whether or not she would like to be a loose woman herself, because she'd never had sex and did not anticipate much opportunity even after matrimony, beyond just the once for the sake of legality. In fact, the whole affair was likely to be dreadfully uncomfortable if not downright mortifying, given her betrothed's preference for the company of men and the fact that everything she knew of female pleasure came from novels.

After taming the dull black waves of her hair and pinning them into submission at the nape of her neck, Elegy selected a pair of coral-and-topaz drop earrings and studied the solemn woman in the mirror who stared back with gray eyes that had been remarked upon as "unsettling" and "far too large in her face." Goodness, had her cheekbones always been so pronounced?

She pressed her fingertips against them, then pinched the skin there until a flush bloomed. It lingered but the space of a breath and then abruptly vanished, leaving her once more as pale as the spirits alongside whom she lived.

Bleary-eyed and in desperate need of tea, Elegy descended the great staircase from the second floor of Thorne Hall and passed wraithlike through the magnificent room that was the heart of the house. If she'd been the daughter to any other father, she would have lit the fire in the hearth herself, but Thaddeus believed it beneath any of their blood and name to perform such menial tasks, and so it would have to wait until the staff arrived, even if it meant they froze to death in the meantime.

Through the dining room she entered the butler's pantry and descended the concealed steps to the kitchen, whereupon she found herself standing quite unexpectedly in a pool of murky water.

Elegy blinked, looked down, and wondered if she were, in fact, still asleep.

"Cook!" she called, and from around the corner to the pantry, the sweet-faced spirit peered, eyes wide beneath the lacy brim of her cap. Cook's eyes were always wide on account of the fact that she existed in a perpetual state of trepidation, the irony of which was not lost upon Elegy. "Where did all this water come from?"

Cook pointed out into the corridor, and Elegy gathered up her poor crepe skirt and waded toward the sound of gushing water until she found the source of the problem: the copper pipes just below the first-floor powder room between her father's office had burst. A plumber

The Spirit Collection of Thorne Hall

would blame their age; Elegy knew it was far more likely that Reed had stuffed a rag down the pipe of the pedestal sink and left the faucet running while the house was sleeping. He had been lashing out of late and harbored an unfortunate fascination with water, which made a certain sort of sense, seeing as how he'd drowned in the lake on the estate in the year 1899.

She *knew* something had not been quite right, and yet she'd gone to bed all the same, and now look at the state of the kitchen.

Damage to the estate by a spirit had ceased to constitute anything extraordinary long ago. It happened almost twice a month now in some form or another, whether it be floorboards torn up in search of something that never was or a bank of stained glass shattered for no discernible reason at all, but what Reed had done, what with her incompetence she'd allowed him to do, was by far the worst of it.

Jeremiah Hart, the local contractor her father kept on permanent retainer owing to the bits and bobs that kept falling off his ancestral home, would be called, and unlike the last incident involving several of the sconces in the dining room having been ripped off the walls and the wires stolen and later found adorning the rafters in one of the third-floor bedrooms, the repairs would be significant indeed.

Men and supplies would be ordered from Boston some two and a half hours away, and the routines of those within Thorne Hall, both living and dead, would be in upheaval for the duration.

The family's actual, living cook—Lucy, who also doubled as maid—would hate preparing their meals in the second kitchen in the butler's pantry for however long the work lasted, and as for Fletcher . . . well, Elegy's stepmother would be positively apocalyptic; her annual birthday fete was a mere eight days away.

But first, the water supply to the house would need to be shut off posthaste, and that meant Elegy must go to the boiler room.

"Take courage," whispered Cook, and she pressed into Elegy's hands a rock that upon further inspection turned out to be a scone that must've fallen behind the stove some weeks ago. Elegy thanked her for it all the same, and when the spirit turned and drifted back into the pantry, she dropped it into the water.

* * *

Amos was a tragedy Elegy had never learned to mourn, sparing as little time and thought on him as possible. He'd been banished to the boiler room many decades ago, on account of the fact that he'd once ripped the face clean off a guest sometime during the summer of 1962, when Alasdair was master and her father Thaddeus was just a boy.

He lacked one of his own due to the accident that claimed his life, a fire at Lenox Iron Works in 1862, and as such, his appearance was far too abhorrent for anyone to stomach for long. The first time Elegy had seen him as a small child of six, she'd vomited, then fainted dead away in the puddle at her father's feet. 'Twas not merely the raw flesh and blackened, peeling skin where his face ought to have been but the terrible things she'd no choice but to feel when he came too near: fear, helplessness, agony. Oh, such terrible agony.

His name was not really Amos, of course, nor had The Mourning been called thus in life, but neither could say otherwise in death, and so the monikers given them by Jasper Thorne had stuck and after so many years had become truth.

Elegy had not seen him in two years; before that, it had been three. The ways she'd accomplished this extraordinary feat were twofold: first, by avoiding every single room in the basement save the kitchen, and second, by virtue of the fact that Amos disliked people both living and dead and was content to leave well enough alone, which suited her and everyone else in the house just fine.

Weaving her way around brick columns and piles of rusted, old tools and equipment, Elegy gave the hulking, coal-burning furnace a wide berth on her way to the pipes along the wall where fresh water was fed to the house from the water tower in the garage by means of a horizontal iron pipe with a bulbous valve housing at its center.

The closing of the valve was accomplished by turning an enormous key over and over again until the valve gate lowered, a task that required both hands and all the strength in her body.

A single lightbulb dangled from the ceiling above the pipe, but even perched precariously upon a moldering apple crate, she could not reach the chain required to light it, nor was she entirely certain it had been changed in, well . . . *ever*, and so she held the flashlight against her shoulder with her chin and began to turn the key. It refused to budge at first, groaning its protestation, until with a mighty shove that sent a jolt of pain up one arm and a hiss escaping between her teeth, it began to move.

She'd rotated the key three times before the hair upon her neck stood on end and the scent of blackened flesh and charred bone and the distant sound of screaming engulfed her senses.

"Stay away," she whispered to the spirit lurking somewhere behind her as she pushed the key with renewed vigor. "Come not near me."

The Spirit Collection of Thorne Hall

The valve gate had nearly lowered all the way, yet Amos was undeterred, and as his presence drew closer, Elegy felt a hot, sickly rush of panic and found it suddenly very difficult to breathe within the restrictive bodice of her ridiculous dinner dress. She turned the key faster, sweat pooling between her breasts and dappling her brow, until the gate slammed to a shut; in the ensuing jolt, the flashlight plummeted to the ground and went out.

Elegy fell to her knees and frantically searched the dirty floorboards with her hands while the sound of Amos's rasping, labored breath grew closer. When her fingers closed around the flashlight's handle, she flipped the switch again and again, and when that did not work, slammed its head against the floor until the light flickered and flared to life.

Expecting to see the blackened, bloody mess where Amos's face had once been, Elegy was relieved to find only the ancient boiler squatting in the distance and the scent of naught but mold upon the air.

"Amos?" she called softly, casting the beam of light into every nook and cranny of the boiler room. But only silence answered, and the lingering scent of smoke.

CHAPTER THREE

By the time Elegy returned to the kitchen, Arthur Griswold was hauling waterlogged chairs out the door and onto the lawn, while his wife Beryl stood with her arm around a distraught Lucy as they surveyed the damage to the stove.

In Jasper's day, Thorne Hall had boasted no less than eight maids, a butler, two footmen, two chefs, and a slew of ground and gamekeepers.

Now there were only four people on staff: Arthur, who managed the grounds; his wife, Beryl, who managed the house; Lucy, who was both cook and maid; and Fowler, Elegy's father's valet, who was sometimes his butler and sometimes his driver and always odious.

"Where am I going to cook?" Lucy wailed. "The second kitchen is tiny, and what about Fletcher's party? She'll be furious."

"It'll be all right," crooned Mrs. Griswold, swiping the tears from her cheeks. "We'll make it work somehow."

Lucy sniffed. "They'll have to hire an outside caterer now, and where does that leave me? She always gives me a bonus for the party, and my mum needs her knee done at Christmas!"

Cheeks aflame and an ocean churning within, Elegy waded into the kitchen, the hem of her beleaguered dinner dress slung over her arm. The shoes, a cunning pair of ivory T-straps with appliques of roses in bloom, were a lost cause and a terrible shame indeed, as they were one of several pairs designed by André Perugia especially for Delilah Thorne at Jasper's request.

"Oh, Elegy—there you are!" exclaimed Mrs. Griswold when she caught sight of her. "What happened to the kitchen?"

"There is a leak in the first-floor powder room," Elegy replied. "I shut off the water, but Jeremiah must be summoned immediately."

Arthur shuffled inside, wiping his brow with the tweed cap that was a permanent fixture upon his head. "Does the master know?"

"Not yet," said Elegy, and her stomach plummeted straight to her toes, sodden and cramped within her ruined shoes. "I'll just go tell him now, shall I?"

"Are you certain, miss?" asked Arthur, with eyes gone soft with the sympathy of one who knew all too well the sharpness of Thaddeus's tongue. "I can do it for you, if you like."

Dear, dear Arthur. Elegy would have loved nothing more than to let him, except the daytime staff knew nothing of the Collection, not even its existence; an enviable circumstance. That the family was eccentric they were well aware, and paid handsomely to ignore, even clothing and language a hundred years out of fashion; even the strange symbols painted in white around the doorframes of bedchambers.

No, the damage had not been done by living hands, and Thaddeus would discover the truth of it sooner or later, if he hadn't already, for there were many amongst the Collection who delighted in Elegy's suffering.

"Thank you, Arthur," she replied. "But I must tell him myself."

Beryl wrapped her arm around Lucy's shoulders. "Let's go see to the second kitchen, shall we? The master will still be expecting his breakfast."

Once they'd disappeared up the stairs to the butler's pantry and Arthur had seized two more chairs and shouldered his way out the kitchen door, Elegy straightened her spine and took a deep breath. "Nothing for it now but to visit my father."

Cook crept once more from the shadows and pressed another stone-hard lump of a scone into Elegy's hand.

* * *

Thaddeus Thorne had never been a tall man to begin with, and so it was especially cruel that death seemed so determined to reduce him further still in his final years. The man lying in the enormous four-poster bed that had seen the births and deaths of dozens of Thornes, Elegy among them, had been handsome once, but bitterness had corroded his features as surely as it had his heart. His nose was long and sharp, his blue eyes cold and shrewd. His endless devotion to the Collection to the exclusion of everything else had robbed him prematurely of any vigor he might've once possessed, as well as any kindness whatsoever, though Elegy very much doubted Thaddeus had ever been kind.

And now, hovering over him with a glass of water at his lips, was Elegy's Night Mother.

Were she possessed of enough good sense to be born during the daylight hours, her father might've provided for her mother a midwife of the living variety—one who had last assisted in the birth of a child prior to the year 1866. But as it happened, Tabitha Thorne's water broke on the grand staircase of the hall at precisely 9:37 on a frigid February evening in the middle of a heavy fall of snow, necessitating the use a mop and bucket to prevent any damage to the gleaming oak and a frantic search by Thaddeus for Hester, the only spirit amongst the Collection who had some experience with medicine.

Granted, it had been obtained during the Civil War and comprised mostly amputations, but it would have to do. No one came to Thorne Hall at night if they knew what was good for them. Not even the staff, meager in number as they were, remained after dinner was served.

To Thaddeus's credit, he *did* agonize for several minutes over whether to have his grandfather's Rolls-Royce brought out of the garage, but even if by some miracle it would start and make the journey through the snow to Lenox, Tabitha's labor was progressing swiftly and mercilessly, her screams sending the Collection into a state quite dangerous, and Fowler had left hours ago and would not take kindly to being roused from his bed at such a late hour. Thaddeus could not leave Thorne Hall, not with the spirits in an uproar and no one but he to command them; thus, Hester would have to do.

After being found in the third-floor nursery, Hester, who was, thankfully, quite docile despite the lateness of the hour and the extenuating circumstances, was brought at once to Tabitha's bedside.

The power lines had buckled under the weight of the midwinter snow, and the room was lit only by beeswax candles, their cloying scent mingling unpleasantly with the copper tang of Tabitha's blood. In a shadowed corner, clinging to the legs of a vanity, another spirit huddled and sang songs of the fields, of birdsong, and of love and betrayal and death. Hester would've shooed her away, so unsettling was her appearance, but Tabitha Thorne adored music and Calliope's voice had upon more than one occasion soothed her troubled soul.

Thus, it was into the hands of a woman long dead that Elegy was born. And Tabitha knew, in the way the living sometimes do, that she was dying, and so she held the squalling infant to her breast and kissed her face and named her for the songs sung by the spirit in the shadows.

And now it was her father lying in that same bed where her mother had died, slowly withering and waiting to join her. Elegy briefly wondered if her mother would want his company when he arrived, then banished the thought as too cruel—too like her father—to dwell upon.

Thaddeus lifted his head, and the grotesque twisting of his thin lips told Elegy far more of his general disgust with her than words ever could. He waved Hester away, and after setting the glass of water upon the nightstand, she glided toward a bank of windows and began to draw back the heavy curtains and let the thin morning light stream into the room.

"My breakfast is late," her father barked. "Has Lucy not arrived?"

"She has."

Her father's piercing blue eyes narrowed in suspicion. "Then where is my breakfast?"

She drew a deep breath, and out it poured. "A pipe burst in the corridor outside the kitchen. It's flooded. All of it."

Hester turned, burgundy velvet slithering from her hands, as a thick, suffocating silence descended upon the room, pierced only by the steady ticking of the mahogany clock upon the wall. Unrelenting, a mockery of that which Elegy feared above all else, even the Collection.

"The kitchen is flooded," her father repeated softly, dangerously, the gleaming edge of a knife poised just above tender flesh, and Elegy flinched, despite knowing the struggle to be futile. Thaddeus had cut her to the quick over far less.

"Yes."

"The Collection are to blame."

"I cannot say for certain—"

"It was not a question."

"I suspect so, yes," she admitted. "But they were settled when I retired for the night, Father, I made sure of it."

"This is unacceptable. And it has been for some time," her father added, and the blade sank beneath her skin. "The damage will cost a fortune, to say nothing of weeks of strangers traipsing in and out of the house. How, pray tell, might I trust you to manage to keep the

Collection at peace through all of that? *You*, who cannot manage the Collection when the house is empty and quiet in the dead of night?"

"Father, I *am* trying—"

"Not hard enough," he snapped, then grimaced, his hand flying to his throat before a torrent of coughing erupted from his mouth. He fumbled for the handkerchief in the pocket of his silk pajamas and pressed it to his lips as the attack overcame him.

Elegy flinched as it went on and on, the terrible death rattle that had settled in Thaddeus's chest two autumns ago and continued to burgeon and choke him, grasping hands within rather than without.

She'd not thought it possible to feel it so acutely as she did now, and Elegy was used to shame; she was a constant disappointment not only to her father but to herself. Heat unfurled like a ribbon from the very heart of her until it prickled behind her eyes, and she willed herself not to blink. Thaddeus found tears detestable as well as most emotions in general.

"I am sorry, Father," she said when at last his coughing stilled and his gray head lifted. He balled his handkerchief and thrust it beneath the blanket, but she'd already seen the blood there, drops of crimson stark against fragile, yellowed lace.

During his last visit to the house, Dr. Winslow had taken Elegy aside and over tea and ginger biscuits informed her that Thaddeus's illness had progressed quicker than he would've liked.

He gave her father a year, perhaps longer if he adhered to a strict regimen of diet, rest, and foul-smelling tinctures.

A year would have been time enough for any other Thorne in the family's long and illustrious history. Money, the most insurmountable object of all for anyone about to inherit a 126-year-old estate whose owners had purposefully eschewed most modernizations save those absolutely necessary, was no object. Jasper Thorne had been a man of frankly ludicrous wealth, and he had made sure the house he built and the family saddled with the macabre task of keeping his collection of fifteen spirits would never want for anything.

There were his various investments, of course, as well as their annuities, and at the time of his death, Jasper owned no less than twenty estates scattered up and down the East Coast from Newport to Newark. But it was Jasper's grandson Felix, Thorne's third master, who, when the Highway Act of 1956 was passed, had had the brilliant idea to sell off some of those estates in order to buy buildings in Manhattan, both residential and commercial. That income alone would sustain generations of Thornes to come.

The Spirit Collection of Thorne Hall

While Thaddeus still insisted upon being the one to correspond with their man of business, Elegy had taken over the household accounts when the cough first stubbornly lodged itself in Thaddeus's lungs, and despite his aversion to modernization and its inevitable consequences, their coffers remained sufficiently padded so as to weather any storm.

No, it was the Collection itself she had proven herself entirely incapable of managing. Case in point: the reason she was currently standing before her father's bed with her hands laced together so that he would not see them shake.

"You should be," came Thaddeus's rasping answer to her apology. "It is entirely your fault. By your age, I had the Collection whimpering at my feet. You can barely get them to come when you call. You're up talking and playing and singing with them at all hours of the night when you should be able to silence them with a thought. It's a disgrace. Were you as capable as you should be, I would not have to burden myself so heavily when my health is so precarious!"

"Father—"

"It is high time that you prove yourself a capable successor," he continued as though Elegy had not spoken.

"I *am* worthy."

"Prove it, then," he challenged, and she did not much care for the glint in his eye as the thought settled. "A test, I think."

"Test?" she whispered.

"Of your ability to manage the Collection."

"Father, I *can* manage the Collection."

"There have been more incidents with the Collection in the last two years than in the last one hundred and twenty-six."

He was, unfortunately, not wrong. "Last night was a mistake," she said. "If you will only allow me to—"

"I have spent *years* allowing. Years *preparing* you—wasted years!" He began coughing anew, and this time he did not bother to conceal the bloody handkerchief, the sigil of her ineptitude, the source of her shame.

And like the diamonds carved upon each hearth in Thorne Hall and set into the plaster ceilings, taken from Delilah's family's ancient coat of arms, a herald of what was to come.

The moment the last, putrid gust of breath left her father's lips, the Collection would pass to her.

And it would not matter that it was Hester's mottled hands that had brought her gently into the world, nor that Calliope had taught her to sing. They were the docile ones. The kind ones.

But there were also the mischievous ones, like Reed and Adelaide.
And then there were the vengeful ones. Like Amos.
And Bancroft.
And worst of all was Gideon Constant.

"You will submit to my test, Elegy," her father said when he had recovered the ability to speak. "And for your sake and the sake of our name, I do hope you are successful."

And what else could she possibly say but, "Of course, Father. I shall not fail."

"See that you do not," her father rasped. And with considerable effort, he threw off the heavy velvet coverlet and swung his feeble legs over the edge of the bed. "I must summon Jeremiah. Has Fowler arrived?"

"I have not seen him."

"Then send Arthur. And go change your dress—you're dripping all over my carpet."

And just like that she was dismissed.

* * *

Jasper's money might've built Thorne Hall, but the house had always been Delilah's.

She'd designed every inch; every room and every stair and every intricate plaster ceiling was so completely and indisputably hers that the house breathed in and sighed out again *Delilah* in such a manner that no one could've possibly doubted it.

A mere summer cottage it might've have been at the start (and Elegy always snorted when she thought upon it, because only a revoltingly wealthy middle-aged white man would consider a thirty-thousand-square-foot Jacobean redbrick manor a "cottage"), but after the Collection were bound, it became the permanent seat of the Thornes. As Jasper became increasingly absorbed with the Collection and training his second son to command them, Delilah took over the management of the estate.

Therefore, of the two offices upon the main floor of the house, Delilah's was the larger and afforded an unencumbered view of the porte cochere. In this manner, she could see who approached and inform the butler in advance of whom to welcome inside and whom to inform that she was not at home.

It was whispered by certain staff with absolutely no sense of self-preservation that she had taken a lover, and that said lover was the butler William Abner, who had listed his formal name as "Sweet William" upon his employment papers and introduced himself as "Willie" when

The Spirit Collection of Thorne Hall

arriving at Thorne Hall for the first time, upon that most fateful and famous night in their family lore.

He'd evidently served the family with great distinction that night and been offered permanent employment on the spot, then risen quickly through the ranks of Jasper's staff, far too quickly not to arouse suspicion. Neither the fact that Delilah quit Thorne Hall only two years after construction had been completed nor that William Abner remained behind as Jasper's butler could do anything to dispel the rumor.

Elegy had no sooner arranged herself at her desk than there was a knock upon the door and Mrs. Griswold entered, bearing a silver tea tray and a thick leather portfolio shoved underneath one arm.

"Don't think I didn't notice you've not had breakfast," she said, shuffling into the room and placing the tray upon the small table near the door where Elegy kept flowers in the seasons she could, sprigs of evergreen and rosemary when she could not. "And I've just had a call from Holcroft."

At the name, Elegy's heart began to race, and hope blossomed in the hollow cavity of her chest. "And what did they say?"

"Mrs. Carmichael is visiting from New York, and she's coming to see you this afternoon."

"Floss!" exclaimed Elegy, and she was so unused to smiling that her delighted expression bordered on painful as it stretched her solemn features. She'd not seen her dear friend Floss since Christmas, and even then, her visit had been all too brief, and full of tears and wailing on account of her husband's most recent infidelity. "Did she say when?"

"Within the hour," answered Mrs. Griswold, spooning preserves from a small crock onto a thick slice of toasted bread. "I've brought the menus for the week, seeing as you'll have to change them on account of the accident."

Elegy sighed. "I suppose I must make arrangements for Fletcher's party as well."

"Lucy's made a list of caterers—I've included it with the menus."

"Thank you, I'll see to it at once."

Once Elegy's breakfast was arranged upon her desk, Mrs. Griswold took her leave, and Elegy left her poached eggs untouched whilst she took a pen and laid waste to all the lovely dishes that could not be prepared in so small a confine as the second kitchen with little more than an oven and four burners.

When that was done and Lucy had (rightfully) stomped down the corridor muttering a litany of curses, Elegy did battle with the Chicago potbelly upright phone on her desk until she'd managed to secure the services of a caterer who did not mind the short notice once Elegy promised them an obscene amount of money for the privilege.

It wasn't as though she had much choice in the matter.

Her stepmother's birthday fete was the only party still permitted at Thorne Hall, and that was only because if Thaddeus didn't provide some kind of proof of life for his wife, people might begin to suspect he was keeping her locked away in the attic, which he absolutely was. Or, rather, she locked *herself* in the attic, and who could blame her? Fletcher had lost one baby, and then another and another, and with each little mound of freshly tilled earth in the graveyard, Thaddeus's patience frayed and his resentment festered. After all, he'd only married her in the hope of having a son, a true heir to inherit both blood *and* name.

Elegy's existence absolved Thaddeus of any blame in the matter (or so he said), and he'd briefly considered divorcing Fletcher and finding another woman of breeding years, but by then his health was beginning to fail him. It was his bitterness, Elegy believed, that had driven the Collection to such a frenzy upon that long-ago night.

The fight had occurred upon the occasion of her sixteenth birthday, and this time instead of merely hurling insults at one another, Fletcher dragged the hand-carved cradle that had once been Elegy's down the staircase into the main hall and took after it with the axe Mr. Griswold used to split firewood.

In retaliation, Thaddeus set the Collection upon her.

Fletcher was never quite the same after that. Her vibrancy turned brassy and sharp, her laughter shrill, and her smiles, smeared with rust, grew wide and wild.

She took the largest of the third-floor bedrooms as her sanctuary, filled it with everything beautiful the house had to offer, and filled her evenings with alcohol and cigarettes and music and spent her days sleeping it off.

The mahogany clock on the wall intricately carved with a pattern of hydrangeas intoned the hour, and in the distance an engine rumbled. Elegy rose, limbs and seams protesting, and pressed her face against the stained glass as a smear of red appeared at the end of the drive, coalescing into the familiar shape of the Abernathys' Maybach as it crested the slope.

She quite forgot herself at the sight of it, leaving her desk in disarray and dashing beneath the porte cochere and down the drive until her ancient heels nearly snapped and she was forced to stand and wait as she always did for the world to come to her.

CHAPTER FOUR

Elegy made her first mortal friends at the exceedingly gerontological age of twelve.

It was not that she had never seen children before. After a great deal of begging, Mrs. Griswold had been granted permission from Thaddeus to bring her grandchildren around to Thorne Hall some six years before, but only the one time on account of one of them getting stuck in the dumbwaiter. That in and of itself wasn't so very terrible—Elegy herself had hidden there several times during games of hide-and-seek with Reed and Adelaide. Rather, she suspected the unfortunate boy had caught a glimpse of something he was not meant to, lurking in the basement. He'd been white as a sheet and trembling when they'd pulled him out, so it must've been Cook or possibly even Bernard. Had it been Amos, he would have been catatonic.

Or possibly missing his face.

That fateful afternoon in her thirteenth year was already the happiest day of her life. Her father had decided to remarry—and the woman in question who was to become her new mother was as fascinating a person as Elegy had ever met.

A car accident had left Fletcher an orphan at the terribly tender age of five, and instead of taking her in as any loving aunt might, her mother's sister had used the meager fortune meant to fund her care on a dismal boarding school upstate that she claimed "built character" but that also contributed to a ranging addiction to all manner of vices.

Once she was free of the wretched place, Fletcher attended Sarah Lawrence on scholarship, majoring in women's studies and French, as one does, and spent several years traveling the world until a chance invitation to spend a summer in the Berkshires with a friend from school led to her attendance at one of the parties Thaddeus had been forced to throw in order to find a suitable replacement for Tabitha.

She was the loudest woman Thorne Hall had ever seen, a terrible mistress for such a house, but she'd fallen in love with it, with the promise of so many salons and the fascinating people who would flock to it and to her, and the intoxication of her excitement spilled over until it surrounded Thaddeus as well. He was handsome if somewhat severe in his appearance, and well read, which she thought was important even if she didn't actually care. That he was the same age as her father, and therefore scandalous, only enticed her further, and two months after they'd been introduced, the ten-carat Thorne emerald adorned Fletcher's finger just as it had Tabitha's.

Even if Fletcher weren't so very striking with her square face, thick brows, and heavy-lidded brown eyes, or so very fashionable, even if she weren't enviably well read and in possession of such forceful opinions, it would not have mattered, for were Elegy's new mother to conceive a child, and particularly if that child happened to be a boy, Thaddeus would surely name *him* his heir.

Even though Elegy would never be permitted to leave Lenox, perhaps she *could* leave Thorne Hall; she could leave the Spirit Collection.

It was a ghastly of her to wish such a cruel fate on another, particularly her own flesh and blood, and years later when she was no longer a terrified, foolish child, she would sicken herself with the memory that she ever had. But in those hopeful days, it had been her dearest wish, the one she'd whispered to herself at night as she lay burrowed beneath the covers while skeletal fingers scratched at her door, begging to be let inside.

After the ceremony that bound her father and his new bride together as husband and wife, Elegy tucked herself into a corner of Thorne Hall's foyer as Thaddeus's guests streamed inside, tossing their furs in Fowler's general direction and seizing coupes of champagne in hands garishly adorned for the occasion.

The lace collar of Elegy's drop-waist mauve satin dress itched terribly, and her stomach growled in protest of the porridge she'd hardly touched that morning out of excitement, but when the bulk of a particularly odious man shifted suddenly and Elegy caught sight of golden curls and sullen eyes heavily lined in burgundy, all discomfort was promptly forgotten. Here, in Elegy's own foyer, amid the splendor of the Berkshires' oldest families in their finest attire, was a girl in a short black skirt and fishnet stockings that disappeared into combat boots laced to her knees. Elegy could do nothing but stare, because she'd never seen anything quite so wonderful as a living child her own age.

The golden-haired vision caught sight of her then and clomped her way across the foyer until she reached Elegy's hiding place. "Are you Elegy Thorne?"

Dumbstruck, Elegy could only nod.

"I *knew* you existed. Ranjit owes me twenty bucks."

"My existence was in doubt?"

The girl regarded her as though she were very stupid indeed. "Well, yeah. No one has ever seen you."

"Plenty of people have seen me."

"You didn't go to school with us," the girl pointed out. "Or attend any of the other parties before this one."

"My father would not permit me."

"We all thought maybe he kept you in the basement," she went on. "Or an attic. Or that he murdered you. Theories abound."

"Well, *that's* quite extreme."

The girl shrugged. "He seems like an extreme kind of guy. Anyway, my name's Floss."

"That's an odd name," Elegy answered, then grimaced at her stupidity. She really was as terrible at this as she had feared she would be. "Sorry, I don't know why I said that."

Floss shrugged, unbothered. "Barbara swears I was conceived in Florence."

They exchanged a smile, and Elegy thought Floss was the most wonderful person she'd ever met despite her vulgar mouth. Or maybe because of it. Elegy couldn't decide, and she also didn't care.

At the far side of the great hall, Fletcher threw back her head and laughed, a garish, barking sound full of rust and white teeth, and Floss sighed. "Your stepmother is so cool."

Pride flared to life in Elegy's chest at the idea that Floss should envy her of anything.

"She is."

"Did you know she came with Thaddeus for dinner at Holcroft last month?"

Of course Elegy did. She'd watched from between the slats of the second-floor railing as her father helped Fletcher into a sumptuous silk evening coat trimmed with mink and guided her into the crisp winter night and allowed herself a rare moment of bitterness. She'd shed no tears, of course, but the little half-moon gouges in her palms did not fade for weeks, because that was the first night her father had left her alone with the Collection.

"She's so clever," Floss continued, tossing her mane of golden curls. "She had everyone in stitches over her stories from Europe. And she actually noticed I exist, which is more than I can say for fucking Barbara."

"Who is Barbara?"

"My mom. Anyway, I want to be just like Fletcher when I get older. Do I look like her a little bit?"

Floss swept her hair up in her hand, piling it atop her head, and tilted her head this way and that as they both watched Fletcher across the room, where two men who were most definitely *not* Elegy's father were falling all over themselves to fill her champagne coupe. The Thorne emerald caught the light as she gestured wildly with her hands, and the men around her laughed at whatever terribly witty thing it was she'd said.

Elegy did not have to look to her father to know his face was pinched in disapproval.

"This place is way bigger than Holcroft," Floss continued, her heavily lined eyes rising with the staircase to the second, then the third floor, lingering on the ornate ceiling above. "How many rooms does it have?"

Elegy shrugged, because she wasn't sure if Floss meant main bedrooms or servants' quarters, bathrooms or parlors, for Thorne Hall had quite a few of each, though most were never used and, without a full staff, the rest were left to gather decades of dust and cobwebs. She finally settled with, "A lot."

"Which one is yours?"

"It's on the second floor," Elegy answered.

"Show me."

Elegy hesitated. She'd never had another living soul her age to show about her room before, and she was desperate to find favor with this peculiar, spectacular girl; however, there was the minor inconvenience of Adelaide, whom she'd left sulking in the corridor when the first crunch of gravel beneath the porte cochere heralded the arrival of Thaddeus's guests.

It was still relatively early in the evening, not yet dark. She should be able to keep Adelaide under some semblance of control were she still lurking about, but perhaps they shouldn't stay in her bedroom for so very long.

The Spirit Collection of Thorne Hall

Elegy nodded. "Okay, come on."

When Floss's fingers threaded through her own, Elegy experienced an unfamiliar yet wonderful sense of warmth that spread throughout her entire being; a broad grin split her face, and together they danced up the staircase, Floss giggling and Elegy shushing her until they at last reached her bedroom and she pushed the door open.

The window seat was occupied by a dark-skinned boy with a face full of freckles and a half-smoked cigarette dangling from his lips. He was a lanky thing with a head of tight copper curls and a large-boned face he would, with luck, grow into. His suit was the deepest purple and, in Elegy's humble opinion, clashed horribly with the mustard shirt with its pattern of white flowers he'd paired it with, and yet, somehow, he made it seem the height of fashion. It was the way he sprawled his legs, Elegy reasoned, so wide and sure, nothing like her, who spent half of her time crouched in preparation to flee at the mere suggestion of a spirit gone willful.

"You're not supposed to be in here," Elegy informed him, once she'd overcome her shock at seeing a boy in her bedroom, however unthreatening. She dared not raise her voice lest Adelaide, wherever she might be—or worse, the playfully mischievous Reed—come investigate the commotion.

"*You're* in here," the boy pointed out.

She bristled because, honestly, how *dare* he. "This is my father's house."

"But not *your* house."

"Fuck you, Hugo." Floss pushed past Elegy and snatched the cigarette out of the boy's laughing mouth. She took a long drag and handed it back to him. "It'll be her house someday."

He scowled at the lipstick she'd left behind but stuck the cigarette back in his mouth anyway, sucking deep before exhaling a cloud of noxious smoke. Then, to Elegy's absolute horror, he smashed the stub against the window casing and left it there to smolder. "My name's Hugo," he told her. "Hugo Prescott."

She tore her gaze away from the smudge of black and took his proffered hand. "Elegy Thorne."

"Elegy," he repeated. "Appropriate, given, well . . ."

"Well, what?"

"Shove over," Floss ordered Hugo, and he drew his knees up so that she could squeeze onto the window seat. From the depths of her bag, she drew a silver flask and unscrewed the cap.

"He means the ghosts."

Elegy froze. Whispers that Thorne Hall had once been haunted were unavoidable. But, considering that there was not a single square foot of land in the Berkshires that was not said to be haunted, it was hardly cause for alarm.

Schooling her features, Elegy inquired, "Who told you there were ghosts here?"

"I overheard my parents talking about it." Floss drank deeply from the flask, dragged the back of one hand across her mouth, and passed it to Hugo. "So, is it true?"

Elegy's eyes fell to her lap, where her small white hands twisted in the same way her stomach did.

"Come on," Hugo wheedled. "You can tell us. We won't say a word to anyone else—we swear, don't we, Floss?"

The girl in question nodded earnestly, and Elegy felt her stomach roil further still. She wanted them to know; she wanted someone else to know so very badly, but what on earth would Thaddeus say were he ever to find out? She'd only just met them. Who was to say they could be trusted with a secret as enormous, or as dreadful, as this one?

In the end, her desire for living friends won out. "I'm afraid it's true: Thorne Hall is quite haunted."

"Fuck me," Hugo said, shaking his head as though he were in a trance. "Seriously?"

"She's just said yes, hasn't she?" Floss rolled her eyes.

"What are they, then?" Hugo continued. "Would your hand go right through them if you tried to touch them? *Have* you tried to touch them?"

Elegy worried her bottom lip. "I can't really talk about them."

"We're not going to tell your dad," Floss offered. "If that's what you're worried about."

"Here," Hugo said, and passed her the flask. "Go on—it'll help."

Elegy's eyes watered at the acrid smell of the liquor, and she fought the urge to pinch her nose closed as she tipped the flask back and swallowed deep. Heat bloomed in her throat and bravery poured into her belly.

"There are fifteen of them," she said. "The first one was collected in 1902, and the rest over the decade that followed, bound to our name and bloodline."

"How old are they?" Hugo pressed. "When did they all die? What do they look like?"

Elegy's head spun with the whiskey and the barrage of questions she'd never been asked and never thought she'd answer. "They died at

The Spirit Collection of Thorne Hall

many different times," she replied. "The oldest death was Gideon's—we cannot be certain of the exact date, but he was hanged sometime in the 1780s. The most recent was Reed—he died just before the turn of the twentieth century. He's the youngest—just five years old. Vivian is the oldest, and the rest are in between."

"And they've lived here all this time?"

"Well, I wouldn't exactly call it living."

Floss took the flask from Hugo and, after shuddering through an enormous swallow, asked, "Why don't you just lock the doors and burn the place to the ground? No offense—it's a nice place and all—but why would anyone want to live with ghosts?"

"We all live with ghosts," answered Elegy. "And anyway, they cannot be banished. Not ever."

"Why not?"

"The man who built this house, Jasper Thorne, he expressly forbade it."

Hugo snorted. "And you *care*? Did he live hundreds of years ago?"

"He died in 1934," she replied. "And we Thornes take such things *very* seriously."

"You could leave," suggested Floss. "Surely they can't follow."

"Some of us do leave," Elegy hedged. "But not the master and his heir—never too far, never for long, and never at once. Someone must always stay behind to manage them."

"Why? What would happen if you didn't?"

Elegy shuddered. "We cannot possibly imagine."

"Do they just wander around the house as they please?" Hugo asked. "Will one wander in *here*?"

"Of course not," Elegy chided. "Do you see the runes around my door? They keep the Collection from entering places they shouldn't; otherwise they would, and often."

Thaddeus himself had drawn the symbols above her nursery door until she was old enough to move into the Ivy Room, which had been her mother's favorite, and on that day, he brought a medium to the house to teach her because he simply could not be bothered.

Elegy remembered little of the medium save that he was kind and patient with so young a student and was possessed of a calming voice. She thought of him sometimes while her fingers, dipped in white, traveled the now-familiar symbols he'd taught her. How had he come to know them? And did this mean that there were other houses like hers containing ghosts from which one must guard oneself? She recollected him as a young man at the time, in his midthirties, perhaps, but no older. He'd taught the runes to Tabitha when she became Mrs. Thorne, and Elegy six years later, but he could not possibly have taught Thaddeus, for he was far too young; so who had?

There was a knock at her door, and the three of them started in shock—and in guilt, for Hugo was smoking another cigarette and Floss had just polished off the rest of the whiskey.

"Shit!" Hugo panicked and, furiously opening the window, tossed the cigarette into the night while Floss hid the empty flask behind a pillow.

It was Mrs. Griswold come to tell them that their supper was ready in the great room.

They were not permitted at their age to dine with the adults, but they were entirely unbothered by the fact. A platter of sandwiches and fruit was presented, and they lounged in the velvet armchairs before the fire, cursing and giggling and stuffing their ravenous faces, alcohol thrumming through their veins and the discovery of one another an even more tantalizing high.

The grandfather clock tucked away in a corner beneath the staircase chimed the lateness of the hour, and Hugo lifted his gleaming eyes. "This is when they're about, yeah? The ghosts?"

"They're always about," Elegy answered. "By day, if you don't know about them, you won't see them. They'll be like a bit of shadow out of the corner of your eye, or the fluttering of a curtain. But at night, they become something else entirely."

"Explain," Hugo demanded, but how could she?

How could she put into words the way the house changed the moment night fell, how it exhaled fetid air that stirred cobwebs that had not been there only moments before, how wallpaper peeled and rot bloomed and floorboards creaked and groaned, traversed by the feet of the dead and worn into familiar patterns of anguish?

"By day, they exist alongside us, hidden and harmless. Some of them are even friendly. But at night, the house is theirs, and it is we who are the trespassers."

"Come on, then," Hugo said. "Let's trespass."

Well, wasn't she the fool? She should have realized this was what they'd wanted all along, and she could not pretend it did not sting somewhat, yet she could hardly blame them. Floss and Hugo might be in the agonizing throes of puberty and taking full advantage of their parents' wealth and indifference, but they were, in this desperate curiosity, still children. The idea of the impossible, the deliciously forbidden, lit their eyes with insatiable desperation, and Elegy was compelled to satisfy it despite the danger. And danger there was if she was not careful.

Elegy's eyes darted to the corridor. The dining room beyond had gone silent; Thaddeus and his guests had long since finished their lavish supper and were likely in the ballroom, where there would be dancing and gambling and drinking until the early hours of the morning. The blazing lights of the chandeliers and her father's impeccable control would keep the more dangerous sort of spirits away from his guests, and the rest he would manage from afar.

If she were to choose one of the more docile spirits, Thaddeus would likely never know, even if her new friends were to run from the manor screaming into the night.

But who to choose?

Children were possessed of loose lips, and these two in particular seemed to pride themselves on being indiscreet. Elegy could not risk that their idle chatter might reach Thaddeus's ears, and so she ruled out The Mourning, despite her being conveniently nearby, tucked as she usually was at the corner of the staircase just before the gallery. One should never make the mistake of falling asleep before the hearth in the great room after dark lest they wake to the spirit's spindly fingers wrapped about their neck, if they woke at all.

They might make it unseen to the basement by way of the servants' staircase, but Elegy could not very well expose Floss and Hugo to Amos. Her new friends were more likely to stay friends with their faces intact, after all.

Hester was the best choice but would disapprove of Elegy telling anyone about the Collection without her father's permission. Cook was sweet and decidedly less judgmental, but Lucy and Mrs. Griswold were in the second kitchen that night and she was likely to be more agitated than usual.

In the end, Elegy selected Calliope. She never spoke, only sang, and while it was true that half her face was caved in, she was no more ghastly by night than many of the others, whose teeth were sharper, their skin decayed and their sunken eyes ringed in rot. Some of their noses had even begun withering away, revealing the odd upside-down heart of the bones beneath.

Elegy led Floss and Hugo up the staircase in silence, bypassing the second floor and climbing to the ruins of the third, where Calliope could usually be found in the Honeysuckle Room. She liked the window seat there, overlooking the grove, and spent her days and nights singing softly for hours upon end until Elegy would put a record on, for she was helplessly drawn to music of any sort.

"Watch your step," Elegy whispered over her shoulder. The third floor had suffered most acutely the ravages of time, and if they were not careful, one of them was likely to lodge their foot somewhere rather unfortunate.

Outside the Honeysuckle Room, Elegy bid her friends to wait and pressed her ear to the door. Sure enough, she heard the spirit's sweet rasp of a voice singing one of the Child ballads of which she was so fond.

Be still, Elegy bid her. *Be sweet and be still.*

The singing stopped as her command settled over the spirit. Elegy took a deep breath and opened the door.

Floss and Hugo followed, blessedly silent, their wide eyes taking in the tattered room with its peeling floral wallpaper and sagging canopy bed, opulence left to putrefaction, for no visitors had come to Thorne Hall and stayed the night since Jasper's day.

The ghost sitting upon the window seat wore white, and always would; it was her wedding dress.

"Oh fuck," Hugo breathed at Elegy's back. "Is that one of them?"

"Yes," Elegy answered, her voice low and soothing, for even though Calliope was ordinarily docile, she'd never brought anyone around her before. "She died at the end of the eighteenth century."

Floss began a whispered mantra of "Oh god, oh god, oh god," and gripped Elegy's upper arms tightly, peering over her shoulders even though she was much taller. And why wouldn't she? She'd just been told that the woman a few feet away from them was dead and had been so for a very long time.

Calliope's song trailed off and her head tilted in their direction, her once-golden hair hiding her countenance.

"Good evening, Calliope," Elegy said. "You've no need to be frightened. I've brought to friends for you to meet."

Calliope rose from the window seat, and as she slowly turned, the moonlight streaming through the window illuminated the ruination her husband had wrought on their wedding night when she'd grown afraid and refused to submit. Barefoot and still clad in her wedding gown, she'd fled from his drunken molestation down the staircase, or at least she'd tried; his fingers had wrapped round her wrist, and the resulting struggle had left her in a heap at the foot of the staircase. To her new husband's chagrin, the fall had not killed her. If it had, there would be no one to speak of his actions that night, of the way he'd manhandled her, of the way he'd caused her to fall in the first place. And so he'd wrapped her beautiful hair around his wrist and bashed her face into the bottom stair until she stilled and slumped into the widening puddle of her blood.

Elegy realized at that moment that Calliope's appearance was, in fact, extremely disturbing; she'd grown so used to it that she'd thought only of her demeanor when choosing her.

Hugo and Floss, however, spared no time to acquaint themselves with the spirit's gentle disposition.

Screaming like a pair of proper banshees, they bolted from the Honeysuckle Room and exploded into the corridor in a tangle of limbs, propelled by terror absolute. Elegy dashed after them, begging them to stop, to wait—*please, wait! Stop!*

She followed them down the stairs to the second floor, and all the while they ignored her desperate pleas.

It had all gone horribly wrong, and she'd no idea how to make it right, particularly with them barreling toward the front door as they were. There was no way to stop them. She could not very well set Bernard upon them or The Mourning; that would only make matters worse. And so Elegy followed them out into the sharp, bright cold of the early-spring night, begging all the while for them to stop, to wait, to *please* not tell their parents or hers.

At last, some forty feet past the drive and into the grove, they stopped. Keeled over with their hands braced upon their knees, they sucked in great lungfuls of air while Elegy stood a respectable distance away and waited for them to regain their composure.

Hugo recovered first, lifting his head to regard her with round, horrified eyes. "Holy shit, that was a fucking *ghost*. That was a fucking dead woman, holy shit!"

"To be fair, you did ask to see one," Elegy pointed out delicately.

"Yeah," he exhaled, the heel of his hand pressed against his forehead. "I didn't actually expect them to be, you know—*real*."

Elegy's brows pulled forward in a frown. "So you thought I was lying?"

"No! No, I believed you—"

"But you didn't really."

"Not until I saw it, no," he answered honestly. "I mean, I kind of did? But this is also a creepy house and you're a creepy girl, so it could've gone either way, really."

"Shut the fuck up, Hugo," Floss groaned. "What he's trying to say is that it's one thing to say it and another to see it."

Hugo threw up his hands. "She's missing half her face!"

"Well, Amos is missing *all* his face, so it could have been worse," Elegy pointed out.

"We could have been killed!"

"Honestly," Elegy sighed. "You're terribly dramatic. I told you, the Collection are bound to the Thorne bloodline, and to the manor—they obey the master and his heir in all things."

"And the heir—that's you," said Floss.

Elegy nodded. "Calliope is perfectly harmless, but if she *had* wanted to harm you, I would have prevented her."

They did not appear convinced, their wary eyes darting between Elegy's pale face and the house. She swallowed over the fear in her throat, the loss she stood to suffer should she remain unable to convince them to stay, to trust her. She'd only just found them, and now the Collection would steal them from her, just as they'd stolen everything else.

"Please," she said, and her voice wavered and broke, but she felt no shame, for the thought of losing them was a far worse thing. "Please don't leave. I swear my father and I will protect you from them—it will be as though they're not there at all. It's just that I've never had friends before. Not any my own age or . . ."

"Alive?" supplied Hugo helpfully.

Elegy grimaced. "I suppose so, yes."

They'd a silent conversation between them whilst Elegy stood and shivered and wished she could read minds until, a decision having been made, they turned back to her as one. She sucked in her breath.

"So, do you think your cook could whip up a few more sandwiches?" Floss asked. "Being scared out of one's mind does tend to work up an appetite."

Elegy exhaled upon a grin, and as the three of them trudged back toward the warmth of the manor and the promise of sweets pilfered from the kitchen, Hugo took Elegy's arm, threaded it through his own, and asked, "So, do they fuck?"

"*What?*"

"The ghosts," he sighed, as though it were exceedingly obvious. "Do they fuck?"

Floss groaned. "Hugo, you absolute twat."

"Oh, come off it—you're as curious as I am."

Curious or not, Elegy would have to disappoint them both, for the truth was she did not know.

It had always seemed impolite to ask.

CHAPTER FIVE

They had been fast friends ever since the night she'd nearly been the cause of their mutual pediatric heart attacks, but it was not like the friendships they shared with others. Visits to their respective homes were rare; visits to Thorne Hall rarer still on account of the Spirit Collection and only ever by day, but just like Elegy, they were moths drawn helplessly to her stepmother's flame.

It was Floss who had the keenest relationship with Fletcher, even taking to dressing like her for a time, wearing her blonde curls in the same haphazard bun atop her head and smoking her cigarettes through a long, silver quellazaire studded with garnets. They often sat often together and spoke of men and sex and the world, and Elegy, who had never before allowed herself to hope that she might experience such things, wondered if perhaps she ought to at least consider them, for surely someone so vibrant, someone so *alive*, would give Thaddeus the boy child he so craved and release her from her terrible legacy.

By her sixteenth birthday, such frivolous notions had been long buried, languishing in the graveyard alongside the five little stones that bore the name Thorne, and Fletcher rarely left the attic in the daylight hours.

Floss and Hugo, sympathetic to her plight, even attempted to downplay the disgusting, fascinating mess that was middle school at a private institution whose yearly tuition rivaled that of most Ivy League colleges. Elegy loved them for it but demanded they tell her *everything*, for it was a marvelous thing to imagine herself as one of them, a regular teenager with a disgusting, fascinating mess of her own.

High school was particularly agonizing. Elegy had by then gone through puberty and existed in a perpetual state of desperate envy at all the (mostly mediocre) sex Floss was having and the (slightly better) sex had by Hugo, because they were having it and Elegy was not and she felt so terribly juvenile. They attended ever so many parties from which she was forbidden, and weeks went by when she didn't see hide nor hair of them, owing to the frequent weekend skiing trips to Vermont or clambakes on the cape. Hugo had a key to his uncle's penthouse on Park Avenue in Manhattan, and since he was frequently occupied with high-class escorts and blow in the south of France, Hugo and Floss spent more and more time away from the Berkshires until their graduation day, which Elegy was not permitted to attend.

Floss went to Sarah Lawrence like Fletcher, Hugo to Princeton, and she saw them at Thanksgiving, at Christmas, and during the summer of their first year and their second. Then they returned to the Berkshires less and less, and although Elegy was never forgotten (she'd a collection of hastily scrawled letters and postcards locked away in a chest on the top shelf of her armoire to attest to the fact), she was certainly not in the forefront of their lives.

She'd become the very thing they'd feared so many years ago.

And now, as the chauffeured Maybach came to rest at last beneath the porte cochere, Elegy sprinted down the steps to meet the woman carefully extricating herself from the back seat. Her youthful flirtation with counterculture fashion long behind her, Floss was, as ever these days, the very picture of wealth and sophistication in a cream sheath dress and cape, her golden hair falling around her shoulders in perfectly styled waves and eyes covered by an enormous pair of round sunglasses, and beside her, Elegy felt small and gray and positively sick with jealousy.

Elegy stiffened as she was pulled into Floss's embrace and surrounded at once by the scent of expensive perfume and cigarette smoke. "I'm so glad you're here," she mumbled into her hair, lifting her arms and patting her friend awkwardly upon the back. "It's been ages."

"It's only been nine months."

"Nine excruciating months. Why didn't you come this summer?"

"Conrad wanted to do the Hamptons. I did try to convince him, but you know how he and my dad get on."

Floss gave instructions to her driver to wait at least an hour, and the two of them sauntered arm in arm into the manor.

The Spirit Collection of Thorne Hall

Mrs. Griswold had laid out tea for them beside a plate of pear and cardamom tarts in the great room before the hearth, but Floss made a beeline for the gleaming mahogany liquor cabinet flanked by two potted palms and grabbed a bottle of Thaddeus's good whiskey.

She filled a crystal tumbler, drank it down in one swallow, then poured another. "Caught Conrad cheating again."

She'd married him to piss off her father when she was just twenty-four, and in the two years since, Conrad had been caught cheating with three different women, though Elegy suspected that there were far more that Floss didn't know about. Conrad was a philanderer despite having very little to offer women other than his bank account. A stodgy, middle-aged man with watery blue eyes and an only slightly bigger than average cock, according to Floss, it was a wonder to Elegy that he never seemed to want for female companionship.

Floss's father had hoped she'd get on well enough with Lionel Westbrook's son that they'd eventually make a go of it and their children would inherit Holcroft, but despite his obvious shortcomings, Conrad had one thing Tobias Westbrook did not: no ties to the Berkshires nor any desire to form any. He owned property in New York City and London, and the moment Floss realized that by suffering his attentions she might live a life of her choosing, she happily let him adorn her finger with a massive Harry Winston bauble.

Floss got out, and Elegy would always hate her just a little bit for it.

"Are you staying a while this time?" asked Elegy, pitiful in her hope. Hugo had been poor company for months now, in Boston more often than in the Berkshires, and otherwise occupied when he was.

"A week, maybe two." Floss shrugged. She poured herself a third glass of whiskey and dropped gracefully into the chair opposite Elegy's. "We should get Hugo round for old times' sake."

"Do you remember Sebastian?"

"Black hair, chubby, quite sweet, actually."

"Not chubby anymore, still sweet."

"I guess so. Why?" At the sight of Elegy's suggestively raised eyebrow, Floss began to laugh. "Oh fuck, I saw this coming. Remember the Blythes' Christmas party last year?"

In fact, Elegy did remember it. Hugo had gotten wasted on rum-spiked eggnog, and Floss and Elegy had found him concealed behind the velvet drapes in the empty library with his cock down Sebastian's throat. At the sight of Elegy's slack jaw and Floss's laughter, Hugo had shoved Sebastian unceremoniously away and affected abject outrage, as if he also had just become aware of the situation, whilst his clandestine lover blinked up at him in confusion.

"How dare you, sir!" shouted Hugo, then stormed off with Floss and Elegy trailing behind him, but not before turning back to Sebastian and mouthing: "Call me."

"So, then your engagement is over?"

"Please don't."

"Tell me you're not going through with it."

Elegy pressed her lips together in a flat line. They bickered over it every time Floss visited and every single time they spoke over the phone in between—and likely would do so until her wedding day. Instead of having Floss serve as her maid of honor, Elegy planned to lock her away in the rectory so that she could not object when old Reverend Thwaites asked if anyone knew of any reason she and Hugo Prescott should not be joined together as man and wife.

Floss settled back in her chair, her finger tracing the rim of her empty glass. "You look worse than the last time I saw you."

"I've missed everything about you but your honesty."

Elegy knew perfectly well what she looked like. She'd always been small, had always been thin; elfin, many said, with black hair and skin as pale as fresh cream. Tabitha's eyes had been the color of sage in high summer, according to Hester, and had she passed those eyes on to Elegy, she might've appeared a modicum less somber. Unfortunately, her eyes were a clear, pale gray. She was memento mori, a living, breathing reminder that all must die, though not all stayed that way.

A fitting mistress for a house such as Thorne Hall.

"Sorry," Floss said, even though she wasn't. "But Jesus, Elegy, when was the last time you left the house?"

Well, *that* was a bit unfair. "I went to town last month."

"Come back to New York with me," Floss begged. "Just fucking leave. I'll get Conrad to pay for school—he owes me after this last one. You can stay with us until you get yourself sorted."

"You know I can't."

Floss's smile was resigned. "Yeah, I know. But I'm not going to stop asking. Every single time I'm here, I'm going to ask until you finally say yes. Until this place finally fucks you up so bad that you can't say no."

Elegy wasn't entirely certain she hadn't already reached that point, and yet, here she was. Here she would always be. Her throat tightening, she reached across the space between them and squeezed Floss's hand. "I'm glad you're back, if only for a little while."

"Me too."

They talked of this and that as Elegy sipped her tea and Floss drank her father's whiskey like it was water because she could not face her parents any other way but shit-faced. And why shouldn't she, when she had her own driver and the excuse of Conrad's infidelity to explain away the sorry state of her?

At last Floss rose unsteadily and kissed both of Elegy's cheeks, her breath heavy with the earthy scent of peat and cloves. "I've got to go. Barbara's having one of her ghastly dinners. But we'll get together soon, yeah? With Hugo?"

"Fletcher's party is next Friday. Will you still be here?"

"Probably. The fucker deserves to sweat for a while."

"Stay," Elegy begged. "Stay until then. Let's get drunk and try on all your clothes."

Floss patted her shoulder. "Yes, let's. Come to Holcroft soon, yeah?"

Elegy stood beneath the port cochere and watched Floss's car until it became a crimson smudge upon the horizon once more as her thoughts turned to the rest of her day, a series of tasks set before her so familiar as to be mundane, and mundane enough as to be a relief.

One could only handle so much ghostly mischief in a single day.

CHAPTER SIX

At two o'clock that afternoon, Elegy bolted upright on the window seat in her bedroom, a first edition of *Northanger Abbey* purloined from the library sliding from her lap to the floor in a heap of pages too old to endure such abuse.

She blinked, and beheld Adelaide's face hovering above her own.

"There are men here," the spirit informed her solemnly. "*Men*."

Elegy scowled. "How did you get in here? The runes—"

"Are worthless if the door is left ajar."

"I didn't—"

"I did." Adelaide beamed, exceedingly proud of herself, as the cheeky thing had been hiding around the corner and rolled a bobbin across the floor just as Elegy pulled the door closed. It had lodged in the jamb, and she'd waited until Elegy had fallen asleep somewhere around the second chapter before sneaking in.

"I watched you sleep," Adelaide continued. "But that was exceedingly boring, so I went through your things instead."

"Well, I do hope you enjoyed yourself, because it won't happen again."

"Doesn't matter. They weren't that interesting anyway."

Elegy did not know whether to be relieved or insulted.

"Reed has been a very bad boy, "Adelaide continued. "I tried to stop him, but he would not listen. He's angry with you."

"Angry with me?" Elegy asked. "Whatever for?"

"He can't remember."

"Well, that is most unhelpful."

From below, Elegy heard the sound of heavy footfalls and male voices before the front door closed. It must be Jeremiah and the men he'd promised he'd bring to consult upon the kitchen. Thaddeus would have met them already, but her presence would be expected to calm the spirits, as several of them did not take kindly to disruptions such as these, even during the day. She smoothed the skirt of her dress, straightened her hair in the desilvered mirror of her vanity, and shooed Adelaide from her room so that she could shut the door properly, allowing the runes to do their work. Adelaide might've found her personal things uninteresting, but that did not mean Elegy wished them to be trifled with.

"I don't suppose you had anything to do with last night's mischief?"

Adelaide's lower lip poked out. "You do know I hate to be left out."

"Calliope," sighed Elegy. "That was you, then."

"It is hardly my fault that she is so easy to rile."

"It is entirely your fault that you used it to your advantage."

"Elegy," whined the shade of a girl long dead. "Don't be cross with me. I only wished for a bit of fun; it's so deadly dull at night. Not like it used to be when there were more of you Thornes."

Thaddeus would have seen Adelaide punished most severely for her transgression and likely had done so many times over the years, given as she was to mischief and entirely unrepentant, however theatrical her pouting. But when it came to the children, Elegy felt nothing but sorrow, and such sorrow rendered her soft in her father's eyes.

"Promise me that you will never do it again and I shall not be cross with you."

They were empty words, for she absolutely would do it again, and Elegy would be no less soft upon that day than she was now.

"I promise," Adelaide declared solemnly, and Elegy pretended to believe her.

They parted ways, Adelaide to the room at the end of the corridor that had once belonged to Delilah and then to many Thorne wives thereafter and Elegy to the first floor to confront their visitors. But when she reached the landing, she stopped.

A man was standing at the bottom of the staircase admiring the scrollwork of the banister.

All Elegy could make out at first were broad shoulders beneath a black T-shirt and a head of disheveled brown hair streaked with gold. At her approach he lifted his face, and Elegy Thorne, who had been surrounded by beautiful things all her life, beheld something that rivaled them all.

He was tall and exquisitely made, perhaps a few years over thirty, with a strong, sharp jaw covered in several days' worth of stubble. When she looked into his eyes, she found herself upon the flat of her back beneath the Painted Grove in the sticky, buzzing heat of late summer, staring up at the rich, dappled green of the sun filtered through a canopy of leaves.

Evidently a person could, in fact, be so beautiful it hurt to look at them, because there was a sharp, sudden twinge behind her breastbone. When the corner of his mouth tilted upward, she wondered if she were having a heart attack. Or had possibly gone insane, because she suddenly had the most peculiar urge to sink her teeth into the perfection of his lower lip.

The man's gaze traveled the whole of her, which, given her pitiful stature, did not take very long, and she could well imagine what he saw: a pale, black-haired young woman in a gown one hundred years out of fashion, coral softly brushing her pale neck and her eyes as dead as her constant companions, one of which was standing mere feet away, watching him beneath a tattered black veil.

She was the daughter of the house, the mistress of Thorne Hall in all but name, and he was but an interloper come to disturb her peace with that *face* and all that brown hair in a lovely disarray, and there was still the matter of the ache in her chest that refused to subside.

It simply would not do.

Squaring her narrow shoulders, she lifted her chin and demanded: "Who are you, and what are you doing here?"

"There's a leak in your kitchen."

Her eyes narrowed. "How do you know that? Are you one of Jeremiah's men?"

"Not exactly."

"Then you do not belong here. Show yourself out at once."

"Jeremiah is my father."

"Jeremiah has no children. If he did, I would know."

"I was raised in Seattle with my mom, and we didn't visit often."

"Then why are you here bothering us when you should be there bothering someone else?"

The Spirit Collection of Thorne Hall

His expression grew thoughtful, and she regretted immediately her impertinence, for she much preferred his smile. "Dad's been ill since summer. I'm here for the month to help him as best I can."

"Oh," Elegy breathed, shame flooding through her veins. "I'm sorry. He's a lovely man; will he be all right?"

"He is," the man agreed. "And I suspect he will be. He's a tough one."

"Are you a contractor too?"

"No."

"What do you do, then?"

"You ask a lot of questions."

She stiffened. "I don't have occasion to meet many people. I'm curious."

"Come down here, then, and I'll tell you."

He was self-assured, comfortable in his skin and altogether too comfortable with her. She should have been affronted, enraged, even!

Later, she would blame her weak constitution on her sorrow at having parted with Floss and the desire to be near someone who neither was dead nor despised her very existence, and she would refuse to consider the fact that she might have been . . . *attracted* to him, which she certainly was not.

She descended one step, then another and another, until she stepped from the last into the foyer and stood before him with hands clasped demurely at her front; the top of her head barely reached his chest.

She lifted her face; the dappled forest of his eyes met the wide, clear gray of hers, and although it was likely only her imagination, she could've sworn his chest jerked as he caught his breath.

"Hi," he said softly.

"Hello," she answered. "I've come as you've asked. Now tell me what you do."

She'd no idea what she'd said that should be so amusing to him, but the corner of his mouth lifted all the same. "What's your name?"

"You've not answered my question."

"And I won't until you answer mine."

Well, *that* was certainly not their agreement, and Elegy was very tempted to walk right back up the great staircase and allow The Mourning to deal with their most aggravating visitor despite the inevitable consequence.

"How about I go first," he offered, and lifted his hand between them. "I'm Atticus."

Her eyes dropped to his fingers, and she wondered if he could see the way her heart fumbled about in her chest at the very idea of touching the warm skin of another living person she'd only just met.

Elegy did not like to be touched, much less by a stranger, but of course he could not possibly know that.

After her mother died, Thaddeus had hired a nanny called Miss Ambrose, a stern woman of seventy-five years and even stingier with her affection than he was, whose favorite pastime was locking Elegy away in her room for hours while she read the Bible.

By the time she passed away and Mrs. Griswold arrived, Elegy outright screamed every time the housekeeper endeavored so much as to hug her. With a great deal of time and patience, she eventually came to accept and even enjoy a bit of affection here and there, even from several of the spirits in the Collection, for she spent far more time in their company than she did with anyone else, but never did she seek it out the way other people did—people who were so perfectly ordinary as to be objects of jealousy to someone who was extraordinary in the worst possible way.

Steeling her spine against what was certain to be a most unpleasant experience indeed, Elegy thrust her hand into his and shook it, hard.

She would have pulled away immediately after, but his fingers, warm and steady, curled around her own, and she shivered in wonder and in delight, her lips parting as she pondered the contrast of his tanned skin against the pale white of hers. She knew few men beyond her father and those who served them, and few were as large or as vital as this one whose hand engulfed her own. His thumb moved across her skin, stroking idly once, twice, and it was an absolute tragedy how much she liked it.

"Ah, Elegy. I see you've met Atticus."

At the sound of her father's voice, Elegy came to herself at once and tore her hand free as though it had been thrust into scalding water.

"Jeremiah and I have business to discuss," Thaddeus continued. "Show Atticus the house."

A command, not a request.

And yet, ever the dutiful daughter, she replied, "Of course, Father."

"Excellent," said Thaddeus, and when their eyes met, his sharp nod told her that the Collection would cause them no trouble, a kindness only ever afforded to guests. He and Jeremiah disappeared into his office, and Elegy was left alone once more with his son, whose hands she could not stop staring at, particularly his left thumb.

The Spirit Collection of Thorne Hall

"Well, then," she said, tearing her gaze away from said offending appendage and folding her hands primly before her. "This is the great hall, of course. Now do try and keep up."

She led him down the gallery, into the butler's pantry, and through the dining room, her pitiful efforts to remain ahead of him—and thus out of sight of his absurdly beautiful face—thwarted by his long and easy strides.

She'd played the tour guide upon numerous occasions since Thaddeus had fallen ill, her knowledge of the house being extensive and far less brusquely delivered under ordinary circumstances, and yet she found herself flustered as she called his attention to the intricate plaster ceilings and stained glass, the original fixtures and furniture and gleaming wood paneling.

His arm brushed hers, and she shivered and forgot the year the first electric lights had been installed. They turned the corner, and the scent of him, leather and spice and warm skin, sent her stumbling into the china hutch.

Good God, was she ever to know peace again?

She did not show him the ballroom. Her father might believe the Collection managed, but a man—a living, breathing man, and one with that *face*, well... Atticus was a temptation far too irresistible to risk parading anywhere near Gideon Constant and his ilk, even if the early-autumn sun still shone defiantly through the banks of milky gold-and-green glass.

"Will the repairs take long?" she asked, as they came once more to the great hall by way of the dining room, passing the grand piano where Vivian watched their journey with rot-ringed white eyes.

"A few weeks, maybe. Longer if the parts are hard to come by."

"Can you spare so much time?"

"Don't sound so disappointed."

"I'm not," she said, too fast, then busied herself with opening the pocket doors. "The library, obviously."

Atticus whistled as he stepped over the threshold, his attention immediately captured by a sheaf of yellowing paper in a lighted glass case. "Are these—"

"Shakespeare's sonnets, yes. Will you be staying with your father?"

"I've rented a place in town for a month," he answered, attention still fixed firmly upon the contents of the glass case. "This *can't* be a first edition."

"Published in 1609," she confirmed.

"'No longer mourn for me when I am dead,'" Atticus read. "'Than you shall hear the surly sullen bell.' Why this one?"

She considered the hallowed pages caged in glass. "I'll admit there are far lovelier poems within this volume, but none speak quite so accurately upon death and the danger mourning too long poses to the living as well as the dead. I suppose I find such a thing fascinating."

If he thought her odd because of it—well, odder than he likely already did—he was polite enough to say nothing as he moved to the nearest bookshelf, his eyes taking in the leather bindings and gold titles stamped upon the spines. He took a copy of *Little Dorrit* in his hands and gently turned it this way and that to inspect the gilt edging, flipped open the cover, put it carefully back.

"You never did tell me what you do," she reminded him as he bent to examine an illuminated manuscript upon a stand, opened to a gilded illustration of trumpeting angels.

"I'm an engineer."

"Well, that's very vague."

He laughed, a husky, throaty sound that sent Elegy's heart ricocheting about within the cold hollow of her chest. "My company designs clean-energy systems."

"You have your own company?"

"Going on six years now."

It occurred to her then that Atticus Hart was quite a bit more worldly than she'd first imagined. He had gone to college; several colleges, most likely. Perhaps he had an office with glass walls and concrete floors and screens that displayed stock prices in neon numbers and lines that rose and fell and crossed one another. She'd seen such a likeness in the *New York Times* one day and decided that every businessman must have an office such as this, as well as a secretary who was blonde and wore very short skirts.

Atticus did not look like a businessman now, with his worn jeans and steel-toed boots, but he was a danger to her nonetheless because she could not seem to stop looking at him, observing and cataloging every detail she could, from the way the muscles of his back flexed beneath the fabric of his shirt to the deliciously rumpled mess of his hair and *especially* the wonderful way the corners of his eyes crinkled when he smiled that told her he did so often.

She decided his smile was the most dangerous thing about him.

In the drawing room, she called his attention to the marble hearth and plaster ceiling, ignoring the grotesque faces and crude gestures made by Eugenia and Mabel from their usual table, and ushered him quickly back into the great hall.

He was appropriately awed at the staircase, and she showed him the landing with its courting bench and medieval tapestries before allowing him a glimpse into the master bedroom, the adjacent suite that had been left empty since Tabitha's death, and the four guest bedrooms with en suite bathrooms, only two of which were actually suitable for use, the other two being smothered in at least an inch of dust and boasting an impressive array of cobwebs.

"We don't often have overnight visitors to the house," she explained.

He did not appear to mind, studying with curiosity the odd metal box affixed to the wall above one of the porcelain sinks. "What's this?"

"A methane lamp."

"A what?"

She gestured to the length of thin pipe that led from the lamp to the toilet. "As you see."

He tipped back his head, and there went Elegy's traitorous heart once more at the sound of his laughter. "Oh, that's fantastic."

"They were not invented to amuse," she told him primly, "but to allow those using the facilities at night to see what they were doing. Men have extraordinarily bad aim even by daylight."

He moved closer to inspect it more thoroughly. "This has to be the weirdest thing I've ever seen in a house."

The thought was so terribly absurd that the corner of her mouth twitched upright before she forced it back down again.

He paused just outside Thaddeus's room to study the painting hanging there, an ostentatiously large portrait of a young, fair-haired woman with gray eyes and a small bird perched delicately upon her fingers.

"Is this one of your ancestors?" he asked.

"I believe so, although I cannot be sure. No one knows who the subject is. One of Jasper's sisters, most likely."

"She has your eyes."

She was far too pleased that he'd noticed such a thing than she ought to have been.

The third floor was off-limits to guests due to the fact that one had gotten their leg stuck in the floor up to the thigh the last time Elegy had given a tour. But Atticus's curiosity was insatiable, and if he wanted to fall straight through the ceiling into the Blue Room, well, she supposed that was his prerogative. Jeremiah could do the repairs and send the bill to his son directly.

This part of the house he observed in silence, and she could well imagine why.

Time donned many guises. It passed both slowly and in haste, flew when one was having fun, waited for no man, and healed all things.

And it could just as easily destroy as it could any of the rest of it.

Rotting floors and peeling wallpaper and crumbling plaster aside, the real trouble was that the exterior walls were caving in on account of the ice and snow that gathered in places and melted come spring, seeping into the house.

"The estimated cost to repair them is great," said Elegy, as Atticus took hold of one of the beams that braced the wall upright, testing its weight. "I imagine we'll have to, one day, but my father has deemed the third floor a very low priority."

"So it's you, your father, and your stepmother—and no one else?"

"There is the staff, of course. The estate is simply too large to manage without them. But we are the manor's only residents, yes." Her eyes narrowed. "Why are you making that face?"

"This is just my face."

"You find fault with the house."

"I don't," he answered immediately. "It's an incredible piece of history."

Warmth blossomed in her chest and spread throughout her cold little body. "Yes, it is. In fact—"

"It ought to be a museum."

Elegy stopped so abruptly her heel sank into a particularly soft spot in the wood, and she found herself stuck. "Surely you jest."

He turned and, upon seeing her predicament, offered her a steady hand whilst she extricated herself and brushed the dust and humiliation from her skirt and stockings.

"There are eighteen bedrooms, and only three of them are occupied," he pointed out as they made their way back to the third-floor corridor. "You said you don't receive visitors, so what do you need all of the extra space for? The cost of maintaining it all must be staggering, and for what?"

"Thorne Hall has been in my family for well over a century," Elegy answered. "It is our home and always will be."

"That you've kept it running all these years is a miracle, but it won't last—not without some serious modernization."

The house was at far greater risk from the midnight mischief of spirits, but of course she did not tell him so.

The Spirit Collection of Thorne Hall

By the time they descended the staircase back into the great hall, Jeremiah and Thaddeus had finished their conversation. They clasped hands, paperwork was exchanged, and Atticus was summoned by his father.

"I'll call Paul in Boston and get fans out as soon as possible," Jeremiah said. "You've got the second kitchen still, yes? You'll need to use it for the time being."

Thaddeus frowned, and Elegy knew he was thinking of Fletcher's party.

"I'll be back tomorrow," Jeremiah continued. "Keep the water shut off to that part of the house until then."

The contractor tipped his weathered cap to her father and bowed to Elegy in an exaggerated show of chivalry. As he ambled to his beat-up black truck, Atticus held out his hand.

Oh, no. He would not get away with it a second time, muddling her head with the warmth of his skin and that stupid thumb of his. She fixed the offending appendage with a withering gaze as she folded her hands primly before her. "Good afternoon, Mr. Hart."

Amusement tugged at the corners of that wide, full, absurdly lovely mouth. "I hope to see you again, Miss Thorne."

Elegy promptly turned and slammed the door shut before he could see the flush that rose upon her cheeks.

Stupid thumb.

The Wife of Usher's Well
Francis James Child ballad #79

There lived a wife in Usher's Well
A wealthy wife was she;
She had three stout and stalwart sons
And sent them o'er the sea.
They had not been from Usher's Well,
A week but barely one,
When word came to this carlin wife
That her three sons were gone.
"I wish the wind may never cease
Nor flashes in the flood
Till my three sons return to me
In earthly flesh and blood."
It fell about the Martinmas,
The nights were long and dark,
Three sons came home to Usher's Well
Their hats were made of bark
That neither grew in forest green
Nor on any wooded rise,
But from the north side of the tree
That grows in Paradise.
"Blow up the fire, my merry merry maidens,
Bring water from the well
For all my house shall feed this night
Since my three sons are well."
Then up and crowed the blood red cock
And up and crowed the gray,
The oldest to the youngest said,
"It's time we were away.
For the cock does crow and the day doth show
And the channerin worm doth chide
And we must go from Usher's Well
To the gates of Paradise."
"I wish the wind may never cease
Nor flashes in the flood
Till my three sons return to me
In earthly flesh and blood."

CHAPTER SEVEN

The remainder of Elegy's day passed exactly as it was meant to.

There were orders to be placed with the manor's usual suppliers, inventories to be taken, wine to be selected, and a great deal of needlework to be done, and she went about it all with the usual quiet determination with which she approached all things, until Mrs. Griswold called her to an early supper. Like the rest of the staff, she and her husband departed before nightfall, and so if Elegy wished her food to be warm, she must make haste. There was no microwave at Thorne Hall and never would be.

It used to be that Thaddeus, Fletcher, and Elegy ate together in the dining room, but that awkward tradition had ceased the more erratic Fletcher became. What had begun as cruel barbs exchanged over candlelight and too many glasses of wine gradually became the throwing of said glasses against the nearest wall, and so Thaddeus had taken to dining at a different hour entirely from the rest of the family and most often in his office.

It happened that Fletcher's behavior was a show put on for Thaddeus's benefit, and so, when he removed himself as the audience, she no longer wished to perform. Instead, she dined alone in her third-floor suite, and Elegy ate at the table in the kitchen, where at least she had Cook for company.

Unfortunately, the enormous hand-hewn table that sat proudly at the center of the kitchen had been removed, its legs requiring restoration after hours submerged in water, and so Elegy ate that night in the dining room, which she avoided whenever possible and for very good reason.

"I hate to think of you here in the dim and cold," Mrs. Griswold fretted as Elegy slid into her chair and reached for her goblet. "I could light the fire for you, if you like."

Elegy shook her head. "That's all right, Mrs. Griswold. It would be a waste, and anyway, I'll be quick. I do not like to remain in this room any longer than is necessary without my father present."

Mrs. Griswold had absolutely no idea what Elegy was on about but smiled nonetheless, and the heir to Thorne Hall was left alone to eat in silence and in the gathering dark. Lucy had prepared Scottish salmon that evening, which ordinarily Elegy would have enjoyed were it not for the imminent arrival of a most detestable dining companion. Indeed, not five minutes had passed after the housekeeper's departure before the shadows at the far end of the room shifted and a man slid from them, pressing himself against the wall as his milky-white eyes found hers.

Elegy stiffened and cast her gaze down to her plate, where she busied herself flaking the tender fish, parceling it into morsels meant to hurry along the process as swiftly as possible; this would be a meal less to enjoy than to endure.

This particular spirit's skin was grayer than that of most of the Collection, owing to the length of time he had been dead before his summoning, though an argument could be made that it matched the perfect emptiness of his conscious, and it was marbled with cracks and fissures of black rot. He moved slowly, sinuously, along the length of the wall, and all the while he watched her with those terrible eyes.

"Go away and leave me be," Elegy murmured, but he did not.

Curling into the corner like ink, he watched as her silverware slid across the antique china and as she lifted a bit of fish or vegetable to her lips. He watched as she alternated between sips of water and wine. And when she refused to look at him, he poured himself into the chair usually occupied by her father and began to mimic her movements, slicing his invisible supper and lifting it to his rotting lips, followed by his nonexistent goblet. He did this until Elegy could no longer bear his company and, enough of her supper eaten to sate her, she pushed her plate away and stumbled from the chair.

In life he'd been a well-to-do merchant with offices in Merchants Row near Faneuil Hall in the late 1840s, where he trafficked in tea and slaves. He'd perished in the Berkshires whilst visiting an elderly aunt whom he hated, a sentiment overlooked by virtue of the enormous fortune he was certain to inherit as her only living kin. He did not live long enough to do so and, to add insult to injury, discovered some one hundred years later that his aunt had never intended to bequeath her money to him, choosing instead to leave the lot of it to her two dogs, to be split evenly between them.

As he had made his fortune fulfilling the depraved whims of people wishing to own other people, Elegy very much doubted Bancroft had been the cheerful sort in life. In death he was oil with teeth, sharp and at the ready.

He watched with a slick black smile as she darted from the room into the great hall. She did not bother to close the doors—he could walk through them if he pleased and whistle while he did so—but Bancroft disliked the great hall and would not likely follow her.

Shivering, Elegy curled up in her usual chair before the marble hearth, a tufted leather wingback far too large for her and far too stiff to be comfortable, and pulled a blanket over her lap. She'd forgotten *Northanger Abbey* upstairs, but it was no matter, for she'd yet to read today's news in the hubbub over Floss's visit and the arrival of Jeremiah and his son.

Mrs. Griswold had left the stack of newspapers in the basket beside the hearth, and Elegy took up the *New York Times*. Beneath were the *Wall Street Journal*, the *Washington Post*, and the *Globe*, her father's required daily reading. Although he refused to allow her access to the world, he despised the idea of her ignorance, lest she embarrass him when they had the occasional guest call or attended the odd country house party.

She had moved on to the *Journal* when she heard the distant slamming of a door and the sound of her stepmother descending the staircase.

"Bernard!" Fletcher barked. "Drink!"

From the butler's pantry came a grunt, and the air was filled with the tinkling sounds of copper and ice and glass as Fletcher made her way down the grand staircase in one of Matthias Thorne's velvet smoking jackets that hung far too large on her tall, willowy frame but at the same time fit her so perfectly that Elegy was certain it had been made for her and her alone.

She was met at the bottom of the stairs with a martini upon a silver tray by Bernard, a farmer who had stumbled into his field drunk and been run over by a plow. How he had become Fletcher's personal mixologist was a mystery for the ages; not even Thaddeus could account for it.

Fletcher had finished half of it by the time she slumped into the other wingback chair.

"I'll take another, Bernard," she called over her shoulder, then fixed her shrewd eyes upon Elegy. "What the fuck happened to the kitchen?"

"Leak," Elegy answered. "Nearly two feet of water."

"And what's being done about it?"

"Jeremiah was here earlier to assess the damage. He brought his son from Seattle. He's an engineer."

Fletcher's rust-stained mouth stretched into a wide grin. "Is that why you're so flushed?"

"I am not flushed."

"Sure you're not," Fletcher laughed, a series of undignified snorts that Elegy's father despised. "How long will the repairs take? My party is next week."

"It'll be lovely."

"God, you're a fucking terrible liar." Fletcher sighed as she rose and made her way to the record player across the room. The rich timbre of Ella Fitzgerald's voice filled the great room and Elegy's stepmother leaned against the wall, closed her eyes, and began to sing in a truly abysmal rasping alto.

The records had belonged to Elegy's mother, contraband she'd smuggled into the manor with her upon the occasion of her marriage. Her dowry, she used to tell Mrs. Griswold. She'd had wonderful taste, in Elegy's opinion, from the gypsy jazz of 1920s Paris to the Beatles and Fleetwood Mac, but there was nothing past the eighties when she'd come to Thorne Hall.

Fletcher kept a great number of the records in her crumbling third-floor sanctuary, and when Elegy was particularly sentimental, she bribed Adelaide to pinch what she wanted. The Collection did not often bother with Fletcher, for Elegy herself painted the runes above her bedroom door, just as she'd done every night since her sixteenth birthday when her stepmother had lost what little remained of her good sense.

"You should invite him," Fletcher said, listing back to her chair and falling down so hard within it that her martini sloshed over the edge of her glass. "Jeremiah's son."

Elegy stiffened. "Absolutely not."

"And why not? You've just said the party will be lovely."

"You know perfectly well why not."

"Because of Hugo?"

"No, not because of Hugo."

"I cannot imagine why, then."

Elegy arched one eyebrow. "Oh, you cannot?"

"Delphine said he was delicious."

"I doubt she used that word."

"She absolutely did."

Elegy snorted. "Pervert."

"Agreed. So fuck him."

"No."

"Then you won't mind if I do? A little birthday treat, if you will."

Elegy knew Fletcher wouldn't. She'd had many opportunities for lovers throughout the lonely years and had not succumbed despite a rampant libido that she did little to conceal. It was for the same reason that Elegy had never attempted to do the very thing Floss spoke of with such enthusiasm when they'd reached an age where such activities became an overwhelming curiosity.

Although the runes forbade the Collection from passing through certain doors, neither Elegy nor Fletcher was convinced that they could not see them all the same. Thaddeus refused to confirm or deny their suspicions, and so Elegy was mortified at the idea that they might see her fumbling attempts at pleasure. Fletcher had no such qualms and, in fact, had told Elegy upon multiple occasions that she was sure she'd given them quite a show. No, for Fletcher it was the fear that, should she take a lover, the Collection would tell Thaddeus and he would punish her. With them. This she could not abide, however much she longed for the touch of another, and so Thorne Hall was perfectly, pristinely, infuriatingly chaste.

"I think you'd better stick to the cake," Elegy said at last, and Fletcher had the good grace to laugh.

Even so, Elegy was forced to recount each and every observation of Atticus that she'd made, until she was sick with longing and furious at herself over the fact. Bernard had slunk off somewhere, and after shouting did not produce him, Fletcher stumbled to the liquor cabinet and poured herself a tumbler of gin. "I'm to bed," she announced.

It was just as well she'd decided to pack it in early. Elegy had a date with a certain young man who had thrown their lives into such chaos with a simple act of mischief.

The Mourning's head turned as Elegy made her way up the staircase to the second floor, passing her own bedroom door until she reached the end of the opposite corridor.

"You've been misbehaving," Elegy whispered into the shadows there.

A face, round and sweet and utterly horrifying, appeared from behind a curtain. Reed had been in the lake for a full day before a search party discovered his body, and the sight of him still made Elegy want to retch. It was his mouth that sickened her the most, the black water that dribbled from his perfect Cupid's bow lips and down his tiny chin.

"I haven't," came his rasping whisper.

"You have."

The spirit of the dead boy lurched down the corridor toward Elegy in silence, leaving behind a trail of wet footprints that better resembled tar than water and vanished within moments.

His face lifted to hers, and in the shaft of moonlight streaming from the leaded glass window, Elegy could see the rot that was spreading beneath his eyes. He had been the last spirit collected, and soon he would be as mottled as the rest of them.

"He said it would make you laugh."

Reed did not need to say his name for Elegy to know exactly whom he meant. She stiffened. "I've told you not to listen to him."

It mattered little what she said or how many times she said it; they *all* listened to him. He was the first of the Collection. Gideon Constant had welcomed the rest of them and won their trust and the adoration of their muddled heads and black hearts. The 115 years that separated his death from the beginning of his captivity should have rendered him even more mindless than the rest, but Gideon was cunning. Ruthless. And only just under Thaddeus Thorne's thumb.

Her father would survive another winter, perhaps, but certainly not two, and then the Collection would be hers.

And Gideon Constant would eat her alive.

Reed's hand slipped into her own, his head low and contrite. "I'm sorry, Elegy."

"That's all right," she told him on a sigh. "Do try to remember what I've said in future."

"I'll try. Elegy, will you hold me for a little while? I'm ever so cold."

Elegy sat on the window seat at the end of the corridor, and Reed clamored into her lap, soaking it through with black water. He wound his skinny arms around her neck and pressed his rotting, cherubic face into her neck and sighed, the sound a death rattle.

"Will you sing for me?" he whispered. "'The Wife of Usher's Well'?"

"Why?" she asked. "Why that particular song?"

"Because it wasn't her fault," he answered upon a sigh. "It wasn't her fault at all."

The Spirit Collection of Thorne Hall

It was one of the Child ballads, of course, for she sang them more often than anything else, but it told a terrible tale of a fine woman who had three stalwart sons, although in some versions it was three little boys. Whether it was to sea they went in the case of the former or to school to study their grammar (or, in several versions, witchcraft) in the case of the latter, they died and her excessive mourning tied their spirits to the earth.

> *The green grass is at our head*
> *And the clay is at our feet*
> *And your tears come tumbling down*
> *And wet our winding sheet*

But however much their mother tried to feed them or bid them sleep in their beds, death was the lord before whom all must bow. And as in so many visitation songs, the cock crowed at dawn, and thus they departed.

Cold seeped from the spirit's tiny body into Elegy's own as she sang, and as the fetid stench of death surrounded them both, Elegy felt the first tear well and fall. They came quickly after that, sliding down her frozen cheeks as she held the body of a boy long dead, trapped within a corpse that would make one of her long before she died.

CHAPTER EIGHT

That Elegy was able to manage the Collection as well as she did was owed not to her father but to a Harvard professor named Francis James Child.

The fact that he had been dead some 125 years was of little consequence.

As a child, she'd watched the way the Collection were drawn to the ballroom upon the rare occasions that Vivian took to the piano, wood brittle and broken with the years, the hammers having lost their suppleness, as though the instrument had been left to sit gathering dust for decades rather than being tuned twice a year without fail. But it was Calliope's sweet, lilting voice they loved best of all, because she sang the old songs, songs they recognized even if they'd forgotten everything else.

Some Calliope had learned from her mother and grandmother, who'd brought them from the Scottish Highlands when America was new, but far more she'd heard within the walls of Thorne Hall over the long years, including the Child ballads, a collection of 305 stories lovingly gathered and meticulously preserved so that they would never be forgotten. Jasper's second son, who had inherited the Collection owing to his older brother's untimely demise, was beseeched by his wife to provide entertainment for their isolated household, shut away as they were with the war raging across the ocean and the pandemic at home nearing its second wave. And so, on a sweltering August evening in the year 1918, a woman named Ida Rose Pritchard arrived at Thorne Hall with a harp and two guitar players in tow. For two hours they performed for the beleaguered family and staff (and other unseen ears), but it was Calliope who was forever changed by that magical evening, so much in fact that while the musicians enjoyed a late supper before their journey back to the village, she rifled through their belongings until she found a folio of sheet music and hid the lot of it beneath a floorboard in the Honeysuckle Room.

One night when Elegy was all of seven years old and ravenous in the way all growing children were, she crept down to the kitchen once the house was abed, in search of the Dundee cake their cook, Clara, had made for tea. Cook was likely to be there, true, but she was more terrified of Elegy than Elegy was of her, and so Elegy cut herself a fat wedge of the rich, fruit-studded cake and sat at the large table in the center of the kitchen to eat it. She'd no sooner shoveled three enormous forkfuls into her mouth when a shadow fell upon her. She looked up, and her fork fell from her slackened fingers with a clatter.

The Shaker farmer with gashes upon his back stood in the doorway with his hands curled into fists, staring at her with his milky eyes narrowed.

She swallowed the cake that had become lodged in her throat and waited for him to pass on as they always did, disinclined to invite their master's wrath by making mischief with his young heir. But rather than drift away down the corridor, he dragged one heavy foot into the kitchen and then another, a low growl rumbling in the great barrel of his chest.

He normally kept to the butler's pantry and to the kitchen, but once she'd seen him at the foot of the staircase in the great hall as the sun was beginning to set, with his face titled upward, listening to the sound of Calliope's voice drifting down from the third floor. And so Elegy took a deep breath and began to sing.

The effect upon him was both immediate and wondrous. He stopped moving toward her, and his fists uncurled until they hung limp and harmless at his sides. The menacing look in his eyes had vanished, and Elegy sagged in relief even as the rest of the cake lay forgotten upon the plate before her.

Cook had peered around the corner of the pantry as Elegy continued the tale of Tam Lin and his brave lover, and soon she'd floated all the way into the room, listening with the same rapt fascination as Bernard. Elegy had a lovely voice, low and clear and with a pleasing timbre well suited for such simple melodies, and soon others appeared: Nathan Bride, the kindly scholar who never left the library; The Mourning, who had once strangled a man deep in his cups who'd fallen asleep in the great hall; Adelaide and Reed, only children themselves, who dearly loved a story.

They watched Elegy until she'd sung the last verse and afterward, as she slid from her chair and saw to her plate. And as she left the kitchen, they slid into the shadows and let her pass with all the deference afforded her position, however young she might be, the mistress of Thorne Hall in miniature.

It was the first of thousands of such nights, when with her songs she did what her blood could not.

Once Reed had slid from her lap and wandered off in search of Adelaide, Elegy bolted to the bathroom nearest her chamber and slammed the door shut. She only just made it to the toilet.

Clutching the ancient porcelain in both hands, she shook and retched until there was nothing left in her stomach, then slid down until her cheek rested upon the cold tile of the bathroom floor. There she stayed until she was certain that she could make the short journey to her bedroom without collapsing.

This was the way of it whenever she allowed any of them to touch her for too long.

According to Child, the Collection would be considered more revenant than ghost, what with the fact that they were corporeal at least some of the time, but the term was never used in any ballad she had uncovered from Ravenscroft to Sharpe, to say nothing of the London broadsides. Their touch was not an uncommon occurrence; fingers brushed against her own in the threading of needles, against her neck when there was no one else to see to her hair or to clasp a necklace, against her cheeks to wipe away her tears when darkness had fallen and there was no one else. But the effects of these were fleeting and easily managed: a cool cloth upon her face, an hour or two of solitude, a song for her and her alone.

But Reed often wished to be held, and she'd never been able to refuse him as often as she should have.

Perhaps it was that he'd lost his mother the day he'd gone into that lake, and she'd never known hers at all.

Perhaps it was guilt that she'd grown from midnight playmate to the cusp of adulthood when he never would.

Whatever the reason, she could no sooner deny him her touch than she could her song, and so she could be found hunched over a toilet at least twice a week.

The Spirit Collection of Thorne Hall

And so, when Mrs. Griswold arrived with tea and scotch eggs for her breakfast the next morning, Elegy felt as limp as a dishcloth freshly wrung and cast aside. Alas, there would be no one to sing her ballads to distract her from the fact that Jeremiah Hart and his infuriatingly beautiful son were due at ten o'clock.

She'd no reason to select her attire for any other purpose than to avoid her father's ire, and yet, on this morning, she found herself lingering overlong in her closet, pulling one dress after another from the rack only to find it wanting for some ridiculous reason or another and shoving it back.

In the end, she decided upon an ivory silk blouse with black piping, pearl buttons, and a high lace collar, and she paired it with a skirt of claret silk with only a minimal bustle. Elegy frowned at her reflection in the mirror, turning this way and that to examine her figure in a way she'd never desired to do before. She came to a rather depressing conclusion:

She looked like a librarian.

In the 1890s.

Elegy pinned her thick black hair in a proper chignon at her nape and tried on no less than a dozen pairs of earrings before she settled upon garnets set in gold, surrounded by a halo of tiny seed pearls.

What little makeup she possessed she'd been gifted by Floss for some Christmas or another, and it was likely too old to be considered sanitary, but she fumbled with it nonetheless, managing to poke herself in the eye only twice.

In the end it proved to be all for naught, because he did not come.

At precisely ten AM, Jeremiah strolled through the front door with two middle-aged men at his back and a smile upon his face.

"Good morning, Elegy." Jeremiah greeted her with a tip of his tweed cap. "I do hope you and your household slept well."

"Tolerably," Elegy answered, her eyes flickering briefly past him to the empty doorway beyond. "I thought your son was meant to help you this fall."

"Atticus? Oh, I expect he will when I've need of him," Jeremiah answered. "I told him not to come all this way to bother with me—he's got his own company, did you know?"

Elegy smiled agreeably, but inside she was positively seething. "Yes, he told me somewhat of it, but I was rather hoping he would come today. I wanted to ask him about sustainable improvements that might be made to the estate."

She most certainly had not and only then remembered the idea as something Hugo had spoken of some years before in his fruitless quest to convince her father to modernize Thorne Hall. Thankfully, either she'd made a valid point or Jeremiah did not know enough about the subject to doubt her, for he nodded sagely. "I've been trying to convince your father of the same for years now. Maybe now that Atticus is here, he can finally change the old man's mind!"

There was nothing more he could tell her regarding Atticus, and so she bid him a polite "Good day" and listened as he greeted her father in the butler's pantry. Then, silence.

Back in her room, Elegy unbuttoned her blouse with shaking hands and thrust it back on the rack, followed by the skirt, slamming the dressing room door with far more force than she'd meant to, but it felt so wonderfully good that she did it again, and then once more. Then she pulled on a dressing gown made of pale-coral velvet and lace and threw herself onto the window seat and took up *Northanger Abbey* once more.

She turned one page, then two, cut herself upon the third, and thrust her smarting fingertip into her sullen mouth.

Why had he not come? She could not claim to be particularly riveting, and the longer she perched in her window and stared up at the patterned plaster of her ceiling, the more certain she was that his curious behavior upon touching her hand was a product of her febrile imagination.

But was she really so very dull as to be avoided entirely?

She turned her attention once more to the page.

Honestly, the infuriating man and his stupid thumb had done her a great service. She had thought of little else since he'd come to Thorne Hall, and it was not to be borne. Fletcher's party was but a week away, and there was the dreadful inconvenience of the kitchen, to say nothing of the darkening circles beneath her father's eyes and his threats of some sort of test . . .

She must keep her wits about her, and Atticus Hart was a dangerous creature indeed as far as her wits were concerned.

Better to think upon *Northanger Abbey* instead. A handful of pages became a chapter, then another, and after an hour passed and she'd had to chastise herself for her thoughts drifting toward a certain engineer from Seattle only eight times, she congratulated herself upon such a successful diversion.

Too soon, as it were, for she'd only just come to the part where Henry Tilney seemingly jilted Catherine with regard to the walk he'd invited her on.

The Spirit Collection of Thorne Hall

And now Catherine would allow herself to be taken in by John Thorpe rather than give Mr. Tilney the opportunity to explain himself. Or at least give him a well-deserved piece of her mind.

Yes, Mr. Tilney deserved one or the other, if not both, and so back into her dressing room Elegy went, and the blouse and skirt were pulled once more from the rack.

At the garden door near the servant's staircase, Elegy laced her feet into a pair of black leather boots and took a black beaded reticule trimmed in sterling that she kept on a nearby shelf to hold the few possessions she needed when she left the house.

She found Mr. Griswold outside the garage, tinkering with an ancient lawn mower, his pants covered in oil.

"I require the car," she told him. "If you would be so kind."

His eyes widened and his mouth went slack before he remembered himself. "Y-yes, Mistress. Give me a moment . . . she hasn't been out and about in a spell."

The *she* in question was her great-grandfather Raymond Thorne's Rolls-Royce Phantom, purchased in the latter half of 1938 and kept running only by the grace of a man in Boston whom Jasper brought out twice a year to the tune of several months' worth of electricity bills.

She waited ten minutes for Arthur to bring the car around and then slid into the driver's seat with the same shock followed by the same thrill that always accompanied time away from the manor.

The day was a pleasant one, temperate and sweet, the air smelling of golden leaves and loam and promise; the very best moments of autumn before the peak gave way to the fade, when the dense morning fog would refuse to burn off altogether, settling heavy and low in the valleys and fields.

Elegy slipped on a pair of aviators her grandmother had prized and hummed to herself as she savored the three miles between Thorne Hall and Lenox, already planning which roads she would travel on her way home so as to make the trip as long as possible without arousing suspicion. Her freedom was a rare, precious thing indeed, and she was determined to enjoy every minute of it.

* * *

Lenox was a small town boasting just over five thousand residents, but as Atticus was not staying with his father, she would be forced to ask around as to his whereabouts.

There would be the inevitable stares, the whispers behind cupped hands that she was, indeed, every bit as small and strange as those who had visited the mansion (however few and far between they happened to be) had claimed.

She would ignore them as she'd always done.

Then would come the louder voices, the questions about her father's health and the state of the manor and, when she was master of Thorne Hall, would she make an effort to better manicure the drive and perhaps host one of the city council's fund-raising events?

Those she would deflect with a somber smile and a suggestion, presented ever so demurely, to contact her father, which they would not do, for they knew by now he would not answer.

She turned onto Church Street and immediately saw Harvey ambling out of the pâtisserie with a croissant in her mouth. If anyone could help her, it would be Harvey.

Thaddeus, obsessed as he was with appearances, loathed Harvey. She was a woman in her sixties with wiry gray hair cut short who always wore matte red lipstick and looked as though she'd allowed a blind child to pick her clothing. Today she was wearing a navy-blue coverall with what appeared to be a rack of military ribbons affixed to her breast, along with a floral blouse beneath and yellow Wellingtons on her feet.

Elegy pulled the car into a vacant spot a few feet away, stretched herself across the passenger seat, and battled with the crank until she'd rolled the window halfway down.

"Harvey!" she called.

Harvey caught sight of her and grunted around the croissant. "Well, hello, Miss Thorne. It's been a while."

"Have you seen Mr. Hart today?"

"Senior?" Harvey jammed her hand against her forehead and peered into the Rolls-Royce with undisguised curiosity.

"The son."

"Visited Hallowed Grounds earlier this morning for coffee. Takes it with a splash of oat milk, if you're wondering. How the fuck does one milk an oat?"

"The same way one milks an almond, I expect."

Harvey knew everything about everyone in Lenox, whether they wished her to or no, and had made it her business to do so for the last forty years. She wasn't a gossip; she did not traffic in speculation or exaggeration. Her word was gospel, for better or worse.

The Spirit Collection of Thorne Hall

Needless to say, she had never been invited to Thorne Hall and had given up begging sometime around 1987.

"Why are you so interested anyway?" Harvey prodded like the old brute that she was.

"Never you mind. Did you see him after that?"

"Went to Parchment and Quill last I saw. Maybe he's still there."

The small, cozy bookstore was just around the corner. Elegy thanked her, then drove the short distance and parked across the street. Inquisitive eyes noted the presence of the familiar ostentatious vehicle and the wraithlike woman emerging from it, but no one waved or smiled in greeting. They gave her the same wide berth that she did many of the spirits that belonged to her family. It was not respect.

It was fear.

Elegy straightened the hem of her skirt and was about to cross the street when the door of Parchment and Quill opened, and there he was. She stopped as their eyes met.

As recognition dawned, his brow rose and his eyes lit with mischief, and all thoughts of giving him a piece of her mind vanished and instead she wondered if she ought to throw herself into oncoming traffic. It was inconceivable that anyone could be so handsome. He'd made a deal with some devil or another for the privilege, no doubt.

"Mr. Hart," she greeted him politely.

"Miss Thorne."

"Why were you not at the house this morning? You said you intended to help your father with the project."

His gaze traveled slowly from her to the Rolls and back, and an absolutely beautiful and utterly infuriating smile spread across his face. "Did you come here looking for me?"

"No!" she answered, too quickly. "Of course not."

"Why are you here, then?"

"Books."

"Books," he repeated.

"Yes, you know, the things you read?"

He gestured to the bag at his side. "I'm aware. Don't you have thousands of those already?"

"Tens of thousands, actually," she sniffed. "But I wanted something in particular."

"Oh really?"

"Yes, really."

"What's the name of the book?"

And damn it all if Elegy couldn't think of a single thing to say. Research into this particular venture she had not expected to be necessary. The jig, it appeared, was up.

Atticus did not seem to mind in the slightest. "Admit you came looking for me, and let's go have a drink."

"I most certainly did *not* come looking for you."

"Right."

"And I most certainly do *not* want to have a drink with you."

He scraped his hand across his jaw. "There's a wine bar, I think, about a block that way."

Elegy shook her head. "Not in public."

"My place, then. It isn't far."

People were starting to take pictures of her car, and so Elegy slid into the driver's seat and jerked her head for Atticus to slip into the passenger's seat. For one brief, terrifying moment she feared it would not start without Arthur's ministrations, but to her very great relief, the engine roared to life, and she took off down the street upon a great plume of exhaust.

CHAPTER NINE

The Queen Anne Victorian Atticus had rented for the month was just off Lenox's main square, and as Elegy carefully extracted herself from the Rolls so as not to tear her skirt, her eyes darted about the street, searching for the crack of a door, the moving aside of a curtain. It was only a quarter after two, but these were the retired sort, sitting in their living rooms with little to do but note and remark upon the comings and goings of others. Elegy was, on her own, a novelty in town, however much she'd hoped it would wear off with age. With a man, with *this* man, she was positively legend.

Ducking her head and shielding her face with her reticule, she followed Atticus up the stairs and waited on the sun-drenched porch while he unlocked the front door and held it open. She'd never been inside such an ordinary place before; she loved it instantly.

In the center of a cheerful foyer, a white ceramic jug filled with sprays of Stargazer lilies sat upon a round table painted pale green. Beneath was a Turkish rug, the bright colors long faded though no less beautiful, and beneath that were wide wooden planks worn by age and shuffling feet.

A set of stairs rose to the second floor, where a round stained-glass window sat proudly at the landing, depicting a magnificent tree as it passed through all four seasons. Beneath it, another smaller arrangement of lilies sat beneath a slag-glass lamp.

To her right was the dining room, and although it was so much more humble than that of Thorne Hall, Elegy had the feeling it was used far more frequently and in far higher spirits. To her left was a small sitting room. A stack of freshly cut firewood sat at the ready beside the fireplace, and above it, around it, upon the faded damask wallpaper, were sketches and lithographs of silhouettes and flowers and all manner of landscapes Elegy had never seen.

There was a television in one corner that even she recognized as terribly old, and a leather Chesterfield opposite with a coffee table, where a sleek, silver laptop computer sat beside a stack of files. She could picture him upon the couch in the evenings, catching up on work while a fire burned in the hearth, a tumbler of Scotch or perhaps whiskey set beside him and a documentary of some sort on the television, perhaps something about physics; she could not be certain, but it seemed unlikely he cared for mindless sitcoms. It was warm and pleasant the way she saw him in her mind, and even though he was alone in this lovely house, she did not think he was lonely; not in the way she was, even though she was never alone.

Atticus said nothing as she stepped into the sitting room and ran her fingers down the gold velvet of a shabby chair, one of a pair that sat squat before the hearth.

"It's nothing like what you're used to," he mused. "But it'll do me fine for the month."

She looked to where he stood leaning his tall frame against the archway between the sitting room and the foyer. "Is your home in Seattle like this?"

"No, nothing like. I'm actually thinking of buying a new place near the ocean once I get back. That's what my company does—hydro power."

"I've never seen it."

His brow rose. "You don't mean the ocean."

"I do."

He did not seem to know what to make of this, and she could not bear to see the pity in the forest of his eyes, so she cast her gaze back to the shabby velvet beneath her fingers.

"Make yourself at home," he said. "Wine?"

"Wine would be lovely."

Elegy removed her shoes and placed them beside one of the chairs as he disappeared, then tried and failed to fold her legs beneath her without splitting the seams of a skirt older than the house she sat in. By the time Atticus emerged from the kitchen with two glasses of red wine in his hands, she had given up and sat primly upon the edge of the chair with her pale hands folded in her lap.

"That cannot be comfortable," he observed, handing her one of the glasses before lowering himself into the chair opposite hers and stretching out his long legs.

"This skirt is very old," she informed him, her tone as stiff as her posture. "It belonged to the first mistress of Thorne Hall."

"And when was she mistress?"

"Eighteen ninety-seven."

"You're kidding."

"I am not."

"And the car?"

"Nineteen thirty-eight," she answered. "It belonged to my great-grandfather."

He took a sip of his wine and studied her over the rim of the glass. "You Thornes hand everything down?"

"Old families like ours often do."

"I thought it was usually money and property," he remarked, and though his tone was light, it ill concealed the distain he clearly felt for such practices. "Not clothing."

"Wait until you find out about our Perpetual Pill."

"Perpetual *what*?"

"Antimony."

"The chemical element?"

"The very same. Fools used to swallow pills made of the stuff in the Victorian era," she explained. "Once swallowed, the pill induced purging. After it had been purged itself, it was cleaned off and put away until it was needed again. They were so valuable that families often handed them down through generations. We've been in possession of ours since the Napoleonic War."

"Please tell me it hasn't been used since then."

She grimaced. "Unfortunately, I cannot. The use of it actually killed my twice-great-aunt."

"Jesus," he said upon a shudder. "What was she trying to cure?"

"Her rather large waistline."

"You're kidding me."

"I am not."

"Well, *that's* horrifying, but it still doesn't explain the skirt."

Damn it all; she'd rather hoped the shocking nature of the Perpetual Pill would've made him forget about her clothing entirely, but it appeared that Atticus was not easily deterred. And so she told him the truth: "My father is very particular regarding appearances. Modern sensibilities do not appeal to him, so he prefers that I select my attire from what is original to our family and to the house."

"And is that what you want?"

"What I want is irrelevant," she answered immediately, for that was how quickly the thought came to her, now, after so many years of forcing herself to accept it. Her father would've been terribly proud.

This Atticus did not care for at all, as evidenced by the furrow of his brow, and Elegy wanted suddenly to climb into his lap, smooth it away with her thumb, and then kiss him until they were both breathless with it.

Her experience regarding the mouths of men consisted of exactly one bumbling attempt with Chauncy (goddamned *Chauncy*) during one of Fletcher's parties after she'd had too much brandy. It'd been Chauncy because he was leaving for college in Paris the next day and she'd never have to look him in the eye again. A good thing, too, because it had been fucking awful. Both of them drunk and neither having the faintest clue what to do with their limbs, he'd thrust about inside her mouth with his thick, slimy tongue until she'd shoved him away and hurled her guts into a nearby vase.

Having absolutely no evidence, she could not say with any authority that kissing Atticus would be any different; however, given the warm, throbbing sensation she suddenly felt about her lips and lower still, she very much doubted it.

She ought to try it, really, just to be certain.

Her eyes fell to the wine clutched tightly in her hand, and as though the glass had suddenly caught fire, she set it firmly upon the coffee table.

"Do you not like the wine?" he asked. "I have a couple of other bottles if you like—maybe a white?"

"No!"

The corner of his mouth quirked upward. "No?"

"That is, the car is quite temperamental, and I must keep my wits about me if I expect to make it back to the manor in one piece."

"Suit yourself."

She cast about for another topic, and her gaze fell upon the laptop sitting open on the coffee table. "You are a self-made man," she said. "Your father is very proud."

Atticus grinned, reclining back with the air of a man with the world in his pocket and himself sure of it staying there. "He tried to talk me

The Spirit Collection of Thorne Hall

into basing the company out of Boston, but I've spent most of my life in the Pacific Northwest and can't imagine living anywhere else."

"Is that where you went to college?"

"No, I went Caltech in Pasadena," he answered. "You?"

No one had ever asked her that before. She almost never met anyone who did not already know about the long history of Thorne Hall and accept whatever she told them of the estate and its need for her constant attention without question or care.

Atticus knew nothing of such things. He saw a twenty-five-year-old woman with the means to do anything she pleased, and why should that not include the enrichment of her mind, attending a university with a building that likely bore her family name, all of them earning degrees and honorifics they would never use.

It was a curious sensation, the prickling flush of humiliation that settled beneath her skin as the silence between them stretched too long.

"I didn't attend college," she answered at last. "Though I would have liked to."

"You still could, you know," he told her gently, as he watched her with what appeared to be pity, and this she hated most of all.

"You're very kind, but I couldn't. My father is not well, and soon the estate will come to me."

"Let someone else manage it."

"Let us simply say it is not possible and leave it at that."

To her very great surprise, he did leave it, and they talked of more pleasant things. She shared with him what she knew of Lenox and, and throughout it all, however ridiculous, he smiled and laughed. She wished she was anyone else, something worthy of the attentions of such a splendid person, perhaps her favorite person despite her knowing him all of two days.

"I suppose you'll leave your father to fend for himself again tomorrow?" she asked him as he walked her to the Rolls, wincing at her own flippancy. She'd never quite learned how to say goodbye, so fiercely did she hate doing so.

"Is that your way of asking if I'll be at the house?"

"No."

Yes.

"Do you *want* me to be there?"

She could manage only a brief nod, cheeks aflame. Then she promptly turned and fled.

CHAPTER TEN

From the bottom of the winding drive to Thorne Hall, Elegy could see, through the fog and drizzle, a car parked under the porte cochere and thought that it must be Jeremiah. However, once she was close enough, she saw that, instead of the contractor's sturdy black truck, their visitor drove a gleaming white sports car as ostentatious as it was expensive.

Hugo!

Forgetting entirely the age and temperament of the Rolls in her excitement, Elegy pressed the gas pedal nearly to the floor in her haste, gravel protesting beneath the tires and exhaust exploding into the fog.

She parked haphazardly just behind Hugo's Audi and was out of the driver's seat like a shot the moment the engine died.

"Hugo!" she cried.

He looked up from where he leaned against his ridiculous car with his usual cigarette dangling from his full lips, and he barely managed to catch her as she threw herself into his arms. They went around her like a vise, and she clung to him hard, until he nearly lost his cigarette in her hair and, laughing, they drew apart and studied each other.

He'd cut his curls shorter than the last time she'd seen them, and the heavy dusting of freckles across the bridge of his nose was more pronounced; he must've spent time in the sun during the long months.

"You look wonderful," she told him, and plucked the cigarette from his mouth, grinding it into the gravel beneath her boot.

The Spirit Collection of Thorne Hall

"Fuck, Elegy!"

"You know my father will have a fit if he smells that," she answered. "Come in and have a drink."

Mrs. Griswold did not seem to be about, and so Elegy busied herself with uncorking a bottle of wine and pouring two generous measures while Hugo selected one of Tabitha's records among the pile that Fletcher had not purloined. The sound of Fleetwood Mac's "Second Hand News" filled the great hall, and Elegy's mouth turned up in a smile. *Rumors* had been one of her mother's favorite albums.

They ascended the staircase to the second-floor landing, tucked away amidst velvet curtains and stained glass. There was a courting chair in shades of burgundy-and-gold brocade, and it was there they sat, facing each other. "So, tell me what adventures you've been up to, and make them good—I intend to live vicariously through you," Elegy insisted.

"I am afraid I shall have to disappoint," he sighed after draining half the contents of his glass in one swallow. "I've been in Boston with Sebastian doing absolutely nothing that would interest you."

"By which you mean you've been doing Sebastian in Boston."

"Cheeky, but you're not wrong," answered Hugo with a mischievous smile. "God, he's such an idiot, but fuck me if he isn't *my* idiot."

A bitterness settled upon her tongue that was familiar and yet no less potent for the years that had passed during which Hugo loved with wild abandon, knowing Elegy's good name would one day shelter him while she wasted her virgin life away within the walls of her legacy.

It was, their parents believed, the perfect solution.

Hugo's taste in lovers was as varied as those to love available were to him; however, to the abject devastation of his parents, he vastly preferred men. Marrying one was simply out of the question, no matter what the law had to say about it, or he would find himself cut off without a cent, and so it was quite fortuitous that he engaged in enough dalliances with women to make it not so terribly unbelievable that he would one day settle down with one, particularly if he wished to continue his family line.

His parents, Phineas and Lavinia Prescott, did not dislike Elegy per se; she was educated, well mannered, and agreeable, which almost made up for her inherent strangeness. But above all, Elegy was desperate (or, to be more precise, Thaddeus was desperate on her behalf), and desperate was exactly what they needed.

As Thaddeus had no living family nor second heir despite his best efforts, it was of the utmost importance that Elegy provide the house with an heir of Thorne blood to keep the Collection under control. And one born in wedlock, of course; whether the child was her husband's or another man's entirely was of no concern, as long as the appearance of propriety was satisfied. Thus was the idea of their marriage conceived: Elegy would marry Hugo and have a child one way or another, and Hugo would be free to dally as he saw fit. So long as they were both discreet in their endeavors and he kept his mouth shut about the Collection, it was an ideal solution.

Well, ideal for everyone save Elegy and the child she bore.

It was in Hugo's nature to wander, the concept of home being as revolving as his amorous entanglements, and Elegy could hardly expect him to waste away the idle hours of his youth within the walls of Thorne Hall with only her and the Collection for company. He would remain with her after the wedding only so long as to maintain the appearance of legitimacy, and by the commencement of the social season, he would be gone to New York or London or Paris and she would be alone.

"I'm glad for you, Hugo," she said at last, touching her glass gently to his. "For you both."

"Oh, you know me." He shrugged. "I'm not one for staying with anyone for long."

"You've been with Sebastian for quite some time now," she pointed out.

"As I said, you know me."

"I do know you. And I think this time it's different."

"And *I* think that we've talked enough about me," Hugo replied. "Now, tell me all about Atticus."

Elegy stiffened. "How do you know about him?"

"Darling, the whole *town* knows about him. Is he hot? He sounds hot." And when he caught sight of the crimson blooming upon her cheeks like wine carelessly spilled, his grin turned positively wolfish. "Oh he *is*—just look at that flush!"

There was a ripple of black lace beneath the staircase, and Elegy reached out and grasped Hugo's corduroy-clad sleeve with trembling fingers. "Quiet," she hissed. "Not here."

"Why? There's no one else here—" The moment the sentiment left his lips, he slammed them shut while his eyes widened. "Fuck, I'd forgotten."

"That must be nice."

She'd not meant to sound so bitter; she'd not meant to say it at all. It must've been all their talk of Sebastian when she'd only just come from Atticus.

The Spirit Collection of Thorne Hall

"I'm sorry—" she began, as he took a vicious swig of wine.

"Forget it," he cut her off. "It was thoughtless of me. Of course you can't forget."

But he could, even when they'd exchanged vows and rings and made shameful fraud of their marriage bed, because he could leave this place whenever he pleased, and she never could.

Hugo never stayed in one place for long, and he wouldn't stay in Lenox. He'd asked her long ago why anyone would want to live with ghosts, especially those who could not be properly managed.

Her reminder sobered them both, and Hugo continued to sit ramrod straight, downing the wine until at last his glass was empty and his cheerful countenance somewhat restored, though she would have had to be a fool, or at the very least a terrible friend, not to see the question in his eyes: he was wondering, and not for the first time, if her life, the life that would purchase his freedom, was worth the string of Sebastians that would inevitably follow.

"I've got to run," he said when the already murky gray of the afternoon outside began to darken further with the setting of the sun. She took his empty glass as he stood and rolled his shoulders. "But I'll see you next week for Fletcher's party, yeah?"

"Of course."

At the door of his Audi, he took her arm and crushed her against his body, knocking the breath from her for several seconds before he drew back and smacked a kiss upon her forehead.

"Take care of yourself till then, El."

She did not ask him to do the same because she knew he would.

He always did.

* * *

That evening, Fletcher decided to adorn herself in a peach satin evening gown and burst into Thaddeus's bedroom, drunk on sloe gin and furious over the state of her party.

Eugenia and Mabel, emboldened by the racket, took to the great hall, where they swung each other around in a dizzying, cackling waltz, and so Elegy led her stepmother back to the third floor and spent the rest of the evening sitting upon an oversized blue velvet pillow with a Montblanc Meisterstück in her hand and a pile of loose-leaf parchment propped up on her folded knees, upon which to take notes of the gravest importance.

"You'll need to consult Bernard. He's been working on the drink menu for a month already," Fletcher slurred, and when Elegy flinched, she added, "Your father did say you needed more time in their company at night. Consider this excellent practice."

"I don't suppose I have a choice."

"You know very well you don't. Now, what's the budget for the caterer? I don't care—whatever it is, double it."

Elegy filled several sheets of parchment with the names of dishes and drinks whilst Django Reinhardt played upon the gramophone and Fletcher danced before the window with various shawls as her partners.

When at last her stepmother fell asleep facedown upon her bed in a heap of limbs and silk, Elegy drew a heavy blanket over her, stoked the embers in the fireplace, and returned to her own room with the half-finished bottle of champagne. It was cold enough to warrant a fire, but there was a wariness in her bones that made her disinclined to bother.

She pulled a heavy velvet coat trimmed with ermine from her wardrobe, jammed a beret over her ears, and sat upon the window seat watching wisps of cloud float past the moon while she savored the warm champagne straight from the mouth of the bottle.

Somewhere in the vast darkness mere miles away in a perfectly ordinary house that was not filled to the brim with the undead, Atticus slept; he dreamed.

It was far too great a thing to hope that he dreamed of her.

She fell asleep right there on the bench, and she dreamed not of Atticus but of a garden.

It was an unruly thing, but so very beautiful, and best of all, it was *alive*, surrounded by a handsome wrought-iron fence, and there were pear trees and apples trained in espalier and even figs. The blackberries had overgrown their trellis, canes bowing under the weight.

Elegy plunged her hands into the dark, moist soil, dragging her fingers through it toward her palm and squeezing, letting it fall in clumps to be gathered again and worked through with fertilizer and warmed by the sun.

She measured the rows and spaced them just so, dropping seeds reverently only a few centimeters from the surface and snuffing them out with soil until, with water and with warmth, they would burst forth, wild and boisterous and so alive.

And although she could not feel it as she slept, a tear slid down her cheek and soaked her hair, because the garden in her dream was beside the ocean, which she had never seen.

Let No Man Steal Your Thyme
(A Sprig of Thyme; circa 1689)
Collected by Cecil J. Sharp in 1903

Come, all you fair and tender girls
That flourish in your prime
Beware, beware, keep your garden fair
Let no man steal your thyme
Let no man steal your thyme
For when your thyme is past and gone
He'll care no more for you
And in the place your time was waste
Will spread all over with rue
Will spread all over with rue
A woman is a branchy tree
And man's a clinging vine
And from her branches carelessly
He'll take what he can find
He'll take what he can find
He'll take what he can find

CHAPTER ELEVEN

"What should I wear if I want to impress someone but I don't want that someone to know I am trying to impress them?"

There was a groan on the other end of the telephone line, followed by a great deal of scuffling, an almighty crash, and copious swearing before Floss spoke, her voice rough with sleep, "Elegy, what the actual fuck?"

The fire in the great hall had not yet been lit, as it was only five o'clock in the morning and quite a cold one at that, and Elegy had cocooned herself in a mound of blankets as she huddled on a chair beside the small end table that held one of only four telephones in the whole of the estate.

"He'll be here in four hours, and I can't decide between the silver Jacque Doucet day dress with the blue sash or the periwinkle one with the beaded bodice."

"Slow the fuck down, Elegy," Floss ground out. "Jesus, what time is it?"

"Five."

"In the morning?"

"Yes, in the morning."

"Wait, wait, wait—who will be there in four hours?"

"Atticus."

"Who the fuck is Atticus, and why are you calling me about your fucking wardrobe at five in the morning?"

Elegy sighed. "Our contractor's son, and five in the morning would be perfectly reasonable had you not stayed awake drinking until two."

"Rude."

"So, which one do you think I should wear?"

"Neither, and since when did you care so much about impressing anyone other than your father?"

"Rude."

"It's five in the fucking morning; you deserve it." There came down the line the rustling of bedclothes and a deep groan of resignation. "So, what does he look like?"

"What does who look like?"

"Don't be obtuse. If you're trying to impress some contractor's son, you must find him attractive."

"I most certainly do *not*," Elegy insisted, though by then her cheeks were so warm that perhaps Mrs. Griswold did not need to light the fire after all. "I am the mistress of Thorne Hall and must dress accordingly."

"Right. In that case, it's still neither."

Elegy chewed upon her lower lip. "You're right."

"I am?"

"I should wear an evening dress."

"No, that's not what I—"

But Elegy had already hung up.

After a breakfast of amaranth porridge and honeyed fruit eaten in the bath and a considerable amount of time and vexation spent taming her thick, black hair, she stood at the center of the wardrobe while Delphine, nearly indiscernible by the light of day, fastened each of the tiny pearl buttons of the ivory Edwardian evening dress with a cunning teal velvet panel just beneath her breasts and a copper marquisette overlay embroidered with falling red leaves and twining branches. She'd not worn it for years, as such a treasure was to be saved for an occasion of great distinction, an increasing irregularity at Thorne Hall, but after finding fault with everything in her wardrobe (the Weeks evening dress in pale-blue silk was missing too many of its glass beads, the Callot Soeurs dinner dress washed her out completely, the lace upon the Herbert Luey bodice had yellowed so much that it clashed garishly against the lilac satin, and so on), she did not object when Delphine herself finally plucked it from the rack and pushed it into her hands.

"You look lovely," Mrs. Griswold said when she emerged from her chamber. "Are we expecting someone?"

"Mr. Hart, of course," Elegy replied, and it was just as well that Mrs. Griswold did not know she meant the younger.

J. Ann Thomas

A heavy knock sounded at the main door, and Elegy's wide eyes met the housekeeper's before she clambered down the staircase as fast as the seams of her dress would allow, nearly barreling into Mr. Griswold on his way to admit their visitors. She positioned herself primly before the banister with both hands folded before her, the very picture of poise and decorum whilst her insides were in a terrible jumble.

The door opened, and men's voices drifted into the foyer.

Arthur greeted Jeremiah and two of his usual men from the village—offering Thaddeus's apologies, as he was not feeling well that morning—and ushered them into the great hall and beyond to the kitchen. And all the while Elegy stood frozen, her eyes fixed upon the door left open, waiting for him to appear.

Where was he? Surely he'd come with his father, so why the delay?

She waited, and she waited, and indignation that he'd not kept his promise turned to disappointment, and then to shame. It had all been a folly, then; she'd feared it so, and here was the proof. She should have known, really, that one such as she could never have truly captured his interest, because why on earth would someone like Atticus, so worldly and lovely with his hair and wide, beautiful smile and low, rumbling laughter, ever think her anything but the daughter of his father's employer with a sharp tongue and strange clothing?

As if the universe wished to remind Elegy that she did not, in fact, know the slightest thing about anything, particularly men, Atticus Hart chose that moment to grace the foyer of Thorne Hall with his presence.

Elegy straightened with a gasp. When he caught sight of her, his eyes gleamed, and there was that damnable grin that tinted her countenance pink.

"Miss Thorne," he greeted her.

"Mr. Hart," she returned. "You're late."

He glanced down at the strange contraption on his wrist that she supposed was a watch, the small black rectangle alight with neon numbers and circles and was that the weather? "Dad said nine."

"And it is two past."

"Waiting, were you?"

"I detest unpunctuality."

"Let me make it up to you, then," he said.

"And how do you propose to do that?"

"How about a walk?"

The grounds suited her very well, for they were safe from both the prying eyes and grasping hands of the Collection. They were also beautiful, but Elegy was hardly particular about that when her choices were a house full of ghosts or paths walked without them.

From beneath the porte cochere, Elegy led Atticus away from the house toward the Painted Grove, where the leaves were most beautiful. The turn had begun in earnest, glowing embers of yellow and russet and scarlet at the heart of stubbornly clinging green. By next week more would have changed, and then, just like that, there would be no more green to be had once the peak was upon them.

"I'd forgotten what it looks like," Atticus murmured almost absently, and when Elegy turned her inquiring eyes upon him, he nodded to the gum and spicebush and oak and sassafras that surrounded them. "A New England autumn."

"How long has it been since you've seen one?"

"A few years," he admitted. "Maybe three. I don't come here often."

"Why?" This genuinely perplexed her. Had she Atticus's freedom, she would likely never visit Thaddeus again in her lifetime, but Jeremiah seemed a kind man and jovial, proud of Atticus and his accomplishments—the sort of parent she imagined her mother would have been had she lived, and her Elegy certainly would have visited in this fairy tale of hers.

Step by step he constructed the story of his life like the engineer he was: a foundation in Lenox, a future built awash in the sun of Pasadena, and what came between and after.

His mother had not particularly cared for the Berkshires. She found it stodgy, ruled by old money and snobbery. And the more desperately she tried to convince Jeremiah of that fact, the more stubbornly he dug in his heels. He was Lenox born and raised, as had been his father and his grandfather before him. It was all he'd ever known, and he feared what lay beyond.

"It's odd." Elegy frowned. "Jeremiah has been to the house with some frequency over the last several years, and he's never mentioned a son. Did he ever visit you out west?"

Atticus's grin was wry. "Dad hates airplanes. And avocados."

"Not even once?"

"Not even once. You know, we don't have to talk about this."

"We don't," she agreed. "But I think you'll find me a keen listener should you wish to do so."

He shook his head. "The way you talk sometimes."

She stiffened, for it sounded very much like an insult, and just like that the warmth of the day vanished. "What is that supposed to mean?"

"No one talks the way you do anymore," he explained. "It's absolutely adorable, and also really fucking strange."

An indignant sound emerged from her throat. "It is not strange, it's proper."

"Can you even curse? I'll bet you don't."

She scowled. "I curse."

"Prove it. Say *fuck*."

"Fuck," said Elegy.

"Look at that blush!" Atticus grinned, and Elegy thrust her nose into the air so as to avoid seeing those aggravating dimples.

"You delight in teasing me."

"I do," he answered. "But you give as good as you get."

A fierce lick of pride flared to life within her cold, bitter chest.

Beyond the grove, before it gave way to the wood that belonged to Elegy's family, was the graveyard that held them. It had once been fine and well kept, with a filigreed fence of wrought iron and a kissing gate. At the forefront of the plot stood a marble mausoleum that held Jasper's remains within a massive sarcophagus upon a dais. Within were benches separated by an aisle where mourners had perhaps lit candles and sat in silent contemplation, but no longer. Mr. Griswold kept the weeds at bay, but time and the elements had rendered the stone structure a pale imitation of what it had once been.

Atticus read the inscription carved above the door with a furrowed brow. "His wife isn't in there with him?"

"Oh, no." Elegy pointed beyond the mausoleum to a statue of a weeping angel, her face stained black by a century of tears. "She's just . . . there. It's strange—by all accounts, Jasper loved Delilah, else Thorne Hall would not stand today, but I suppose in death he wished to be worshiped as the deity he believed himself to be."

Behind Jasper's shrine stood a single tree, an English yew as old as the estate itself, surrounded by the stones that marked the final resting places of his progeny. The stones themselves were weathered and dark with age and the ravages of rain and snow, the names of those who rested beneath barely visible.

"They are symbols of Hecate," Elegy explained, gesturing to the towering shrub with its glossy green needles and clusters of bright-red berries. "Said to purify the dead before they reach the underworld. Jasper thought it fitting. Don't eat the bark, though. Or the berries, for that matter, unless you wish to die a ghastly painful death."

"I'll bear that in mind."

The Spirit Collection of Thorne Hall

"This is my mother's grave," Elegy told him, resting her hand atop an elegantly carved stone bearing the name Tabitha Thorne, the delicate script below proclaiming her to have been a wife and mother, taken too soon. "She died giving birth to me."

"Elegy, I'm so sorry."

"Sometimes I think it was easier that way, because I don't miss her. You can't miss someone you never met." She ducked her head. "I've never told anyone that before. You must think me wicked."

"Not at all," he answered. "I doubt she would want you to grieve."

"Oh, no. The dead do not care for that sort of thing at all."

It was out of her traitorous mouth before she'd thought better of it, and now he was staring at her with curiosity burning brightly in his eyes. "Sonnet number seventy-one," he said.

She did not cry, refused to do so, in fact, and yet in that moment she thought as though she might.

And that simply would not do at all.

"Indeed," she answered with a brisk nod, and turned away under the pretense of further examining the grave while Atticus shoved his hands in his pockets and meandered about until he came to a stone set apart from the rest in the shade of a cypress tree. He sank down to better see the inscription upon it, but there was no such thing carved there—no name, no date, nothing at all but the image of a small bird in flight.

"Who is buried here?"

"We don't know, actually," Elegy confessed, crouching down beside him. "There is quite a detailed account of those laid to rest in this graveyard—all Thornes, of course, either by blood or marriage, but there is no mention of this grave at all."

Atticus snapped his fingers. "The portrait of the woman holding the bird. Maybe it's her pet buried there."

"I thought the same when first I saw it, but no . . . I think this is someone of great importance," Elegy replied, touching gently the white petals of the flowers that covered the lonely plot. "These are anemones. They're planted upon graves to honor sacrifice."

Whose sacrifice she did not know, and likely never would. She'd inquired after the inhabitant of the grave when she was young, and her father either could tell her nothing or refused to do so, and once Thaddeus had made up his mind about a thing, he did not unmake it. They left the stone behind them and continued on down the path around the east side of the manor, past where the corpses of three massive greenhouses rose beyond a low-hanging fog.

J. Ann Thomas

"What's in there?"

Elegy followed his gaze and realized with a start that she'd led them in the entirely wrong direction. She'd meant to take him the short way around the grove to the house, but at some point she'd taken the path leading to the walled garden. She hadn't been within for years, and ivy had grown up around the red brick such that she was surprised he had seen it at all.

"A place I loved once," she murmured. "But I could not get it to live."

She would've left it well enough alone, but while she continued down the path, he did not. And when she turned, she found him with his hands in his pockets, staring at the door just visible beneath the glossy green leaves.

"I want to see it," he said.

"There is nothing to see," Elegy answered. "Nothing but dead things."

"You said you loved it once."

She turned her confused gaze upon his face. "So?"

"So, I want to see it."

Jasper Thorne had built the walled garden along with the greenhouses; the trouble was, he'd done it *after* he'd bound the first of the Collection. Prior to that fateful Samhain night, the estate had flourished. The trees were a riot of color, the lawns pristine, and the flowers grown in the hothouse were always at the ready to decorate any surface of the manor with pride and prestige.

But after that, nothing could be persuaded to grow that had not already been there. Jasper hired innumerable experts from Boston and New York, who tried everything they could, but everything shriveled and died within a matter of months. Failure followed failure. Eventually the garden was hidden behind the shame of brick and key.

This had not stopped Elegy from trying.

She'd spent months huddled in the library, studying books on horticulture and botany, furiously filling crudely bound sketchbooks with ideas for plots and ways to amend the soil and ensure proper irrigation. Then she'd approached Mr. Leeds at the general store and convinced him to order seeds and starts and shrubs and trees from Burpee and Johnny's and Monrovia.

She'd done the work herself. Had she enlisted Mr. Griswold in her plot, her father would've been furious, and besides—she needed to prove to him that she could bring the garden to life upon her own merits.

She'd created paths with stone and shrub, planted climbing roses at the base of the brick archway at the garden's center, and scrubbed clean the stone benches at the perimeter. She'd filled the cracked and mossy topiaries, chosen a number of fruit trees for their shade and for their bounty, along with elderberry bushes on account of the syrup, and arranged beds of flowers according to season so that at any time the garden would be saturated with color, teeming with life; an anathema to the halls of her home, a sanctuary.

Even after everything she'd planted in the first year of her experiment withered and perished, Elegy had refused to admit defeat. She smuggled from the house a pocket watch of no mean worth and bought new seeds and new starts and new trees. These lasted a mere handful of weeks until they too succumbed, and this time Elegy allowed them to be swallowed by ivy and moss and weeds, for she'd not the heart to try again when failure was all but certain.

She'd hidden the key behind a loose stone close to the door so that none of the Collection could steal it from her, and it was with shaking hands that she retrieved it, shoved it in the rusty lock, and pushed the door open. It was no easy feat; she'd not set foot in the garden for five years.

It might as well have been twenty for how it had decayed.

Elegy lowered herself onto a stone bench now crawling with tendrils of black moss and watched as Atticus walked a lonely path of stones deeper into the overgrown tangle that had been beautiful for a time, however short. It was far worse now than it had been the day Elegy first arrived armed with her trowel, as if she were being punished for her audacity all those years ago; for believing that a place so horribly tainted could be purified.

"Why is it like this?" Atticus asked at last.

"Because it was never meant to live."

"I thought that was the point of gardens."

"Not this one."

He was determined to find a lie in her explanation, and so she stayed upon the bench and watched as he examined slowly and methodically every brittle trunk and branch and rotting patch of would-be flowers, lingering longest beneath a tree she'd hoped would bear golden apples and instead seeped worms from its blossoms, black and wriggling and swallowed up by the tainted soil beneath.

"Do you remember when you asked me about college?" Elegy unexpectedly found herself saying.

"I do."

It emerged from her in a rush: "I thought that if I somehow coaxed something to grow here, my father might see the use in me studying horticulture. I even had a program picked out. He just laughed at me and told me I was wasting my time."

He rose abruptly and turned his gaze upon her. "What kind of a father laughs at his own daughter's ambitions?"

"The sort I've got. And anyway, he was right. I tried for years. Nothing grows here."

"Here?" he asked, and then his gaze drifted beyond where she sat to the redbrick walls of the manor behind them. "Or there?"

He did not know about the Spirit Collection; he did not need to. Like others who had spent more than a handful of moments within the house, he knew there was something wrong with it. It stood to reason that he would eventually surmise that there was something wrong with her too. She had been planted in cursed soil, denied sunlight and water, and emerged small and frail with a frightened soul and a sharp tongue.

Elegy rose from the bench. "Let's continue on, shall we?"

In that same strange way in which Atticus always seemed to know when she wished to speak of a thing and when she did not, he followed her silently from the garden, waiting as she locked the door and stored the key safely within its stone prison.

"If it had worked," he asked as they walked, "if you could've grown anything, what would it have been?"

"Flowers," she answered immediately. "The only ones we've ever had in the manor have come from a shop in Pittsfield, and they're too perfect. Like the ones in your foyer."

"You prefer the imperfect ones."

"I like the ones that grow by the roadside and in the fields," she admitted. "Sometimes I smuggle them into the house and keep them in my office."

"What else?"

"Fruit trees," she answered, remembering what she'd planted and how she'd seen it all again in her dream. "Apples and pears, mostly, but figs too, and blackberries and herbs. Oh, and carrots. I imagined there is something wonderfully satisfying about pulling them, though I've never done it."

There was ever so much more, and he coaxed it out of her as they walked beneath leaves round and round the estate, giving the dead garden a wide berth. Somewhere near the curve of the path where they were once more surrounded by autumnal splendor, Elegy became aware that Atticus was watching her with eyes gone soft and bright.

The Spirit Collection of Thorne Hall

"What is it?" she asked, looking immediately to the state of her dress, and when she found nothing wrong with it, she came to the next most logical conclusion. "Have I said something foolish?"

"Not at all," he returned. "It's just that I've known you three days now, and this is the first time I've seen you smile."

Her features immediately schooled themselves into a scowl, and he laughed at the sight of it.

"Let me see it again," he said.

Everything stilled save her furious heart, and the cursed thing threatened to shatter her ribs with its infernal beating. "I've nothing at all to smile about."

"Nothing at all?"

Her lips threatened to turn up into a traitorous smile, and she looked away so that he would not see it. "Not a thing."

By the time they arrived back under the porte cochere, Jeremiah had been waiting for Atticus for half an hour, placated only by several helpings of Mrs. Griswold's shortbread. Atticus apologized, all the while grinning conspiratorially at Elegy over his father's head, and when it was her turn to bid him farewell, she shook his hand in a manner most professional.

"Thank you for the walk, Miss Thorne."

"And you for taking it with me."

"What are you doing tomorrow?"

Oh, the usual, she thought, and wanted to laugh at the absurdity of it because tomorrow, just like any other day, she would walk among ghosts that belonged to her father and would one day be hers.

She did not laugh. Instead, she asked, "Why do you wish to know?"

"Meet me at my house."

Her cheeks flamed, and she grabbed the sleeve of his sweater in a white-fingered grip.

"Keep your voice down!" she hissed.

"Say you'll come, and I will," he said with a smile.

Elegy released his sleeve and stepped a respectable distance away as his father appeared at his side, then she fled back into the manor before anyone could suspect she was entirely undone by a simple walk, a simple conversation, a simple request.

She went about the rest of her day ignoring her duties entirely in favor of dithering back and forth between knowing full well she ought not to let this strange, wonderful thing between them go any further and deciding that it absolutely must, and she made up her mind and unmade it again and again before Mrs. Griswold called her down to dinner.

CHAPTER TWELVE

It was past dark, and Elegy was surprised to find her father in the dining room sitting at the head of the table and Fletcher at the other end wearing a peacock harem costume complete with beaded headpiece. Some color had been restored to her father's hollow cheeks, no doubt owed to Dr. Winslow's tinctures, but it was impossible to miss the way his hand shook when he raised his wineglass to his lips.

Elegy took her place at the middle of the table between the two and lifted the cloche covering her plate. Lucy had prepared venison that evening with a sauce of wine and cherries and a lovely gratin of root vegetables, and Elegy, safe from Bancroft by virtue of Thaddeus's presence and hungry after hours spent out of doors, took in after it with enthusiasm.

"How are the repairs to the kitchen coming?" Fletcher asked, sipping long and slow from her goblet of wine.

A perfectly sliced piece of venison poised at his lips, Thaddeus glared down the table.

"Now, dear, I'm sure Elegy has discussed this with you, but it will not be ready for your party."

"Yes, *dear*, Elegy was kind enough to inform me," Fletcher returned. "A pity you did not, for at least it would have shown that you cared."

Thaddeus placed his fork and knife upon his plate with such force that Elegy flinched. Fletcher, however, was no such coward. She stared down the length of the table at her husband and raised her glass, drinking long and deep once more from the claret within.

"I don't care. But as you will make my life a fresher hell than it already is should I deny you, the party shall commence. I trust Elegy has already made arrangements."

It was not a question, and he did not even look upon her as he said it even though she sat mere feet away.

"I want to invite more people," said Fletcher.

"That is out of the question."

"If we are contracting an outside caterer, it should be no trouble."

Thaddeus's mouth pinched. "Have you already forgotten why an outside caterer is needed at all?"

"Invite them," Elegy said in an attempt to placate them both. "It's my fault, so invite them and I shall see that the Collection behave themselves."

Her father raised a mocking brow. "You believe yourself capable?"

"I shall endeavor to try."

"You shall endeavor to try," he repeated, the disdain in his voice dripping like venom from the fangs of a snake. He did rather look like one in that moment, with those cruel, beady eyes of his.

Beneath the table her hands clenched into fists. "I can do it, Father."

"We shall see."

"Excellent," said Fletcher with a nasty smile. "I think I shall invite more young men. All the men in *this* house are dead or on their way to it."

"Invite all the young men you want, but none of them will want you any more than I do."

Her stepmother stood so suddenly her chair toppled backward. She took up her wineglass and stalked toward the door but stopped behind Elegy's chair first. Fletcher's hand curled upon her shoulder like talons, her long fingernails digging painfully into her skin through the fragile silk of her ancient dress. Her wine-soaked breath tickled the shell of Elegy's ear as she lowered her mouth, and she whispered, "Invite the contractor's son to my party. That is not a request."

She straightened, squeezing Elegy's shoulder one last excruciating time, then departed the room without a backward glance. Thaddeus bunched up his napkin and threw it upon his plate in disgust before he rose, and then collapsed again, helplessly ensnared in the grip of another attack. Wet, rattling coughs filled the room as he gripped the edge of the table with both hands so tightly the bones beneath nearly pierced the veil of his sickly skin.

Elegy was out of her chair in an instant, curling her hands around her father's shoulders in an attempt to take the weight of him, but he would have none of it, recoiling as though her touch were akin to that of the Collection.

"Let me help you, Father," she begged. "You are not well—"

"I require rest, that is all."

But when she reached for him again, he wrenched his arm away so quickly she stumbled into the table, his departure from the dining room heralded by the tinkling of glassware and the shivering of silver.

Elegy's appetite had vanished along with him, and so with shaking hands she gathered plates and cloches and half-drunk goblets of wine, and as she stacked them in the dumbwaiter for Lucy come the morning, there came from the corridor the sound of heavy feet dragging upon the wood.

Elegy turned and beheld Bernard's hulking form in the doorway. He was a solitary sort of spirit save his unfathomable devotion to Fletcher's cocktail preferences and a strange, almost sweet devotion to the harried Cook; he spoke to Elegy rarely, and it was always to deliver a message from *him*.

The spirit opened his blackened lips, and the subterranean growl of his voice sent the bare skin of her arms prickling: "Come."

No further elaboration was needed; she knew who summoned her, and her anger flared.

"He's no right to summon me."

But Bernard was as stupid as he was gentle, and although he could make an excellent martini, he did not understand that anyone should not heed Gideon Constant when he called, even the living, and so he remained where he stood, patiently waiting for her acquiescence.

"Fine," she said, voice taut as a bowstring. "Lead the way, then."

Elegy tried to divert her eyes from the ghastly wounds upon Bernard's back; she had no idea whether he'd been dead before the plow or after, but the gashes stubbornly wept blood as black as tar that soaked his simple linen shirt. She followed him to the ballroom, the place she never went, so terribly did she fear it because it was *his* domain.

And he was holding court tonight there, just as he did every night.

Gideon Constant.

The first.

Gideon was golden, and even in death with skin mottled gray, he was handsome, making a mockery of the uniform he wore. He'd been executed for betraying it and the men under his command. He had been no ordinary foot soldier in the war but a captain, and, in the end, a coward.

He might've chosen a less conspicuous place to frequent at night, but it had been his second birthplace—indeed, the second birthplace of them all—and Elegy supposed she understood somewhat the draw he must feel, more potent than all the rest experienced for the fact that he'd been summoned before them.

"Elegy," said Gideon upon a welcoming smile when she entered the ballroom. "I am exceedingly glad to see you."

He slouched indolently in a high-backed chair upon the dais that in brighter days long past was where bands and orchestras had serenaded the fabulously wealthy and frivolous. There was but one lone piano there now that, of all the spirits, only Vivian and Calliope knew how to play. The former was perched upon the bench, fingers whittled to little more than bones resting upon the ivory keys as she waited upon Gideon's whim.

This room more than any other in the manor was changed by the darkness; Gideon bade it so. There was no light at all save what little might be had from the slice of moon through the windows, and the walls seemed determined to swallow it before it spread. They were pale blue by day, trimmed in cream and gilt with sunken alcoves hung with gold and crystal sconces, but by night they were the same pallid gray as the skin of those who gathered there, paint peeling and mottled with black rot.

The gleaming wood floors suffered the same ill treatment, stained here and there with dark patches that might be decay and might also be blood or even tar, and as Elegy picked her way gingerly toward the dais where Gideon waited, they groaned and creaked and threatened at any moment to buckle.

Mrs. Griswold would've despaired to see the way the chandeliers above dripped with cobwebs, so pristine did she insist they be despite the fact that very few saw them, but the Vengeful Ones preferred it so. It never lasted past the breaking of the dawn; with the light came the restoration of the manor to its rich, lustrous splendor.

"You ought not to summon me," Elegy informed the leering man, whilst maintaining a respectable distance should she be forced to flee. "It is I who command you and not the other way around."

His terrible grin widened. "And yet here you are! Tell me—did you like my surprise? It was, after all, for you."

"I assume you mean the destruction of our kitchen. Yes, what an amusing thing indeed," she answered flatly. "Leave Reed alone. And Adelaide. They are just children."

"Dead children," he countered. "And before you they were never so susceptible. That is why you are my favorite of your bloodline, Elegy. You're so deliciously inept. I look forward to managing you the way your father manages us, which will, in fact, be very soon."

Her fury at having been summoned dissolved into fear, and what little color she possessed drained from her face. Had he said such a thing to Thaddeus, he would've found himself confined to some closet or another for a month for his audacity.

But Elegy was not her father, and Gideon Constant well knew it.

"You could bind me to this room, but only for however long it takes you to escape it," he continued. "Perhaps you could even reach a doorway with your ridiculous runes. But you cannot punish me the way he can. The most formidable master over us since Jasper himself is Thaddeus."

"Take care what you say," she said. "My father yet lives."

At Gideon's feet, Bancroft lifted his head and stretched his black lips thin, a grotesque mockery full of pointed teeth and sneering. "Not for long. We can taste it, child, like a festering sore, and the taste of it is so sweet."

Elegy lifted her small, white hand and pointed at Bancroft's detestable face.

"*Leave.*"

As Bancroft was seized by invisible hands and drawn helplessly toward the wall, he squealed like a gutted pig and begged Gideon to allow him to stay because he wanted to watch, to drink in Elegy's failure and humiliation, the herald of an age to come.

But even if Gideon could prevent Bancroft's banishment and temporary confinement to the dining room, which he could not, he seemed disinclined to do so; in fact, he was rather enjoying the spectacle, as he always did when it involved the pain of others, even his servants. In death Gideon was as loyal as he was in life, which was to say, not at all.

With one last high-pitched, sniveling whine, Bancroft disappeared through the ballroom wall and was deposited in a heap in a corner of the dining room.

He would not remain there for long.

The moment Elegy retired to bed, Gideon would allow him to slink back beneath the cobwebs and dull crystal and grovel at his feet while whichever amongst the Collection felt disinclined to pass the evening drowsing in shadows danced to his tune.

Gideon cocked his head and regarded Elegy with cruel amusement. "You know, I do so enjoy watching you playing the master."

"I am not here for your entertainment."

"But you *do* entertain me."

"Do not summon me again. I am not yours to command." She'd meant to sound haughty, dignified, in possession of even the smallest shred of courage, but instead it came out in a pained whisper.

Gideon bowed low with a nasty, glittering smile. "My sincerest apologies," he mocked. "But do come again soon, my dear. I miss you when you're away."

A mournful melody, played upon a piano that was in tune by day and out of it come nightfall, followed Elegy down the corridor as she left Gideon's following to their revels, and at the threshold of the dining room, Bancroft wiggled his fingers at her as he slid back into the shadows with a smile.

CHAPTER THIRTEEN

When Elegy asked for the car the following morning, Arthur Griswold's eyes nearly bulged from his head.

"Twice in one week?" he stuttered. "Well, I don't know . . . What will the master say?"

"He'll be glad of the fact, because it is on Fletcher's behalf that I must go to town," Elegy replied.

Arthur scratched his chin. "Is this about that party of hers?"

"It is."

There was not a single soul within Thorne Hall living or dead who did not know that Fletcher's annual birthday celebrations were to be regarded as the most important occasion of the year, even if they very obviously were not. As such, Arthur brought round the Rolls without further complaint and waved the oil-stained cloth often kept in his back pocket at the car as it retreated down the drive toward town.

October was, to the Berkshires, a certain sort of religion.

Once they'd ripened on the vine, pumpkins populated every roadside farm stand and were just as quickly snapped up to be artfully placed upon stone walls at carefully measured intervals and to adorn porches alongside urns full to bursting with chrysanthemums, towering cornstalks, and decorative hay bales.

October did nothing for Elegy but to remind her that Samhain was coming, and Elegy hated Samhain. Forbidden from using the colloquial

The Spirit Collection of Thorne Hall

Halloween, Thorne Hall saw no grinning Jack-o'-lanterns or buckets of candy to deposit in the pillowcases of children dressed as comic book characters she did not recognize (Thorne Hall, being isolated as well as viewed with a healthy dose of fear from the local population, received no trick-or-treaters).

Rather, on that odious night in celebration of their summoning and binding, the Collection behaved more appallingly than usual, and Elegy passed the evening mollifying them.

Without a glance spared for the strands of white polyester stretched around shrubs and the poor imitations of gravestones littering the ground, she drove into Lenox and straight to Atticus's rented house. Elegy had, at Fletcher's insistence, written each and every invitation by hand more than a month ago, reserving a few in the likely event that her stepmother wished to include additional guests. She'd not used any of those; she'd written Atticus's the night before.

She rang the bell, then stood back and waited, her fingers worrying upon the edges of the invitation until the door opened, and there he was.

Elegy's breath caught in her chest, and she clasped the invitation to her breast. "Hello."

"Hi," he answered, and leaned against the doorframe with his arms crossed over his chest as he took her in.

Delphine had paired a high-necked burgundy blouse with sleeves far too ostentatious for this century with a teal houndstooth skirt and burgundy leather gloves and boots to match. The boots were made for far smaller feet than Elegy's and pinched terribly, and although she was not an amply bosomed woman by any stretch of the imagination, Delilah must not have had anything at all, for the silk was uncomfortably tight and Elegy feared losing a button—or several—at any moment. Her head ached both from the weight of her hair gathered at the nape and from the pins that secured it to her scalp such that a terrible throbbing was beginning to form behind her eyes. In short, she was miserable.

"But fashionable," Delphine had told her, which was apparently a worthy trade when calling upon a man.

Said man appeared infinitely more comfortable in a pair of jeans and an ivory cable-knit sweater that looked so soft she had the terribly mad urge to rub her cheek against it.

She did not. Thankfully.

"Good morning, Mr. Hart," she said primly. "I have come at my stepmother's request to issue an invitation."

She thrust the vellum into his hands, and he took it, scanning her calligraphy with an amused tilt to his lips. "Ah, the famous party I've heard so much about."

"She wishes for you to attend."

"Does she now?"

"You don't have to if you don't want to, of course, but you should know that invitations to Fletcher's birthday fete are quite coveted in these parts."

He said nothing to this, only grinned and pushed his tall body away from the doorframe, dropping the invitation upon the green table in the foyer and gesturing for her to come inside. A cursory glance about the neighborhood revealed naught but the odd plastic skeleton watching, and so she stepped over the threshold and closed the door.

Atticus disappeared, presumably to the kitchen, and as Elegy made her way to the sitting room, a brilliant riot of color gave her pause. Gone were the lilies in the pitcher upon the foyer table. In their place an enormous bouquet of wildflowers sprouted: Queen Anne's lace, cornflowers, spears of blinding goldenrod, and best of all, clouds of tiny, pale-purple asters that were her favorite.

He simply wished for a bit of color, that was all; he'd not thought of her at all when he'd gathered them. And gathered them he must've done, for he could not have found such flowers in Lenox save by the roadside and in the fields.

Atticus was still rummaging about in the kitchen, so she made her way into the parlor. The room was unchanged since her last visit other than that Atticus's laptop was open and a mess of papers were scattered around it upon the coffee table. She moved to inspect them and recognized her own home. The floor plan was very old, yellowed and crumbling about the edges. Thaddeus must've given it to Jeremiah; she could not imagine he would've trusted anyone else with such a priceless treasure.

The contractor knew her home, knew every floorboard and pipe and casing and stair.

He knew what it meant to preserve it; to honor it.

She wondered what Atticus saw when he looked at Thorne Hall. He probably wanted to burn the lot of it to the ground and build something square and hideous made entirely of windows and steel.

Elegy was attempting to arrange herself into the yellow velvet chair, holding her blouse together with both hands so that it did not split in two, when Atticus appeared in the doorway with two ceramic mugs in his hands.

"We'll have none of that," he said, setting the mugs on top of the blueprints of her home, and for a moment she stiffened at the casual way in which he treated even an image of Thorne Hall and thought to chide him for it, but she did not because he was pulling his sweater over his head, the worn white T-shirt he wore underneath riding up so that a small stretch of his taut abdomen was revealed.

Really, someone ought to arrest him.

"That blouse is absurd," he said, and held out his sweater. "Put this on."

Her eyes fell to the offering in his hands, then lifted to his. "I can't."

"Yes, you can," he answered, pushing it gently into her hands, and it was every bit as soft as she'd imagined it would be. "Put it on."

Atticus turned his back, and she stood stupidly for too long simply holding his sweater before it became apparent he would not turn around again until she had done as he asked, and so she unbuttoned the burgundy blouse with shaking hands and, after folding it carefully and setting it upon the arm of the chair, pulled Atticus's sweater over her head and *oh*.

It was comically large, but she loved it because nothing had ever felt so wonderful upon her skin, to say nothing of how wonderfully it *smelled*. She seized a handful and brought it to her nose, inhaling deeply.

"All set?" he asked over his shoulder.

Elegy flushed and smoothed his sweater back into place, lacing her hands before her as though she had not prior to that moment been shamelessly drinking in his scent. "Yes, I'm all set."

He turned, and she could have sworn his eyes darkened with something very much like hunger and could not account for such a thing at all. Didn't men usually prefer women to be less dressed, or at the very least, with their clothing hugging each and every curve to the point of absurdity? She'd absolutely no curves whatsoever to speak of, and what she *did* have was enveloped in Aran wool a lovely shade of ivory, and yet he looked as though he might die if he could not touch her.

Then again, the room was rather dim and she had no experience whatsoever to speak of, so it was quite possible she was mistaken.

She had been mistaken about a number of things regarding Atticus Hart.

Elegy crawled into what she now considered her chair even though she'd sat in it all of one time before, and Atticus handed her one of the mugs.

"Tea," he explained, and she exhaled in relief. There was little chance of her imagining impure things about the man lowering his magnificent body into the chair opposite hers over a cup of tea.

Elegy breathed in the warm scent of cinnamon and orange rind and took a tentative sip, and then another. "It's delicious."

"Good."

She nodded toward the floor plans on his coffee table. "I see you've been studying the house."

"I have, yes."

"You must despise it."

His laughter began as a low rumble in his chest and emerged rich and throaty, and it was the best sound she had ever heard. A pity that in a world in which ghosts might walk alongside the living, one could not capture sound. Were it possible, she would keep Atticus's laugh in a bottle in the drawer of her bedside table and take it out in the small, dark hours when she could almost believe she was alone.

Perhaps she could also capture his scent; his smile with that infuriating dimple; that stupid, stupid thumb of his. She would collect him just as Jasper had collected spirits and enjoy him at her leisure once he'd disappeared from her life entirely.

"No, of course not," he said. "Thorne Hall is beautiful. Beautiful and completely impractical. Why won't your father modernize?"

"Because he cannot."

"Cannot or will not?"

Elegy's brow furrowed. "Both, I suppose."

He was watching her in that steady, patient way of his, elbows braced on his knees and fingers tangled loosely as he waited for her elaboration, and she thought about what she might say to him that was enough of the truth that he would believe it. He was too cunning, too discerning; she should have run long ago, and now there was a vise around her heart such that, should the terrified animal of herself attempt to flee, it would grip tighter and tighter until the poor thing burst in her chest.

There was no sound in the little room other than the ticking of the clock on the wall; she drew breath and lifted her eyes.

"The man who built Thorne Hall—Jasper—he made his son and all other sons and daughters to come swear an oath that no change would ever be made to the house save what was absolutely necessary."

His head tilted thoughtfully. "What has been considered necessary?"

"Wiring, mostly, and plumbing. Telephones, though, mind you, they're still very, very old. My great-grandfather bought the car, and his son bought the mower . . ."

"What about the internet?"

Her nose scrunched. "Of course not. My father would *never*."

"But you *do* know what it is."

"Of course. I do have friends, you know."

"From school?"

"I wasn't allowed to attend. Tutors came to the house from the time I was three until eighteen."

"Jesus." He scrubbed his hand across his face, and she thought, then, that he was beginning to understand. "So these friends of yours..."

"The sons and daughters of my father's friends, or his father's friends," she said. "Of course, they were never allowed to come round for playdates or anything like that because of the—" She caught herself. "My father. Because of his illness. But I was allowed to visit them on occasion, and, of course, there are the parties."

"Like the one you've invited me to."

"Just so," she answered. "But anyway, they have iPhones and computers and such. I know what email is, and Instagram and all that, though I hardly see the point."

"On that, we can agree," he chuckled. "And what did you study with your tutors?"

There was Latin and the classics, of course, and politics and geography. She did not much care for mathematics, but she did like science, particularly biology and horticulture. She'd had an art instructor for several years, and an old woman so insubstantial that one good gust of wind would've blown her straight over who taught her the piano. And, of course, there was the needlework she learned from Delphine, although she didn't tell Atticus anything about *that*.

"You put my public education to shame," he said when at last she finished.

"Oh, but I envy yours so much better! You got to have *recess*."

He let out a bark of laughter at that and shook his head, eyes gleaming and smile wide as he took her in. "Christ, Elegy, the things you say."

Elegy knew she was far from worldly, particularly to one such as Atticus Hart from Seattle who owned a business and probably wore expensive suits and drove a fancy car and had a sickeningly attractive secretary. Still, she had not imagined he would fling it back at her in such a cruel way and was horrified by the way her face went all aflame.

"I am glad I amuse you," she managed at last to say, rather proud of herself for the way her voice only slightly wavered.

"I didn't mean it like that."

"How did you mean it, then? Because it sounded to me as though you think me quite the child."

"No. Fuck, no." His hand plowed through the glorious mess of his hair and scraped across his jaw. "The opposite, in fact."

Elegy answered slowly, "Then you think me... old?"

His grin returned, as did his dimples, the ones that had for the last handful of days been a bane worse than Bancroft's oily sneer, for at least she could easily rid herself of that.

"Do you know what I thought when I first saw you?"

"I am almost afraid of the answer."

"I thought you had the most ancient eyes I had ever seen." He paused. "And the saddest."

"You did not."

"I did," he continued. "And then you marched right down those stairs, gave me hell, and I haven't been able to get you out of my head ever since."

She blinked. Then blinked again.

"Well, that cannot be right."

"Why not?"

"I'm as prickly as my namesake and every bit as unwelcome, for you see I've no sweetness to reward the effort. No one thinks of me and if they do, 'tis not kindly."

Any trace of his easy smile had vanished, and he appeared almost stricken as he set his cup down upon the coffee table and closed the distance between them. She'd twisted her hands into a tight ball of white flesh in her lap, and to her mortification, when he knelt before her and attempted to pry them apart, she resisted. She was so rarely touched by anything living that she suspected the Collection had cursed her somehow; cursed her to want it but to have it so little that she could not bear it.

With that stupid, stupid thumb of his he coaxed her gently to release her grip upon herself, and once it was done, he threaded his fingers through hers. "You are not prickly."

In contradiction of his statement, her features pinched themselves into a tight scowl.

"You can't fool me," he continued, undeterred. "I've seen your smile. That fucking beautiful smile. You don't give them away for free, but that's okay—I'd rather earn what I have than inherit it."

And wasn't that just a swift kick in the neck followed by a knife to the heart for good measure.

"I should not have been cross with you that day," she said softly, her eyes still fixed determinedly upon where his skin met hers. "It's only that you made me feel something I am unused to feeling and I resented you for it."

"And what is that?"

For the second time in two days, she found herself smiling in his presence as she answered softly, "I think you shall have to earn it."

"Then you'll have to keep coming to my house."

"That is no hardship. I have never felt so safe anywhere in the world."

She immediately regretted her candor as he drew back, his oft-smiling mouth pulled into a flat line.

"Safer than Thorne Hall?"

"Of course not," she answered, too quickly. "Thorne Hall is my home."

"Then why do you feel safer here?"

She very nearly told him, so great was her desire for someone separate from it all to know, particularly this man whom she had come to regard so highly in such a short amount of time, but it was a bleak impossibility, and not because there was a very good chance that Atticus with his extraordinary, clever mind would not believe such things were he not to see them with his own two eyes, but because Thaddeus would learn of her disloyalty. The ways in which he could punish her far outweighed the momentary relief it would feel to confide in someone other than Floss and Hugo.

Discerning that he likely believed her fear to stem from abuse, and of the familial nature and not the supernatural, Elegy felt she must give him *something* so that he did not go running to the nearest police station.

She tightened her fingers around his. "Thorne Hall is very old. And within it, terrible things have happened throughout its long history, things that have left indelible stains. And I know this might offend your scientific sensibilities, but I feel them. I feel them all the time, and it frightens me."

He said nothing for a very long time. Outside, a chill mist gathered, heavy and fragrant with the promise of rain, and yet it was as stubborn as he and refused to yield. It grew swollen in the sky.

"Okay," he said at last upon an exhale. "You would tell me, yeah?"

"Of course I would," she lied.

"I have to review a few things for a client," he said as he lifted his eyes to hers once more. "Stay and read with me?"

Her voice emerged as little more than a squeak. "I've brought nothing with me to read."

"But if you had, would you stay?"

Elegy cast her gaze down the length of her person. "You've made me more comfortable than I've ever been. How could I say no?"

He disappeared, but only briefly, and when he returned, he held a tattered paperback that she took from him with skepticism. Turning the book over in her hands. she read the title out loud: "*The Shadow of the Wind.*"

"Have you read it before?"

"I cannot say that I have."

His smile was reassuring. "You'll love it."

They sat together in perfect silence for an hour.

She stole frequent glances at him, and each time he discovered her, he gifted her with a smile. He watched her too, and she was far less graceful upon the discovery of his attention. At first, she flushed over having been found out, then scowled because she could not seem to stop and this made her feel quite foolish, and it was entirely his fault for being so . . . himself. And she liked himself very much; *too* much.

The clock upon the mantel tolled the hour. "I've got to go." She sighed as she rose and placed the book upon the chair. "I've been gone too long. Will you turn around so that I can change?"

"I will not."

Rather than filling her with the indignance she ought to have felt, the idea quite thrilled her instead.

"Why not?"

"Because it's yours." She should have refused.

She did not.

Holding a large black umbrella over them both, Atticus walked her to the Rolls and saw her safely inside with her poor burgundy blouse bundled into the passenger's seat.

"Will you accept it, then?" she asked.

"The invitation, you mean."

She nodded, hands gripping the steering wheel, for it had not occurred to her until then that he might say no, that after what she'd told him about the house, he would not wish to return.

"I'll be there," he promised. "Stains be damned. Will you come see me again tomorrow?"

The notion of seeing him again after she'd told him so much, of sitting once more in the yellow tufted velvet chair, more herself than ever before, was so visceral a desire within her that her chest ached and in the most extraordinary way; not as something to fear, but to want, desperately. But Elegy was not allowed to want anything; not for herself, anyway.

"I shouldn't," she said. "I've been away from the house too much already."

"If you change your mind, and I hope you do, you know where to find me."

It wasn't until she was halfway back to Thorne Hall that she realized she'd imagined his hands all over her an appalling number of times that afternoon and all she'd had to drink was a cup of tea.

The Three Ravens
Francis James Child ballad #26

There were three ravens sat on a tree
Down, a down, heigh down, heigh down
They were as black as black might be
With a down
The one of them said to his mate
"Where shall we our breakfast eat?"
With a down, derry derry derry down down
"Oh down in yonder green field
There lies a knight slain under his shield
His hounds they lie down at his feet
So well they do their master keep"
His hawks they fly so eagerly
There is no fowl dare nigh him come
Oh down there comes a fallow doe
As great with young as she may go
She lifted up his wounded head
And kissed the wounds that were so red
She got him up upon her back
Carried him to earthen lake
She buried him before the prime
And was dead herself ere evesong time
God send to every gentleman
Such hawks, such hounds and such woman

CHAPTER FOURTEEN

It had been far too great a thing to hope that Gideon and Bancroft were somehow wrong about her father, but the dead seemed to sense in a way the living never could when the veil was thin and the other side beckoned. Thaddeus could neither stop nor slow the inevitable, but that certainly did not prevent him from putting forth his best effort.

Elegy was in the butler's pantry making a count of the silver serving spoons when she heard him fall, heard his hoarse cry and the sound of his body striking the second-floor landing, and The Mourning watched impassively as she barreled into the corridor like a gust of chill wind, wild and biting and positively frantic.

"Mrs. Griswold!" she called when she reached her father's side, his emaciated form swallowed by his fine wool suit. With little effort, she turned him onto his back and pressed two fingers to his neck. "Call Dr. Winslow at once!"

"I *told* him not to get out of bed, but he insisted he had important work to do," she wailed.

"Never mind that now, just call the doctor—and find Arthur. I'll need his help to get him back upstairs."

The good doctor arrived not a half hour later with a deep frown etched between his peaked gray brows, and Elegy was unceremoniously relegated to a chair in the corridor, where Mrs. Griswold brought her a cup of tea. By the time the doctor emerged from her father's room, shaking his head and muttering to himself, it had grown cold.

"Dr. Winslow," she said, nearly spilling the tea all over herself as she shot to her feet. "How is he?"

"Ah, Elegy. I've just come from . . . well, that is . . ." He trailed off, unable to find the right words and disinclined to try any further.

Fear took her into its icy grip, frost blooming within her blood and spreading until she shivered and shook, and the good doctor, bless him, mistook it for sorrow and folded his warm, papery hands around hers.

"It is very grave, then?" she whispered.

"I'm afraid so," he answered upon a heavy sigh. "His illness has progressed at a rapid rate."

"How long?"

"Three months perhaps, if he is lucky. Two if he is not. I'm so sorry, Elegy."

Two months.

Far below them in the shadows of the ballroom, Gideon's chuckle rumbled like the quiet thunder of a storm upon a gray horizon.

"Is there nothing that can be done for him?"

"Are you the praying sort?" the doctor asked.

"I am not."

"Then there is nothing that can be done."

He shook his head and shuffled past her down the corridor, and Elegy was left standing mere feet from her father's chamber door. From within came the sounds of a man dying: terrible hacking coughs and gasping breaths, groans and muttered curses, and when it had at last subsided, when he could speak once more, he called her name, but she could not seem to bid her body cross the distance to his door.

Coward, whispered a voice unseen, and then another, and another and it was Gideon's and it was Bancroft's and it was Hester's. The cacophony echoed throughout the corridor, followed and taunted her as she turned her back on that room, and not even when she left the house, not even when she was safely locked within the Rolls barreling down the road at far too great a speed to be considered safe could she escape it, because while it was their voices, it was also her own.

* * *

Elegy had not been to Brightleigh for nearly two years; she'd no cause when Hugo was so rarely at home, but the seat of the Berkshire Prescotts was exactly as she remembered it: all honey stone and towering columns in the Venetian style surrounded by meticulously groomed arborvitae and gardens so spectacular they'd been featured in numerous magazines.

She was met at the front door by Stiles, the Prescotts' butler, who informed her that the young master of the house and his . . . *guest* were to be found by the pool.

The midautumn afternoon was a balmy sixty-two degrees, and yet Hugo and Sebastian reclined shirtless on identical white loungers, drinking martinis while plastic floaties shaped like pineapples and avocados drifted upon the steaming water of the heated pool, occasionally bumping into one another and then whirling quickly away.

"Elegy!" Hugo exclaimed once he'd caught sight of her teetering unsteadily across the manicured lawns. He pushed his sunglasses up into his wild copper curls and grinned. "Join us, will you? We were just wallowing in ennui."

"You look nice," said Sebastian as Elegy sat stiffly on one of the empty loungers, her fingers threaded together tightly so neither man saw how terribly they shook. "A bit old-fashioned, though, isn't it?"

"It is," answered Hugo fondly.

She could not make small talk, had never excelled at it even under the best of circumstances, and now, with her heart thundering in her chest like a veritable heard of the wild and exotic, she was certain her attempt at a smile made her look constipated.

Hugo swung his legs over the lounger, swallowed the dregs of his martini, and thrust the glass into Sebastian's chest. "Seb, be a dear and tell Stiles to make us another round. And maybe some caviar and blinis, but only if it's beluga. If it's not, then gougères, but only if they're made with Gruyère. And see if there are any of that foie gras left from last night."

Grumbling, Sebastian dragged himself off across the lawn while Hugo grabbed hold of Elegy's lounger and pulled it toward him until they were knee to knee.

"Tell me," he demanded.

"It's my father," Elegy whispered. "He's dying."

Hugo's smile was indulgent. "Darling, he's been doing that for years."

"He collapsed on the staircase this morning. Dr. Winslow was called to the house."

His smile slipped, and beneath his freckles, Hugo paled. "What did he say?"

"He estimates my father has two months left, perhaps three, but certainly no more."

"Fuck," Hugo said faintly.

"Indeed."

"Well, I suppose we knew this was coming eventually, and the timing is actually perfect."

Elegy lifted her head, eyes wide with surprise. "Is it?"

"My parents have been harassing me about announcing the engagement to the public and setting a date since I got back from Boston. They'll be thrilled to move things up a bit, even if the circumstances are a bit grim."

"But Sebastian," Elegy stammered. "Won't this complicate your relationship?"

"I don't see why it should. He knows we're only doing it to appease our parents. He doesn't necessarily agree with it because he's so fucking *good*, but he's not about to leave me over it."

"Then it *is* serious."

Hugo sighed dramatically, but his eyes twinkled with something it took her far too long to realize was happiness, so rarely did she see it. "Go on, then—gloat. I know you want to."

If circumstances were different, if her father were not gasping for fetid air in a dark room while spirits restlessly prowled the halls of his house waiting for the breath that would be his last, she would have reminded him of the time he proclaimed himself deathly allergic to monogamy.

But so much had changed since, and what had once seemed so very far away was now upon their doorstep.

"I'm happy for you, Hugo," she said. "Truly, I am, but doesn't Sebastian think it strange that I can never leave the house? That we must have a child if our arrangement is solely to please our parents?"

"About that . . . I haven't told him *everything*, exactly. Not yet. He's only just gotten used to the idea of being with a married man. He won't know what to make of the rest of it."

"You cannot keep it from him."

"I know. And I'm not going to; I just need more time."

"Time for what?" she asked. "We have precious little of it now."

Whatever his answer, it never came. Sebastian was making his way back across the lawn with a heaping pile of food, and Stiles followed close behind with the martinis balanced perfectly upon a silver tray. Elegy had quite lost her appetite for gougères, Gruyère or otherwise, and so she made her excuses and fled, promising to see them both at

Fletcher's party. Sebastian mumbled a cheerful goodbye around a mouthful of foie gras, but Hugo was thoroughly occupied by the golden facade of his ancestral home.

Rather than the longing she expected to find in his eyes, Elegy saw only loathing and could not account for it at all.

* * *

At the end of the drive beyond Brightleigh's open gate and rows of meticulously trimmed arborvitae lay a choice: were Elegy to turn left, the road would take her back to Thorne Hall; back to her father, to the Collection and her duty, the albatross round her neck she would never be rid of.

But if she turned right, she would eventually find herself in Lenox, near a particular Queen Anne Victorian just off the main square.

When the first thought that entered her head that morning was of Atticus, she'd arrived at the troubling conclusion that he had become a very great addiction in a very short time and that she should most certainly *not* return to his lovely home and sit in her usual chair beside the fire and drink his tea and steal glances at his absurdly beautiful face. Honestly, how dare he be so wonderful to look at, particularly when he smiled. Look at the state of her because of it, to say nothing of the fact that she could not seem to stop imagining the most *indecent* things.

And she who had quite gone out of her way never to think of sex for fear the Collection would somehow know and torment her endlessly. It simply would not do.

She ought to forget such temptations and turn left, keep a vigil at her father's bedside; hold his hand and read aloud from Tolstoy or Dostoevsky and pretend she wasn't suffocating under the weight of expectations far too heavy for anyone to reasonably bear.

She turned right.

* * *

The black velvet dress and coat Elegy wore had been fashioned as a set by Callot Soeurs in 1925, long sleeved and in the drop-waist style popular at the time, with intricate gold lace trim upon the hem and sleeves, and Elegy had been convinced by both Delphine and Adelaide that she looked quite sophisticated.

Unfortunately, it came at quite a cost. The lace itched, the seams that joined lace to velvet were worse, and for some ridiculous reason she'd worn a string of jet beads with a knot at the end that were so heavy her neck was sore.

She was standing over her usual chair in Atticus's sitting room trying to decide how best to situate herself within it whilst keeping the seams of her skirt intact when he appeared at the threshold with a bundle of pale-pink cloth in his arms.

"I wasn't sure you'd come back," he explained. "But just in case you did, I went to Pittsfield last night and bought these for you."

Her head tilted and her lips parted and she could not quite reconcile the notion in her head. He had bought clothing meant just for her.

Shock rendered her utterly useless, and so he was forced to cross the room and place the bundle in her hands. It was the softest thing she'd ever felt.

"Bathroom is down the hall," he told her upon a soft, golden smile. "Tea?"

She hugged the bundle to her chest. "Tea would be lovely."

The first-floor bathroom was light and airy with what she supposed was a shower (for she'd never seen one without a bathtub beneath) and an antique vanity topped with marble, where she spread out Atticus's offering, then hastily shed her own clothes, hanging them primly upon the hooks meant for towels. She had the good sense to be embarrassed by the moan that escaped when she felt the brush of the fabric upon her skin, but only just, for she'd never felt anything so wonderful, and it was all her own.

No one else had ever worn these clothes before.

She slipped quietly from the bathroom and padded down the hallway to the sitting room, where she stood at the threshold and watched as Atticus set two cups of tea upon the table and situated a fresh log upon the fire. He straightened, his hand rubbing the back of his neck, and as though he'd felt her there, he turned, and that wide, wonderful grin of his nearly split his face in two.

"They're so soft," she blurted out.

"I know. I tried them on before you got here." Upon the coffee table his phone began to dance with an incoming call, and he scooped it up, his face falling as he registered the caller.

"I'm sorry, I have to take this. I'll be right back."

As he retreated into the foyer, Elegy clambered into her usual chair, sinking into it with such deep contentment she felt it through muscle and sinew; felt it settle within her bones.

What a joy it was to be able to tuck her legs beneath her with ease and not worry about a ripped seam! She indulged in a moment of contortionism while Atticus was away, flopping about and stretching herself this way and that just because she could. When he returned with the tea, she was on her back with her head dangling over the seat of the chair and her legs hooked over the back.

Upside down, their eyes met.

"I would appreciate it if you never spoke a word of this to anyone," she said most gravely. "Ever."

"Too late, I already told half the Berkshires."

"I couldn't resist. I haven't worn anything so comfortable in ... well, it's been a very long time."

"I'm going to buy you ten more just like it," he declared once she was properly resettled, tea between her hands, letting the warmth of it steal beneath her skin and seep into the depth of her.

"Don't be ridiculous," said she. "I'll have no use for them after you're gone."

The easy smile remained frozen on his face, but it no longer lit his eyes; she might've felt guilty were it not something of which he should have been well aware.

He'd saved her place in *The Shadow of the Wind* with a small scrap of paper, and while he answered a few emails on his laptop, she read in utter bliss. And this time, when he caught her staring, she did not look quickly away and busy herself within her pages, but studied him in easy silence while he did the same.

When their cups were emptied, it was she who stood and stretched, then headed through the dining room into the kitchen, where she found a tin of black tea sachets with bits of orange rind and cinnamon and a kettle on the stove gently steaming. While she waited for the tea to steep, she poked about in his fridge and cabinets, fascinated by the clear plastic containers that bore the name of a posh organic grocery store in Great Barrington.

The porcelain sink, no doubt original to the house, was situated before a great, wide window, and as Elegy filled the kettle, a rustle of black feathers drew her attention to the fence that separated Atticus's garden from the neighboring plot. She beheld a raven perched there, fastidiously grooming his glossy black plumage with its prominent beak.

There was a Child ballad regarding ravens; a gruesome tale it was indeed, but the melody was a particular favorite of hers, and she quite forgot herself as she hefted the kettle to the stove.

The Spirit Collection of Thorne Hall

There were three ravens sat on a tree
Down, a down, heigh down, heigh down
They were as black as black might be
With a down
The one of them said to his mate
"Where shall we our breakfast eat?"
With a down, derry derry derry down, down

The kettle whined, a dissonant harmony, and Elegy busied herself with pouring the boiling water into their cups, forgetting that she was not within the walls of Thorne Hall and that 'twas not only spirits who heeded her song.

She must've been singing louder than she realized, for when she happened to lift her gaze, she found Atticus leaning against the doorframe of the kitchen and startled herself so badly she nearly scalded herself.

"What song is that?" he asked.

"'The Three Ravens,'" she answered, suddenly finding the sachets of tea in their tin quite fascinating indeed. "It's one of the Child ballads—number twenty-six."

"You have a beautiful voice."

Elegy flushed, unaccustomed to praise, for the only other person who'd ever complimented her singing was dead and had meant it sardonically, she was certain. "I've no idea how I ended up with it," she said. "My mother loved music, but she was tone-deaf, and my father . . . well, you've met my father."

"Will you sing something else for me?"

"No!"

He chuckled at her horrified expression, the way she shook her head so frantically—'twas as if he'd asked her to show him the Collection. "Why not?"

"Because you're right there!"

Now he laughed outright. "I've been here the whole time."

"Yes, but I couldn't *see* you."

"I'll turn around, then."

"It's still no."

"That's too bad," he said. "I could listen to you sing all day."

"I love to sing," she told him, a truth to distract him from a much greater one. "My songs are a comfort, and much more besides."

"Where did you learn them all?"

"Mrs. Griswold," she lied.

"How old are they?"

"Some are very new—perhaps one hundred and fifty years or so. Others are far more ancient. Many have been lost to time, and it hurts to know I'll never hear them."

"Only you would think to call something one hundred years old *new*."

"The oldest Child ballad is six hundred and twenty years old."

He laughed softly. "No shit."

"Shit," she answered primly.

When it came time for them to say goodbye, Elegy found she had become stone.

"What is it?" he asked at the door to the Rolls. "What's wrong?"

"How do you know anything is wrong?"

He rubbed his thumb gently across the crease between her delicate brows. "This little line just here." He moved to her temple, tucking an errant lock of hair behind one ear. "Tell me."

"I hate to say goodbye."

"Then don't."

"I've been gone long enough to be missed."

"Come back tomorrow, then."

"I can't," she said upon a groan. "I wasn't even going to come *today*, and look how spectacularly I bungled *that*."

"Then I'll make sure my father needs me tomorrow."

Her poor heart did not know what to do with itself, and so she turned upon her Pinet embroidered heel and ducked inside the Rolls so that she did not do something exceedingly foolish like kiss him.

She did not believe herself capable of stopping were she to begin.

CHAPTER FIFTEEN

On the day of Fletcher's party, the Spirit Collection of Thorne Hall observed from the shadows as Elegy and the Griswolds prepared the manor to receive Fletcher's guests, denizens of the Berkshires distinguished enough to mollify Thadeus and entertaining enough that Fletcher should wish to spend an evening in their company.

For the more agreeable spirits, this was done with wistfulness, as they were perhaps reminded what it was to be amongst friends; to drink and dance and laugh. For others of a less agreeable nature, such gatherings only served as a reminder of what they had lost. These, Thaddeus would pay the most care to that night, for it would not do for a guest to find himself helplessly turned about looking for the powder room and wander into a darkened corridor where the covetous dead lay in wait.

When at last Mrs. Griswold announced that there was little more to do than had already been done and thoroughly inspected, Elegy locked herself in the bathroom and soaked so long in the tub that her fingertips began to prune. She emerged in a silk robe and a cloud of steam and saw Adelaide sitting against the opposite wall with her gray arms crossed over her pinafore and a scowl on her face.

"I wish you'd let me in when you take a bath," she sulked. "You know I love the smell of that pink stuff in the bottle, and you always shut it away after."

"Yes, because *some* little spirit kept leaving puddles of it all over the manor." It was after Mrs. Griswold had slipped on one such puddle in the foyer and nearly broken her hip that Elegy had begun locking her toiletries in a chest. "I'm off to dress—would you like to watch?"

The ghost nodded with such earnestness that Elegy's heart ached because, dead though Adelaide might've been for 150 years, she would forever be a little girl who had loved watching her mother prepare for the evening, smiling at her in the mirror and letting her try on her satin gloves so long as she was careful. She'd felt so grown up during those times, she'd told Elegy once, and she could scarcely wait until it was her turn to sit at the dressing table, wearing ballgowns of silk and taffeta, with jewels dripping from her ears and gleaming at her throat.

Her father had always come in to fetch her mother when their guests arrived, bending to kiss her cheek and telling her how beautiful she looked.

"He was the very best of papas," Adelaide had confided wistfully. "He was ever so tall and had black hair and a black moustache. He was kind and gentle and had a lovely, deep voice. He used to read me stories before bedtime. I wished to marry a man just like him."

Jasper and his bloodline had made certain she would never forget that illness had stolen such wishes from her.

Back in the Ivy Room, Adelaide flitted about Elegy's wardrobe, pulling skirts of satin and taffeta around her shoulders like capes and rifling through the mahogany jewelry chest, while Elegy fumbled with an ancient pair of curling tongs and a 1948 edition of *Modern Woman* open to a page depicting a young woman in a dress similar to the one she'd chosen for that evening, a treasure she'd discovered hidden inside a dusty garment bag at the back of her wardrobe. The zipper was so damaged she'd had to cut the dress free, and when she had, crimson satin had poured into her hands, rich as blood and supple as skin, a dress for a woman who wished to be seen.

Elegy observed her reflection in the desilvered mirror as Delphine gently fastened the hooks in the back: the plunging neckline and diamanté broach at the cinched waist, the gentle caress of the fabric, the skirt that rippled gently when she moved. Her black hair, deeply parted to one side, fell softly in waves down her shoulders, and her lips were painted a deep, rich burgundy, darker even than the gown she wore.

It was not an austere mistress who stared back with eyes ancient and sad, but a young woman on the cusp of something both terrifying and wonderful.

The Spirit Collection of Thorne Hall

"I suppose I shall allow you to borrow these for the evening," Adelaide said as Elegy rummaged through her jewelry box for a suitable pair of earrings. She held out her mottled gray hand, where unfamiliar diamonds glittered in her palm, and Elegy wondered how long she'd had them in her possession. "But *only* for tonight. I'll want them back after the party is over."

Once Elegy had given Adelaide her word and donned jewels far too beautiful to be hidden away, she slipped from her room.

Thaddeus had hired a band for the ballroom, but it was Tabitha's record collection that serenaded Fletcher's guests as they arrived: Benny Goodman, Django Reinhardt, Édith Piaf, Louis Armstrong, Glenn Miller, Duke Ellington, and many more. Below, Fowler met Fletcher's guests as they arrived, taking their coats and welcoming them into the warmth and gaiety of the great hall where Elegy's father and stepmother waited.

Dr. Winslow had brewed a tonic of unusual strength for the occasion, and while Thaddeus still leaned heavily upon his cane, his gait slow and stilted, his coughing could be managed by a subtle turn and a handkerchief held to the mouth. Unfortunately, there was no such remedy for his ghastly appearance, and a great many guests whispered their concerns for his sunken eyes and sickly pallor behind his stooped back.

Of course, it did not stop them from enjoying the very best their host had to offer.

Two fully stocked bars stood ready to accommodate the whims of the fifty guests who had been invited that evening, while trays of champagne and wine were industriously circulated along with various amuse-bouches, and every gleaming inch of the dining table was covered by mountains of shellfish on ice, cheeses, and accoutrements on chilled marble slabs—pâté and foie gras with tiny toast points, caviar and blinis, and even lamb chops and mint jelly, Fletcher's favorite.

Gripping the railing tightly with both hands, Elegy scanned the crowd, searching for a familiar head of tousled brown hair among the glittering jewels and silks, the dark suits and crisp white collars, but did not find Atticus among them. Perhaps it was just as well. An eclipse of moths had taken up residence in her rib cage, velvet wings fluttering against the prison of her bones, and she wondered if the red satin gown had been a good idea after all, if it was not putting on airs she did not deserve. Perhaps she ought to go and change before anyone saw her.

At that very moment, there was a knock upon the front door, and Elegy's breath caught as Fowler admitted the new arrival. He was so tall, so handsome in a three-piece charcoal suit and black wool chesterfield coat, that he drew the eyes of Fletcher's guests even though he'd not sought such attention, and he was as disinterested in them as they were fascinated by him. His green eyes looked here and there amongst them, and Elegy hoped that it was she whom he sought.

Fletcher, resplendent in a black velvet gown with a plunging neckline and ruby earrings the size of quail's eggs spotted him at once from across the room and was at his side in an instant, bracing her hands upon his arms and tugging him down to kiss one cheek and then the other, and Elegy bristled when he spoke into her ear.

Fletcher straightened and looked around the great hall, her gaze finding the staircase and then the landing, and Elegy knew she could no longer hide because Atticus's eyes had followed, and he'd caught sight of her at last.

The future mistress of Thorne Hall took a deep breath and began her descent.

CHAPTER SIXTEEN

Atticus's eyes were not the only ones that drank her in, but they were the only she saw, and they were the anchor she so desperately needed, because whispers had suddenly broken out amongst the crowd. They did not recognize her, she realized, and were desperately trying to place the black-haired young woman in a gown the color of blood one hundred years out of fashion.

She was a stranger in their eyes that night, and Elegy found the idea both peculiar and appealing in equal measure. Perhaps she might be able to enjoy herself for once, and to enjoy him as this new version of herself at least for a little while.

When at last she reached the bottom of the staircase, he was there, towering over her, his head low so that his lips nearly brushed her ear; she shivered.

"You are so beautiful I can't breathe," he told her, the low rasp of his voice sending shivers dancing down her neck.

"Well, we cannot have that," she replied, bold as brass and yet so she felt certain it was his hand and his hand alone that kept her from sinking to the floor in a puddle of satin. "So perhaps you should look away."

"Not a chance."

"Atticus, I am so glad you could join us tonight!" Fletcher piped up, thoroughly ruining the lovely moment between them, and Elegy glared at her as she drew away from the solid warmth of his body. Her stepmother hardly noticed; she was far too busy swooning. "I told Elegy to invite you as my personal guest, you know. And here you are!"

His smile was easy and thoroughly indulgent. "Here I am."

"And Elegy—I hardly recognized you! If I'd known you had this stunning number stashed away in your wardrobe, I would've stolen it long ago."

Atticus laughed, but Elegy did not. The likelihood of the red satin mysteriously going missing come morning was an almost certainty.

Elegy hoped Fletcher would leave them be and mingle with her other guests, but she seemed perfectly content to make a fool of herself hanging upon Atticus's arm and smiling up at him with a wide, wild smile stained with rust.

A tray of champagne hovered nearby, and Atticus seized one for Elegy and one for himself, and Elegy drank the lot in three deep swallows and asked if she might have another. He gave her his own glass; he seemed to know that she needed it more than he did.

And thank goodness for that, for a jovial voice piped suddenly, "Well hello, gorgeous!"

It was Hugo, dressed in a teal velvet tuxedo and keen for the sort of mischief they usually got up to at these sorts of gatherings. At Fletcher's thirty-eighth birthday he'd brought edibles, which they'd consumed in the library, where the spirit of the scholar Nathan Bride was quite eager to discuss Socrates and Plato and Heraclitus. He never left the library because he'd died in one, and he was happy to have done so, surrounded by that which he found most beloved. He was excellent company, though easily given to fits of panic when his thoughts grew too large for his head and he wanted for someone to share them with, someone to challenge him the way a scholar should be challenged. He could also be terribly skittish, particularly when there were intruders amongst his beloved books.

The night they'd crashed his sanctuary, Hugo broke a chair by attempting to dance a jig upon it, and poor Mr. Bride was so traumatized that he tore out every page in a first edition of Darwin's *Origin*. Elegy was far too terrified to admit the truth of the deed to Thaddeus, and to make matters worse, she hadn't even *had* a brownie, so she could not even blame her ineptitude on being inebriated. In shame, she burned the evidence in her bedroom hearth, and as an act of contrition, Hugo stole a much-younger copy of *Origin* from his family's own library. Elegy waited with a knot in her chest for nearly a month for Thaddeus to recognize her deception, only to discover that her father did not actually read books.

In fact, he rarely ventured into the library unless a guest to the manor specifically asked to see it. Thaddeus loved *owning* books, just as he loved owning everything else in the manor, but rarely paid them any mind save what others thought of them.

"Hugo!" Fletcher trilled, and pulled the young man toward her even as half her martini coated the back of his jacket. "I'm so glad you could make it! And here's Floss!"

Floss appeared behind Hugo, her arm threaded through Sebastian Blythe's, a tumbler nearly full to the brim of what Elegy suspected was her father's finest whiskey. The silver sequined dress she wore was as shockingly low in the front as it was short, and with her golden curls blown out and eyes deeply lined, she was certainly a sight to behold. Fletcher greeted them both with the same enthusiasm she'd shown Hugo, then swung around to Atticus with a dazzling smile. "Atticus, these are dear friends of Elegy's and of our family: Hugo, Floss, and Sebastian."

They inquired politely after the renovations at Thorne Hall, at which point Fletcher began to lament the pitiful state of the food that evening, as they'd been forced to bring in an outside caterer. She was humored as both hostess and guest of honor until she grew bored and traipsed off to find a fresh martini and more entertaining company, and they all let out a collective sigh at the sight of her sashaying backside disappearing into the crowd.

"Good old Fletcher," said Hugo fondly. "I am so glad she is still relatively sane. Now then." And here he turned to Atticus, his expression gone positively ravenous. "Where were we?"

It was quite clear that Floss, Hugo, and Sebastian wished to positively devour Atticus, and Elegy was more than a trifle nervous. He was an enigma; a man who earned his own money rather than inherited it and was in the business of modernization rather than perpetuation.

An anathema to their world.

"Hugo! There you are—we've been looking for you."

The new voice belonged to one half of the duo known affectionately as the Kapoor Twins, owing to the fact that they disliked nearly everyone and liked no one so well as each other. They were long past the point where their parents would've preferred them married and in possession of heirs of their own, but whenever one of them exhibited even the mildest of romantic interest in someone, the other inevitably found fault with them and that was that. Elegy hadn't seen them in an age; they kept mostly to Boston, a respectable distance from their prying parents but close enough should they need to make an emergency trip to the Berkshires to mollify them, should talk of bestowing their inheritance upon a far more deserving cousin arise.

Hugo turned to them, wearing a broad grin. "Amar! Anaya! To what do we owe this pleasure?"

"We're here for the leaves," Anaya deadpanned.

"And the booze," Amar added.

As if she were the mistress of Thorne Hall and not Elegy, Floss leaned over the bar and extracted a bottle of whiskey whilst Hugo procured a stack of tumblers, then led the troop away to a corner of the great hall, where Floss filled their glasses until the bottle was empty. "Cheers to old friends and new," she said, smashing her glass against everyone else's, then downing half the contents.

Everyone else followed suit, save Elegy, who only sipped her own whiskey because her head must not under any circumstances be so muddled that she could not hold her own against the Collection, should the need arise.

"So, Atticus," Hugo said once his glass was empty. "You own your own business."

"Correct."

"So, what's it like working for a living?"

Elegy flushed as the rest of them snickered, for while Hugo was partially serious, fascinated as he was by the lives of others, it was usually because he thought himself above them and sought to prove it.

Atticus rolled his broad shoulders in an easy shrug and drank long and slow from his glass. "I've never minded it."

"I'm sorry," Anaya interjected. "Who the fuck is this?"

Hugo opened his mouth, but Elegy was faster. "This is Atticus Hart, my father's contractor's son from the West Coast. He's in sustainable engineering."

It was at that moment that Elegy remembered that Atticus was much older than the rest of them—thirty-two, seven years her senior. How dreadfully insipid he must find them. None could be introduced by their profession for not a one of them had a real job and, save Floss, all resided in lavish mansions owned and unfortunately still occupied by their parents. "You must hate Thorne Hall, then," Amar mused.

"Nobody hates this house," Floss declared, refilling their glasses to the brim. "It's too fucking pretty."

"It *is* pretty," Sebastian slurred; he was already halfway drunk.

Just as Hugo suggested a rousing game of asshole despite the fact that no one had a deck of cards, Elegy felt Atticus shift beside her, and his quiet voice drifted into her ear. "You know, I still haven't seen the ballroom. Care to show it to me?"

She could have kissed him.

She wanted to kiss him.

"Oh my God, you have to see it when it's all done up," Floss gushed. "And Thaddeus always hires the best bands for dancing."

Hugo's howl of dismay was drowned out by the enthusiastic agreement of the rest, and Elegy was relieved beyond measure when they rose, even if they did leave behind their empty tumblers in a stack on a nearby banister.

The band Thaddeus had booked for that evening played the Great American Songbook atop the platform in one corner of the ballroom, and in the opposite was a small bar serving classic cocktails in crystal coupes and tumblers and highballs. At the center of the gilded room, couples stepped and twirled beneath chandeliers of gold and crystal commissioned by Jasper for his Delilah.

Despite being within the most cursed room in the manor, Elegy felt a fissure of excitement at the simple notion of wearing a beautiful dress and standing arm in arm with a man who made her heart fumble about in her chest while the lyrics of Cole Porter were crooned in a magnificent baritone.

They claimed a table, the five of them, and drank gimlets and Sazeracs and watched the dancers until the piano tinkled the opening chords to "Someone to Watch Over Me" and a woman with a voice like warm honey began to sing. Atticus reached over and gently plucked the glass from Elegy's hand and offered his instead.

"I may never get the chance again," he said. "Dance with me?"

He drew her into her arms when they reached the center of the room, and she shivered at the warmth of his palm on the small of her back as she slid hers to his shoulder. Their other hands met, fingers tangling together, and rather than holding hers aloft as so many others surrounding them did, he held them against his chest, over his heart.

Elegy felt him bend, felt him envelop her, and when she lifted her head, her lips nearly brushed against his jaw, so close was he. They studied one another, he in certainty, she in wonder, and the five minutes that followed were the best of Elegy's life—and although she could not account for it at all given the horror within which she existed, also the most frightening. Perhaps it was because she knew it was fleeting.

Perhaps it was because he was wonderful, and she wanted him, and she had never wanted anything for herself before.

Whatever it was, for those five minutes she was a young woman in a beautiful dress dancing with a man who stole her breath and made her stupid while the chandeliers blazed above them and the band played on, and she memorized every second of those five minutes so that in her lonely bed when darkness fell and the Collection came with teeth and claws, she could replay it in her mind, feel him upon her skin and in her heart.

It was a gift that he would never know he'd given her but that she would cherish for the rest of her miserable life within that house.

The song ended, and as the couples around them politely applauded the beauty of the performance, Elegy reluctantly drew away from Atticus, her fingers sliding reluctantly from his; they were in company, after all, and had garnered quite a few stares by that point. A new song began and he reached for her again, but she saw nothing but Hugo, striding toward them with a glass of whiskey in one hand and a forced smile upon his face.

Floss was fast on his heels, as was Sebastian, and Elegy did not like at all the way Floss's mouth was pinched in apprehension.

"Well, that was lovely, wasn't it?" Hugo said brightly, and tipped the remainder of his drink down his throat. "Really, thank you, Atticus, for looking out for my fiancée. I would've offered, but you beat me to it."

"Hugo," Floss hissed. "What the fuck?"

But the damage was done. Atticus's entire body tensed.

"Fiancée," he echoed, looking to Elegy as though waiting for her to smile, to confirm that it was, indeed, a terrible joke, and that any moment the lot of them would burst into gales of laughter.

But she could do nothing but stare at her friend with a face frozen in perfect horror as what little she'd known of perfect happiness evaporated in an instant.

Her silence was all the confirmation Atticus required. He let fall the hand that rested upon her back and offered it to Hugo. "Congratulations. I didn't know."

Hugo had clearly not thought of anything beyond his shocking announcement, because he appeared entirely unsure of what to do. Tentatively, and with the furious eyes of Floss upon him, he took Atticus's proffered hand and shook it.

"Thank you," he answered, and cleared his throat. "Much appreciated."

The Spirit Collection of Thorne Hall

"I should go," Atticus said, flexing his hand upon his thigh once Hugo had relinquished it. "It's getting late. Please give my best to Fletcher."

And then he was gone, leaving Elegy's heart in pieces upon the floor and Floss angrier than she'd ever seen her.

"You fucker," Floss seethed. "Hugo, you absolute fucker."

Hugo's cheeks stained pink, but he remained stubbornly indignant. "How was I to know no one had told him?"

As the two of them began to argue in the middle of the dance floor without a care as to who heard them, Elegy could not stand to spend one more moment in their company for fear the champagne she'd consumed would decorate the floor. She gathered the red satin of her gown and fled from the ballroom and down the corridor, pushing aside those in her way until she reached the great room.

Frantically she searched the crowd for his tousled head of brown hair standing far above the rest, but she did not see him. In the time it took Elegy to recover her wits, he'd made his escape and was no doubt glad to be rid of her.

Fowler was no longer at the door, and she pushed it open, stepping out into the frigid night, the sweet tang of woodsmoke hanging in the air.

One of the hired valets had just brought his car around, the rental she'd seen parked in front of his apartment in Lenox, and he was just about to duck inside the open driver's side door when she gathered her courage, and her voice.

"Wait!"

His shoulders tensed beneath his heavy wool coat, and his head swung around, eyes finding her at once.

"Atticus, please," she said when he made no move to extract himself from the car. "A moment is all I ask."

The valet had the good sense to mumble something about other cars to see to, despite the fact that they were the only two not inside, and shuffled into the darkness. Atticus closed the car door, then leaned back against it with his hands shoved in his coat pockets, a guarded expression upon his face that her own deception had put there.

"A moment, then," he agreed.

Her relieved exhale was a shaky intimation of a laugh. "It's really, really not what you think."

"Then why don't you tell me what it is."

"Hugo and I are not in love with one another."

"Yeah, I figured that out what with his tongue being down Sebastian's throat all night."

"His parents do not approve," she continued. "They have demanded that he enter into what they refer to as a respectable marriage with a woman, or he will forfeit his inheritance. By marrying me, Hugo will satisfy his parents and the conditions of his inheritance, and I've assured him that he will be free to love as he wishes so long as he does not make a public display of it."

Atticus folded his arms across his chest, brows drawn together in blatant disapproval.

"And what exactly do you get out of this?"

"Hugo knows what will be expected of me when I am mistress of Thorne Hall, and all of the limitations that accompany it." Here she took a deep breath, because she could not tell him why. "I cannot leave this place. Ever. I do not expect you to understand, but Hugo does. It's a solitary life I will live, that *we* will live, and Hugo is willing to pay that price. No one else would. Certainly not someone like you."

Atticus exhaled long and slow, and she did not blame him at all for the dazed expression upon his face. She imagined it sounded completely and utterly ridiculous. "Well," he said at last. "That's a lot to take in."

"I know."

"And I think there is a lot you're not telling me."

Lips pressed thin, she could only nod with miserable agreement. "I'm sorry."

"And this is what you want?"

It was less a question than a demand that she must say it. Aloud and to his face.

She did not want to marry Hugo.

She did not want to stay in the Berkshires.

She did not want to inherit Thorne Hall, and she most certainly did not want to inherit the Collection and live with them each day, as if it were a perfectly normal thing to live amongst the dead and to become one of them herself with each day that passed.

"It is not about what I want," she said at last.

"You've said those words to me before."

"And I meant them."

Silence fell between them, and Elegy knew they had come to it at last, to their moment of parting, for he could not want to see her now that he knew, and with so little understanding.

The Spirit Collection of Thorne Hall

"Your choices are not mine to make," he said at last. "If this is what you want, far be it from me to judge you."

"But you do judge me."

"No."

"You do."

They were at an impasse; he smiled, and it was a sad smile, a smile of resignation and acceptance.

"Well, I guess that's it, then," he said, and Elegy's heart splintered.

"I suppose it must be."

He nodded, and she hated more than she had ever hated anything the anguish in his eyes.

"I don't think I should come back to the house."

She'd expected it and was still surprised by how dreadfully it hurt. "I understand."

"But if you change your mind," he went on, and she, who had only ever seen his hazel eyes smiling, was stunned by the storm she saw there roiling within their depths. "If you decide to stop caring about what everyone else wants and do what *you* want, you know where to find me."

CHAPTER SEVENTEEN

Elegy discovered Hugo still in the ballroom, sitting alone at a small table in the periphery with a sullen expression upon his face and an empty tumbler dangling from his limp fingers. The sound of her heels on the polished wood drew his attention, and the moment he registered her approach, he was out of the chair like a shot.

"Elegy, I'm—"

"Why did you do it?" she demanded, horrified at the trembling in her voice. For fuck's sake, Thaddeus was right; she couldn't even properly confront a man who'd wronged her without dissolving into tears. "*Why?*"

He recoiled from the rage that poured from her small frame, but it was not guilt that twisted his features. If anything, he seemed as angry as she. "We're engaged, Elegy, and here you are parading around in front of your father's friends and mine with another man who spent the entire night devouring you with his eyes."

Heat flooded her face, both at the unfamiliar sensation of arguing with a friend and with the guilt that his words provoked. "He did no such thing," she lied, because he most certainly had and, what was more, she'd wanted him to. She'd adored it.

"He did," said Hugo flatly.

"It doesn't really matter, does it," Elegy snapped, the words bitter in her mouth. "He's not staying here, and I'm bound to this place."

"Then why didn't you tell him?"

"Because I'm mad for him, Hugo!" There, she'd admitted it, and to someone other than herself. "He's different. He doesn't know anything about this place, about them. When I'm with him, all he sees is me and not what use I might be to him. Just me. I've never been so myself with someone."

She could think of no other way to explain the way in which she felt both perfectly still and content and yet so desperately alive.

"I regret the way I handled things tonight," Hugo admitted. "But, Elegy, he needed to know, and frankly, you needed the reminder. However much you feel like yourself when you're with him, you can't really be with him."

"You don't think I know that?"

"Maybe you don't, because earlier tonight I swear you would've let him fuck you in the middle of the dance floor if he'd asked."

Had she been Floss, she'd have slapped him. Had she been Thaddeus, she'd have set the Collection upon him. But because she was Elegy, snappish, solemn, sad little Elegy, she flinched; she *flinched* when he was the one who should have cowed before her.

"I'm sorry," he said, properly contrite. "That was uncalled for."

"That was cruel."

"I know. But Elegy, you've only known him, what—a week?"

"One week and two days," she whispered.

"Exactly. And if you feel this way, spending any more time in his company will make it all the worse when he eventually leaves."

"And what about Sebastian?"

"What of him?"

"You cannot possibly think me so obtuse," she said. "You are in love with him."

"Fuck you."

"Likewise."

Hugo tossed back the rest of his whiskey upon a grimace. "Fine. *Fine*, yes. Yes, I'm in love with him."

"And yet you haven't been truthful with him either, so you've no right to lecture me."

Hugo dropped his face into his hands, scrubbing his palms back and forth over the freckled skin, and when he lifted his dark eyes to hers, they were utterly desolate. "I can't do it, El. If I do, he'll leave. He's the gentlest person I've ever met. Not like me, and definitely not like you."

"Not like me," she echoed.

"Look, El, you and I both know you're weird as fuck—always have been, and I love you for it—but you've survived this place. You haven't let it make a monster of you like your father, or a lunatic like Fletcher. I wish I had your strength, but I just don't."

Strength? No, it wasn't strength.

It was because a little part of her had been cut out. Whether she'd taken the knife to herself or the Collection had, she could not say, but it was lost all the same, and so she was different; not gentle.

"You cannot trap him in a lie," she said softly. "Tell him the truth or let him go. It would be a kindness."

"If I tell him, I'll lose him."

"You don't know that."

Bitterness twisted Hugo's face. "Why would he stay?"

Elegy would have told him exactly why if Floss had not sidled up to the table with a plate in one hand and a bottle of champagne in the other, followed by Sebastian.

"Here." Floss pushed the plate across the table to Elegy. "You haven't eaten anything all night."

She'd hardly the stomach for it, but at Floss's insistence she nibbled on a canapé and sipped champagne, all the while stealing glances at Hugo. Wretches were they both, destined to each be half a person.

At half past midnight, Thaddeus rose from his seat and, leaning heavily upon his cane, bid good-night to the men with whom he had been conversing, and looked across the room to where Elegy sat, his blue eyes heavy with the command he need not speak aloud.

She felt it, the shift in the air and the heaviness as it settled: the relinquishment of command by one and the taking of the mantle by the other. They'd done this before, father and daughter, but never like this; never when there were so many about and so very much at stake should she fail.

She'd told him she could manage the Collection for Fletcher's sake. Here, it seemed, was her test.

Floss saw it first, the stiffening of her spine and the widening of her eyes, and followed her gaze to see Thaddeus hobbling slowly down the corridor.

"We should go," Floss announced, reaching out to squeeze Elegy's hand. "Elegy looks exhausted."

They would be a distraction to her, which Floss knew full well. Hugo and Sebastian, however, shared a look between them that suggested they were uncomfortable with the idea, perhaps reluctant to leave Elegy before their friendship was fully mended. She gave them as reassuring a smile as

The Spirit Collection of Thorne Hall

she was capable of and told them to nick a few bottles of wine from the bar on their way out.

Floss enveloped her in a suffocating embrace of sequins and sweat and perfume. Sebastian gave her an awkward hug, followed by an even more awkward pat on the back, and then she was in Hugo's arms blinking away tears as he gripped her tight and whispered in her ear that she was strong, so much stronger than she knew.

Once they'd gone, the ballroom emptied rapidly.

The band had long since left, but small clusters of guests had lingered in the relative silence, gossiping and flirting amongst themselves. Now they drifted away into the great hall, where sudden bursts of laughter suggested a game was being played, and they spared only a glance for the black-haired girl in the red satin gown sitting alone at the edge of the ballroom until there was none but her.

Then she stood, took hold of her chair, and dragged it across the floor until it was positioned directly in front of the door to the great hall. She locked the ballroom from the inside, then sat down, folded her hands in her lap, and waited.

The chandeliers remained blessedly ablaze, as did the sconces in the alcoves, bathing the room in wealth and in light. While the mirth and revelry continued outside her door, Elegy sang to pass the time, stories to amuse herself and melodies to soothe. The Elfin Knight, Tam Lin, Robin Hood; she altered a melody here, used a different variation upon the lyrics there.

The Collection did not appear to be in any great hurry to rouse themselves in spite of her father's absence. But she did not fool herself into thinking they might stay docile. No, they would stir themselves up again long before the final guest departed. And then Elegy would be put to it.

The grandfather clock in the great hall tolled one in the morning, and the first of the two chandeliers above flickered once, twice, then died.

The ballad she was singing at that moment was the first ever collected by Cecil Sharp.

Elegy had fallen desperately in love with the language of flowers after first hearing Calliope sing it, scouring the library for books regarding botany and the meanings attached to all manner of herbs and plants and blossoms. Thyme stood for courage and strength, and rue for regretting the theft of it, although in her case thyme might have also been *time*, the blush of her youth lost in a single syllable: Thorne.

She thought of the flowers Atticus had collected by the roadside and placed in his foyer: Queen Anne's lace for refuge, goldenrod for peace, bachelor's button for protection . . . aster for love. Things she'd had for at least a little while; things she would never have again.

Bitterness coated her tongue as she began again to sing:

Come, all you fair and tender girls
Who flourish in your prime

The other chandelier dimmed, and the next words caught in her throat. Beyond the door at her back, Elegy heard the sound of laughter, Fletcher's bark easily distinguishable above the rest. There was a thud followed by the tinkling of breaking glass; more laughter. *Leave*, she thought. *Oh, please, leave.*

"*Beware, beware,*" she sang, "*keep your garden fair—*"

The second chandelier sputtered and died. All that remained to chase away the shadows now were the ten gold sconces tucked away in their alcoves.

"*Let no man steal your thyme,*" she sang, and willed the sconces to stay lit; *please stay lit.*

Please do not leave me in darkness.

"*Let no man steal your thyme.*"

The first sconce sputtered and died.

Elegy's fingers curled around the seat of the chair and gripped tight as the second and third began to dim. *He* was playing with her. The way a cat played with a mouse before devouring it. And this time, there would be no Thaddeus when it went too far.

"*For when your thyme is past and gone, he'll care no more for you. And in the place your time was waste—*"

The second and third sconces were snuffed out in the same breath, and she heard laughter in her ears, softly echoing in the darken corners.

"*Will spread all o'er with rue, will spread all o'er with rue.*"

"Will it now?"

The vile whisper was at her ear, and her body shuddered violently.

The fourth sconce died and the fifth quickly followed, and Elegy, at the beginning of the third verse, fixed her eyes upon those which remained, those which she willed to stay alight with the heart hammering in her chest, fit to burst through her pale flesh, as much as with her voice.

"*A woman is a branchy tree,*" she sang, her voice clear and sweet, but only just, fear seizing her throat the farther the darkness spread. "*And man's a clinging vine. And from her branches carelessly—*"

The Spirit Collection of Thorne Hall

The sixth and seventh went then, followed a moment later by the eighth, and she began to shake because her song was at an end and so, too, was her peace.

Gideon Constant had come, and she was not ready.

"Well?" His voice coiled about her, his teeth at her throat, her jaw, the shell of her ear, and she shuddered when he demanded: *"Finish it."*

She stared straight ahead, did Elegy, at the last two lights blazing in defiance of the dark, and sang:

He'll take what he can find
He'll take what he can find.

All of the light in the room vanished. And with it, something else—something she'd not known had still lingered there upon her—was lost as well. Her father's protection was gone entirely. She felt it torn from her body like a cloak ripped away by hands far too eager to discover what lay beneath. And beneath, she feared, was nothing at all.

Was this the test?

Or something worse . . .

Could her father, frail with illness, exhausted from the party, have died in his sleep at that very moment?

From the darkness, Gideon Constant emerged, clapping his hands with excruciating slowness.

"You've a beautiful voice, Elegy," he taunted. "Like my daughter did, but she's been gone a very long time."

Elegy said nothing, but when she thought, *Come no closer*, he heard and obeyed.

Come no further.
Come no further.
Come no further.

Over and over she thought it, and for a long time, for a very long time, it held.

But then, when he found he could not remove his chains or at the very least loosen them a bit, he began to summon the others.

Bancroft came first; of course he did. He relished madness such as this, adored seeing her frightened, and he seeped from the shadows like oil poured upon the floor, a mouth full of teeth stretched in a gruesome smile. He came as close as he could, darting back with a gleeful cackle when she exerted her will upon him, diverting her attention from Gideon.

And all the while, Fletcher entertained her guests at Elegy's back, the sound of their jubilance a long and fearsome barb that burrowed beneath her skin.

Eugenia and Mabel came next, together as they always were; they were so inseparable that, even in death, when they were summoned, they came as one. She'd felt sorry for them in her youth, forced as they were to disguise themselves as friends, as spinster roommates, unwanted and pitiable, when all the while they had been lovers in a century when such a thing was considered an abomination.

Indeed, they deserved her pity, and in the light of day 'twas easily given, but not now, not in the dark of night when they came at his call.

Amos would not come; he never left the boiler room. And yet this was of little comfort; Amos might be no threat to Elegy herself from where he lurked in his hideaway, but thus he was the greatest danger to others, should one of Fletcher's guests accidently take a wrong turn or deliberately sneak away, as too often happened, to search for the manor's rumored ghosts in its darkest nooks and corridors.

Cook was drowsing in the kitchen; Elegy could feel her there, as she could Nathan Bride in the library, and Adelaide in Elegy's empty bathtub, inhaling the remnants of her scent while Reed turned the tap on and off in the sink nearby, passing his putrid hand back and forth beneath the stream.

Delphine, helplessly drawn by the attire of Fletcher's remaining guests, hovered in a corner of the great hall, partially obscured by the heavy curtains framing the windows that led to the veranda, and Bernard was in his usual place in the butler's pantry, waiting for Fletcher's instructions that would not come, but wait he did. Vivian lay upon the moldering bed in the Honeysuckle Room listening to Calliope sing, and Hester . . . dear Hester.

She stood sentinel at the top of the staircase where the string quartet had long since retired, while The Mourning remained at her usual post down below.

And thus did Elegy know that her father was not dead. Were he gone and the Collection fully loosed, not one would be able to resist Gideon's summons.

And so, this must be her father's test.

Far away in the library, she felt a jolt, a pull, a restlessness. Nathan reached for a tome most beloved to him—Kant's *Critique of Pure Reason*—and Elegy felt his horror as he was forced by Gideon's will to lay the book open upon one of the reading tables. He took hold of the corner of a page with trembling, rotting hands and began to tear—

Stop!

The command cost her dearly; Bancroft slithered across the floor, his rotting fingertips a hairsbreadth from the red satin of her gown before she regained her wits.

The force of her unspoken command sent him reeling backward, but slippery thing that he was, he planted his hands upon the floor and curled his claws until they sank into the wood, which had gone fetid and soft with the night. He lifted his head, eyes gleaming and teeth bared; he would try again.

Gideon's delighted laughter rang out, and the rest echoed him. Elegy sat perfectly still and held them each in her thoughts, pinning them where they stood, and let Nathan Bride thoroughly destroy his beloved Kant.

Once each and every page had been torn from the binding, Gideon released his hold on the poor, trembling scholar, who then lifted fistfuls of ruined parchment to his black lips and sobbed into them.

It was just a book, Elegy told herself.

Gideon regarded her with sly triumph, and if she let him see how much the loss of it pained her, he would most certainly repeat the performance, and so she schooled her features into an indifferent mask he'd forced her to craft long ago when she should have been allowed to care for naught but frivolous things.

Steps in the great hall. The sound of a door opening—the front door leading out to the porte cochere. And voices, including Fletcher's. She was bidding farewell to guests.

Elegy did not allow her attention to become divided. She kept her tormentors pinned like insects to the board. Bancroft squirmed and writhed, Eugenia and Mabel whimpered and sobbed, and Gideon, well . . . his was the indulgent smile of one content to let her imagine she'd prevailed.

"Will you not sing for me, Elegy?" he whispered. "Like you do for poor little Reed? I can crawl into your lap, if you like, and clutch your hair in my fingers, and burrow my face into your breasts. Please will you sing to me? Hold me and sing, and when all the warmth is gone from your body and you're vomiting your guts upon the floor, that will be the sweetest music yet to my ears."

She did not know how long he tormented her thus, until the front door closed upon the last of those who had reveled at Thorne Hall that night. Then Elegy watched through The Mourning's eyes as Fletcher turned and sagged against the wall, her head tipped back and her stained mouth agape; she was drunk or high, perhaps both.

Stumbling to the bar, she took a bottle of champagne and traipsed up the grand staircase, never bothering to shut off the lights, for she knew that if Elegy did not do it, the Collection would, so keenly did they prefer the dark. She rounded the stairwell to the second floor, wedging the cork from the neck of the bottle as she went, and as she listed toward the third-floor staircase, she drank long and deep, foam dribbling past her lips and down her velvet front. Her plodding footsteps ascended and grew fainter; in the distance, a door creaked open and slammed shut.

At last, Elegy was alone with the dead.

And now was her chance.

She bolted upright from her chair and shoved it in Gideon's general direction before she unlocked and threw open the ballroom door, fell into the corridor beyond, and slammed it shut behind her.

In the shadow of the great staircase, black lace rippled as The Mourning's head slowly turned in her direction.

Elegy ran.

Down the corridor, into the great hall, up and up and up the stairs she ran, and they watched her as she went, those most docile amongst them, and sympathetic, and yet no help at all. Though they might be disinclined to see her come to harm, they would not cross Gideon that night or any.

At some point upon the stairs, she lost a shoe and stumbled, then kicked off the other and left them both behind. They would be shreds upon the morning.

Adelaide and Reed stood together at the far end of the corridor when she reached the second floor, and hand in hand they watched her hysterical dash to her chamber door, where she grappled with the doorknob until she pitched forward through the threshold in a glittering heap upon the floor.

The spirits were not quick, in thought or movement, but she could hear them scrambling up the staircase in pursuit of her; she could hear their ravenous howling and the gnashing of their teeth. She kicked the door viciously closed, then dashed to her bureau.

The bottom left drawer contained a pot of white paint. Coating her fingers, she traced the runes that already decorated the frame of her door, making certain each rune was properly reapplied with no mistakes or gaps.

The Spirit Collection of Thorne Hall

The empty pot fell to the floor as the first of them reached her door, and she stood barefoot and helpless as they clawed and scratched and howled, furious that they could go no farther.

Protected though she might be from any danger to her person, the runes did little to dampen the fury that rolled off of them like smoke, enveloping her in anger so thick and suffocating that each breath was a battle hard fought. They'd been denied their prize, for they'd expected her to fail; perhaps Thaddeus had guaranteed it.

She felt the moment when at last they grew bored with her and withdrew, skulking back down the staircase to the ballroom where Gideon waited, never having left himself, for 'twas they who served him, and he never bothered visiting her himself.

Silence fell, and Elegy pressed a hand to her chest, the skin there cold and clammy. Her heart thundered.

There she stood for untold minutes until her breaths came slow and easy again. Then she pulled at the straps of her dress and let the red satin puddle at her feet. It was the first time she'd worn it, and it would be the last. Fletcher could have it for all she cared. She'd worn it for Atticus, and as she was never going to see him again, she'd rather not see *it* again.

Made weary by fear and such terrible misery, Elegy leaned over to douse the light upon her bedside table, and her eyes fell upon an unfamiliar lump of cream-colored fabric upon her neatly made bed. It was not until she reached out to touch it that she realized it was a pile of unscoured wool yarn.

The remains of Atticus's sweater.

CHAPTER EIGHTEEN

The catering staff returned the following morning to Thorne Hall to retrieve their equipment and, under the expert supervision of Mr. and Mrs. Griswold, cleaned the manor so thoroughly that no one would ever have supposed a party had taken place the evening before, aside from the young woman on the second floor still abed at ten o'clock. Anyone unfamiliar with her particular situation might've attributed her condition to overindulgence rather than the exertion of holding back a fright of ghosts.

At half past the hour, there was a great crash outside her window, the result of carelessly stacked racks of glassware, and Elegy was dragged unwillingly from the blissful oblivion of sleep.

Tangled in her sheets, she lay prone upon her bed and stared at a crack in the ceiling of her bedroom while the sound of the caterers and the cleaning crew bustling about outside filtered in and out of her consciousness. It wasn't until she heard her name being called from below by Mrs. Griswold that she dragged herself to her wardrobe.

The red satin gown mocked her from where she'd left it pooled on the floor, and she thrust it away back in the black shroud from whence it came before she began to sift listlessly through rack after rack of beautiful things, despising every button and seam as she did.

Because she felt as though she'd lain down beneath the port cochere and let Arthur run her over several times with the Rolls, she donned a pale-yellow chemise and a black velvet dressing gown trimmed in gold medallions. Once she'd emptied the contents of an entire pot of tea into her mouth and taken in after the leftovers from the party, she might consider actual clothing, but at that moment she felt very sorry for herself indeed and was determined to wallow appropriately.

Her makeup had left her gray eyes smudged with black and lurid, and she scrubbed it all away in the bathroom while Adelaide prattled on about the party and which dress she'd liked best. It was Mrs. Brewer's lavender tulle with the corset top, as a matter of fact. Elegy hadn't even recalled seeing Mrs. Brewer, and her mind had been so occupied that she likely would not have noticed if her gown was lavender or pink or chartreuse or if she'd worn nothing at all.

Adelaide pretended to style her hair, tilting her head this way and that in the mirror while Elegy combed her fingers through the black tangle of her own. When Elegy considered her reflection in the mirror, a ghost stared back, and it was not Adelaide but her.

"You look tired," Adelaide observed delicately.

Elegy frowned into the glass and pinched her cheeks as hard as she could. She turned to the little girl's spirit. "What about now?"

Adelaide shook her head solemnly.

"Well, fuck."

See, Atticus? she thought bitterly. *I can curse. I can curse just fine.*

Just the thought of his name was a sharp, sudden ache. She rubbed her sternum, fingers kneading the flesh there as though to loosen it, but it persisted.

She wandered down the staircase, her rumbling stomach spurring her on toward the second kitchen fridge, where the leftovers from Fletcher's party had been stored. But when she arrived on the final landing and the great hall came into view, she froze.

The shriveled figure of her father stood before the fireplace, his hands clasped behind his back as he stared into the flames. The previous evening had taken its toll: he was still clad in his striped pajamas, a deep-blue velvet dressing gown, and matching smoking slippers. At the sound of her footsteps upon the landing, he turned his head a fraction, and beneath his sunken eyes the fragile skin was bruised in exhaustion.

He turned back to the fire. "Come here, Elegy."

The journey consisted of twelve stairs, a turn, and five more, and yet it felt as though she'd walked for miles, so heavy were her steps. When at last she stood before him, Thaddeus better resembled one of the Collection than he did a living man, his skin so translucent she could see the veins beneath and his cheeks so hollow his bones protruded as though straining to escape their sallow confines. The medicinal smell that had clung to his skin since he'd begun taking Dr. Winslow's tinctures was so pungent her eyes begun to water, and Elegy wondered how much he'd taken in order to remain upright.

"You should be in bed," Elegy said when at last she found her voice. "You look unwell."

"And you are entirely the cause."

"Your test, you mean."

"You failed."

"I kept them from Fletcher's guests."

"You were weak!" he snapped. "You allowed them near enough to touch you without your consent. They should *never* be allowed such liberties!"

"It was one time. I slipped—it won't happen again."

"No," he agreed. "No, it will not. Tonight at precisely midnight you will report to the ballroom, and there you will stay until sunrise. If any of them touch so much as a hair upon your head without your permission, you will repeat the exercise the next night and the next until you are successfully able to keep them from your person."

She did not quarrel with him; there was nothing to be gained from it. If she did not come to the ballroom that night, he would send them after her, and her defiance would be punished.

She merely nodded her understanding.

"And this afternoon you will see to the damage caused by the Collection due to your failure. I suggest you begin in the library. You will need to catalog every book damaged by Mr. Bride and order replacements in the exact specifications."

"Yes, sir."

"Excellent." He took in, perhaps for the first time, her attire, with narrowed eyes. "I thought I'd made it perfectly clear what is expected of your appearance as mistress of this house, Elegy."

"You did."

"Then go change. *Now*."

"I'm tired—"

His brittle hands curled around her forearm and squeezed, tight and then tighter still, until she gasped and stared up at him in pain and in shock. Thaddeus had not touched her in many years; had gone to great lengths, in fact, to avoid any physical contact with anyone in the house whatsoever. He had never hurt her before.

"Go upstairs at once and change," he repeated, and his breath upon her face carried the stench of death. "You've disgraced this house enough."

She could not escape fast enough, flinging herself up the staircase on shaky legs, and by the time she reached her bedroom, they gave way entirely and she collapsed in a heap on the rug.

From the window seat, Vivian observed her with only a vague interest. "You're on the floor, dear."

"I am well aware."

"If you'd have bothered to consult *me*, I would have told you those are night clothes."

"Again, I am aware."

Vivian sniffed.

"Wait—how did you get in here?"

"Adelaide and a—"

"Bobbin," finished Elegy with a groan. "Fuck."

"Language!"

"Oh, go to hell, Vivian."

Vivian smiled dreamily. "One can hope, my dear."

* * *

Elegy eventually extricated herself from the floor and changed into a pleated blouse trimmed with lace and a long gray skirt. At Vivian's urging, she plaited her long, black hair into a braid slung over one shoulder, though out of petty defiance she jammed a newsboy cap onto her head.

Nathan Bride was consumed with guilt, and she was not at all surprised to find him in a corner surrounded by empty leather spines and piles of paper resembling drifts of snow.

"I didn't want to do it," he whispered. "He *made* me do it."

"I know," said Elegy as she pushed aside several books' worth of paper so that she might sit beside him.

"I'm ever so sorry," said Nathan, tugging fitfully at the ends of his long, stringy brown hair. "I can still hear the sound, Elegy—all those lovely pages!"

He alternated for several long moments between keening and muttering before finally dissolving into heaving sobs, and all the while Elegy patted him upon the shoulder and promised that she would find replacements.

When at length he calmed himself to the point where his sentences were punctuated by only the occasional hiccup, she left him and stumbled listlessly to her office. The bouquet of rudbeckias and cow parsnips she'd collected earlier that week had wilted and died; she opened the window and dumped the entire vase out onto the grass below, and when she turned, her eyes fell upon the bird.

Lying at the center of her desk was a sparrow, claws curled stiff and feathers fluttering gently in the breeze from the open window. Sometimes they got in through the third floor where the ceilings had rotted away, but she'd never seen one on the first floor—how had it gotten into her office? Taking a handkerchief from the desk drawer, she lifted its tiny, broken body and recoiled when its head lolled to one side.

Its neck had been snapped.

Her breath came quickly, dread slithering down her spine, and she stumbled toward the window and flung both bird and handkerchief into the cold, gray damp beyond.

Had the bird's neck already been broken, or had one of the Collection taken its fluttering pulse between their decaying fingers and snapped the delicate bones? And was leaving it upon her desk meant a warning, or something far more insidious? If she were the bird and Thorne Hall her cage, had it been the prison that killed her, or a desperate flight toward freedom?

Night fell, and she slept a pitiful handful of hours fully dressed atop the covers, dreaming of beating wings and a ruinous fall.

When there came a knock upon her door, she rose and found Reed standing silently with his hand outstretched. Side by side with their fingers entwined, they walked in silence to the ballroom, where she found her father standing beside a solitary chair at the center of the floor, a white circle painted around it with a diameter of no less than ten feet.

"Ah, Elegy," he said when he caught sight of her hovering in the doorway. "Do come in and sit here—just here."

She did as she was bid, with her ankles crossed and her hands in her lap, songs at the ready and determined not to allow the Collection an inch.

"Let none of them come within this circle," Thaddeus instructed. "If they do, you will repeat this exercise tomorrow evening."

"And if they do not?"

"Then tomorrow night I shall draw a larger circle, and a larger one the next, and so on until they move no further than the perimeter of the room at your command."

He left her then, and Gideon Constant took his place, a wide smile full of teeth and glee upon his face.

At first, she commanded him with thought and with will, and only turned to song when the night was darkest. And all the while he prowled about the perimeter of the circle, speaking to her so insouciantly about whatever seemed to cross his mind, which consisted entirely of her faults and failings. When at last she began to sing, he punctuated the end of each ballad with hearty, mocking applause.

"Even better than last night, in my humble opinion. I like the older songs best. I recognize more of them. Which is my favorite?" he continued. "Well, Elegy, I am flattered that you asked, and of course I shall tell you."

He did not need to. His favorite was Child's ballad number twenty-three: "Judas." It was the oldest ballad in the history, or some said, and unusual in that it cast Christ's betrayer in a sympathetic light, the thirty pieces of silver given him to purchase the bread and wine for the last supper having been stolen by his wicked sister while he slept.

She'd only ever sung it once.

"You know, I've thought quite a lot about you since last night. About that dress. Your tits are too small, but you managed well enough. Some men even like that sort of thing, did you know?"

She ignored him and continued singing. Seeing as how the Collection were quite keen on any ballad regarding the dead, particularly those in which they returned to beleaguer the living, she chose "The Cruel Mother," even though she did not care for it.

"*He* must like it," Gideon continued, clasping his hands behind his back and rocking upon the balls of his feet. "I caught him staring several times. Oh, did you not know I was watching? I was, of course. I always am." He sighed. "How tedious this is. He wished for me to wait, but I rather think I've waited long enough."

One by one they slunk forth at his command, Bancroft arriving first as he always did, Gideon's faithful second, and Eugenia and Mabel shortly after, for they adored chaos however it came. And then, to Elegy's surprise, came Vivian, who disliked most of the other spirits for some reason or another but abhorred Bancroft most of all.

Spine stiff with fear, Elegy curled her fingers around the seat of the chair and sought awareness of those who would not come, whose small act of rebellion against Gideon Constant was her only comfort.

Adelaide and Reed, huddled together on the floor of the moldering nursery writing crude words on an old Etch A Sketch; Calliope, who sang; Hester, who listened; Delphine, who drew needle and thread through cloth by the light of a single candle; Nathan, muttering in the library as he rifled feverishly through book after book, his agitation growing as he could not find what he sought; Cook, who wrote menus she would never prepare and that no one would ever enjoy; and Bernard, who could not read but looked over her shoulder as she put pen to paper and nodded as though he could.

The five spirits pressed round her, prowling the circle like a pack of wild dogs waiting for a wounded buck to end its death throes and go still so they might feast. Elegy tried to pin them with her thoughts, to no avail. She commanded them aloud: "Stop! Be still!"

Not once did they set foot across the white line upon the dark floor, and although they paced unceasingly, turning this way and that, ready to spring forward should her attention waver for even a moment, never did they advance.

And so Elegy passed the night, the white circle unbreeched. Thaddeus resumed control of the Collection sometime after the fourth hour of the morning—well before dawn, but not out of kindness. Like most men his age, particularly the sickly sort, he retired early and rose even earlier.

Back in her chambers, behind the runes on her door, Elegy slept soundly despite thunder rumbling in the distance, the portent of a storm so dreadful 'twas rarely seen more than once in a lifetime. The smell of it, the heaviness, had hung about the air since Fletcher's party; like Elegy, it was only a matter of time before it broke.

* * *

"I smell it on you," Gideon crooned, making a show of inhaling the air. "Your fear. Lord, but the smell of it is sweet."

"Those who came before me mastered it well enough, and so will I," she answered from the same chair as the previous evening, the white circle wider, just as Thaddeus had promised.

"Many masters," he agreed. "No mistresses."

"There will be no son to follow my father," said she. "So I suppose I shall be both master and mistress."

He laughed as though he found her terribly funny.

To her horror, Bernard and Cook answered his call this night, and so his company swelled to seven. They did not prowl but were still as stone, staring at her with white, sightless eyes and leaning forward, forward . . . pressing upon her will, ready to strike the moment they sensed even the slightest weakness.

Elegy sang with bravery, but still they drew close, far closer than they should have done, and once Gideon began to speak, the rest crumbled like ash in the hearth.

"I must confess I am having a difficult time discerning what the contractor's son sees in you," he mused, hands clasped behind his back as he alone strolled leisurely around the perimeter of her father's crudely drawn circle. "You really were such an ugly child. Such a tiny, skinny, sour thing, nothing like your father's sister. Now *she* was a beauty even from the cradle—not you. It took *years* until you drew my eye."

And so he continued, hour upon hour, and never could she just ignore his words, for letting her mind wander for even a moment would be to fail the test. She had to focus upon him, and all of them, attentive to their every movement and thought and desire. And the only desire they had was to seize her, to grab her and claw her, to tear her apart; they had no other desire in the dark hours of the night than what Gideon allowed them: a bitter, consuming hatred.

* * *

She woke at noon the next day with her throat inflamed and her eyes red rimmed and watering. Mrs. Griswold brought her a pot of tea with lemon and honey, and after drinking the whole thing from the spout, she fell asleep again upon her desk and startled awake at the unpleasant sensation of fingers upon the tender nape of her neck, only to find herself alone save for the relentless ticking of the clock upon the wall, a drum beating relentlessly against her skull.

"Do you know what song you should sing?" asked Gideon on the fourth night. "'Once I Had a Sweetheart.' Because you did, and now you do not."

Elegy met his mocking smile with a face of stone, at which he laughed most heartily.

"Oh, Elegy, you are such delightful fun. Now, let's see—how does it go again?" And he began to sing in his clear, melodious tenor: *"Once I had a sweetheart, and now I have none. Once I had a sweetheart, and now I have none. He's gone and left me, gone and left me. Gone and left in sorrow to mourn."*

And thus another beloved ballad was relegated to the expanding list of those she would never sing again, for it would forever remind her of Atticus and the tufted yellow velvet chair beside the fireplace.

Elegy slept until noon the next day, still clad in a black silk evening gown by the House of Worth, so heavy was her exhaustion. When Delphine gently helped peel it from her body, her pale skin was riddled with angry red welts from the cane sewn into her stays.

When she collapsed into the chair at her desk later that afternoon with dark smudges beneath her eyes and her lips cracked and dry, there was a tray waiting for her courtesy of Mrs. Griswold. She tucked into the meat pasties with such enthusiasm that she nearly missed the small white envelope propped against the teapot. Brushing the crumbs from her mouth, she slid the card inside free.

Then she called for the car.

* * *

"I'm so glad you haven't gone back to the city," Elegy told Floss as they embraced on the steps of Holcroft, and if Floss found it at all odd that Elegy knotted her skinny arms around her middle and squeezed, she did not show it.

Barefoot and clad in nothing but a short silk kimono belted at the waist, Floss held her cigarette away from Elegy's back until they'd drawn apart, then took a long drag before dropping it on the steps. "I would've, but Barbara has been so fucking emotional lately, and I've been worried about you. Come on—let's have a drink."

Elegy politely declined any sort of liquor in her coffee but did accept a dollop of whipped cream from a delicate crystal bowl the elderly housekeeper presented on a silver tray.

As they sipped their coffee, Elegy recounted her father's test on the night of the party, her subsequent failure at said test, and the past four nights she'd passed in repentance.

"What you need is a match and a gallon of gasoline," Floss answered dryly before draining her cup. "Have you spoken at all to Atticus?"

Elegy's insides twisted tighter and tighter still. "No. He came to the house once to help his father, but it was very early in the morning, and I was . . . indisposed."

Floss swallowed the last of her coffee, which was mostly liquor, and set the empty cup aside. "Here's my advice: tell Hugo to fuck himself, take Thaddeus's money, and buy a one-way ticket to Seattle."

"I can't do that to him."

"Yes, you can—Thaddeus is a dick."

"I meant Hugo."

Her eyes studying Elegy, Floss sucked her cigarette to the filter and slowly exhaled a stream of smoke before crushing the butt into the delicately painted ceramic dish she used as an ashtray; Barbara would no doubt succumb to a fit of the vapors should she ever see. "You are not responsible for Hugo's happiness at the expense of yours."

"He's our friend."

"And what about you?" said Floss. "Aren't you our friend too?"

"Floss?" a shrill voice called from down the hall, and Floss groaned.

The Spirit Collection of Thorne Hall

"Fucking Barbara. Stay here; I'll go see what she wants."

Floss left the door open in her wake, and as Elegy sipped her coffee and waited for her friend's return, she became aware of the distant sound of a piano.

The melody was haunting and terribly, terribly sad, and yet there was such beauty in it that she was helplessly in its thrall. She stood, spellbound; waiting. A man began to sing, and she was certain: it was "The Unquiet Grave."

The majority of the ballads collected by Child and Ravenscroft and Sharp were, while lovely, tediously ordinary and served little purpose other than to entertain. The Collection liked these well enough, for there was little other amusement to be had save mischief. When they grew restless and could find no comfort, these were the songs that soothed what remained of their troubled, fractious minds and stayed the worst of their impulses.

Then there were the other ballads, those whose words and melodies held a peculiar, sometimes frightening sort of power. These Elegy wielded in much the same way her father did his will alone. With these, she could captivate the spirits—the docile ones, at least—and gently bend them to her own desires and purposes.

Of these, there were five that had been classified by Child as revenant songs: ballads in which the dead returned to the living, either to torment them or to plead for release.

Four of them Elegy sang only when she must, for they were potent and took as much from her as they gave.

And then there was "The Unquiet Grave."

Her intentions had been perfectly innocuous the first and only time she'd sung it—the satisfying of a curiosity and nothing more.

Calliope had long since memorized every note of Ida Rose Pritchard's sheet music, and over the years the fragile, yellowing pages had borne the brunt of her occasional bouts of madness and now lay strewn about the Honeysuckle Room in pieces; all save one. Elegy had found it hidden away beneath a rotting floorboard that had cracked beneath her heel, and when Calliope clapped eyes upon it, she began shrieking and wailing and tried to rip the pages from Elegy's hands.

A sullen teenager at the time, with tragically few opportunities for petty rebellion, Elegy, desperate to know why the song should have provoked such rage in the usually docile Calliope, darted past her and fled to the great hall, where the Steinway grand squatted in a corner between the dining room and the veranda. She set her fingers to the keys and played the melody, and finding it simple enough and rather beautiful if terribly sad, she began to sing.

At the bottom of the staircase, The Mourning's head turned. There was a creak upon the stair, a soft gust of wind as a door opened and then another, but Elegy was far too engrossed to notice as one by one the Spirit Collection drifted into the great hall until, somewhere in the middle of the second verse, she felt the weight of their eyes upon her. She lifted her head and nearly toppled backward off the piano bench.

She had never seen so many of them in once place before—and in daylight no less!—but what was far more disconcerting was the desperation in their eyes and the hunger that poured from them like smoke, thick and suffocating.

"Leave me alone," she whispered. "Please, go away!"

A door opened in the nearby corridor, and swift footsteps carried Thaddeus Thorne from his study into the great hall. "Elegy!" he called. "What on earth—"

She'd scrambled to her feet as he rounded the corner, and when he saw what was the matter, his spine went taut. He did not utter a single word, merely a thought, and they drifted away quite innocuously, as though they'd not a moment before been hell-bent on swallowing her whole.

"What is the meaning of this?" demanded Thaddeus. "What were you doing to anger them so?"

"I was singing. That's all, I swear it."

"You sing in front of them all the time. What's so different about this time?"

Her eyes slid to the pages sitting innocently upon the music rack. "It was a song they'd not heard before. Perhaps they did not care for it."

After he'd returned to his office, she shut the lid of the piano and tucked the pages away inside her bodice. She'd no intention of ever singing "The Unquiet Grave" again, but neither could she bring herself to dispose of them, and so she hid them away inside a leather hatbox upon the top shelf of her wardrobe, where they had remained for the last eleven years.

The man who was presently singing the piece in question had a deep, gravelly voice that was surprisingly pleasant if unrefined, or perhaps it was pleasant because of it, and her feet began to move, carrying her down the corridor as though the music itself had possessed them.

Upon reaching the music room, Elegy stopped short at the sight of a man with bronze skin and a wild tangle of black hair and a beard to match, hunched over the keys of the Steinway grand; his long, nimble fingers traipsed about them with frenetic grace.

He appeared rather odd for a piano tuner, but there was no doubt as to his profession; the lid of the instrument had been removed and rested upon a thick blanket of red velvet below, surrounded by various levers and mutes.

The last notes of the accompaniment played, only his voice remained, pitched low, and as it faded into the air, the deep-brown pools of his eyes met her own startled gray. A curious expression crossed his face as he beheld her there, a sort of thoughtful appraisal that suggested he knew exactly who she was, though she could not recall meeting him before.

"The tuning is done," he told her with an easy smile, his voice every bit as captivating in speaking as it was in singing. "Give me a minute to set things right, and I'll be out of your hair."

"There's no need to hurry," Elegy answered. "I've not heard 'The Unquiet Grave' in a very long time. You sing it beautifully."

His brow rose in tandem with the corners of his mouth. "And how do you know of that old tune?"

"I love the old tunes."

"Do you now?"

"Very much."

His eyes took on a rather feral sort of gleam at that, and he gestured her forward with the crook of a finger. He was possessed of craggy features, sharp and strong; high cheekbones, a prominent nose, full lips. She'd thought his age to be near forty, but as she drew closer and the lines upon his skin deepened, she placed his age at least ten years beyond that. His hair was thick and dark, with strands of gleaming silver throughout, and although he was not handsome in a conventional way, he was a striking person.

There was enough space beside him at the bench, but she would have none of it, and so she stood within the bend of the instrument.

"Come and tell me—what other old tunes do you know?"

"I know every Child ballad," she answered. "And many of Ravenscroft, even if he was a repugnant excuse for a human being."

He stroked his short beard thoughtfully. "And what of Sharp?"

"A few, not many."

"You know, old Cecil visited the land I once called home at the turn of the eighteenth century."

"And where is that?"

The tuner grinned. "The Appalachian Mountains. He collected quite a few variations on a lovely ballad I've a soft spot for, that came across the sea with some ancestor of mine or another. It's called 'The True Lover's Farewell.'"

Elegy's skin prickled. "And is it a tragic song?"

"Exceedingly."

"The key?"

"Aeolian in B."

"Have you any paper? Perhaps a pen?"

He reached down and shuffled around inside the satchel at his feet until he unearthed a pad of manuscript paper and a pencil. "There you are."

There was no need to scratch out sharps or flats in the key signature for the most sorrowful of all the modes; she would add them later as the scale ascended, curling around the lyrics, binding them like vines.

She lifted her gray eyes to his own dark, fathomless ones and nodded; she was ready.

He set his long, agile fingers upon the keys, and that wonderfully gruff voice of his filled the music room once more while Elegy scribbled furiously with her pencil, capturing fragments of lyrics and fragments of notes. When the song was finished, he promptly began again, and each time she captured more and more, until at last the tuner's voice faded away and silence swallowed the music room once more.

"How dreadfully sad," said Elegy. "But beautiful at the same time."

"The best ones always are."

Indeed, for her purpose she could think of nothing better.

She tore the pages from the manuscript pad and handed it back to him, along with the pencil. "Thank you. You helped more than you could possibly imagine."

"Would you like my notes upon 'The Unquiet Grave'?"

"No," she answered firmly. "Thank you, but I do not sing that song."

The door on the southern wall opened, and as two men outfitted in coveralls strode into the room, the tuner slid off the bench and tipped his head in a nod. "I am happy to have been of service. Good day, Elegy."

She made her way back to the parlor where Floss would expect to find her, the pages clutched in her hands like priceless treasures. And when Elegy found Floss and her mother arguing upon one of the cream brocade couches, she realized she had not asked the kindly piano tuner his name, nor given hers.

The Spirit Collection of Thorne Hall

And he'd known it all the same.

* * *

Her father did not summon her until ten o'clock that evening, which left her time enough to finish her supper and nap for an hour or two but also bestowed upon the Collection several unfortunate hours of darkness within which to grow restless and in want of amusement; specifically, theirs at her expense.

This had been his intent, no doubt.

She took her place in the chair, the circle painted so wide around her that it left a border of scarcely one foot at the perimeter of the room. Then she drew from the folds in her skirt a small leather folio, the manuscript paper with the tuner's song within. That particular melody she was saving for last, when her strength faltered and her throat grew dry; there was power in it that would see her through, of that she was certain.

All save Amos and Hester had gathered in the ballroom for the last night of Thaddeus's punishment, plastered against the walls like the black rot that covered them come nightfall.

Naturally, they were upon their very worst behavior for the occasion.

She began with Child's ballad number one, "Riddles Wisely Expounded," and continued on in order while the taunting and hissing of the Collection grew into a cacophony. Sometime after the grandfather clock in the great hall gave two dull clangs, Gideon at last overcame the enchantment of her voice and the emotions bound up in her songs. With a long hiss between blackened teeth, he ripped the attention of his company away from Elegy like a ravenous beast ripping flesh from bone. They silenced themselves and turned the full force of their seething malice upon her; even gentle Nathan, even the children. All were lost to her and bound wholly to his will.

"You think tonight is the end of your test," whispered Gideon into the silence. "But you are a fool, my sweet Elegy, for it is only the beginning. Once your father is dead and gone, every night will be just the same as this one. This is what your life will be, night after night and year after year, on and on without end. You alone against all of us."

It was then that she took the leather folio upon her lap and opened it to reveal the tuner's song.

He fell silent at once, and his hold on his company wavered. They lifted their faces, looking this way and that, scenting the air as if they could taste the promise of *new*, of a story they'd never heard; a melody she'd never sung.

And she began to sing.

> *Oh fare thee well, I must be gone*
> *And leave you for a while*
> *But wherever I go, I will return*
> *If I go ten thousand mile, my dear*
> *If I go ten thousand mile*

Helplessly beguiled were they, ensnared by the lament of two who must be parted from each other—of one who makes a promise to return and the other who doubts it.

> *Ten thousand miles it is so far*
> *To leave me here alone*
> *Whilst I may lie, lament and cry*
> *And you will not hear my moan, my dear*
> *And you will not hear my moan*

It was sorrow; it was a vow. And when she'd finished, they begged to hear it again. And again, and again.

The sun rose, and the circle remained unbroken.

* * *

The next morning, she stood on trembling legs in her father's room and stared at a patch of damask wallpaper behind his left ear because she could not look him in the eye, lest she throw herself across his bed and claw his eyes out.

Five nights she had endured, five nights she had suffered, and he said only, "You performed satisfactorily."

She left before she was properly dismissed, the only rebellion she had left in her, and rather than return to her chamber for sleep so desperately needed, she strode down the gallery into the great hall and out the front door of Thorne Hall.

CHAPTER NINETEEN

Arthur Griswold's tweed cap had fallen low over his brow as, head down and hunched, he swept away the leaves on the veranda that had been deposited there that morning, and he did not mark Elegy's approach until the pointed toes of her boots came within his line of vision.

"Jesus," he gasped, gripping the handle of the broom and then sagging upon it with a great sigh of relief. "You just about made a ghost of me."

"Good afternoon, Arthur. I require the car."

"Now, Miss Thorne—"

"Now, Arthur," said she, no longer meek and amiable but no less polite. "I require the car and will likely require it many times over the next several weeks. As the mistress of the house and your future employer, I expect you to provide me with the car whenever I request it and to say nothing to my father, other than I have gone to visit Mrs. Carmichael or Mr. Prescott, and only should he ask. Have I made myself clear?"

Her speech was met with the further plummeting of Arthur Griswold's jaw, and she did not wait for his words to follow. Striding down the steps, she headed for the garage, and thank goodness, he followed. To be perfectly honest, she had expected him to refuse and had intended to use his future employment at Thorne Hall as collateral to buy his silence, then break down when he did not believe her because, of course, it was a hollow threat; he would know it.

The car was brought round, and Elegy sped toward town with her hands gripping the steering wheel, and as she pushed the Rolls far beyond reasonable capability, she rehearsed what she might say once she arrived upon his doorstep.

"Atticus," she said to the road. "My coming might appear strange to you given the manner of our parting, but I can no longer deny my feelings, and given your behavior these past weeks, I have come to believe that you might share them. If you do, perhaps we might pass an idle hour or two engaged in . . ."

In what, exactly? Sexual congress? Activities most amorous? The divestment of her loathsome innocence?

It was far too formal, and she could never hope to remember it all; it would come out terribly jumbled and making very little sense, and were he to shut the door on her, she would not fault him for it.

"Atticus," she began again. "I regret the way we parted. My circumstances have not changed, and neither have my feelings for you—wait, that should've come first. I have feelings for you, and although my circumstances have not changed, I still want to be with you. Well, not *be* with you in a relationship—I mean, I *do* want to be with you in that way, but I can't. I'm here now, though, so we should . . . be together."

She was as hopeless at this as she was at commanding the Collection. Upon a sigh she closed her eyes, and when she opened them again, she saw blots of yellow and purple here and there along the roadside, blooming in defiance of the cold and absence of light, and remembered the jug of flowers in the foyer he'd picked for her: refuge, peace, protection . . . love.

"Atticus . . . you told me that when I decided to do what I want rather than what everyone else wants for me, I should come and find you. I'm here now, and what I want, what I want more than anything, is you, even if it is only for a little while."

Yes, that was it. That was what she would say, and either he would invite her inside or he would never see her again, but at least she would have said it.

The matter at last settled, she began to sing as the first fat droplets of what promised to be a spectacular storm came thumping down upon the windshield, and she pulled up in front of Atticus's house just as lightning split the sky overhead.

She flung herself from the car and sprinted up the walkway, a feat not easily achieved wearing three-inch heels the width of a fountain pen, and rapped three times in rapid succession upon the door.

The Spirit Collection of Thorne Hall

She did not wait long.

The door opened and there he was, clad in a sweater every bit as delicious as the one the Collection had ruined. His hair was its usual wreck, and as he always did when he laid eyes upon her, he smiled.

She opened her mouth and promptly declared: "I want to have sex with you."

What the actual *fuck*? The speech she'd rehearsed in the Rolls had been so lovely and sincere, and now Atticus was staring at her as though she'd grown a second head.

Oh well.

Boosting herself up on the pointed toes of her absurdly uncomfortable boots, she gripped the front of his sweater and pulled his mouth down to meet her own.

It was a fumbling, desperate thing, the tangling of her lips with his, and she was grateful when his hands came up to frame her face and with patience taught her the proper way of it: a languid slide, slow and unhurried, somehow both tender and filthy, and she was both utterly consumed by it and possessed of a desire to consume.

If she could have but burrowed beneath his skin, she would have made a home for herself there and never come out again.

He drew her inside and kicked the door shut behind him with his foot, then he slid his hands down to the backs of her thighs and lifted her effortlessly. Her back hit the wall of the foyer, and instinct bid her wrap her legs around his waist.

The sound of fabric rending split the air, and she drew back, swollen lips parted in shock.

Oh fuck, what part of her dress was *that*?

She didn't care, she realized with a breathless laugh, and neither did he, for he bit her lower lip gently, sucked it between his own, and grinned against her mouth as she did something she'd been longing to do since she saw the glorious mess of his hair at the foot of the staircase before she'd ever seen his face. She plowed her fingers into it and tugged; he groaned into her mouth, and she swallowed the sound.

Delicious.

A heady drug it was indeed to elicit such a response from such a man, and Elegy, who had never had much power of her own nor cared to wield what she *did* possess, was suddenly quite keen to discover what other responses she might wring from him, and to that end set out upon a most thorough exploration indeed.

At some point Atticus had the good sense to remember himself, and she whimpered as he drew back, his pupils blown wide. "Are you sure this is what you want?"

She nodded her head frantically, tightening her fingers in his hair and trying to guide his mouth back to hers. Now that she'd decided she had to have him, she could think of little else save removing his clothes and hers and then . . . well, she might've learned all she knew of the subject from books and pictures and the vicarious lives of friends and acquaintances, but she *did* know one needed to be naked first, and so her hands fisted the bottom of his sweater and attempted to pull it up the length of his body.

His hands stayed her own. "Wait, Elegy—"

When he resisted, a small but fearsome growl erupted from her throat, the sort of sound she'd never thought herself capable of making, and he laughed as she wrapped herself around him like a vise, like ivy, and refused any space between them.

His forehead dropped to rest gently upon her own, and her eyes fluttered shut. "Are you sure this is what you want?"

"I have never wanted anything more," she replied, and because she knew that he would understand more than anyone, she brushed her lips against his and whispered against them, "I choose this."

Up the stairs they went, scattering clothes and shoes in every direction, laughing breathlessly as their mouths came together and apart and together again. The clasps of her wool skirt were exceedingly difficult to manage, but she forbade any further ripping of it, and so he turned her to face the wall, flattening her palms against the faded floral wallpaper while his capable fingers went to work. With a few deft tugs it loosened and fell, and her forehead dropped forward as he moved to the high lace collar of her blouse and the delicate pearl buttons there, undoing one, two, three, then gently parting the fabric. Her eyelids fluttered shut as his mouth settled upon the newly revealed skin at the nape of her neck, and there it stayed, nipping and sucking until her breath came fast, sweat misted her skin, and the ache between her legs grew positively untenable.

The blouse tossed aside, he turned her around to survey his handiwork. His eyes darkened as they fell on the flimsy stockings she wore, one of only two pairs of Pretty Polly hold-ups made of Lycra that had been all the rage in her grandmother's tenure as mistress.

"They're called hold-ups," she explained in a voice gone rather whispery. "They were invented in 1967—quite revolutionary, actually. One did not need a garter to—"

The Spirit Collection of Thorne Hall

Having evidently decided a lesson in vintage hosiery was entirely unnecessary, he ducked his head and, taking hold of the elastic encircling her upper thigh, began to draw the first one down.

"Hold them up," she finished weakly, as he tossed it over his shoulder and started upon the second. "You see, garter belts tend to leave dreadful lumps under fabric, and while I cannot deny they have aesthetic appeal, particularly to members of your sex, they *oh*—"

Both her stockings now discarded, he was quite enamored with exploring the tender skin of her thighs, fingers stealing beneath the hem of her chemise until he reached that place even she'd not dared touch and found it slick and swollen and positively wanting.

His breath left him upon a shuddering sigh. "Perfect."

"Bedroom," she panted in reply. "Posthaste."

By the time they stumbled into his room with their hands and mouths absolutely everywhere, she watched with wide eyes and her lip between her teeth as he unbuckled his belt, pushed his pants down over his hips, and kicked them away. He stood before her fully himself and without shame and let her study each and every inch of him.

Elegy had seen naked men before, of course—Hugo's father possessed a vintage pornography collection that was both impressive and disgusting in equal measure—but it was a different experience altogether to have one before her, warm and willing and hers at least at that moment, and she was shameless in her perusal.

Her fingers mapped the warmth of his skin tentatively at first, and then, when she felt his breathing hitch and grow unsteady, she leaned forward and pressed a kiss upon his heart.

His fingers delved into the heavy arrangement of her hair at her nape, and pins were sent scattering as inky black tumbled about her neck and down her shoulders. He took hold of it, twisting it around his hand and tugging until her neck was bared and her lips parted to be captured by his own.

This kiss was not meant to instruct but to devour, and she surrendered herself to it wholly and completely, to the slow slide of lips and tongues. The soft cry she uttered when his mouth left hers became a gasp as he took her earlobe softly between his teeth, then sucked gently at the skin where her jaw met her neck, and she discovered that she was, in fact, incredibly sensitive just there. He'd evidently made a similar discovery, informed no doubt by the way her nails dug into his shoulders, and, scoundrel that he was, pressed his advantage.

His fingers had been busy indeed while his mouth and teeth and tongue rendered her senseless, and she felt suddenly the chemise loosen and fall at her feet, leaving her in nothing but her underwear, and he discarded them alongside the rest, far more interested in what lay before him.

They fell together upon his bed in a tangle of flesh, and Elegy sunk her fingers once more into the mess of his hair whilst he made a thorough exploration of her neck, her jaw, her collarbone. She feared he would find her small breasts a disappointment—no doubt he'd seen far more impressive figures than hers—and yet he touched her with reverence, and then with hunger, first with his fingers and then with his mouth, and any doubt as to his enthusiasm ceased entirely.

"I know I said I wanted to try everything, and I do, I just . . . I have no idea where to start."

He pressed a kiss beneath her ribs and looked up with green eyes dark and gleaming. "I know where *I'd* like to start."

"Do you?" she said faintly, as he continued to kiss his way down the flat plane of her stomach.

He hummed his assent against her hip bone, parting her legs so that he could nuzzle the soft skin of her thighs, and it was then that she realized what it was he wanted to do. She'd read about it, of course (there was a first edition of *Lady Chatterley's Lover* in the Thorne Hall library, after all), and Floss had waxed endlessly nostalgic about it (once she found a partner more adept in performing the act than her college boyfriend, who ostensibly sucked everything into his mouth *but* her clitoris). But reading and being told were nothing to experiencing a thing, and she *very* much wanted to experience this particular activity, and so when he did something with his tongue that robbed her of all rational thought, she carded a hand through his hair and let herself surrender to it entirely.

His satisfied groan ghosted across her skin before he returned to his task with shameless abandon, with tongue and teeth and fingers, until her sweat-sheened skin twisted helplessly in the sheets, a plea upon her lips as she canted her hips just so, just there—oh, please, *there*—

And then she was coming, coming and *laughing*, which was, evidently, a perfectly normal thing to do if one was Elegy Thorne, and if Atticus thought it strange, he did not say so.

As she sank languidly into the pillows, he placed his perfect mouth upon each and every inch of her quivering skin that he pleased, from her hip bone to the edge of her jaw, where his teeth grazed and his tongue soothed the ache, and all the while she marveled that such a thing had existed all this time and she'd never known.

"Everything," she murmured. "I said I wanted everything, and I meant it."

"You're sure?" Atticus asked against the taut skin of her rib cage. He asked the question once more with his hands sliding across the warm soft of her skin until he framed her face, that stupid, wonderful thumb of his caressing her lower lip.

Her teeth bit gently down; acquiescence.

He shifted up to his knees, and Elegy heard the sound of ripping foil and had the good sense to panic for at least a second before—oh, right. One of those.

His forehead dropped to hers, and in that steady, patient way he did all things, with his brows drawn together and his lower lip caught between his teeth, he slid in; and in, and in. Her lips parted upon a gasp as he withdrew, then canted his hips forward slowly, fingers tangled in her hair, thumb pressed to her lower lip, and eyes upon hers. When at last she'd taken him fully, a sudden thought occurred to her.

"Atticus," she said, "I do believe I am a loose woman after all."

"Elegy," he rasped. "The things you say."

He set about robbing from her the ability to speak, moving slowly and quite at his leisure, and she did her best to meet him, awkward and fumbling at first but easily mastered, requiring little skill at all save to chase one's pleasure, and that she did with enthusiasm once she'd the hang of it. He helped her with his hands beneath her hips, lifting her just so, and they moved together in a sweat-slicked tangle of flesh, the pleasure they found so acute she thought she might actually die if he were to stop.

There was a moment toward the end where she thought she'd done just that.

And when it was over, she blinked dazedly up at the ceiling as he lazily kissed and sucked at the flush and salt of skin that felt new.

Together they'd made a terrible mess. Between her thighs was slick and throbbing, and she could not seem to stop twitching nor breathe in a manner that did not leave her light-headed. Several pillows had been displaced in their enthusiasm, and her head was now lodged between two of them, to say nothing of the disarray of her hair and the tangles it would take an age to comb through.

In short, the whole affair had left her absolutely, positively ruined, and she had never felt so wonderful in her entire life.

"Let's do it again," she said to the thorough dishevelment that she'd made of his hair, and when he lifted his head, the grin upon his face was blinding.

CHAPTER TWENTY

Elegy woke not because it was day but because it was night, and without the distraction of Atticus's mouth upon hers, she became suddenly aware of the fact that she was not within the walls of Thorne Hall and could not feel the Collection at all. She'd no phone of her own, but his was lying upon the nightstand nearby, and when she lifted it, she gasped upon beholding the hour: half past ten.

Behind her, Atticus was a veritable furnace, his mouth pressed to the nape of her neck and their hands tangled together beneath her rapidly beating heart. His was the deep and untroubled sleep of one who had not been roused so often by the mischief of ghosts that her rest better resembled a half-life: never dreaming, seemingly always upon the verge of wakefulness that left her exhausted upon the morning.

He only briefly stirred when she slithered from beneath the heavy weight of his arm, stepped into the puddle of her chemise, and slipped the straps over her shoulders. Casting one last look at him lying there so deliciously rumpled, she tiptoed from the room.

Elegy gathered the rest of her clothing in the darkness as quietly as she could and dressed in the foyer before stealing out into the night with her shoes clutched tightly to her chest.

Standing upon Atticus's porch, she took in the horrifying sight of rain pouring sideways on account of the heavy gusts of wind and knew she was being punished for wanting so much and daring to take it for herself.

Had she the luxury of good sense, she would've promptly turned around, gone back inside, and crawled back into the warmth of her lover's bed. It was not that she'd ever spent a night away from the manor; on the contrary, during her youth her father had oft sent her away to Holcroft on account of Elegy being a dreadful nuisance during his search for a second wife. But that had been before, when she'd only lived side by side with the dead and not commanded them, before her father's health was failing.

Now she must return at once, storm or no.

The drive was a precarious one, made all the worse by the frantic hammering of her heart, a steady pounding in her ears not even the rain could drown out. She'd never been in Lenox past dark and had some difficulty sorting out the unfamiliar streets, and once she reached the open road, the rain was a relentless downpour and the ancient tires sent her sliding, forcing her pace to slow and her panic to rise.

How could she have been so thoughtless, so consumed?

The windshield wipers were useless, made worse as her vision blurred with tears of sheer terror as she gripped the steering wheel and began to shake. He would flay her for this.

Thaddeus was unforgiving, and she'd no excuse this time he would accept.

It took an age, during which the car spluttered and nearly died as she careened around a corner, but at last the familiar drive came into view and Elegy burst into hysterics, laughing and crying in equal measure.

She parked the Rolls beneath the porte cochere and breathed slow and deep, swiping her hands across her face until she might appear merely tired with her red-rimmed eyes. The car had broken down upon the side of the road, she would tell her father, and she'd been forced to rely upon the kindness of strangers to set it to rights again. The excuse was as flimsy as one of her silken nightgowns, but he could not prove she'd not been stuck in a ditch somewhere the past several hours, and to this small sliver of hope she clung as she pushed the door open.

The house was dark and silent when she slipped through the door and closed it silently behind her. The fire in the hearth had long since gone out, the tang of woodsmoke hanging faintly in the chill air, and Elegy saw no one save the whisper of The Mourning's black veils as she turned her shrouded gaze upon her.

"Where is my father?" Elegy asked, for it seemed unimaginable that he should not be there, lying in wait with a dressing gown hanging from his shriveled shoulders as he roused the embers with a poker.

The spirit lifted one gray mottled hand and slowly unfurled the rotting bones of her fingers until she pointed up the staircase.

Hope beat its wings frantically against Elegy's ribs. "Abed?"

A slow, deep nod was her answer.

She would have found her own bed were it not for the sudden awareness of Bernard's broad shoulders at the threshold of the gallery, watching her with rot-ringed eyes gone white with the hour. He'd brought no cocktail, for Fletcher was long asleep. No, it was for an altogether different reason he was there.

Elegy was being summoned.

Gideon Constant waited not in his usual place upon the dais but at the center of the room with his hands clasped behind his back and a wicked smile upon his handsome, terrible face. At the perimeter of the rotting corpse they'd made of the ballroom gathered the whole of the Spirit Collection, save two.

The first was Amos, of course, who had not been seen aboveground since his summoning.

The second was Hester.

Elegy's chest constricted with pain so sharp and unrelenting that she gasped and nearly stumbled. With the Collection gathered as they were in one place, surely she did not fear for Fletcher's safety or her sanity, and yet she had not come. She had left Elegy there to face them all alone.

It was cruelty she would not have thought Hester capable of had the loss of her not proved it.

"Ah, Elegy," said Gideon, greeting her as a friend when she was no such thing. "How wonderful of you to join us at last. Your father was really quite worried, you know."

"He needn't have been," she answered. "I was—"

"At the Prescotts', yes. Thaddeus called there, and your dear friend was ever so obliging in assuring him that you'd simply fallen asleep after too much talk of weddings and the like."

Oh, Hugo. He'd saved her, the wonderful, infuriating, desperately ridiculous man, and she nearly cried again, this time in gratitude, but she would not give herself away.

Elegy lifted her chin, braver now with an alibi that Thaddeus could not possibly contest.

The Spirit Collection of Thorne Hall

"Yes, I was at the Prescotts'."

Gideon's grin rent his face in two. "You've always been such a wretched liar, Elegy. I know where you've been, and it wasn't with your patsy. It was with *him*."

"I've no idea what—"

"Yes, you do." He prowled closer, and Elegy commanded him silently away, for the night was young and she would not waste her songs on him so soon. "And you *gave* yourself to him, didn't you? That innocence that you've been guarding so fiercely is gone. Filthy little slut—"

It was the first time she'd ever willingly touched him.

The sound of her palm connecting with his dead flesh echoed throughout the room, and yet no one flinched but she, shocked at her boldness and at his.

"You will not speak of me thus *ever*," she said.

His answer was a slow, stretching grin. "Oh, Elegy, I was merely encouraging your honesty."

"I do not owe you my honesty. I owe you nothing at all. It is you who answer to me, and you would do well to remember it."

"And what of this man to whom you gave yourself, whose clothing you kept in your chamber? What loyalty do you owe him?"

She'd known he'd ordered the destruction of Atticus's sweater; Bancroft was too stupid to have thought of it on his own, and none of the rest of the Collection were that vindictive.

"Who was it, then?" she asked him. "Which of them did you manipulate this time?"

He did not answer but bent slightly at the waist and extended his mottled palm. "Dance with me, Elegy," said he. "Dance with me, and I won't tell your father you kept another man's clothing in your chamber."

It was the cruelest torture, for she knew she would be sick if he so much as touched her, but should Thaddeus discover that she'd visited Atticus and kept his sweater, his wrath would be far worse than five days sitting within a circle of white upon the ballroom floor.

"Don't do this," she said, and although her voice bore the edge of a command, it was a plea and she hated herself for it.

"Dance with me, and it will all be forgotten."

Vivian was at the grand piano. She set her bones upon the keys, and when she began to play "Someone to Watch Over Me," Elegy nearly retched upon the floor.

"What will it be, Elegy?" asked Gideon with the ease of one with nothing to lose, for no matter what decision she made, either caused her pain, and he loved her pain. "My hand, or your father's wrath?"

Elegy touched him willingly for the second time as she slid her hand into his. Revulsion slithered down her spine, and he delighted in the way her body shuddered and trembled as he drew her close. The scent of another man was still upon her skin, as was the ghost of his touch, and between her legs she ached, sweetly so; she clung to it like armor against the stench of decay and the desperate, desperate cold, for it was far worse to be touched by him than it was Reed or Dephine or Hester, and she was not altogether certain she could endure it.

To be touched by Gideon Constant was to be buried alive without the kindness of a coffin: freshly turned earth in her hair and in her mouth as the weight of the world bore her down into nothing but darkness and silence and *alone*. She'd never felt such a terrible, devouring emptiness as his embrace.

Her breath came fast, but it came nonetheless, and if she could breathe, she could dance, and if she could dance, she might survive that night.

Like Thaddeus, Gideon cared little for modern dances. It was a two-step they performed instead, achingly slow and far too intimate, with Gideon's cloudy eyes fixed upon her and his putrid scent surrounding them both, coating her throat in bile.

"I've wanted this for a very long time, Elegy," he whispered into the shell of her ear, and the first tear slid down her cheek. His black tongue licked it away, and another followed. "When your father is dead, we will dance like this every night while your husband fucks another in your bed. Perhaps we will do the same, right here on this floor where I was born again."

"You cannot touch me," she whispered.

"I am touching you even now."

"I've allowed you the privilege."

Gideon spun her out, his black-tipped fingers a tremulous tether until he drew her back again, and his lips lowered back to her ear. "And you will again, I think."

"Never," answered she, and her voice cracked and broke into nothing.

"Never is an awfully long time, Elegy . . . and all we have together is time."

The Spirit Collection of Thorne Hall

"Elegy?"

No.

Oh God, no.

Her back was to the door, but Gideon's was not. His terrible gaze slid away from hers and over her shoulder, and a fearsome delight spread across his face.

She knew what she would see, and yet the sight of him stole her breath all the same as she turned in Gideon's arms.

Atticus Hart stood at the threshold of the ballroom, clutching the door with white knuckles and wild eyes, his hair a disarray and all the color gone from his face such that he might've been one of them.

She'd stopped dancing at the sight of him, but Gideon had not, and when she attempted to free herself from his sickening embrace, to cross the ballroom until she was safely wrapped in Atticus's arms, she could not, for Gideon tightened his hold.

"Elegy," croaked Atticus. "What the fuck am I seeing?"

"This is him, isn't it, Elegy?" Gideon's voice was positively gleeful, and when he laughed, she felt it against her back. "The owner of the sweater and your innocence. Welcome, friend! Welcome to Thorne Hall!"

But Atticus's eyes were fixed upon her own, begging, pleading for her to tell him that he was walking as he slept, or dreaming, still wrapped around her body beneath his sheets, miles away.

Her lips moved, mouthing his name, and yet no sound emerged.

"You must be Atticus," Gideon continued, and one of his hands slid lazily up Elegy's front, brushing over the swell of her breast beneath her dress, and she and Atticus stiffened as one, his tall frame vibrating with rage and hers with shame. "I've heard ever so much about you from them."

At this, he tilted his head toward the Collection at the edges of the ballroom, watching the scene unfold with unbridled glee, for even the finest amongst them count not resist the lure of the *new*; this was a scene they'd not yet seen played out, and they were positively in raptures over the way it might end.

Atticus's eyes swept over them all with mounting horror and dawning understanding.

"Atticus," Elegy whispered. "Look at me. Only at me."

An age passed before he obeyed, an age in which he saw what no man should see, and when at last his eyes met hers, she did not recognize them, and it was all her fault. She should have left him alone, should never have imagined that she could have him and not be punished for it.

Something vital within him had been rent just then, and although he might hold both savaged halves together until they healed, the whole of it would never again be true.

"This," he said, and the words caught in his throat and emerged strangled. "This is what you wouldn't tell me about this house."

"*Couldn't*," Gideon answered in her stead, and all the while his hand climbed steadily. "And would you have believed her if she had? Better to see with your own eyes what she lives through every night, though you could never hope to understand it."

Elegy arched and gasped as Gideon's hand reached her throat, mottled fingers curling around her fragile windpipe, and Atticus let go the casing.

"Get your fucking hands off of her!"

Gideon's answer was to snake his other arm up her torso and squeeze her breast, digging his fingernails into her soft flesh. A scream tore unbidden from her lips, and at the sound Atticus charged forward with murder etched upon his face.

"*No*."

Elegy's voice echoed within the gilded space grown gray and hollow. A command, but not for Gideon.

Atticus's footsteps faltered and stopped. "Elegy—"

"You need to leave," she said, Gideon's thumb digging into the soft skin beneath her throat and tilting her face upward to the cobwebs above them. "You need to leave this house right now."

He shook his head. "No. *No*, I'm not leaving you here with . . ."

"Us," finished Gideon, and his laughter vibrated through Elegy's body strung taut against him. "Lad, we've been with her since the moment she was born. And we will be at her bedside the moment she dies."

Elegy lowered her face, despite the jabbing pain of Gideon's thumb, and her eyes were clear as she and Atticus regarded one another across the ballroom. "Leave," she said. "They cannot hurt me so long as my father lives, but they *will* hurt you."

For far too long he stood with his hands clenched in fists at his side as his mind worked furiously to solve the terrible conundrum before him, but the equation remained terribly, perfectly balanced: to attempt harm upon Gideon was to guarantee Gideon's wrath upon *her*.

"Please trust me," she said softly.

The Spirit Collection of Thorne Hall

With agony upon his face, he slipped quietly from the ballroom in wretched concession.

Gideon held her against him by the throat as Atticus's footsteps echoed down the corridor to the great room. They drew breath together, and in the silence came the creak of hinges and the heavy thud of the front door.

"Don't touch me!" The words erupted from Elegy's throat as she threw herself from Gideon's arms so violently, she nearly smashed her face upon the ballroom floor. "Don't ever touch me again!"

"Oh, but I *will*," said he. "Once he dies, whenever I want."

Elegy shed no tears as she left the ballroom. She was saving them for someone who had hurt her that night far more than Gideon, far more than the Docile Ones who had cowed to his whim and watched her humiliation in silence.

She rounded the corner on the second floor past the Lovers Landing and ascended the staircase to the rotting third floor where she could feel Hester lurking in the shadows, and still she did not cry.

Not yet.

Not until she'd faced her.

Hester was not outside Fletcher's door, nor was she in the sewing room where she sometimes sat with Delphine. Elegy threw each of the three guest bedroom doors open so hard they rattled in their hinges and the third splintered entirely from its frame and collapsed with a crash. Still no one emerged to face her, living or dead, and the hot sting behind her eyes thundered forward, threatening to spill over before she was ready; before *she* saw what she had done.

The servants' hall lay just beyond the top of the stairs, and Elegy thrust open the door that separated it from the family hall and charged inside.

"Hester!" she shouted. "Show yourself, Hester!"

She was near; Elegy could feel the sturdiness of her, the stalwart comfort that had accompanied her presence since she'd first drawn breath in her arms. The most agreeable among the Spirit Collection did not often disobey her (and although Hester was firm, she was always agreeable), and yet the black stillness around her remained stubbornly, bitterly barren.

"What have I done?" she asked. "You've never stayed away so long, never when I needed you most, and I needed you tonight."

Surrounded by rot and cobwebs and silence, Elegy waited until her limbs grew stiff with cold, but no one answered.

The Cruel Mother
Francis James Child ballad #20

There was a lady lived in York (*all the lee and loney*)
Fell in love with her father's clerk (*down by the Greenwood sidey-o*)
She loved him up, she loved him down
Loved him till he filled her arms

She leant her back against an oak
First it bent and then it broke

She leant her back against a thorn
There she had two fine babes born
She took out her reaping knife
There she took those fine babes' lives

She wiped the blade against her shoe
The more she rubbed, the redder it grew

She went back to her father's hall
Saw two babes a-playing at ball

"Oh babes, oh babes, if you were mine
I'd dress you up in scarlet fine"

"Oh Mother, oh Mother, if we were yours
Scarlet was our own hearts' blood"

"Oh babes, oh babes, it's Heaven for you" (*all the lee and loney*)
"Oh Mother, oh Mother, it's Hell for you" (*down by the Greenwood sidey-o*)

CHAPTER TWENTY-ONE

Elegy dreamed of flesh.

At times it was hers, desperate and hot and pliant beneath Atticus's hands, quivering and straining until it erupted, hot and throbbing and so wonderfully good that she thought of nothing but to chase it without shame while his name tumbled joyfully from her lips.

Sometimes it was his, shoulders and arms peppered with the half-moon scars of her fingernails as she came undone beneath him and he above her, the groan torn from deep within his chest setting her aflame, the answering flush blooming beneath her pale skin.

And sometimes it was theirs, rotting, cloying, dead and yet living, even though it was a half-life to be sure, however long.

At the center of a midnight ballroom, she wore a red dress and danced in the arms of a beautiful man. Round and round they went to the muted strains of a band that played from the shadows, and she was so full of happiness that her poor heart could scarcely hold it all.

And then the song changed, sliding discordantly from the soft, muted brass to the tinkling of a piano long fallen out of tune, and her stomach plummeted, for she recognized it at once.

Would she ever be rid of it, that cursed song?

The arms about her tightened, and when she looked up, it was not Atticus who held her now but Gideon Constant, the cloying stench of rot that clung to the Collection turning her stomach in revulsion. She struggled; he laughed, and only held her the tighter for it. And in her ear in a slithering rasp, he sang:

The fairest flower that e'er I saw
Has withered to a stalk.

With the tip of his finger, he lifted her chin, the black of his lips so close they might've brushed her own.

She whispered, "I'm the ghost now."

Elegy woke in the dull gray of early morning with the vestiges of his laughter still echoing upon the air.

The Griswolds had not yet arrived, and the household was still abed as Elegy lurched down the staircase clad in the same thing she'd worn the day before. She knew she looked a fright with her tangled black hair and face swollen and red, streaked with salt and sweat and fear, but none of it mattered because she had to see him, had to explain as best she could.

Of course, he might not even be in Lenox any longer; after what he had witnessed, she'd not have blamed him for driving straight to the nearest airport and leaving the lot of it behind.

But in case; just in case—

Elegy threw open the front door and made to dash out beneath the porte cochere where the Rolls was still parked but came to an abrupt stop when she saw the sleek black car parked alongside it, and leaning up against the door, with his hands in his pockets and red-rimmed eyes beneath the disheveled mess of his hair, was Atticus.

"You came back," she breathed.

"I never left."

The strangled sound that emerged from her throat was muffled by his sweater as he tugged her to him and enveloped her in his arms. His lips settled atop her head, and she was surprised to find that he felt quite unsteady when he had only ever been solid.

She let him hold her as much as she did him, and when he could speak at last, it was to rasp into the tangle of her hair: "Elegy, what did I see last night?"

She lifted her head, taking in his raw countenance. He'd not slept, that much was certain, but it would not have mattered if he had, for surely he would have dreamt of them and woken himself screaming.

"Not here," she murmured.

He lifted his gaze, and she realized that he was looking for them in the windows just as she did when others came to the house. How differently he must see it now; how differently he must see her: with pity she did not want and revulsion she most certainly deserved.

Elegy took his hand and led him away from the house, through the Painted Grove, and into the dense forest that surrounded three sides of the estate, smears of yellow and russet and scarlet amongst the evergreen trees. There was a clearing that Elegy had discovered as a child on one of her wild rambles, and it was there she led Atticus, where the dead would not see them and the living would not find them.

He had sobered somewhat by the time they reached it, his eyes appearing a modicum less wild; however, he also appeared less inclined to be near her, keeping an almost wary distance between them that cut her far deeper than the spirits ever had.

"You were never meant to find out that way," she told him once they'd reached the clearing amid a grove of bigtooth aspens, the chill morning wind setting the golden leaves aflutter. "I would have told you in my own time, but not like that."

"I'll say this, you never cease to surprise me," he replied. "Tell me there is a perfectly logical explanation for what I saw other than what it is I *think* I saw, because that would be *ghosts*, and they're not real."

"Extraordinary claims require extraordinary evidence," Elegy answered.

"She's quoting Carl Sagan," Atticus said to no one but the trees. "Fuck me." Then he snapped his fingers as a sudden thought occurred to him. "Ventilation!"

"I beg your pardon?"

"Hallucinations caused by toxic mold or carbon monoxide. The ventilation in Thorne Hall must be ancient."

"They are not hallucinations."

"They're not *ghosts*."

"It will not be perfectly logical, but I *will* explain as much as I am able, if you only promise to listen."

His broad shoulders sagged under the weight of what he'd seen and the struggle to make sense of it, to say nothing of the sleepless night he'd no doubt passed in his car on her behalf.

She stole forward, a wraith wrapped in the early-morning fog, and took his hand.

"Okay," he said, his voice hoarse and catching. "I can do that."

They sat together upon a log that Elegy had oft used for reading, and her heart shriveled when he withdrew his hand from hers and fisted it upon his knee.

She smoothed her own hands upon her silk dressing gown. How *did* one explain to a scientist the existence of ghosts when she hardly knew herself how they had come to be summoned; why they'd been forced to remain? She'd never had the luxury of considering them a novelty. For her they'd always existed. They simply were.

"The man who built this house was named Jasper Thorne, and he had a desperate fascination with the occult."

"Séances," he said.

"One must applaud their ingenuity, but those were always fake. I mean *true* spiritualism."

Atticus gave a harsh exhale. "There is no such thing as spiritualism."

"Atticus," she admonished softly.

"Fuck," he said, raking his hand through his hair. "*Fuck.*"

"Would you like me to stop?"

"Yes," he said. "No. It's just—I'm not a spiritual man, Elegy, never have been. I'm a scientist, and this—"

"This changes everything."

"Yes." The word was torn from his chest, raw and pulsing with anguish. Both of his hands delved into his hair. "Okay, tell me."

She told him of a frigid Samhain night when a true medium, along with her four kinswomen, summoned and bound the first spirit in the Collection: Gideon Constant, the man within whose dead, rotting arms Atticus had found her dancing the night before. And she told him how, in the six years that followed, Jasper Thorne had collected fourteen more.

"Why would someone want to own a bunch of dead people?"

It was a question she'd pondered for much of her young life. "If he'd a reason other than the inherent greed that defined men of his class, I cannot fathom it," she answered.

"And you've lived in that house with them—"

"All my life."

He dragged his hand across his face. "Christ, Elegy. All this time when you were telling me you felt stains, felt the past, you meant literally."

"Yes."

"I've been to the house several times these past weeks, and I never saw any of them."

"No one ever does. They are quite innocuous by day, faint and non-corporeal, and most people can look right at them and not see them, particularly if you've no knowledge of their existence. But by night, well . . . you saw them."

"Tell me about them," he said. "Tell me about all of them."

She listed them in order of acquisition as the crisp morning wind ruffled the leaves, and she told him when they had died and how, and the places in her home they typically haunted depending on the time of day or night or who might be visiting. Sometimes she smiled, even laughed, for some were as familiar to her as friends, and as beloved. They'd taught her to cook and sew and how to be still and vigilant; how to sing.

He sucked in a breath when she confessed that it was Calliope and not Mrs. Griswold who had taught her so many songs, and who was responsible for her name.

And when she told him of Hester, into whose hands she'd been delivered, he let that breath out. "I am so sorry," he murmured. "I am so, so sorry."

"They belong to my father now," she said at last, picking up a perfect golden leaf that had fallen on his shoulder and twirling it between her fingertips. "He commands and controls them. And to a certain extent, so do I."

"How do you mean?"

"The Collection heeds the master of Thorne Hall in all things. They obey his every whim despite their basest impulses, and cannot harm those within his care," she answered. "It is my father they answer to now, but when he dies, it will be me. And I have proven myself entirely incapable of managing them."

"Elegy—"

"They heed me, but only just, and only because my father still draws breath. And there are the songs. But when he dies . . ."

The rest was lost to a gasp, a shudder, and Elegy put her face into her hands and cried, hot, bitter tears pooling in her palms and sliding past her fingers as he cupped the back of her head in his hand and held her against his chest. She'd not cried in front of another living person since she was a child.

It was not an experience she'd missed nor cared to repeat.

"They're not supposed to touch me," she sobbed into the wool of his sweater. "Not without my permission. But once he's gone—"

"No," said Atticus firmly. "No. They will never, ever touch you again."

"You cannot promise me that. You'll soon be gone, and I'll be here forever because I can never leave this house."

His large hands, capable of so much, cupped her face and tilted her chin so that their eyes met, and within the forest of his she saw certainty, conviction. "Let's get one thing straight: I won't be gone, because I am not leaving you here with *them*."

"You don't know what you're saying."

"I do. And I am not leaving you."

"I'm bound to this place for the rest of my life, Atticus," she sighed. The tears upon her lips had dried in the autumn chill and her tongue tasted salt as she wet them.

"Why? What would happen if you just left?"

"With no one to manage them, the Collection will torment each and every living person who sets foot in that house."

"Burn it to the ground."

"They will dance upon the ashes." She laughed, and it was a bitter, hollow thing. "None of us know what might happen should there not be a master of Thorne Hall, or walls to hold them. Considering they've been responsible for the deaths of at least half a dozen people, it isn't a risk I'm willing to take."

"Hugo," he said suddenly. "That's why you're marrying Hugo."

She nodded miserably. "I must have an heir, and his parents have made his inheritance contingent upon our union. The Thorne money will shield him, he will do his duty by me, and I hate it. I *hate* it."

Her breath escaped in a shudder, and she swiped her palms across the hot spill of tears that had overborne their confinement. "Any child of mine will not have asked for it any more than I asked for it or my father did or his father before him, but they'll do it just as I have because we've no choice."

His body stilled, and beneath her ear she felt his heart begin to race. "What if you did have a choice?"

"I cannot imagine what you mean."

"What if there is no Collection to command?"

The air in the clearing stilled as the weight of his words settled upon Elegy's narrow shoulders. "No," she said, bracing her hands upon his chest so that she might face him properly. "No, that's not possible."

But something had taken hold; the engineer within, she supposed, searching always for a solution. "You said they were summoned," said Atticus. "Could they not also be banished?"

"No."

The Spirit Collection of Thorne Hall

"How do you know?"

"You think you're the first to want them gone? My father is quite insistent that it's been tried and is impossible."

"Have you ever considered he might not be the most reliable source of information?"

"Atticus." She closed her eyes. "You know nothing of this world."

"Is there anyone else who has ever interacted with them other than you Thornes?"

Elegy sank her lower lip into her teeth. "There was a man who came to the house long ago to teach me the runes of protection that keep the Collection from entering a room without permission."

"Where is he?"

"The first and only time I made his acquaintance, I was six years old. I do not know where he lives or *if* he lives. I can't even remember his name."

"So we find out. Your father must've had a way to contact him. Maybe he still does."

"Thaddeus has been mostly abed these past few days," she answered, something small and quivering within her chest that felt very much like hope.

"That will definitely make things easier."

In the distance there was the sound of gravel crunching beneath the tires of Arthur Griswold's car. "You can't stay," Elegy murmured. "Arthur's probably already wondering why your car is here."

His forehead rested upon hers. "I don't want to leave you here."

"I've survived here for twenty-five years."

"Surviving isn't living. When can I see you again?"

"I need to avoid arousing my father's suspicion," she answered. "Hugo came to my rescue yesterday, but Thaddeus will expect to see me today. And tonight, with the Collection."

"No," he ground out, his brows drawing low in his anger.

"I have to, Atticus."

"I know. But if he tries to touch you again, give him hell."

She answered softly: "I will."

* * *

Elegy sat before the fire in the great hall for some time after Atticus's car ambled down the drive toward Lenox with her dirty feet tucked beneath her and a reckless, terrible longing thundering about inside her chest. That Atticus would tear the manor apart brick by brick in his attempt to free her, she'd no doubt. That the Collection could be banished, she doubted completely, and yet the glimmer of it stubbornly remained, even as she dragged her weary body up the staircase to her room to dress for the day.

Her father's coughing filled the corridor with discordant agony. A loving daughter might have comforted her father during such a time, soothing him with cold water and a small hand upon his back as he eased onto the pillows; with a song, her voice fading to a whisper as his breathing grew slow and steady with sleep.

But Thaddeus had seen fit long ago to make Elegy a dutiful daughter, not a loving one. She stood still outside his door surrounded by the sludge of his illness and turned her thoughts to the Collection.

In the Rose Room across the hall, Adelaide played at painting her face while Delphine sewed a pattern of hydrangeas upon a skirt in seed pearls that had spilled from a woman's shawl the night before when it had snagged on a chair. She'd collected them herself while Mrs. Griswold stood mere feet away dusting fixtures, blissfully unaware.

Calliope had drifted into her own head while at the piano the floor above and had not stopped playing "The Cruel Mother" for fifteen minutes. It always made Reed desperately sad to hear it, for while the Wife of Usher's Well had lost her babes to illness or, in some variations, at sea, the Cruel Mother had killed hers with a penknife from which she could not clean the blood; in fact, the harder she scrubbed, the redder the blade became. And so Reed took Calliope's hand and called her name until she blinked her single eye and looked down at him in sweet bewilderment. "Sing 'Sweet' William's Ghost,'" he begged. "I love that one."

"I know you do."

Calliope led him away to the Lovers Landing and positioned him on the floor before the couch where, with a silent command, she insisted he stay and not climb upon her lap. She began to sing softly the tale of Lady Margaret, who loved her dead fiancé so fiercely that he was pulled back from the grave and, as in "The Unquiet Grave," could not sleep peacefully. Wretched with it, he visited her bower one night and begged her to release him from his promise. After wandering her father's hall and over the hill to the graveyard and the chapel beyond, Margaret took the cross from about her neck and placed it upon William's chest.

And as it always followed in visitation songs when the dead were peacefully laid to rest, the cock crowed upon the morn, and together Calliope sang the sweetest verse:

The Spirit Collection of Thorne Hall

And it's time for the living to depart from the dead
So, my darling, I must away
My darling, I must away

As the spirit's voice died away, the shadows at the end of the second-floor corridor rippled softly and, with a sigh, they parted to reveal Hester standing there, gazing upon her with milky eyes ringed with rot.

Spirit and mistress faced one another with Thaddeus's door between them and far more besides.

"Why?" Elegy whispered. "Why weren't you there last night? Why—" Her throat began to close around a terrible thing she could not swallow down, and what emerged was cracked and broken, pitiful just like her. "Why did you let him touch me?"

"You let him touch you."

"You could have saved me."

"I have saved you long enough."

Mrs. Griswold had mothered Elegy as much as she was able, being devoted first to the house and second to the solemn child who dwelled there, and even Fletcher had tried in her own unusual, frenetic way, but Hester . . . Hester, into whose hands she'd been born . . .

Nothing Gideon Constant could have said or done, even when he told her he would fuck her upon the ballroom floor, even when he had licked her tears with his blackened tongue, nothing could have hurt her more than Hester's absence in those dark hours.

"You kept away to punish me for my weakness."

"You are not weak," Hester rasped.

Elegy shook her head. "If I were not weak, I could better control them."

"You could have brought that room to its knees."

She imagined them kneeling before her in the ruinous dark, bent to her will and chained to her whims. Absurd.

"I'm not my father's equal," she confessed.

"Indeed not," rasped the spirit. "Nay, for you are far more than he could ever hope to be."

Elegy thought, then, of two tufted yellow velvet chairs before a fire. Of cups of wine and of laughter; of warm skin and the sweetest ache—of the soothing of it. She thought of books to be read and countries to be visited; of gardens to tend and of the deepest, maddest sort of love, the sort she'd known for mere days; what wouldn't she do to keep it?

J. Ann Thomas

"I don't want to bring the Collection to their knees," she said.

And in that moment the peace of certainty settled heavy upon her shoulders, a welcome weight, for she knew at last what she must do, and that what she stood to gain was worth the price should she fail.

"I want to end them."

CHAPTER TWENTY-TWO

Elegy discovered the medium by virtue of a phone number scrawled upon a bit of parchment shoved into Thaddeus's address book with the note *runes of protection*.

The number was not for the medium himself (he had no electricity and, therefore, no telephone) but for a woman named Winter, who had only to hear Elegy's name before she agreed to meet her and Atticus at Hallowed Grounds on a cold, dreary morning thick with mist.

Winter appeared to be in her forties, with lustrous, dark skin, tight black curls elaborately arranged atop her head, and a colorful scarf wrapped several times around her neck to ward off the chill. She ordered chamomile-and-lavender tea and told them that her services, as well as those of others adept in what she called the craft, were sought far more often than Elegy could have imagined.

To commune with the dead was a common request and was almost always denied, for no good could possibly come of it. Case in point: Thorne Hall.

Almost as frequently sought were love potions, and these too were rarely granted upon the grounds that 'twas enslavement indeed to force another's affection.

Then there were more permissible applications of the craft that could be bought for a pretty penny: a bountiful harvest, the conception of a child, the soothing of the nerves. That which could only help and never harm.

When Atticus asked if they might meet the medium who had taught Elegy the runes, Winter stared at them over the rim of the glazed ceramic mug before lowering it between her cupped hands. "Dorian does not often receive visitors. He prefers to be the one to do the visiting."

Elegy and Atticus exchanged a glance before Atticus leaned forward on his elbows. "The conversation we'd like to have is a private one."

"Private from Thaddeus Thorne?" Winter asked.

Elegy's eyes narrowed. "If you'd like."

Winter laughed in response, low and rich. "You do not much like me prying."

"I hardly see the need for it."

"Dorian is dear to me, and as such, I am protective of him."

"You know who I am," Elegy answered. "I mean him no harm."

Winter regarded her thoughtfully. "Yes, I know exactly who you are, Elegy Thorne, and I know all about that house of yours. You may not mean anyone harm, but harm follows you just the same."

"Perhaps Dorian should be the judge of that, seeing as how he has actually been inside Thorne Hall and you have not," Elegy replied, then immediately paled. "I'm so sorry. I have no idea what came over me."

"Anger," answered Winter with a knowing smile playing about her lips.

"Then you understand why I must see him."

Winter did understand, which was how Elegy found herself sitting in the passenger seat of Atticus's car as they traveled the winding dirt roads into the forest, following a hand-drawn map scrawled on a napkin.

Dorian Everwood resided in a cottage with no address in the middle of the woods some thirty minutes east of Thorne Hall. The walls were made of small round stones stacked together, and several shingles belonging to the steep shaker roof were missing; the rest were in various states of decay. There were two floors and plenty of windows, the glass within the panes was grimy, and here and there were large patches of moss and lichen.

The dwelling sat upon the bank of a stream, and to one side of it was what Elegy had learned from horticulture books was a witch garden, for what grew within could heal, but could also harm, even kill. There were kitchen herbs that Elegy recognized immediately: creeping thyme and bushels of sage, rosemary that withstood all, hearty mint, and more-fragile plants such as borage and chamomile and fennel.

The Spirit Collection of Thorne Hall

There were others that Elegy knew only from books: creeping nightshade and hellebore, vervain and yarrow, monkshood, lady's mantle. All ancient; all quite poisonous. She felt a frisson of unease and wondered just what else Dorian got up to when he was not teaching little girls runes to guard against spirits.

At the sound of the car approaching, the man rose from a vegetable patch beside the witch garden and pulled the roughened gloves from his hands. He was likely the age of Thaddeus, though the years had been considerably kinder.

Dorian's hair was spun silver and gold, and his prominent nose looked as though it had been broken at least once in his lifetime, though not so completely as to render him anything less than handsome in a gentle sort of way. Elegy thought at first that his eyes were a pale sort of blue, but once she stepped out of the car and they began to walk toward each other, she realized they were gray. Although she could not account for it at all, since she'd been all of six years old when last she'd seen him, she recognized them instantly.

"Hello, Elegy," said he. "It's been nineteen years, and yet I would know you anywhere. How are you with your runes after all this time?"

"They are as familiar to me as my own name," she said.

The medium's gaze shifted to Atticus, standing at Elegy's back. "And you must be Mr. Hart."

"Atticus, please. Thank you for seeing us."

"Let's have a cup of tea, shall we?"

Immediately upon entering the medium's dwelling, Atticus became engaged in a battle with the ceiling of the cottage's first floor.

"How old is this place?" he asked, hunching his shoulders so as not to smack his head upon one of the many bundles of dried herbs that hung from the thick, rough-hewn beams crossing the ceiling.

"Two hundred and forty-five years or so," answered Dorian. "The year the town was settled. People were quite a bit shorter back then, I'm afraid."

Two handsomely carved wood benches topped with lumpy cushions stood opposite each other before a hearth so old it bore no mantel, only a wrought-iron sconce upon either side holding a stubby candle, hand dipped. It was there that Dorian led them with the order to make themselves at home before he shuffled off in the direction of the kitchen.

The cushions were worn but comfortable and the fire was warm, as was Atticus's hand in hers, and so Elegy allowed herself to settle and better take in her surroundings.

Between the two benches was a rickety table, laden with stacks of books, slips of paper shoved between their pages to mark Dorian's place, and Elegy's eye twitched slightly at the sight of it, she who always finished one book before taking up another.

There was a dining table with six mismatched chairs opposite where they sat, a pewter jug full of wildflowers at its center amongst a strange assemblage of ceramic and wooden bowls holding various sprigs of herbs, mostly lavender.

Dorian emerged a moment later bearing a heavily laden tray, which he set carefully upon the table between the two benches before he poured tea from a squat brass pot into cups that had seen better days or, indeed, better centuries. A plate bearing currant-studded scones and a jar of clotted cream accompanied the tea, and Atticus broke a scone in half, slathered it thoroughly, and pressed it into Elegy's hands.

"Eat," he urged, and to placate him she nibbled at one corner, then shoved an enormous chunk into her mouth on account of it being actually quite delicious.

"Now, then," said Dorian. "Winter tells me you have a peculiar situation requiring my assistance."

It was Atticus—who had never before dwelled in this strange world of theirs—who did not beat about the bush.

"I have absolutely no idea how, but Thorne Hall is full of ghosts."

Dorian's gaze slid to Elegy. "You've told him?"

"He's seen them."

Dorian leaned forward, elbows braced upon his knees. "Is that so? And what did Thaddeus say to that?"

"He doesn't know," Elegy answered. "And I would very much like to keep it that way."

Dorian's brows knit together in confusion. "Of course, but what have I to do with that?"

"How do we get rid of them?"

A thick silence fell upon the room after Atticus's blunt question, save for the occasional pop and hiss of the logs in the hearth.

"Get rid of them," Dorian repeated slowly.

"Banish them," Atticus corrected. "Whatever the term is. I'm new to all of this."

"Impossible."

"Ghosts exist," countered Atticus, undeterred. "Nothing is impossible."

The Spirit Collection of Thorne Hall

"Well, I certainly cannot fault your logic, but if you've come to me to perform this miracle, you will be most disappointed indeed."

Elegy straightened, drawing the medium's strange gray eyes. "You taught me how to protect myself against them, and my mother before me. How could you have done so without some knowledge of them?"

Dorian settled back upon the couch and regarded them both thoughtfully. "How much has Thaddeus told you about me?"

"Nothing at all," answered Elegy. "He's not spoken of you since the day you came to teach me the runes."

"I don't suppose he wished you to think too much about someone who knew about the spirits before you did. What I might know."

Dorian crossed the room to where a wooden shelf held far too many books, some with spines of leather and others bound far more crudely. He crouched down and extracted a folio full of loose-leaf parchment, which he placed gently upon the table before Elegy.

"The name of the woman who summoned and bound the Spirit Collection of Thorne Hall was Sparrow, and she was my great-great-grandmother."

He opened the folio, and there were the runes that decorated the frame of Elegy's bedroom door.

"Of all her canny craft, her runes of binding are lost to time, as are the words of the promise made that night," Dorian continued as he resumed his seat. "When I was a much younger man, I mounted a search for the runes she used to summon them in the first place, but it was to no avail."

"Canny?" Elegy asked upon a frown, for she'd not heard the word before. "What is canny?"

"Do you know, it's been a very long time since anyone has asked me that." He folded his hands in his lap and reclined against the carved wooden back of the bench. "Canny is the ability possessed by certain folk to do extraordinary things beyond the limits of the natural world. Blood, bone, earth—these are its tenets. And while it can be shaped with runes and song, it is as instinctual to the practitioner as it is defined by them."

"Are you talking about magic?" asked Atticus, whose normally healthy pallor had gone as pale as Elegy's own.

"If you like." The medium shrugged. "We who are canny practice it by plying what we call craft. It was craft that summoned and bound the Collection."

"Your ancestor," began Elegy, as Atticus dropped his head into his hands whilst muttering a litany of what sounded like scientific nonsense as he struggled to explain away canny the same way he had the Collection. "The woman who summoned and bound the spirits—did she ever say why Jasper bid her do it?"

Dorian sighed heavily and turned the folio slightly so he might look upon the bold strokes of black there. "I have pondered this even longer than you, and I am sorry to say I have little answers to offer you. She lived a modest life by all accounts, though she did have an excess of siblings, so perhaps it was the money. Or perhaps it was the craft itself; no practitioner living or dead has ever seen its like. But then there is the promise . . ."

"What promise?"

"The particulars have been lost to time," Dorian answered. "But she meant for us all to keep it, the Thornes and the canny folk of her family, and a binding agreement of this sort is an ancient one, and powerful. Thus, I believe there was a much more compelling reason for Sparrow to have cursed us to honor it."

"More compelling than Elegy's freedom?" demanded Atticus. "Than any of her family's freedom?"

"I cannot say, because I cannot fathom what consequence may come of breaking a promise like Sparrow's."

"What I *fathom*," said Atticus, "is that most of the people in Elegy's life have failed her in one way or another, you included. And I don't intend to be one of them. If you won't help us, I'll find someone who will."

Dorian lifted one hand. "Peace, friend. I do not disagree with you, but if it were a simple matter of craft, some Thorne or other would have done it long ago. Thaddeus may be stalwart in his devotion to the promise, but there have occasionally been members of the family who contemplated a way out. That it has not yet been accomplished either means that it simply cannot be done or that the price is too high."

"I understand that I will most likely fail," said Elegy, who had been silently contemplating how best to describe the small seed of hope that had been planted within her that day in the clearing and had since grown so wild and ungovernable that it had burrowed into every nook and crevice, strangling her bones and sliding into her veins. "But I must try."

Dorian exhaled long and slow. "I can promise nothing, but I will need the help of others. And time."

"How long?" Atticus asked sharply. "She's not safe in that house."

The Spirit Collection of Thorne Hall

Elegy rested her hand gently upon his thigh, and he seized it at once, threading their fingers tightly together. "I will be safe enough. As long as my father lives, they can do me no real harm."

"How much time?" Atticus asked the medium again.

"A few days, perhaps. Winter deals primarily in tinctures and remedies, but her wife, Mavis, is a historian and she may know something of use, although the Spirit Collection is unlike any craft we have ever seen."

As Dorian saw them out, Atticus's phone chimed.

He glanced down at the screen with a frown. "I need to take this."

"Elegy will be quite all right with me," answered Dorian. "Come—when you were young, you were very interested in gardening. Would you care to see mine?"

Her answer was an enthusiastic yes, so he led her through the rickety gate, where she wandered the neat rows of beets and turnips and spears of kale, planted late in summer for autumn's harvest. He'd several patches of winter squash, and she stepped delicately amongst the flat, green leaves and gourds of varying sizes and colors on her way to the vines heavy with grapes.

"Try one," he said, breaking off a handful of deep-purple globes. "They're muscadine—they can be eaten raw or made into wine."

She shoved the lot of them into her mouth at once. Sweetness exploded on her tongue, and she ate another and another until her mouth was full of seeds. She spat them into her palm and shoved them into the pocket of her skirt.

Elegy wandered past the grapes to where several wooden boxes were stacked atop one another, crawling with honeybees, their low hum pleasant and soothing. "May I ask you a question?"

"Of course."

"Who taught my father the runes?"

"My mother taught Thaddeus when he was a child," Dorian answered. "And he could have just as easily taught yours, but she was pregnant and wished to know if there were any runes stronger for the child."

"Me?"

Dorian took up the basket he'd been filling when they'd arrived, then took hold of a spray of green fronds and pulled from the soil a fat, stubby orange carrot. "No," he said, avoiding her gaze as he placed it into the basket. "The child before you."

Elegy stilled, numb fingers clutching his sleeve lest she topple backward into the cabbages. "There were children before me?"

Dorian's steadying hand came over hers. "There were no living children before you," he answered softly.

"Why did Thaddeus never tell me?"

"I imagine he did not wish to dwell on what never was."

"You knew my mother, then," said Elegy.

A wistful smile softened Dorian's face. "Yes, I knew her."

"Can you tell me about her? Anything at all will do—it's just that he never speaks of her."

Several carrots scattered dirt as he plucked them from the earth while he seemed to consider his answer. "She was . . . well, she was incandescent. She'd a keen mind and an even more fearsome heart. She was very much like you, in fact."

Elegy shook her head. "I am not fearsome."

"That you deny it does not mean you do not possess it, just as she did."

"Please tell me more," she pleaded.

When at last Atticus came to fetch her, Elegy had learned that her mother loved strawberries, sunny days, and dining outdoors, as well as music, but of course she'd already known that.

What she'd not known was that Tabitha had loved to dance, and that her father had been, to her very great surprise, a marvelous dancer in his courting days. They'd met at a rather stodgy house party, the sort Thaddeus loved best, where a chamber orchestra played Strauss and they danced most of the waltzes together. Elegy had difficulty imagining her father participating in such a frivolous exercise or her mother finding anything particularly charming in her partner, but evidently Thaddeus had been a different man in his youth, else Elegy would not have been born, now, would she?

"It was a terrible thing he did to her." Dorian sighed. "What he's done to Fletcher; what all the Thorne men have done to the women they've ensnared over the years."

"Whatever Jasper's reason for this terrible mess he's put us all in, I cannot think of anything worthy of it. He must've been mad."

Dorian's gaze fell upon Atticus striding toward them, tucking his phone back into the pocket of his coat. "I think you will find there are many things that might drive a man to madness. Sometimes we seek such things knowing how it will end, what we will become, and yet we seek it all the same."

CHAPTER TWENTY-THREE

In the days that followed Elegy's visit to Dorian's cottage in the woods, Thaddeus rarely left his bed.

He could scarcely walk, even with the assistance of his cane, and mindful that another tumble down the great staircase might actually do him in, he remained shut away in the moldering dark, drinking broth spoon-fed to him by undead hands while Elegy was left to play the dutiful mistress.

She rose from her bed at precisely six in the morning and dressed in a manner befitting the heir to Thorne Hall: a red Jaques Doucet dress with silver beading; a dusty-rose Edwardian gown with black velvet trim and an applique bodice; a green Directoire-style velvet coatdress trimmed in bronze leaves.

She let Delphine style her hair with all manner of pins and combs despite the relentless throbbing in her head when she took them out in the evening and did not complain a whit.

Whatever meals were prepared for her, she ate. Whatever newspapers arrived for her, she read. She conversed with the Griswolds by day and with Fletcher by night, and throughout it all, the Spirit Collection grew increasingly erratic, their usual mischief devolving into something far more sinister.

Another dead bird appeared, this one left on her favorite chair before the hearth, then another at her place at the dining table, and another outside her bedroom door, their necks bent at unnatural angles. She had only just managed to dispose of them before any of the staff saw when one appeared on her pillow, a pearl hatpin piercing its breast. So she would not have to explain to Mrs. Griswold why blood was smeared all over the yellowed lace, Elegy thrust it frantically into the fire.

Two days later, an epithet appeared on the dining room wall, the words *Scarlet was in earthly flesh and blood* scrawled in the very same. It was a line from "The Wife of Usher's Well."

Elegy lugged a bucket of soapy water from the butler's pantry and scrubbed away at the ghastly sight until the water was stained red and her hands were wrinkled and aching.

Throughout it all, work continued on the kitchen, and Jeremiah and his men were often at Thorne Hall.

Sometimes Atticus came with them.

Within the manor he and Elegy behaved as though they were indifferent acquaintances. He greeted her with the deference she was owed as the lady of the house, and she answered with aloof superiority.

Outside of it, far from the eyes of the Collection and the cloying stench of death that clung to the walls of her father's bed, they stole what little time they could and put it to *very* good use within the decrepit walls of the abandoned gamekeeper's cabin.

Having deemed the wrought-iron bed frame entirely unsuitable even for lying side by side in perfect stillness, Atticus had flung the lumpy mattress on the floor, whereupon Elegy pounced upon him; he'd only just managed to catch her before they both tumbled backward. The floor groaned its displeasure, far too old for such amorous tomfoolery, but such protestations were lost to the sound of clothing hastily removed and gasps of relief once skin met skin.

On a cold, misty afternoon four days after Dorian promised to send word, a visitor came to the door and asked for the lady of the manor. They refused to give their name to Mrs. Griswold, who would surely have sent her away for the slight had Elegy not been descending the staircase at that very moment.

A sharp-featured sort of person waited beneath the porte cochere, hands shoved into the pockets of a long, tan wool coat buttoned to the neck. They were shorter even than Elegy, with hair so fair it was almost white, angled to their chin in front and clipped short in the back, and eyes of rich chestnut, a startling counterpoint.

"Thistle," they said, thrusting out one hand. "Dorian sent me."

"Elegy Thorne," she answered, wincing as the delicate bones in the hand she'd offered in return were promptly crushed in a vigorous greeting.

"Meeting's tonight," they continued. "The Golden Hind, seven o'clock."

Elegy blinked. "I've never been to a pub."

They raked their eyes up and down the stiff periwinkle taffeta of Elegy's half-mourning dinner dress and snorted. "Yeah, no shit. Wear something a little less conspicuous or this'll all be over before it's begun."

"Even if I could sneak past the household at such an early hour, how am I meant to get there? I cannot risk using the car."

"Meet me at the bottom of the drive at half past, and I'll take us."

"You've been invited?"

Thistle grinned impishly, flashing Elegy a row of perfectly straight white teeth. "Dorian and I go way back. And if you want my opinion, your old man should've come to me for craft, because his are too soft. Mine have a little . . . *bite*."

"I am certain I will regret asking this, but what do you mean by *bite*?"

"Let's just say they take a little something out of whoever is foolish enough to cross them."

Elegy felt queasy. "What sort of somethings?"

"Oh, this and that. Memories, usually, or maybe the ability to see a certain color. Hear a certain sound, the tinkling of bells, perhaps. Or the taste of ripe blackberries from the vine."

"You're positively wicked."

"Why thank you."

"And the man," said Elegy, eager to steer the conversation back to the point of Thistle's call. "The man who came with me to Dorian's cottage. Has he been made aware of the meeting?"

"Dude has a cell phone. You *do* know what those are, right?"

Elegy's eyes narrowed as Thistle flashed another quicksilver smile, and then they were gone, hands shoved deep into their pockets once more as they whistled their way down the drive.

* * *

Elegy spent the rest of the day oscillating with nauseating swiftness between excitement and dread, unable to settle upon either or, preferably, neither. The Spirit Collection grew increasingly agitated with each length of her chamber paced, until finally she was besieged by Delphine, who begged her to stop because Calliope had taken to banging her head repeatedly against the window casing of the Honeysuckle Room.

The torrential rain that had drenched her desperate flight from Atticus's bed had turned into a miserable drizzle that came and went with the seemingly endless days and left the ground in a state of perpetual quagmire. Had she any sense, she would have avoided it entirely, but the manor, for all that it was vast, felt as confined and dreary as a prison cell. She kept to the path, passing through the Painted Grove and beside the graveyard and walled garden with her hood pulled tightly around her face, and even so, she was properly saturated by the end of it.

She'd only just kicked off her mud-splattered boots and unwound the scarf from her neck when a shadow appeared in the doorway, and she startled to see Bernard's hulking shoulders filling the narrow passage. And with him, his large hands upon her quaking shoulders, was Cook.

They were nearly translucent with the early hour, and although Elegy had upon occasion seen Bernard slide in and out of shafts of light as he ambled from the kitchen to the butler's pantry and about the dining room, she had never seen Cook aboveground during the day.

"What is it?" asked Elegy, quite alarmed. "What's wrong?"

Bernard gave Cook a gentle nudge forward. "Go on," he urged, his low, rumbling voice surprisingly gentle. "Tell her."

"Tell me what?"

"Duck," murmured Cook.

Elegy frowned. "I beg your pardon . . . duck?"

"*Lacquered* duck."

Elegy's stomach plummeted, for she knew at once what the matter was.

Lucy's lacquered duck was a particular favorite of Lavinia Prescott, who had many times attempted to coax the recipe from Thorne Hall's chef when Elegy and Hugo were children, to no success. The day her husband and Thaddeus clasped hands over their children's betrothal, she had insisted not only that it be served at the wedding supper, but that the Thornes make a gift of the recipe to their family in honor of the occasion.

"And how many place settings has my father asked for this evening?"

Cook whispered: "Six."

There could be no mistaking the reason for the Prescotts' visit; in fact, Elegy was surprised they'd waited this long, what with the

The Spirit Collection of Thorne Hall

nightmare she imagined planning a society wedding to be. But that it should happen tonight of all nights was a tragedy of lamentable proportions. How was she possibly meant to escape the house unseen with so many living witnesses present, and in the middle of dinner, no less? Thorne Hall was, it seemed, determined to thwart her every plan.

"Thank you for telling me," Elegy said at last. "You've been most helpful."

At that moment there came a great deal of vigorous discourse from the great hall, and it so startled Cook that she vanished right through the floor. Elegy darted past Bernard's looming frame and through the gallery in time to see Dr. Winslow descending the stairs and, upon his heels, Mrs. Griswold looking most put upon indeed.

"Are you absolutely certain he should be out of bed for the length of a dinner?" Her hands were as frantic as the shrill pitch of her voice, wringing so tightly they'd gone white. "They do tend to be quite long with the number of courses he's ordered,"

"As his doctor, I assure you he will manage," Winslow answered. "I've given him a stronger dose."

"Not one of your blasted tinctures!"

The doctor reared back as though she'd struck him. "My tinctures are quite effective, madam!"

"So says you. He's thinner each day than the one before, to say nothing of the state of his face, all purple and sunken. He looks like death without the warming over!"

This continued all the way to the front door, where Fowler stood with the good doctor's overcoat, hat, and umbrella. If Elegy hadn't already been informed of the impending dinner, the butler's presence would have certainly been an indication that the Thorne family would not be spending their evening alone.

"I've left another bottle with him should he feel peaky," Dr. Winslow said to Fowler, perhaps anticipating that should Mrs. Griswold be the sole keeper of this information, the bottle might vanish entirely. He then tipped his hat and departed beneath the porte cochere.

"Mrs. Griswold," said Elegy. "Tell me what the matter is."

Mrs. Griswold started, hand clutching her heart. "Oh, Elegy! You nearly gave me a heart attack. Your father has invited guests to dinner tonight. I went to your chamber to tell you when I ran into that snake oil salesman."

"At what time are they due to arrive?"

"Six o'clock sharp."

From the grandfather clock came the mournful toll of the fifth hour, and Elegy felt her heart slam against her ribs so hard that when the black lace of The Mourning's veils rippled, she was certain the spirit had heard it.

"Elegy, child, are you all right?"

The fear in her chest seemed to have traveled to her throat and settled there, for Elegy could not seem to swallow around it. At length, she managed to croak out, "I'm fine."

The housekeeper's face softened. "Do you need any help dressing? Lucy's a right mess in the kitchen with the short notice, but I suppose I've a minute . . ."

"No, no—I'll be fine. Please, go and help Lucy."

As Mrs. Griswold scurried away, Elegy dashed up the staircase and careened into her chamber. There was nothing for it, she thought grimly as she dropped to her knees and searched near a pile of hatboxes for the leather valise that lay collecting dust. She would have to claim illness and make her way through the basement to the game room and climb through the egress there. If she hurried to dress for dinner, she might have enough time to hide a change of clothing there, and then the darkness and vestiges of the rain would do the rest; a mist had just begun to settle upon the grounds and would become a thick fog come half past six. It was hardly an infallible plan, particularly if Amos decided he was in a murderous mood, but it was the best she could fashion given how little time she had left.

The most inconspicuous item of clothing within her wardrobe was a black silk dress with three-quarter-length sleeves and a hem that fell to her knees. Having been meant to be paired with a tangle of long necklaces or a brocade coat, it had no ornamentation and could almost be mistaken for the sort of simple sheaths fashionable women in the city might wear. No one might fault her for wearing Wellingtons when one needed to slog through several inches of water to cross the street, and if she pulled the pins from her coiffure and wore her hair down, enough of her face would be concealed that, with dim lighting and the haze of alcohol, no one would recognize her at all.

No, it would be the sneaking back in that would be the trouble, and for that she would need Hugo.

Elegy shed her houndstooth trousers and high-necked white crepe blouse and chose a Callot Soeurs evening gown of peacock and celadon green with gold-and-black beaded trim and black patent-leather T-strap shoes. The earrings that were meant to complete the ensemble were masterpieces of art deco craftsmanship, designed by Cartier and boasting two enormous emerald teardrops. They had also been missing going on a decade now, presumably hidden under some floorboard by Adelaide and long forgotten, and so she was forced to settle for diamonds and onyx.

When she was suitably adorned for their guests, Elegy hugged the leather valise close to her chest and sneaked down the servants' staircase to retrieve her coat and boots, which were still muddied from her earlier walk, then crept further still to the basement, where the kitchen was in a right uproar.

Fowler and Lucy were shouting at each other over the state of the silver, which had, given the last-minute nature of the Prescotts' visit, evidently not been polished to his exacting standards. Elegy took full advantage of the racket to seek out the rotting corpse of what had once been a bowling lane. Dereliction had encouraged the curling vines of the ivy that grew at the base of the manor on the eastern side, and without proper shoring up, the fragile glass had fallen to their invasion. Moss covered the damp brick walls and the once-gleaming floor that had played host to a great many of Delilah's amusements until Amos was summoned. Even though he kept mostly to the boiler room, the very thought of him was enough to ensure the entire southern wing belowstairs were emphatically shunned.

Her coat wrapped around her hand, Elegy shattered the remainder of the glass still clinging to the largest window's frame, then dragged the sturdiest crate she could find below it so that she might have an easier time of it. Upon it she placed her boots and valise, then she covered the lot of it with her coat and hurried back upstairs, pulling cobwebs from the beaded accents of her dress as she went.

A quick glimpse of her countenance in the mirror of the bathroom adjoining her father's office revealed a flush high on her cheekbones and a wildness in her eyes that could be mistaken for a fever. Excellent.

When at last she presented herself in the great hall, the hour was five minutes until six. Fletcher was standing before the hearth, wearing a French evening dress by House of Worth, originally for Delilah's honeymoon in Europe. The rhinestone capelet and black trimming and tassels that adorned the pale-apricot silk, as well as the enormous bow below the right breast and the elegant fall of the fabric, kept the dress from being too ancient to be considered fashionable, particularly when paired with the full effect of Fletcher's wild, unbound mane, heavily lined eyes, and rusty lips.

She'd a martini in one hand and a cigar in the other, even though Thaddeus expressly forbade smoking, as he found the practice unforgivably distasteful.

From the record player poured the mournful crooning of Edith Piaf.

"The sacrificial lamb has arrived," said Fletcher over her shoulder. "Bernard left you a drink—I had him make it a double, given the circumstances."

"You should have it," Elegy answered. "I'm not feeling well this evening."

"Suit yourself," came the reply as her stepmother wrapped her lips around the cigar and hollowed her cheeks. The smeared red gash of her mouth opened, and a thick plume of smoke emerged. "I thought you might need it."

"I'll manage."

A terrible, hacking cough drew their attention to the staircase, where they beheld Thaddeus upon the second-floor landing, leaning heavily against the gleaming mahogany railing. If Death were ever inclined to attend a dinner party, Elegy imagined he would look somewhat like her father did that evening. His black formal evening attire hung from his gaunt frame, and though he was freshly shaven and had clearly taken pains with his hair, it did nothing to temper the ghastly way his eyes and cheeks had hollowed. Despite his appearance, Dr. Winslow's tincture appeared to have helped somewhat, for he was able to descend the stairs upon his cane with nary a tremor in his step.

"Snuff that out at once," he barked to Fletcher. "Have you no shame, defiling my house with such filth before our guests arrive?"

Fletcher rolled her eyes but crushed the cigar into a crystal dish nonetheless, just as gravel crunched beneath the porte cochere and Fowler opened the front door to reveal the Prescotts' Bentley.

Hugo emerged in a suit of midnight blue with a mustard cravat and, ever the dutiful son, offered his hand to his mother and drew her from the car.

His father followed, and they were met at the door by Fowler, who took the heavy mink cape from Lavinia's shoulders. She'd worn it to appease Thaddeus, for anyone who had ever dined at Thorne Hall knew that whatever the occasion, the host and his family would be outfitted in priceless vintage couture and they must present themselves in similar splendor, even if it was newly purchased and therefore did not require several spritzes of perfume to cover the lingering scent of mothballs.

The Spirit Collection of Thorne Hall

The sumptuous garment seen to, Hugo's mother set upon Elegy and, swooping down, pressed a kiss upon her cheek. "You look ravishing. I cannot *wait* to plan every detail of your special day, my dear—I assume no expense will be spared?"

"Of course not," Thaddeus said as he shook hands first with Phineas and Lavinia, then with Hugo. "Nor were any spared this evening."

Lavinia pressed her hand to her bosom in delight. "Do not tell me—"

"Oh indeed."

"You *do* spoil me, Thaddeus."

"Doesn't he just?" said Fletcher, and Lavinia seemed to only just then notice that she was also in the room.

She nodded stiffly. "Fletcher."

"Lavinia. A treat as always."

A bell chimed in the distance, and Thaddeus looked to his wife. "Shall we?"

Fletcher crushed her rust-stained lips together, then spread them wide in a smile. "We shall."

Thaddeus offered his arm grudgingly, and she took it with equal disinclination. Together they led the way into the dining room with the Prescotts following and Elegy and Hugo left to bring up the rear.

"Wait," Elegy whispered, seizing his sleeve. "Before we go in, there's something I need you to promise me."

"What's that?"

"I'm planning on being ill midway through dinner."

"Now, I know my mom's conversation is far from titillating—"

"And I need you to say that you checked on me and found me sleeping."

Hugo blinked, realizing all at once that she was, in fact, quite serious. "What's that now?"

A swift glance into the dining room revealed that Fletcher and Mrs. Prescott had already been seated, Fletcher's martini drained, and the glass borne away by Mrs. Griswold as Fowler began to pour the wine for the first course. "I can't explain it all now, but I will, Hugo, I promise you. Just please do me this favor."

"The way I did you a favor the other night when you spent the night at his place?"

Elegy's face heated. "You speak to me of favors?"

"This dinner is important, El," he said, as though it were any sort of excuse for his behavior. "Your dad is a dead man walking, and my parents—" He broke off, scrubbing his hand roughly across his jaw. "Jesus, what is it about this guy?"

"It isn't just him, Hugo. There are things I cannot say. Not yet anyway. But I need you to trust me. *Please* trust me."

"Hugo?" Mrs. Prescott's voice drifted from the dining room. "Hugo, darling, where are you?"

"We'll be right there," he called back. Then, to Elegy, he said with a sigh of resignation, "Of course I trust you. But you owe me an explanation."

Relief barreled through her so fiercely that she threw her arms about his middle in an awkward embrace. "Thank you."

"Hey," he laughed, and when he pulled back, he chucked her upon the chin. "We'll get through this."

She entered the dining room on his arm and, like a dutiful wife, allowed him to pull out her chair and see her arranged in it, napkin laid artfully across her lap, before he saw to himself.

The first course, scallop crudo with citrus and ginger, was accompanied by champagne and banal pleasantries, and Elegy hardly stomached either. This was, she supposed, for the best, as in precisely twenty minutes she was due to suffer an ailment so dreadful as to confine her to her chambers during this most sacred event.

"The Forscythes' daughter is said to be engaged to some tech billionaire in Boston," said Mrs. Prescott as her empty plate was removed to make way for the soup course. "I believe she plans to wed in July, which is utterly ridiculous if you ask me, given the heat, so we were thinking May for your wedding, Hugo—"

"Not soon enough," Thaddeus barked, setting his spoon down with a clatter.

Mr. Prescott cocked his head. "How soon do you suggest?"

"As soon as possible."

Elegy's eyes met the mirror of Hugo's, and she expected to see her own self reflected there. But not only had he suddenly taken a very great interest in his fork; the skin beneath the freckles dusting his high cheekbones was turning an alarming shade of pink.

"A winter wedding, then," said Mrs. Prescott. "The ceremony will be held at Trinity, of course, and the reception here at Thorne Hall as you have requested, Thaddeus, though I suppose we will be limited as to the number of guests. I wish you'd reconsider letting us host the reception at Brightleigh."

The Spirit Collection of Thorne Hall

"How many people are you inviting that this place can't hold them?" asked Fletcher. "Elegy hardly knows anyone, and isn't this *her* party?"

"Hers," agreed Mrs. Prescott. "But it is also Hugo's, and he knows a great many people, don't you, darling?"

Hugo, who had been in the process of draining his wineglass, nodded. "Whatever you want, Mother. The more the merrier."

"How many can we fit, darling?" Hugo's mother asked his father.

"How should I know?" he grunted around a spoonful of soup.

Thaddeus brought his fist down upon the table. "Both the ceremony and reception will take place at Thorne Hall. I'm afraid I must insist upon it."

If Mrs. Prescott was disappointed at his insistence, she handled herself with the grace possessed of all socialites turned wives in their income bracket. "Of course, we understand, but perhaps we might hold the ceremony outside? We could purchase heaters, oh—and Elegy could wear a fur cape!"

"You hear that, Elegy?" snickered Fletcher. "A fur cape."

Would the Spirit Collection watch from the windows? she found herself wondering. Eugenia and Mabel would have a right cackle about it, of that she was certain. She imagined Gideon smirking down at her through the glass as she spoke her vows in a gown he'd seen upon her ancestors.

With that terribly depressing thought, Elegy rose. "I'm so dreadfully sorry, but I am not feeling very well at all."

"Oh no!" exclaimed Mrs. Prescott, while her husband murmured his sympathies into his plate before he took up his knife and fork. "Yes, you *do* look a little pale, dear."

"Elegy always looks pale," said Hugo. "But yeah, you should definitely go sleep it off."

Thaddeus had steepled his hands and was staring at Elegy over their peak with baleful eyes. "This is most inconvenient, Elegy. We've matters of great importance to discuss."

Fletcher gave an enormous bark of laughter. "No one was including her in the discussion before, so I doubt you'll miss her."

"Are you sure it isn't just nerves?" asked Lavinia. "A wedding can be an overwhelming event, especially amongst our kind."

Fletcher snorted into her wineglass.

Hugo laid the back of his hand upon Elegy's forehead and affected a worried frown. "You do feel hot, El. Maybe you ought to go lay down."

"But you shall miss our discussion regarding the flowers and the cake!" Mrs. Prescott wailed. "I've booked The Gilded Rose, and Esme Bettincourt herself is going to do the cake, but what with the abrupt change in date, we shall have to schedule a tasting immediately!"

Thankfully, Elegy did not have to pretend at illness as she pushed her chair away from the table and stood, for she did not possess Hugo's natural inclination toward theatrics. The blistering panic flooding her body rendered her so light-headed that her shaky steps to the door were entirely sincere.

"I really am so terribly sorry," she said. "Please excuse me."

Casting one last parting glance at Hugo, she slid quietly from the room as the conversation turned to the five-course wedding supper that Mrs. Prescott had discussed with a French caterer in Boston.

"She's even agreed to replicate the lacquered duck, isn't that wonderful?" she trilled, to which Thaddeus demanded to know why his own cook should not be good enough to prepare the duck for the wedding herself.

Up the stairs Elegy went, her steps heavy for the benefit of anyone in the dining room still paying her departure any mind, and as she went, she cast her awareness of the Collection into the shadows of the second floor. Calliope lay upon the window seat in the Honeysuckle Room, tracing idle patterns on the glass with what remained of her fingertip, while across the room Vivian lay tucked beneath the faded coverlet and beside her in a chair missing several of the spindles Delphine read aloud from an old issue of *Harper's Bazaar*. They were easily managed, content to remain in their habits and with little care for the goings-on below.

It was Adelaide who whined and stomped her dead little foot when Elegy bid her ascend to the third floor where Reed played noughts-and-crosses with himself in the thick dust covering the floor of one of the servant's rooms.

"But why must I go?"

"Do not ask me questions."

Adelaide pouted. "You're leaving again, aren't you?"

"No, I am simply unwell and wish to rest undisturbed."

The petulant little spirit did not appear remotely convinced, but neither could she deny Elegy's command, and so once she'd thoroughly sulked her way up the stairs and settled herself, Elegy made a show of opening and closing her chamber door before stealing down the corridor.

Down the servants' stairs she went, her steps swift and soft, and in the darkness of the moldering bowling alley Elegy carefully shed the

The Spirit Collection of Thorne Hall

dress meant to garner attention and replaced it with another meant to conceal: a mourning dress.

She pulled the pins from her hair and the emeralds from her ears and had just shrugged on her coat when she felt a heaviness in the shadows behind her, and with it came the stench of burning flesh and screaming.

CHAPTER TWENTY-FOUR

Amos almost never left the boiler room, and yet the mass of blood and bone and blackened skin where his face had once been hovered in the darkness behind her.

She could hardly afford the delay, but neither could she afford the disaster that might unfold should Amos decide to terrorize the second kitchen on this rare night when Lucy and the other staff were still on duty after sunset. And so she stepped away from the broken window and bid her racing heart to still as she faced him. Amos, more than any other spirit in the Collection, could unearth her fear, however hard she tried to conceal it.

"Good evening, Amos."

He could not speak, owing to his general lack of lips (and, Elegy suspected, his tongue as well, though she'd never actually seen inside his blackened mouth), but he could make unintelligible sounds, and he did so then, a discordant, subterranean groan that set Elegy's flesh all ashiver.

"Return to the boiler room," she whispered. "And be still. *Please* be still tonight."

But he did not turn and disappear into the shadows as she'd bade him. Instead, he crossed the damp and the dark of the bowling room, and with each heavy drag of his feet, Elegy's breath quickened and she fought to quell the desperate fluttering of her heart.

The Spirit Collection of Thorne Hall

"Amos," she said. He was close enough now that were he to lift the blackened and twisted remains of his hand, he could caress her cheek, and the urge to shudder with revulsion at the thought was so great she nearly bowed to it. And yet he attempted nothing of the sort, and although the silence between them was palpable, it held no malice.

"I must leave the manor tonight," she ventured in that silence. "But only for a little while, and then I will return."

His head tilted ever so slightly, almost inquiring, and when he remained still, Elegy realized that he was waiting. But for what? Even now Thistle likely waited at the end of the drive, ready to spirit them away into town.

"I am meeting some most unusual people in a tavern not far from here," she told him. "They mean to help me, and I will be perfectly safe amongst them. I will return as soon as I am able."

It should have been enough, the words and her intention, to command him into submission, and yet he remained before her, waiting.

"The person meant to take me waits at the end of the drive," she continued. "And if I do not appear, they will surely leave without me and then my chance may be lost."

Still, he did not go, and all the while his head remained tilted as though she'd yet to say the right thing, as if he knew there was far more to it than she was letting on and would not allow her passage unless she confessed it all.

"I seek a way to rid myself of you. Of all of you. And you will be rid of *me*. This is why I must go, and you must let me."

For one terrible moment she could not feel him at all, could not ascertain his intentions or discern his mood, and she wondered if she were about to lose her face or something far worse. A shudder passed through his stout, ruined body before he turned and slowly lumbered back into the darkness of the corridor until he was swallowed entirely by it.

She'd little time to ponder such an extraordinary event. Thistle waited, and so she pulled herself through the window, hands grasping wet ivy as her pathetic arms brought her to the surface, and she wiped them clean on the grass as best she could. Then she turned up the collar of her coat against the frigid gusts of wind that violently rent what was left of the peak from their branches. An old Honda Accord sat in wait at the end of the drive, and its driver glared as Elegy made her way around to the passenger side door and slid inside.

"You're late," they announced.

"My father invited my fiancé and his parents for an impromptu dinner that I escaped by feigning illness, and then I was detained by a ghost with a penchant for ripping people's faces off, whom I was forced to mollify in order to prevent that very thing from happening to said fiancé."

"Well, fuck."

"Indeed."

Thistle threw the car into gear, and Elegy barely managed to buckle her seat belt before they were flying down the road toward Lenox, a barrage of drums and screeching guitars blaring from the speakers. Clumps of wet leaves smacked the windshield and were pushed away by the furiously sweeping wipers, leaving wet smears and pieces of themselves as they went.

"You might slow down," advised Elegy, gripping what Floss lovingly referred to as the "oh shit" bar above the window, but Thistle only chortled and went faster.

The Golden Hind was one of the original buildings in Lenox. Situated upon a corner near Main Street, it was made of red brick and leaded-glass windows with an ornately carved and mirrored back bar boasting hundreds of liquor bottles crammed together below racks of glassware.

Wide-eyed, Elegy clung to Thistle as they weaved their way through the press of bodies, most of them tourists and entirely ignorant as to the identity of this small, strange wraith of a woman and thus not giving her the wide berth to which she'd become accustomed.

"Where are they?" asked Elegy as her foot was nearly trodden on by a man quite unsteady upon his own.

"Private room in the back," Thistle answered. "This way."

At the end of a long and narrow hallway hung and lined with all manner of lamps and chandeliers and fixtures with no discernible theme, they came to a door painted black and bearing a brass plaque with the image of a deer upon it. Thistle knocked three times, and a moment later it opened, and Winter gazed out at them with one perfectly groomed eyebrow raised.

"You're late."

Thistle tilted their head in Elegy's direction. "Her fault. You going to let us in or what? And you'd better have ordered me a good IPA."

"The bitterest they had."

Thistle grinned. "Excellent."

The Spirit Collection of Thorne Hall

They stepped over the threshold, and Elegy nearly tripped into their back in her haste to follow, because she could not wait one moment longer before . . . *there*. There he was.

Atticus lifted her clean off her feet and her arms went round his neck; the room fell away and they held fast, breathing the other in.

"Are you okay?" he asked, lowering her to her feet and taking her face gently in his hands.

She nodded. "Well enough."

Atticus guided her to the chair beside his, and once she was seated, he took hold of her hand under the table, lacing their fingers together.

The room in which they sat had no windows, only walls covered in green and gold damask wallpaper and a stone fireplace with a flue that had not been cleaned in quite some time, given the amount of smoke that seeped into the room. She would need to air out her clothing upon returning to Thorne Hall so as not to arouse suspicion, for Mr. Griswold would never allow the chimneys of Thorne Hall to become so thoroughly clogged.

Along with Dorian, Winter, and Thistle sat two strangers at the table. The first was Winter's wife, a woman in the full bloom of her middle years with a riot of apricot curls and skin awash with freckles and flush. Her name was Mavis, and the moment Winter spoke to her of meeting Elegy at Hallowed Grounds, she had insisted that she simply *must* attend their gathering.

"That's a bit of canny," she explained. "The feelings."

Elegy would have pressed her further regarding these feelings, but her eyes alighted upon the last occupant at the table, and her mind emptied of all other thought but that she recognized him instantly.

The piano tuner looked every bit as rumpled as he had the first time she'd seen him in Floss's ballroom. He smiled and tipped his head, and she wondered if his extraordinary ear might be attributed as much to his canny gifts as to natural talent.

"I'm Brio," he said, leaning across the table to take her hand in his own rough, calloused one. "Nice to see you again, Elegy."

"How *did* you know my name that day?"

Brio winked.

Dorian regarded them curiously. "You've met before?"

"Yes, at Floss's—that is, at Holcroft. Brio happened to be there tuning the piano, and he was playing the most peculiar version of a song I know well."

Dorian went very still. "What sort of a song?"

"One of the Child ballads, 'The Unquiet Grave.' He also taught me a lovely piece called 'A True Lover's Farewell.'"

"Do you know many such songs?"

"I know every Child ballad, as well as several of the Ravenscroft ballads and the London broadsides, though some are more effective than others. It's really to do with the lyrics and how the melody shapes them and the other way around, and of course who I am singing to and why. In fact, 'True Lover's Farewell' was marvelously effective the other night . . ." And there she trailed off, for every eye in the room was fixed upon her, their expressions ranging from thinly veiled curiosity to rapt interest. Brio, she noted, wore a perfectly satisfied smirk, as though he were already in possession of some knowledge the others had only just begun to suppose.

"And what do you do with these songs," asked Dorian, "that they must be 'effective'?"

Elegy looked to Atticus with a growing feeling of unease. The way they'd reacted was most peculiar indeed.

Beneath the table, his hand squeezed hers. "They can't help if you don't let them," he murmured.

"Well," she began, looking about the table at the expectant faces of the canny ones gathered there. "I suppose you all know about the ghosts."

They did, in fact, know all about the ghosts and had for some time. Jasper Thorne's Collection was well known amongst canny ones, for it was an exceedingly rare sort of craft indeed that could summon the dead, and a rarer one still that could bind them for so long to one place, to one bloodline.

"There have been four masters of Thorne Hall, and they have all managed the Collection with ease, even if they did not care for the doing of it," she said. "I have never been able to do the same without songs. At first, I sang because I was scared and the songs soothed me, but eventually I discovered that they soothed the Collection as well, rendered them more amenable to my will."

Brio laughed, his dark eyes alight. "I *knew* it. I could feel it the moment I met you."

"Knew what, exactly?" Elegy asked, almost afraid of the answer.

"Brio," Dorian warned.

"*You*," the piano tuner declared, slapping his palm soundly atop the table, "are canny!"

Elegy's eyes went round. "I am *not*."

"Which of your parents was it?"

"I beg your pardon?"

"It must've been your mother," Brio continued, as though she'd not spoken. "Because I've met Thaddeus, and no man has ever been less inclined to the canny arts."

Dorian's voice, when he spoke, was quiet, but so firm that all eyes were drawn to where he sat at the head of the table with his hands folded before him. "Tabitha Thorne was not canny," he said.

"Well, maybe I underestimated Thaddeus," Brio said, undeterred in his certainty.

"Why are you so certain I am canny?" Elegy asked. "Is it because I command spirits?"

"It is *how* you command them that has captured my friend's attention," answered Dorian. "You see, song has been intimately entwined with the canny arts since there have *been* canny arts. And before spirits could be summoned."

Brio's shoulders shrugged under his frayed blue jacket. "Why do you think so many of us are named the way we are?"

Brio, Elegy thought. It was a musical term that meant vivacity. And Dorian, that was a mode. "Elegy," she said slowly. "A lament for the dead. And the rest of you?"

"Do you recall the tenets of which we spoke?" Dorian asked, and Elegy nodded. "The canny arts are entwined with the natural world."

"But how did your parents *know* you would be canny?"

"They didn't," said Mavis. "Our names always seem to find us all the same."

"I'm telling you," Brio said, slumping back in his chair with a beer in one hand and a knowing smirk upon his lips. "She's a canny one and make no mistake."

From the end of the table, Winter spoke: "Whether or not the girl is canny, that's not why we're gathered here tonight."

"Another subject for another time," agreed Dorian. "Now, then. Back to the ghosts."

He had already informed them all of Elegy's wish to rid herself and future generations of the Spirit Collection, and their thoughts upon the matter were, at first, as dismal as Dorian's: it simply could not be done.

"However," said Winter, leaning forward conspiratorially. "Dr. Singh, the curator who manages the historical archives at the library, is an old friend, and was kind enough to allow me access."

Elegy's heartbeat raced. "And did you find anything of note?"

"As a matter of fact, I did: The society pages mentioned a fete held at Thorne Hall on Samhain night, 1902, in which five women of the same bloodline played at summoning the dead for the entertainment of the master's guests."

Several different newssheets had, in fact, reported upon the event, Winter went on to say, some even quoting witnesses that claimed to have been present that evening, but of the summoning itself little was written, save that which made it sound quite innocuous indeed, just another of the false séances the wealthy often paid charlatans for, for the benefit of scaring their guests shitless for an evening.

And then Winter happened upon the name Willie Abner.

"Yes, I know of him," confirmed Elegy. "He was a young footman on loan from another estate that night, and he must have made quite the impression upon Jasper and Deliliah, for he was made a member of the permanent staff on the spot."

Winter nodded. "And by the time the final spirit in the Collection was summoned, he was Jasper's valet. Quite an unusual and commendable feat for his humble beginnings, but it might've been mere coincidence were it not for the journal."

Here was something quite rare indeed, a detail about the history of Thorne Hall that Elegy knew nothing of, and she listened with rapt attention.

"Unlike most young men in service," Winter continued, "Willie Abner could read and write, and when he was belowstairs, did so quite often. Apparently a kitchen maid who had tried and failed to arouse his interest harbored a grudge and told everyone he must've been touched in the head to ignore her in favor of a dusty old book."

"She was also a horrid gossip," her wife added. "And that was how word of the journal spread."

"What sort of things did he write in the journal?" Elegy inquired.

"The maid only ever caught glimpses over his shoulder here and there, but evidently in addition to what she called gibberish, there were drawings of symbols in the round."

Elegy's eyes found Dorian's at once. "Perhaps that was why your ancestor did not keep a record of her own—this young man did it for her."

"We've no way to know what he wrote at all, because the journal has never been found," he replied. "It is entirely possible that its destruction was ordered to prevent the very thing we have gathered here tonight to discuss."

The Spirit Collection of Thorne Hall

"*Or,*" said Thistle, "and hear me out—what if he held on to it instead? Big old mansion like that, there are probably a million places it could've been hidden."

Atticus spoke at Elegy's side: "So we find it—then what? Can you all reverse-engineer whatever craft Sparrow did and send them back wherever they came from?"

"It would be a vast undertaking, to say the least," Winter replied thoughtfully. "The craft used to summon the Collection was and still is the most complex any of us have ever known. How she managed it could be far beyond the skill of any gathered here tonight."

"And you will need more than our help," Dorian warned. "Sparrow was assisted by her kin, several of whom were rumored to be canny themselves."

"She has you," answered Atticus. "And she has me."

"It will not be enough."

"I have a very dear friend, Floss, who has not yet returned to New York," Elegy said. "And I've Hugo, of course."

But did she really have Hugo? Uncertainty twisted deep inside as she remembered his reticence to help her escape the manor that evening and his miserable face at dinner when the matter of finances was discussed.

"Whomever you have, nothing can be done until we find the journal," Dorian reminded her.

Elegy nodded, quite determined. "I'll begin searching for it first thing in the morning."

"There is another complication, I am afraid," said Winter. "The summoning of the first spirit, arguably the most difficult bit of the craft, was done on Samhain night, the strongest of our sabbats. The same potency will be required in this endeavor."

"But that is only ten days away!"

"We'll find it," declared Atticus.

Thistle gave Elegy a feral grin over their nearly empty pint glass. "Maybe you should ask the ghosties. I'll bet they know every inch of that place."

Oh, Elegy was quite certain they did. But was there really any amongst them who would not give her up if Gideon Constant should grow suspicious?

"Not all of them can be trusted," she answered upon a frown. "Their loyalty lies with my father above all, even the ones I call friends."

Dorian regarded her sternly down the length of the table. "Don't put yourself at risk."

"I'm afraid a little risk may be unavoidable," she answered, worrying at her bottom lip, the wine she'd been nursing gone even more sour in her stomach than it had been to begin with.

It was agreed that Elegy would search for Willie Abner's journal while the rest of the canny ones sought answers in the archives and the memories of others.

"Come home with me tonight," Atticus murmured as those gathered around the table drained their glasses and rose, pulling on coats and winding about their necks thick, brightly colored woolen scarves that looked as though they'd been knitted by the same person.

Elegy could think of nothing she would rather do than twine her pale limbs around him in the dark and feel the steady beating of his heart beneath her ear after he'd thoroughly exhausted her, but she knew she could not.

"I want to so badly," she whispered.

He plowed his hand through the wreck of his hair with a sigh. "Yeah, I know."

At that, her brows drew tight. "Are you still absolutely certain about all of this?"

"More than ever."

"Why?"

"You really don't know?" At her befuddled expression, he huffed a soft laugh. "You really don't."

"Perhaps you might put me out of my misery, then."

The smile that spread slowly across his face was so sweet she ached at the sight of it. "I think I'll let you figure it out yourself."

* * *

Every single light had been extinguished at Thorne Hall, and thus Elegy made her way up the drive by the illumination of the firmament above, the storm having passed while she sat in the pub, leaving behind sharp black skies, a waning moon, and the cold glint of stars.

Back through the broken window and into the bowling room she went, taking a good deal of mud and leaves with her, and when she slipped and landed upon the crate with far more momentum than she'd meant to, her foot went right through it. Her eyes immediately flew to the doorway and found it blessedly empty. Amos had heeded her advice.

Once she'd extricated herself from the crate and shed her muddied coat, she took up the valise that held her dinner costume and used the servants' passage once more to reach the second floor. Reed and Adelaide were hunched over the remains of a bird, the poor thing no doubt having found its way into the manor through the broken panes of a third-floor window.

They lifted their little heads at her approach, and Elegy pressed a fingertip to her lips. Reed waved in greeting, then turned his attention back to the bird. But Adelaide stared at her with a sullen expression until Elegy had disappeared quietly into her chamber.

A piece of paper lay on the floor, ostensibly having been pushed under the door, and Elegy unfolded it with shaking fingers.

I told everyone I found you sleeping, so you're welcome.
We need to talk.

—H.

Sweet William's Ghost
Francis James Child ballad #77

Lady Margaret, she lay in her fine feather bed
The midnight hour drew near
When a ghostly form came to her bed
And to her did appear
"Oh, are you my father the king?" then she cried
"Or are you my brother John?
Or are you my sweet William
Coming home from Scotland along
Coming home from Scotland along?"
"No, I'm not your father the king," then he cried
"Nor am I your brother John
But I'm your own sweet William
Coming home from Scotland along
Coming home from Scotland along"
"Oh Margaret, oh Lady Margaret," he cried
"For love or for charity
Will you give back to me that plighted troth
That once I gave to thee
Oh, that once I gave to thee?"
"No, I'll not give you back that plighted troth
Nor any such a thing
Until you take me to my father's own hall
Where oft times we have been
Where oft times we have been"
"Fare thee well, my own true love
Cold the wind does blow
High, high the moon is o'er the moor
Woe that I must go"
So he took her to her father's own hall
And as they entered in
Well, the gates flew open of their own free will
For to let young William in
For to let young William in
"Oh Margaret, oh Lady Margaret," he cried
"For love or for charity
Will you give back to me that plighted troth

That once I gave to thee
That once I gave to thee?"
"No, I'll not give you back that plighted troth
Nor any such a thing
Until you take me to yon high churchyard
And there marry me with a ring
And there marry me with a ring"
"Fare thee well, my own true love
Cold the wind does blow
High, high the moon is o'er the moor
Woe that I must go"
So he took her to yon high churchyard
And as they entered in
Well, the gates flew open of their own free will
For to let young William in
For to let young William in
"Oh Margaret, oh Lady Margaret," he cried
"For love or for charity
Will you give back to me that plighted troth
That once I gave to thee
Oh, that once I gave to thee?"
So she took the troth out from her breast
She placed it on his chest
Saying, "Here is you back that plighted troth
And in heaven may your soul find rest
And in heaven may your soul find rest"
"Now the north wind blows and the moorcocks crow
It's almost the break of day
And it's time for the living to depart from the dead
So my darling, I must away
My darling, I must away"

CHAPTER TWENTY-FIVE

Having thought Elegy so terribly ill that she'd left a dinner where her own wedding was the topic of conversation, Mrs. Griswold was appropriately shocked to find her descending the stairs with the dawn, looking as bright eyed and determined as she'd ever seen her.

"I did feel dreadfully unwell," Elegy said, doing her very best to appear contrite. "And I am sorry to have missed whatever was spoken of in my absence, but as you see, a full night's rest has done me a wonder of good. Now—what's for breakfast?"

Having missed the lacquered duck the evening before, Elegy devoured a plate of eggs and sausages before throwing herself headlong into the search for Willie Abner's missing journal.

She began in the most reasonable place to find a book, Nathan Bride drifting in and out of the stacks as insubstantial as steam fog upon the surface of a morning pond, but as she'd suspected, there was little to be found in the way of personal accounts amongst the leather-bound first editions in Jasper's collection, and so it was to Thaddeus's office she went next.

He kept the chatelaine there with its dozens of mismatched keys, most original to the house, and once she'd broken in using a pearl hatpin, she tried them all on the drawers of his desk and cabinets, to varying degrees of failure.

The Spirit Collection of Thorne Hall

By the noon hour when Jeremiah and his men came to Thorne Hall, Atticus found her in a most foul mood indeed, sitting in the middle of one of the ruined third-floor bedrooms surrounded by the rotting corpses of old boxes, their contents strewn around her in a mess of yellowed parchment.

"No luck?" he asked.

Several unruly locks of hair had escaped their confines, and she blew them away from her face in frustration. "Unless by luck you mean that I found nearly three decades' worth of grocery lists, then no, I've not."

She took the hand he offered and rose, shaking those three decades' worth of dust from her skirts.

"Where else have you looked?"

She ticked them off on her fingers. "The library, Thaddeus's office, all the second-floor bedrooms save his, and most of the third floor. I've two more rooms here to search, including Fletcher's, and then I suppose I shall start upon the basement."

"My dad will need me, I think, but I'll pop in when I'm able."

They parted ways, him to the basement with a sprig of juniper tucked in his pocket for protection and her to Fletcher's chamber, but not before she'd looked about to make sure there were no spirits lurking and then tugged his mouth down to meet hers in the briefest of kisses. And then one more because she could not seem to help herself as far as he was concerned.

And he did not seem to mind.

* * *

Fletcher did not come to the door when Elegy knocked, and when she eased it open after several moments had passed, she found her stepmother asleep behind the ocher-and-crimson drapes that hung from her four-poster bed, an unmoving lump under a velvet coverlet. The smell of incense hung heavy in the air, mingling with the sharp tang of woodsmoke, and when Elegy glanced into the fireplace and saw the bed of coals still gently glowing, she knew her stepmother had not been abed long.

Her steps quiet and swift, Elegy crossed the room to Fletcher's bedside table and coaxed it slowly open, finding only loose cigarettes within, as well as the pair of familiar emerald earrings she'd been searching for the previous evening.

Well, fuck you, Fletcher, thought Elegy, and shoved them into the pocket of her skirt.

Beneath the bed offered nothing but a thin layer of dust, Mrs. Griswold having cleaned only recently, and there was no second nightstand to search, for Fletcher had taken hold of one of the legs during an argument with Thaddeus two years into their marriage and smashed it against the opposite wall. If there was a journal in it at the time, Elegy could only hope someone had had the good sense to rescue it.

The trunk at the end of the bed was full to bursting with silks and satins, as were the bureau, the armoire, and the closet, and Elegy dug through shoes and unmentionables and cases full of jewelry she'd not seen for years but found nothing of note. The desk squatting before the bank of grimy windows yielded a far more interesting discovery.

Evidently Fletcher fancied herself a writer.

She'd liberated the Woodstock No. 5 typewriter that had for years gathered dust in what was once Delilah's office, and it was now surrounded by stacks of paper that, from what Elegy could decipher, told the story of a woman imprisoned by a cruel man in a house full of ghastly things.

It was florid and melodramatic and surprisingly gripping; really, Fletcher ought to publish it. No one would ever believe it wasn't a product of her feverish imagination but rather an overindulgent memoir.

"Elegy?" slurred her stepmother, still in the throes of sleep, and Elegy froze. "What time is it?"

"Noon," she replied, easing the pages back to their original state.

A grunt emerged from the velvet cocoon. "Too early. What the fuck are you doing in here? Did Thaddeus finally die?"

"No. And I shall, for your sake, decline to mention that you said such a thing the next time I see him."

"I don't give a fuck if you do."

"I seek a journal. It would be quite old and filled with runes—the sort we use to repel the spirits from our chambers."

The lump shifted, rose, and through the dull-brown chaparral of her hair, Fletcher regarded Elegy with bloodshot eyes. "What?"

"A journal," Elegy repeated.

"Full of what?"

"Runes."

Fletcher groaned and fell back against the pillows. "No."

"No?"

"No, I haven't seen it."

Elegy moved the armoire. One of the doors was hanging by a hinge, and she gingerly pushed it aside and peered into the darkness within. "Perhaps it was here when you took the room as yours."

"The only thing here was a cradle." Fletcher flung back the covers and swung her pale legs over the side of the bed, hunching over with a groan. "And you remember what I did with it."

"And you're certain there was nothing else?"

Fletcher groped blindly about the nightstand until her fingers curled around a tumbler full of clear liquid. She brought it to her nose, inhaled deeply, and evidently finding its contents suitable, drank the entirety of it in three hearty swallows. "I'm certain. Fuck, help me up."

Elegy clasped the limp hand Fletcher proffered and pulled her upright. Once she found her footing, she stumbled to the armoire and extracted a teal kimono dressing robe. "Dinner was a crashing bore after you left," she said, cinching the belt tight at her waist. "All talk of the wedding and the prenuptial agreement and nothing else."

"I suppose all the decisions have been made?" Elegy asked as Fletcher pulled a half-smoked cigar and a Venetian brass lighter with a charming design of flowers out of the dressing gown's pocket.

"Nary a loose end in sight." A plume of smoke curled up from her stepmother's lips. "It all worked out rather well, don't you think? Everyone gets exactly what they want. Well, except you, of course, but none of us Mrs. Thornes ever do. I would say Mrs. Prescott, but I doubt Thaddeus would approve."

Upon her knees before the armoire, Elegy paused, her hands lost in a sea of moth-eaten silk.

"I hope you enjoy pale blue," Fletcher continued, sinking onto the chair at her desk. "That's what they chose for the wedding colors. And Lavinia is insisting on roses."

The only rose that belonged in a winter arrangement was a Lenten one. Hellebore, white with black centers, and spiny blue sea holly; a bit of Limonium, perhaps; stephanotises shaped like stars.

But Elegy would not have chosen a winter arrangement for herself; she would have married in summer so that when she crushed her bouquet against her chest with breathless anticipation, the aroma would be of peony, phlox, and sweet pea; honeysuckle and orange blossom warmed by the sun would fill her senses, heady as the occasion. Her gown would not have been worn by anyone before her, there would be no lacquered duck to speak of, and her name when it was done would not be Prescott but Hart.

"I'm sure white roses will suit," she said at last. "And whatever else Lavinia has decided."

Fletcher set her cigar in a tarnished silver dish and regarded Elegy with an eager glint in her eye. "I can't wait to see what happens when you finally snap."

"I have no idea what you mean. Are you certain you've not seen the journal?"

Fletcher began typing upon the Woodstock, slow and deliberate and so very final in the stale air of her sanctuary, and Elegy knew her business there to be complete.

Her hand was upon the doorknob when Fletcher spoke: "Save me a front-row seat."

Elegy's brow wrinkled. "For what?"

"When it happens," answered Fletcher around a mouthful of cigar. "Because it will—it's only a matter of time. I should know."

* * *

Lucy made her Shropshire fidget pie with Spitzenburg apples from trees in Esopus grown gnarled with the passing of so many centuries.

There was fruit to be found on the Thorne estate—a small grove of Northern Spy, which connoisseurs agreed was the far superior fruit for any pie, sweet or savory—but around the time Elegy was born, a peculiar black moss had begun to grow upon the stately branches, and although the fruit appeared quite ordinary upon the surface, when cut into, the mealy flesh was gray and riddled with maggots.

The search for Willie Abner's journal had left Elegy even more pale and insubstantial than usual, and so Lucy left two enormous wedges upon a cloche-covered plate beside a pot of tea and a note that begged her to leave behind not one crumb or she would waste away to nothing.

The repairs on the kitchen nearly complete, Elegy ate her supper there once more, blessedly alone save for Cook's soothing presence as she drifted here and there, examining every new plank and nail and fixture with wariness, as though they might come alive at any moment just like the toaster. Eventually Bernard ambled down the stairs in search of a fresh bottle of gin, and Elegy decided to follow Thistle's advice.

"Cook. Bernard," she said, pressing the back of her fork to the crumbs of pastry left upon the china. "Do you recall ever seeing a journal about the house? It would be very old—as old as Thorne Hall itself, if not more so, and it contains markings, the ones that keep you from our bedchambers. Have you seen such a thing?"

The Spirit Collection of Thorne Hall

Bernard shook his head slowly, as she'd known he would, and Cook, the dear thing, began to search the pockets of her apron as though she'd been carrying just such a journal upon her person.

"Bernard!" Fletcher's voice echoed from inside the dumbwaiter, sending Cook into such a state that she flew into the pantry. "Are you down there, Bernard? Where's my drink?"

Elegy sighed and slid off her stool. "I'll make Fletcher's drink, Bernard. Please see to Cook."

In the butler's pantry she gathered a cup of ice, then she passed through the dining room, where Bancroft was so thoroughly shrouded by darkness where he lurked in the far corner that she hardly noticed him at all.

In the great room she mixed a martini that would have tranquilized a small bear and brought it to the parlor, where Fletcher was engaged in a game of bridge with Eugenia and Mabel, with Adelaide as her partner. It was clear by her sullen glare that Elegy was not yet forgiven, and so when Fletcher barked at her to pull up a chair, she sat herself directly beside Adelaide and helped her win several hands. It was only fair; Eugenia and Mabel were cheating as usual.

In the great room the clock tolled the hour, and Elegy, weary and ladened with defeat, bid them all good-night and began the climb to the second floor, where she wondered if it was possible to smother herself in her own bedclothes. She was nearly there, fingertips upon the doorknob and a sigh upon her lips, when the skin prickled at the back of her neck and the smell of burning flesh filled her nostrils.

She'd never bothered to worry about whether or not Amos could leave the basement, because in 126 years, he never had.

Evidently this was something to which she should have given far more thought.

He stood at the end of the corridor near Thaddeus's bedchamber, the gleaming floors at his feet gone black and fetid as though he'd pulled his cursed self up through it. The tendrils of black that clung to him in perpetuity now filled the hall, coiling into every corner and crevice, smothering the very air she breathed with heat and soot and agony.

"Amos," she whispered. "What are you doing here?"

He remained unmoving as the black crept ever closer, languidly curling toward her toes; she took one step back and then another, and still they followed.

And then Amos lifted the bones of one blackened hand and pointed it right at her.

Elegy's heart leapt into her throat and lodged itself there. "Return below," she said, her voice a strangled rasp. "Return below at once."

He took one step forward, then another, his ghastly hand still extended, and songs flooded Elegy's frantic mind.

Before she could pluck one from the jumble, he lunged toward her, closing the distance between them with shocking speed. She bolted, stumbling over her own sluggish feet, and had nearly made it to her father's door when there was a sharp tug on her skirt and she was sent careening to the floor, managing to avoid dashing her face upon the floor only at the expense of her palms. Twisting onto her back, she beheld Amos looming over her; she could taste burnt flesh in the back of her throat and began to gag.

Well, there was nothing for it; her father would have to be made aware of her imminent demise. Elegy opened her mouth, but the scream gathering there died upon her lips, because Amos was not reaching for her face; he was not reaching for her at all.

She'd fallen between the Hydrangea Room and her father's chamber, just below the portrait of the unknown woman with the bird, and it was upon the canvas that Amos placed his hand, charred bones pointing to the small, feathered creature perched delicately upon the woman's fingers.

"I don't understand, it's just a—" Oh. Oh, she really was quite daft, because it wasn't just a bird, it was a—

"Sparrow," she breathed.

The name of the woman who summoned and bound the Spirit Collection of Thorne Hall was Sparrow.

A great sigh racked Amos's body, and then the floor at his feet swallowed him whole, leaving only tendrils of smoke in his wake. Elegy blinked at the place he'd been, then scrambled upright and dashed down the corridor, taking the stairs two at a time until she reached the great room and continued into her office. Upon the mantel was a stoppered bottle of long matches that Mrs. Griswold used to light the fires, and Elegy seized them before making for the door to the back patio, the sound of her heels striking the wood floors drowned out by the raucous laughter from the parlor. She took one of the wrought-iron lanterns left from Fletcher's party and threw herself down the steps into the grass.

Somewhere between the manor and the graveyard, her heels became a liability, lodging themselves into the sodden ground, and so she wrenched them off and threw them somewhere into the dark. The relentless drizzle of the afternoon had settled into an icy haze, and when she breathed, cold air hit the back of her throat and emerged in puffs of white.

She could see little before her but the lawn and the vague inclination of barren branches by the fickle light of the waxing gibbous, a treacherous reminder of how very little time she had left, but her heart knew the way and pounded in time with her stockinged feet, which were now soaked past the ankle. Soon enough, Jasper Thorne's looming sepulcher came into view. Elegy's hands fumbled with the latch on the gate, and she slipped and stumbled into the graveyard, wet tendrils of hair sticking to her face.

She made for the cypress tree in the far corner, to the grave covered in white anemones, and fell to her knees before it. Her fingers made stupid by the bitter cold, Elegy fumbled with the matches until she managed to extract one and strike true, the tiny flame blazing to life before sputtering out as quickly. Three more matches suffered the same unfortunate fate before she finally managed to light the lantern, and she held it aloft, bathing the gravestone in a soft pool of golden light.

Her fingers passed over the bird carved there—the *sparrow*—and fell to the ground beneath it. If Amos was to be believed, the woman buried there and the woman in the painting were not only one and the same but Dorian's ancestor no less, the canny one who had summoned and bound the Spirit Collection. But why was she here, buried amongst the Thornes? And why would Amos tell her such a thing now unless—

Elegy lifted her hands from the ground and stared at the dirt upon her overturned palms.

Blood, bone, earth—these are its tenets, Dorian had said. *And shaped by song.*

Bones and earth were beneath her, blood and song within.

If Brio was right and she *was* possessed of some modicum of canny, could the bones tell her of themselves and of the woman she once had been? Of course, the song would have to be very specific indeed; a song of inquiry, but dear to the task at hand. She smiled when the answer came easily (and quite cleverly, if she did say so herself), and she rested her palms gently upon the soil once more.

> *Lady Margaret, she lay on her fine feather bed*
> *The midnight hour drew nigh*
> *When the ghostly form came to her room*
> *And to her it did appear, appear*
> *And to her it did appear.*

J. Ann Thomas

Unbidden, her hands sank into the soil, then farther still to her elbows, and a garbled scream was ripped from her throat as she tore her hands away, folding them to her breast as she sucked in great gasps of bitter air.

When she eased them away and examined them by the light of the candle, she was shocked to find no dirt upon them whatsoever, for she could have sworn she felt the grasping earth still, pulling her down to Sparrow's final resting place. Unsettling though it might've been and quite beyond her ability to comprehend, it appeared she was in no immediate danger of being dragged underground and left there to rot alongside Sparrow. And so she began again, and when she again felt herself falling once more, she welcomed it.

As the smell of loam filled her nostrils, she was enveloped by the cold and dark, and with her eyes opened wide, she saw the lid of a coffin made of wood and etched with runes, for certainly it would have rotted away to nothing after so many long years. Were Sparrow's bones within? And what of the journal of William Ezra Abner?

Elegy asked:

"Are you my father the king," cried she
Or are you my brother John?
Or are you my love, my sweet William?
From Scotland has come home?"

And sweet William himself answered:

"I am not your father the king," he said
"Nor am I your brother John
But I am your love, your sweet William
Come home to you again."

* * *

"I need you to come to the manor at once."

Elegy had shut herself into her father's office upon returning from the graveyard, stripped to her underthings and wrapped in a blanket, as the rest of her clothing would've left frightful marks upon the upholstery. Atticus had answered her call upon the second ring, and his voice at such an hour, deep and rasping, did perilous things to her general sense of well-being.

"Hello to you too."

"Did you hear me?"

There came the sound of rustling sheets, and Elegy imagined him sitting up in bed, chest gloriously bare. "I heard you," he said. "I just didn't think you were serious."

"Do you remember the grave with the bird upon it?"

"Yes."

"I think the journal is buried there, and I need you to come and help me dig it up."

"How do you know it's there?"

Elegy clutched the telephone receiver tightly to her ear. "Atticus, I fear Brio might have been right about me after all."

"About your being canny."

She whispered: "Yes."

A long, heavy silence followed, and she feared that *this* would be the thing that would break him; that he could not believe. Then—"Where do I meet you?"

Relief was swift and sweet. "The graveyard."

* * *

An hour passed, and Elegy wrapped herself in a man's overcoat far too large for her frame but wonderfully warm.

Rifling around in the coat closet nearest her office had yielded only a dusty top hat perched upon a shelf, and although it was far too ostentatious for her purpose, the moths had not gotten to it yet, and best of all, it covered her ears. After jamming it upon her head to ward off the rain, she'd donned a proper pair of Wellingtons and slogged back to the graveyard. Once more she lit the candle in her lantern and waited beside the graveyard gate.

A light bobbed between the slender black trunks of the Painted Grove and then another. Flashlights, she realized, and a moment later Atticus emerged from the darkness with two shovels slung over his shoulder and accompanied by Dorian himself.

"You're here," she breathed when she saw the medium.

"Indeed," he replied. "This one roused me from my bed and told me the most curious story of my kin being buried in your graveyard, and possibly with Willie Abner's journal, no less."

Elegy explained what had occurred in the second-floor corridor regarding Amos and the portrait of the woman holding the bird and the way she'd sung and sunk and *seen* the journal encased in stone.

"Very well," said the medium with eyes gone bright. "Let us discover the truth of it."

J. Ann Thomas

They took to the earth with grim determination, piling it behind themselves as they burrowed ever deeper in their pursuit of Sparrow's final resting place, and all the while Elegy stood gripping the handle of her lantern tightly, poised between desperate anticipation and abject fear.

When at last shovel met wood and struck dull and true, Elegy fell to her hands and knees before the grave and watched as Sparrow's coffin came into view at last, exactly as it had appeared before, when she might've only dreamt it. Atticus had not brought a crowbar, and so he used his shovel and his own considerable strength to pry open the top, and with the crack of splitting wood, it was torn free.

They peered inside.

All that remained of Sparrow were piles of dust and the impression of a black gown, atop which sat a box made of stone.

Stone and earth and blood and song.

Dorian lifted the box and, with reverence, passed it into Elegy's trembling hands. She laid it upon the ground amongst the anemones as Atticus pulled himself from the pit and fell to his knees at her side.

Elegy rested her hand upon it and confessed softly, "I am afraid."

Atticus took her chin gently in his fingers and turned her face toward his. "Have you figured it out yet?"

Ah, he meant that night in the pub. She'd pondered it a great deal in the days since and had arrived at the following two conclusions:

The first was that Atticus thought himself in love with her.

The second was that he was wrong.

Still, there was no trace of doubt to be found in his steady gaze, and it gave her the courage to nod and, with a deep exhale, remove the lid.

Sealed away within a tenet of the canny arts was a book no larger than her hand, bound in crude leather and wrapped in muslin that was not really muslin at all but a whisper that dissolved in Elegy's hands at the first touch.

Its pages were filled with runes; they formed circles upon the floor and surrounded doorways, and beside them in a crude hand were Willie Abner's ruminations upon them.

"These are the same runes handed down by my ancestors," murmured Dorian, tracing the designs that decorated what could've been any of the doors in Thorne Hall. "But *these* . . . I've never seen before."

"Can you decipher them?"

"And, more importantly, can you invert it?" asked Atticus.

"Yes to the first," Dorian replied. "As to the second, well, that is the question upon which all of this hinges."

The Spirit Collection of Thorne Hall

Atticus climbed back into Sparrow's grave to set things to right while Dorian and Elegy pored over Willie Abner's notes.

The first page of the journal was dated October 31 and contained a rough sketch of runes in a circle, and with them five women, one at the center holding a knife and the other four behind her, all wearing long gowns, their hair unbound. One was holding what appeared to be a bone, one a small pouch, and another a shard of stone.

"I'll take this back to the cottage," said Dorian. "Once I've copied the runes and any of Mr. Abner's notes that might prove useful, I will send it back."

"Certainly not," replied Elegy. "Not until I have read it."

"I can well understand your curiosity, but this is hardly the time or place."

He was not wrong; they were all of them soaked to their skin, and one of the flashlights had gone out.

"There is a chapel just beyond the entrance to the wood. No one has used it for a very long time, but it will shelter us."

They made their way through the copse of trees to the small stone church once used by the Thorne family for silent contemplation. Atticus kept hold of Elegy's hand, lifting branches out of her way and keeping her upright when she stumbled over this root or that encroaching shrub.

Dorian trailed behind them, the occasional rustle of paper an indication that despite having no light to speak of, he was unable to resist leafing through the pages.

In the long years of its abandonment, the forest had sought to claim the chapel for its own: ivy climbed the crumbling stone, pushing its way inside through the three lancet windows along each of the longest walls, and small saplings sprang from the roof. Still, the stone stood stalwart, stubborn, even, as it was swallowed, much like the family who had built it.

The heavy wooden door groaned its displeasure as they entered, and Elegy was relieved to see that no one had bothered removing the candles from the sconces and alcoves about the room. Some were little more than puddles of beeswax, but two still boasted sturdy wicks, which Elegy lit using the candle from her own lantern, then she handed them to Atticus and Dorian.

They joined Elegy upon the pew nearest the altar, where she smoothed the pages of Willie Abner's journal open upon her lap.

"'October thirty-first in the year nineteen hundred and two,'" Elegy read. "'I have witnessed a most remarkable occurrence this Hallowe'en night, while in the temporary service of Jasper Thorne for a splendid party.'"

Mr. Abner went on to describe the lavish evening, culminating in a ritual in the ballroom in which a woman dressed in black shed her blood upon runes on the floor and, with the help of her kinswomen, summoned the spirit of a soldier named Gideon Constant and bound him to the manor and the Thorne bloodline.

"'Mam always said canny craft could not be used to raise the dead,'" Elegy continued. "'But they sang the same way she does, and it feels the same way in my bones when she does it.'"

She looked up and met Dorian's eyes. "Abner's mother was canny."

"I would wager he was as well, even if he was never made aware of it," he replied. "Read on."

The pages that followed chronicled the summoning of the Spirit Collection at intervals of six months, on Samhain and Beltane, the two most important sabbats of those who practiced the canny arts. Familiar names and circumstances and temperaments blurred together upon the pages, and even the occasional face (or lack thereof), Willie being an artist of no mean skill.

And yet they said nothing of the promise and gave no answer to the question Elegy had asked since the moment she'd first become aware of the spectral presences that shared her home. With hasty fingers she turned page after page, and when she reached the end of Willie Abner's journal, her heart sank, for rather than answers, there was nothing at all: the final pages were missing, torn away, leaving behind nothing but ragged edges.

Elegy sagged against the back of the pew. "I can't believe it," she said faintly. "All this time, and it's not here."

Atticus took the book gently from her slackened hands and flipped to the back, taking in the missing pages. "What's not here?"

They were looking at her like the little fool she was, for what she'd sought was of use to no one but her and had absolutely nothing at all to do with ridding herself of the Collection. And so she swallowed around the lump that had lodged in her throat and said: "Banishing runes. I'd hoped Mr. Abner might've included them. It might've saved Dorian a bit of trouble, that's all."

It was not a lie; banishing runes would have been exceedingly useful.

"Perhaps Jasper suspected one day that one of his progeny would go searching for a way to rid themselves of the Collection," said Dorian.

The Spirit Collection of Thorne Hall

"Then why not destroy the journal altogether?" Atticus asked upon a frown. "Especially if there was a chance another canny one might get their hands on it."

Dorian appeared troubled by this conundrum. "I could not say. Perhaps once I have examined the journal more thoroughly, I will have an answer to that question."

But it was not the answer she craved, and as Elegy passed the journal into Dorian's hands, she tasted the bitter tang of defeat at having lost a battle she'd not realized she'd been fighting.

CHAPTER TWENTY-SIX

The repairs to the kitchen were, at last, complete.

Bile rising in her throat with every step, Elegy led the feeble, fetid body of her father down the grand staircase so that he might pronounce it satisfactory, for he would never be so gauche as to effusively praise Jeremiah's fine work. Thaddeus was little more now than a collection of bones, and it seemed as though he'd quite forgotten the use of them. He shambled, elbows askew and back bowed, a skeleton in a fine, ancient suit, and Elegy's body shook every time his papery skin brushed her own.

Her heart leapt right into her throat at the sight of Atticus standing beside his father, and when once he might've given her a wink bordering on scandalous, the way he regarded her now, steady and serious and without any sort of ease, gave away no clue that he knew her at all.

Thaddeus listened absently as Jeremiah explained how they had preserved the kitchen's original design, ordering materials from architectural salvage stores up and down the East Coast, and when the tour was at last concluded, he gave a nod of approval that might've appeared solemn but was actually his wasted spine's inability to hold his head up properly.

For such a large man, Atticus certainly could move with astonishing silence. The solid warmth of him was at her back and his words were in her ear, but she dared not turn, not while so many people were about.

The Spirit Collection of Thorne Hall

"As soon as you can, meet me at the bottom of the drive. Dorian is expecting us."

She could only nod.

A miserable hour passed during which Elegy saw her father back to his chamber and tucked away once more inside blankets that, however often Mrs. Griswold changed them, smelled of the sour fear of death. The Collection could not tell him what lay beyond, for they remembered nothing but their mortal lives, and even those memories were little more than a series of vignettes hopelessly out of order, and thus he was left to imagine what might lay at the end of his mortal coil.

Thaddeus did not care for poetry, nor could she recall ever having seen him read a novel, and so she sat at his bedside and read aloud from the collection of newspapers Mrs. Griswold had brought up that morning while the clock ticked relentlessly upon the wall. When his breathing was at last a slow, steady rattle, she set the paper aside.

She'd drawn the blankets to his chin and was making to leave, to flee, when his hand shot out and took her by the wrist so tightly it wrested a cry from her lips.

"I know you think me cruel," he rasped through lips cracked and flaking.

And because he could not rise from his sickbed, she answered, "You *are* cruel."

"Not for nothing."

"No, not for nothing," was her bitter reply. "For the Collection."

"*Yes*," he hissed, his fingers tightening until she could feel the brittleness of his bones beneath skin as thin as paper. "There must always be a master of Thorne Hall, but not for the manor or the money or the silk upon your back."

"Father," she said, for she could not stand to hear it.

"You *know* what they are capable of!" Flecks of spit flew from her father's wrinkled lips, and sweat beaded upon his forehead with the effort of his declaration. "I made the promise, Elegy, as did my father and his father before him, all the way back to Jasper. And very soon, it will be your turn."

"You should rest," she told him as she made once more to rise, for the stench of death had rendered her quite light-headed. Although his words were an all too familiar refrain, she could not quite deflect them the way she could before; before she'd had a hope and a plan and an accomplice waiting at the end of the drive.

"My great regret is this," he said upon a tortured sigh. "That Tabitha did not survive to give me a son. That Fletcher could not give me a son."

Through the pain of her father's jagged fingernails sinking through the thin crepe of her sleeve and into her arm, she said answered bitterly, "Because a son would manage the Collection far better than I."

"No woman with Thorne blood has ever managed the Collection so well as you."

Elegy blinked. And when he did not take it back, she wondered if Dr. Winslow had, in fact, spiked her father's medication with hallucinogens. "You might've told me."

"You might not have worked so very hard."

And *there* was the father she knew and did not love.

Yet he did not let her go but tightened his grip further still as he forced the words through lips gleaming with saliva and blood. "The Collection is a cruel mistress, but I cared for your mother in my own way, and she loved you, so I would have spared you, if I could."

He began to cough again, blood flowing down his chin and soaking the stiff collar of his nightshirt, and Elegy pried his fingers from her arm and walked on shaking legs from the room, slamming the door upon the terrible, wet gurgle erupting from her father's throat.

She'd nearly made it to the stairs when a ripple of gray upon the balcony above caught her eye and Adelaide's face appeared between the bars, a pout heavy upon her lips.

"You're leaving again."

"I'm only taking a walk," Elegy lied. "And you should not be about. There are men below."

"You promised last time you left that you'd play with me, and you haven't," Adelaide continued. "Because you're always leaving."

Elegy rubbed at the headache beginning to bloom behind her temples. "When I return—"

"You'll be gone for ages. You always are."

She could not soothe Adelaide's agitation when she herself was a bundle of raw nerves herself, but little by little the spirit grew hazy and slid with a sigh between light and shadow to lie in wait until night beckoned, and only then did Elegy continue on her way.

Atticus emerged from the car and plucked the umbrella from her hand before bundling her into warmth that smelled like him. She sank into the seat as he pulled onto the road, and then she made the mistake of resting her forehead against the window, of closing her eyes.

The Spirit Collection of Thorne Hall

Only for a moment, she told herself, just until the stench of her father's deathbed had abated and her stomach settled.

Warm, calloused fingers touched her temple, brushing her hair gently away from her face. "We're here," said Atticus.

Through heavy eyes Elegy beheld Dorian through the rain-dappled windshield, standing at the door of his cottage with Willie Abner's journal in his hands and a haggard countenance that spoke of little sleep. Under his arm, Thistle's sly face appeared, and their welcoming grin was full of mischief.

In the kitchen, Mavis fussed with a plate of sandwiches while Winter poured hot water from a dented copper kettle over bits of dried rind and herbs, and before the hearth Brio's lanky form was stretched out on one of the couches, his feet dangling over the end and one hand flung over his eyes.

Thistle nudged one foot with a disingenuous cackle. "He was drunk when I called him. Looks like the hangover's setting in."

"I also had company," he grumbled in response. "So thank you for that."

Mavis set the tray of sandwiches down upon the table between the two couches with far more force than necessary. "Stop your grousing. We're here to help Elegy, remember?"

Brio mumbled something unintelligible, hauled himself upright, and shoved an entire sandwich into his mouth.

"Heathen," Mavis clucked with a shake of her head.

Tea was poured, and the rest took their seats.

"As I am sure you have surmised by the presence of our friends," Dorian began, "what I discovered in Mr. Abner's journal was of such import that it required more than one pair of canny eyes."

Beside her, Elegy felt Atticus's spine stiffen. "What did you find?"

Dorian set a scroll upon the table, and as he unrolled it slowly, a drawing familiar to Elegy's eyes was revealed, copied in the medium's own hand from Willie Aber's journal: the woman with long, unbound hair kneeling within a circle of runes, four others at her back wearing the same stiff, high-necked gowns.

He pointed to the runes. "This is the craft Sparrow used to summon the spirits, guided by blood and by song, strengthened by her own kin. But she did not invent it—not entirely. The foundation existed over one hundred years before Sparrow was born. It was Mavis, actually, who recognized it."

"I grew up in Waldren," she explained. "Once while playing hide-and-seek with my brother in a graveyard, I stumbled upon the ruins of a burial shrine to a canny woman named Rowan, who had been put to death in the late 1670s for raising spirits to terrify a man who had wronged her."

Winter raised one perfectly groomed eyebrow. "I can think of far less worthy reasons."

"I was fascinated by Rowan and made a thorough study of what documentation remained of her craft. The moment I saw the journal, I knew they were too similar to be a coincidence."

From a colorful canvas satchel at her feet, Mavis drew several sheafs of paper and placed them beside the scroll.

"Rowan did not bind the spirits she summoned. Once they'd served their purpose, she dismissed them. It was that bit of the craft that Sparrow made her own. Of course, having a physical place to bind them to as well as the Thorne bloodline made it infinitely easier."

"To say nothing of those who bore the tenets for her that night."

Dorian traced his finger over the figures of the four women. "Her grandmother, aunt, sister . . . and daughter."

"And music," piped up Brio from the floor. "Do not forget music."

Dorian pointed to the staves of music on the scroll. "It appears I was correct—Mr. Abner was possessed of some measure of canny himself, even if he was never formally trained in the craft. He managed to approximate quite well Sparrow's melodies and even a bit of harmony here and there."

"And must I sing this particular song?" asked Elegy.

"Not at all. In fact, I would not recommend it. Sparrow chose this song to summon and bind them, while yours must lay them to rest."

"Then the song is mine to decide."

"Yes, but take care. As you discovered the other night at Sparrow's grave, not all songs accomplish the same end. It must suit your canny, and it must suit the tone of the task. You alone will know by what words and by what melody you might lay them to rest."

Elegy thought of the way some songs entertained them, brought them a swoon or laugh or even a tear, a rare and precious thing in far too many lifetimes of nothingness. She thought of those they took comfort in, those songs that soothed what feral impulses were left in them when all manners and courtesy had faded with time and memory.

And although she would rather not have, she thought of that which cut them deepest, which inspired such ravenous hunger she'd nearly been devoured by the singing of it.

The Spirit Collection of Thorne Hall

While she worried at her lip and avoided Brio's piercing stare, Atticus leaned forward.

"You mentioned blood. Whose, and exactly how much are we talking?"

Dorian exchanged an uneasy look with Mavis. "Each spirit was summoned and bound with Sparrow's own blood. The same must be for Elegy."

"Yeah, I don't like that."

Elegy laid her hand atop his and laced their fingers together. "I'm sure it will not be too much, else she would not have been able to do it so often."

She thought a shadow passed across Dorian's face, but she imagined that any talk of shedding blood when the outcome was far from certain was enough to give even the most stalwart of men pause.

"In conclusion," said Thistle, "we have the runes and presumably we'll have a song—all we need is the kinswomen and this fuckery has an actual shot of working."

Elegy's heart stuttered. "But I've no kin."

"You've friends, have you not? They will suffice, if the bond is strong enough," Dorian answered. "And I will be anchoring the craft, so you'll only need three others."

Floss would agree, of that she was certain. She was less certain of Hugo, particularly after his behavior at the dinner she'd fled halfway through. He had far more to gain from their arrangement, but they'd always been in agreement that living with the Spirit Collection was going to, for lack of a better colloquialism, suck.

"I'll invite them to Thorne Hall tonight," said Elegy. "Floss is sure to be departing soon back to New York, so I shall call it a going-away party. We'll go over all of the details of the ritual two nights hence."

"I'll be there," said Atticus. "But shouldn't we invite them to my place instead? We don't want the spirits listening in."

"No, it must be Thorne Hall," said Elegy firmly, though her brow furrowed in worry.

"Floss and Hugo may know of the spirits, but they've never experienced them like you have. It would be wrong to ask them to take part in the ritual when they have no true idea what awaits them."

Atticus nodded in understanding, but his eyes darkened with concern.

"And you?" she inquired of Dorian. "I expect they will wish to hear the particulars."

"Then I will be there as well."

Over the hour that followed, Brio pulled an old guitar from the case he'd brought, strung with steel and its sound rich and full. He and Elegy sat before the fire and sang several songs together while Atticus stretched his long body out upon one of the couches and listened with a grin upon his face. She wrinkled her nose at him and affected an exaggerated sigh here and there, but it was impossible to deny that she was hopelessly, irrevocably in love with him, and whatever he asked her to sing, she would.

Meanwhile, Winter and Mavis usurped Dorian's kitchen and impressive collection of herbs to prepare a sleeping draft that would ensure Thaddeus had no inkling of who visited his house that night. It would, unfortunately, also render him unable to command the Collection for the duration.

Which was where Dorian came in.

He had, amongst Mavis's research, come across runes that he believed could be fashioned to keep something *in* rather than *out*.

"Only for a short time, mind you," he warned. "An hour, perhaps two. And you will need to gather them in one place."

"Oh, I think I know just where to put them."

Brio was the first to leave once the late morning began to stretch into early afternoon, and Mavis and Winter followed shortly after delivering into Elegy's hands a tiny, stoppered glass bottle filled with clear liquid.

"Into his evening tea or the water with his dinner tonight," murmured Winter. "Good luck."

The window above Dorian's kitchen sink was open, and Elegy watched their respective cars rumble down the drive before reaching for the heavy, wrought-iron handles.

"If this does not work, then what will you do? Surely you cannot remain in Lenox."

Elegy froze. The voice was Dorian's, and she knew at once whom he was speaking to.

"It will work," answered Atticus.

"And if it does?"

"What do you mean?"

They were speaking of her, she was certain of it. She pushed the window open a bit farther and leaned forward until she saw them standing together off to the side of Dorian's front porch.

Dorian seemed to carefully consider what he wished to say next. "You want her to return to the West with you."

"It isn't that simple."

"I daresay none of this is."

"Every single aspect of Elegy's life has been controlled by her father, right down to the clothing she wears. I am not about to be another man who steals her choices, however much I want her with me."

"Because you love her," said Dorian.

Elegy's breath caught, and her heart became a bird, wings beating madly against its confines. She longed for and feared his answer in equal measure.

He gave it without hesitation. "I do. And whatever path she chooses, even if it isn't me, she'll have a friend who will do anything to help her."

And oh, if that wasn't the end of her poor heart, taken flight through the window.

"Eavesdropping, are we?"

Elegy nearly jumped out of her skin and whirled around to see Thistle lounging against the kitchen doorframe with their skinny arms crossed.

"I've no idea what you're talking about," she replied with as much dignity as she could muster, and shouldered her way out of the kitchen in search of her coat. Tracking down Hugo and Floss would take time, to say nothing of convincing them to abandon whatever their plans might've been for the evening.

She tugged her coat on and stepped into chill afternoon air, the scent of stale leaves and woodsmoke filling her nostrils and settling in the back of her throat. "Atticus," she called. "I must return."

Dorian clasped Atticus's forearm. "I will see you both this evening."

"Seven o'clock," Elegy answered in reply. "Do not be late, for I will not have long."

CHAPTER TWENTY-SEVEN

Immediately upon returning from Dorian's cottage, Elegy placed a call to Holcroft, only to be told by the family that Mrs. Carmichael was not at home, having checked herself into a spa in Poughkeepsie. An attempt at calling Floss's cell phone, which was most likely switched off and stowed away in a changing room bin, resulted in an immediate answer by her voice mail. The phone book, however laughable Floss found its continued use in Thorne Hall, successfully yielded the phone number of the spa in question, and Elegy managed to catch Floss between a mud wrap and something called a white caviar facial.

"Why are you paying someone to put fish eggs on your face?" she asked.

"Because my mother ages me and I'll never find a new husband if I look like an old crone," Floss replied. "I'm due back home on Halloween—I'll call you then."

"It cannot wait. I need you to come back *now*."

"Why? What's happened?"

"Floss, there's a chance I can end all of this."

There was a beat of silence on the other end of the line. "Please tell me you mean what I think you do."

"Yes."

"Damn it all to fucking hell."

"Well, I mean some of them, probably, but that's hardly the point."

The Spirit Collection of Thorne Hall

Floss agreed to cancel the rest of her trip at once, pointing out that if the banishment worked, they could *both* return to the spa to have fish eggs put on their faces, and she promised to call Hugo on her way back to town.

The ornate mahogany grandfather clock in the corner of the room tolled the five o'clock hour. After setting to right everything on her father's desk and locking the door behind her, Elegy descended to the kitchen, where Mrs. Griswold was readying supper trays for the family.

"Would you like me to prepare your tray in the dining room, Mistress?" she asked. "Or would you prefer to eat here in the kitchen?"

"Here would be lovely," answered Elegy. She reached into her pocket and withdrew the stoppered bottle Winter had given her that morning. "I happened upon Dr. Winslow when I returned from my walk this afternoon. He asked that this be given to my father with his evening meal."

Mrs. Griswold took the bottle with a grimace. "That old charlatan—I ought to empty the lot of it down the drain right now."

"No!" cried Elegy too quickly. "That is, I know his methods are questionable, but I do believe my father has made excellent progress of late."

The lie tasted dreadful in her mouth, acrid and sharp and entirely unlike the ones Elegy told throughout the years to keep Mrs. Griswold and her husband safe. She would have liked to believe with this tincture that she was doing the same, but time would tell and she hoped it would not make a liar of her.

With a knot in her gut, she watched Mrs. Griswold uncork the bottle and pour the entirety of it into her father's water glass, then take up the tray. "I'll be back for Mrs. Thorne's supper, Mistress, then I'll be departing for the evening."

"I'll take the tray to Fletcher," Elegy said. "And don't worry about my tray either. The rain is expected to turn quite torrential, and I am sure Mr. Griswold would prefer to make an early start home."

Another lie. It was not even raining, so far as Elegy was aware, but Atticus was due to arrive any moment, and if he should cross paths with the Griswolds, questions would no doubt arise to which she had no believable answers.

She waited until Mrs. Griswold had disappeared into the servants' elevator to fetch her husband, then made her way to the cellar, where she plucked a dusty bottle from one of the liquor racks. It might've been Scotch or perhaps was whiskey—the writing on the label had long ago faded away—but Fletcher would not mind. Not after three or four glasses, anyway.

The bottle balancing precariously upon the tray, Elegy made her way to the third floor. Through Fletcher's door the rapid striking of typewriter keys mingled with the muted brass of Glenn Miller and His Orchestra.

Elegy shifted the supper tray in her arms and struck the door with the foot of her boot.

The typing abruptly stopped. "Griswold?"

"No," answered Elegy. "It's me. I've got your dinner, so open the door before I drop it."

There came the exaggerated scraping of chair legs over floors already terribly scratched and scuffed. A moment later the door was flung open, and Fletcher appeared in a gold velvet dressing gown with a high neck crowned in lace, a cigarette dangling from her lips. "What are you doing up here?"

"It's going to rain later, so I sent the Griswolds home. Let me in—this thing is heavy."

Fletcher pushed the door open to allow her passage, snatching the dusty bottle off the tray as she did. "What the fuck is this?"

"You cannot come downstairs tonight," Elegy told her. "And Bernard cannot bring you a cocktail."

"Why is that?"

"I've business with the Collection," answered Elegy. "Another exercise father wishes me to perfect."

"He's still not dead, then."

"We Thornes are nothing if not persevering," Elegy answered, setting the tray and dusty liquor bottle atop the trunk at the foot of Fletcher's bed.

Fletcher studied the bottle and grunted in approval. "Pillaging daddy's cellar now, are you?"

"As everyone keeps reminding me, he's not long for this world. If he's not going to enjoy them, someone else might as well."

* * *

Elegy had no sooner returned to the kitchen than there was a short, succinct knock upon the servants' door. She opened it to reveal Atticus with a thick scarf wrapped around his neck and a brown paper bag full to bursting in each hand.

His lips parted in greeting, but no sound emerged as he took her in.

The Spirit Collection of Thorne Hall

"Does it not suit me?" she asked uncertainly, smoothing a hand down the yellowed lace of the ancient high-necked blouse she wore. It was amongst the oldest pieces of clothing in the house. Her father would certainly have approved.

Less so the pair of trousers she'd paired it with, nor the suspenders that held them up.

She'd been confident when she'd chosen it, determined to present herself as the master of her own fate, but now, under his piercing gaze, she wondered if she shouldn't rather have worn the silk evening dress with the beaded overlay Delphine had set out in her wardrobe.

He cleared his throat. "It suits. A little too well."

"Really?" Flushing with pleasure, she turned this way and that, lifting her foot so he might see the way she'd rolled the cuffs of the trousers up to reveal a pair of leather boots with cunning heels that laced to her knees. "Aren't they clever?"

"Very clever. Now put them away before I pull them off you with my teeth."

"Do you promise?" she asked, and when he groaned, Elegy relented and lowered her foot. "Oh, very well."

Atticus set the bags he'd brought upon the table, and together they unpacked meat and cheese and all manner of accoutrements she'd asked him to retrieve from the fancy grocer he favored, for Lucy was shrewd and would surely notice if such things were to go missing from Thorne Hall's larder. Elegy could not very well invite guests and not provide them with refreshment.

"Perfect," she said upon a satisfied nod. "I'll arrange it if you'll fetch me a platter from the pantry."

Atticus turned—and promptly let out a strangled shout at the sight of a fine porcelain plate extended to him by a dead woman in a cap and apron.

Elegy started. "Wait, Atticus—"

But she was too late.

Cook was so terribly frightened she dropped the plate and bolted back into the pantry as it shattered upon the floor.

"Oh, for pity's sake," sighed Elegy.

"*Fuck*," Atticus swore, his gaze darting between the shards of porcelain and the place where Cook had disappeared. "I'm sorry, it's just . . . that was a *ghost*."

She could certainly understand the sentiment.

Elegy laid one hand upon his jaw and gently turned his face until their eyes met and the shock and revulsion within his calmed somewhat. "I know you must feel as though you're dreaming," she said softly. "Or perhaps you think it a nightmare, but please believe me when I say she will not hurt you and is, in fact, quite a lovely person."

She turned and called into the pantry: "Cook? Do come out, for I've someone I wish you to meet."

They waited an age before Cook finally appeared, her bony fingers curling around the doorframe before she came peeking round it and finally shuffled out with her cap pulled low upon her head and her hands clasped tightly before her.

"Cook, this is Atticus. He is very dear to me and would not harm you even if he could, so there is no need for such theatrics."

"Can she talk?" asked Atticus as Cook drew closer, peering up curiously at him beneath the lace trim of her cap.

"Certainly she can. But she is very shy, so do not expect a scintillating conversation. Cook, please bring the broom and pan."

While Atticus assisted Cook in the sweeping up and disposing of the unfortunate platter—at a respectable distance, of course—Elegy fetched another. There came another knock upon the door, startling Cook back into the pantry, and Elegy opened it to reveal Dorian standing there holding a plate covered with a colorful, threadbare cloth. Sitting upon the stone wall to his side, a grinning Thistle perched, swinging their legs.

"Good evening, Elegy," Dorian greeted her, before handing her the plate. "It's a cake made with honey from my bees. Too humble for Thaddeus's table, but your guests might enjoy it."

Thistle swung themselves down and nudged Dorian none too gently. "Don't listen to him; that shit's amazing."

"Thistle?" called Atticus from the kitchen beyond. "Is that you?"

"Atticus, my righteous sir!"

"Come in and help me with this, would you?"

Elegy felt it the moment Thistle and Dorian crossed the threshold into Thorne Hall. Atticus they knew, even before that terrible night when he'd found her in Gideon's arms; the Collection had felt him so often within the walls of the house over the past several weeks that he went nearly unnoticed, even with the lateness of the hour. Drowsing in the shadows, they'd barely stirred at his arrival, but at the arrival of these new guests, these two fascinating strangers with the scent of the canny about them, they lifted their eager heads and showed their sharp and gleaming teeth.

The Spirit Collection of Thorne Hall

"They know you're here," she said. "We must bind them now before they get up to mischief. Have you brought it with you?"

Dorian rummaged around in his pocket and withdrew two small pots of white paint. "Lead the way."

Leaving Thistle and Atticus to finish preparing that evening's refreshments, Elegy took Dorian up the servants' staircase and down the corridor to the ballroom.

"Wait here," she told the medium.

Her heart appeared quite determined to take up permanent residence in her throat as she placed her palms upon the doors, closed her eyes, and pushed them open.

Vivian sat at the piano, her long, skeletal fingers drifting over keys gone out of tune with the falling of the night.

"Why, hello dear. You look dreadful."

"Thank you, Vivian. Playing 'Judas,' I see."

"Oh, yes," she answered. "It's his favorite."

"Indeed it is."

She'd known he was there; she'd felt the shadows positively quiver with delight the moment she'd entered the room. But her skin prickled all the same as he stepped to the center of the ballroom, bringing with him rot and the terrible ravages of time in the mere space of a heartbeat, their gilded surroundings crumbling to ruin with every jaunty step.

"How lovely to see you, Elegy," he said. "To what do I owe the pleasure? I'd have thought you'd be below with *him*. Oh, yes, we know he's here, as are two others. Is your father aware of the fact?"

"My father is not much aware these days."

A cunning smile stretched Gideon's blackened lips. "Oh, he is more aware than you believe. And so am I."

A frisson of unease quivered through her. "Aware of what?"

"I don't think I shall tell you. It is far more entertaining to watch you squirm, wondering what it is that I might know." He paused. "And how I might have come to know it."

Her control over the situation was slipping away, and quickly. She could not allow him another word. Elegy lifted one hand, closed her eyes, and cast her will and her command into the far reaches of the manor, to the dark places where the spirits dwelled. Great splotches of black rot and mold bloomed upon the walls of the ballroom, growing and swelling until, as if punctured, they burst and spewed forth their terrible burdens: Bancroft, The Mourning, Eugenia and Mabel.

Elegy was gratified to glimpse a flicker of shock upon Gideon's face as he beheld them climbing to their feet, blinking their milky eyes in confusion, for in her twenty-five years, she'd never summoned them. Taking advantage of their disorientation, Elegy took one step backward and then another until she was past the threshold of the ballroom.

Then she slammed the doors closed.

"Now," said Elegy. She and Dorian coated their fingers in white and began to paint, and while they did, the six spirits howled, pleaded, and when Elegy refused to relent, they struck the doors, tearing at the wood with their fingernails, snapping and snarling. And yet they were helpless in the face of Dorian's craft, meant to ensnare them within for exactly one hour and no longer, for she'd plans for them that night.

They returned to the kitchen to find Thistle perched upon the counter with their mouth wide open and Atticus at the table holding a jar of green olives. He threw one, and when it missed Thistle by several inches and bounced off the wall, three groans could be heard: his, theirs, and Cook's. Elegy's poor cold heart constricted to see the spirit arranging a pretty little dish of Marcona almonds beside a wedge of French brie.

"One more try," Thistle begged. "I'll get it this time, I swear."

Atticus held up a finger in warning. "One more, but *only* one more—I've wasted enough perfectly good picholines on you tonight."

Thistle rubbed their hands together. "Okay. Okay—go!"

He lifted an olive, positioned it just so, and let it fly right into Thistle's open mouth. Their eyes went wide and they threw their hands over their head as Atticus shouted in victory, and even Cook smiled at their infectious joy.

"You saw that, right?" asked Thistle when they caught sight of Elegy and Dorian lingering in the doorway. "Tell me you saw that."

"I saw it," Elegy said as she drifted to where Atticus and Cook were putting the finishing touches on the charcuterie. "Wow, that looks amazing."

"What can I say, Cook here is one hell of a chef."

"Thank you for being kind to her," Elegy said softly. "Have you become used to it, then?"

His laugh rumbled deep in his chest. "Absolutely not."

A cursory glance at the clock reminded her of the imminent arrival of her friends . . . and how little time she had left before the runes would allow Gideon's company to walk free and how much there was to say before there was no time left to say it.

The Spirit Collection of Thorne Hall

"I should go up and prepare for my friends' arrival," she told Atticus. "They'll be here soon, and the craft will wait for no one."

He pulled her close, threading his fingers through the hair at the nape of her neck and resting his forehead upon hers. "Everything is going to be okay."

"I feel as though I might be sick," she confessed upon a shaking laugh, clutching the front of his sweater with both hands.

He pressed a lingering kiss upon her forehead, and as her eyes fluttered closed, she wished it was all said and done; that the Collection were no more and she were an ordinary woman who loved an ordinary man, standing with him in their kitchen at the end of a long and fruitful day. Their kitchen would no doubt be much smaller and significantly less haunted, but there would be a jug of wildflowers on the hand-hewn table and beeswax candles casting a soft glow upon the walls she'd painted butter yellow, for she'd become quite partial to the color, and perhaps they'd have a glass of wine. Perhaps they would dance, and not to a song involving child murder or lovers returned from the dead; what a novel thought indeed!

It was the conspicuous clearing of Thistle's throat that forced her lovely rumination to an end, and with great reluctance she stepped away from the warmth of Atticus's body.

"We'll be right behind you," he promised.

"I know," she replied.

In the great hall she banked the fire, lit the candles in the sconces and upon the mantel, and fussed with the flowers until they began to shed their petals. Then she busied herself at the bar cart, mixing gin martinis until she heard the crunching of gravel beneath the porte cochere.

As she neared the door, she paused at the mirror to take in her reflection and blinked in surprise at the living woman staring back. She was still hopelessly pale to be sure, but there was a flush upon her cheekbones and a liveliness in her eyes that had not been there before . . . well, before a great many things. She fingered a stray curl that had escaped the lose braid slung over her shoulder but did not tuck it away.

She drew a deep breath and opened the door.

Upon the stoop stood Floss and Hugo, arm in arm, and behind them, to her absolute horror, stood Sebastian holding a bottle of Dom Pérignon.

"Hope you don't mind me crashing. It's already chilled," he said, thrusting it into Elegy's hands. "And an *excellent* year."

She clutched it to her chest and stared back at him with eyes gone round with shock.

"I love what you've done with the new you," said Hugo, completely oblivious as he looked her up and down. "Very turn-of-the-century lady tycoon."

"You look fucking fantastic in pants," said Floss. Then, swooping in under the guise of pressing a kiss to one of Elegy's cheeks, she whispered, "Sorry, Hugo practically shoved him into my car."

"Welcome," Elegy stammered as Floss drew back. "There's no Fowler tonight, I'm afraid, so we'll be fending for ourselves. Lend me a hand, Hugo?"

While Floss and Sebastian hung their coats and scarves upon the rack, Elegy seized Hugo's treacherous sleeve and dragged him over to the bar.

"What the fuck, El," he grumbled, smoothing down the wrinkles she'd made.

"Why did you bring him here?" she hissed. "Didn't Floss tell you why you had to be here and why it had to be tonight?"

"She wouldn't say," he muttered, seeming to suddenly find his shoes of the utmost fascination. "Not in front of Sebastian."

He'd known it must be something to do with the Collection, for nothing else could make Floss hold her tongue. And so he'd brought poor, hapless Sebastian with him as a shield, deliberately trying to thwart whatever conversation Elegy might have planned.

As she pondered whether or not Atticus might be persuaded to help her bury Hugo's body after she murdered him, the man himself emerged from the dining room holding the platter, Thistle at his heels with several sleeves of assorted crackers. Dorian brought up the rear with his honey cake and a small stack of plates and mismatched silver forks.

Elegy stepped quickly forward. "Hugo, Floss, Sebastian—you already know Atticus. Please allow me to introduce Thistle and Dorian. Thistle is a recent acquaintance, but Dorian and I are old friends."

Dorian bowed graciously. "It is a pleasure to meet any friends of Elegy's."

It was Sebastian who moved first, a smile upon his face and his hand outstretched.

"Likewise. Absolutely chuffed. The name's Sebastian Blythe."

There was a great deal of hand shaking and the repeating of names, and all the while no one seemed to know quite what to do with Sebastian, who was, himself, oblivious and perfectly delighted to be so.

The Spirit Collection of Thorne Hall

There was nothing for it; she hadn't time to waste worrying over Sebastian. He was here whether she liked it or not, and whether *he* liked it or not, he was now a part of the endeavor.

Gripping the stem of her glass tightly in her fist, she drank the exorbitantly priced champagne in three swallows, set it aside, and stood.

They all fell silent as she made her way to the hearth.

"Thank you all for coming this evening," she began. "I am pleased that you all could make it. *All* of you, for I have something quite important to share."

At the bar, Hugo's head snapped up, eyes round and martini poised halfway to his lips.

"Elegy—"

Ignoring him, she turned her gaze upon Sebastian; poor, hapless Sebastian, who looked up at her with such a sweet, cheerful smile upon his face that she almost felt sorry for what she was about to do. Almost. "I do apologize for what I am about to tell you, though to be fair, Hugo was not meant to bring you tonight, so, really, it's his fault."

Sebastian fixed Hugo with an expression of deeply taken offense. "You said I was invited."

"You *were*," Hugo replied, smiling through gritted teeth.

"No, you weren't," said Elegy. "But that's all right—if you and Hugo are going to be together—though after tonight I would be very surprised if you were—you're going to find out eventually."

"Find out what?"

She spoke the very same words she had all those years ago, when she first told Floss and Hugo about the Collection. "I'm afraid Thorne Hall is quite haunted."

A moment passed, and then he laughed at what he clearly thought was a jest, what with how ridiculous it sounded coming from a grown woman and said with such sincerity. But as he looked about and realized no one else was laughing, that they were all staring at him with various degrees of pity in their eyes, and that Hugo would not meet his eyes at all, his smile began to fade.

"Very funny," he said with an awkward laugh. "You all got me, well done. Big old house like this one, it wouldn't be difficult to believe."

"It's not a joke," said Floss.

"Yes it is."

"No," answered Elegy softly. "It isn't."

"Yes it *is*. Of course it's a joke, isn't it, Hugo?" And when Hugo refused to lift his gaze from the polished tips of his brogues, Sebastian began to panic. "Fuck you all, this isn't funny anymore. Someone tell me what the hell is going on."

"My great-grandfather Jasper Thorne and a medium called Sparrow, who it just so happens was Dorian's great-great-grandmother, summoned and bound fifteen ghosts to the house and the Thorne bloodline," said Elegy without preamble. "They have been passed down from Thorne to Thorne, and upon the death of my father will come to me."

"It's true," added Atticus. "I've seen them."

"So have Hugo and me," said Floss.

Sebastian's nostrils flared. "You're all assholes."

"I only just met them, so I can't say for sure," said Thistle upon a shrug. "But they're telling you the truth. Just ask Dorian."

"Not only have I seen them," Dorian agreed, "but I am the one who taught Elegy the runes by which she has kept herself and others safe from them."

Sebastian leveled his gaze upon Hugo, who had finally deigned to look up from his shoes. "Assuming I believe any of this bullshit—which I don't—why did you bring me here tonight?"

It was Elegy who answered. "He brought you here tonight hoping it would keep me from speaking of the Collection at all, but I am afraid I must, because the truth is there may be a chance to banish the spirits forever."

"Nonsense," declared Hugo, turning back to the bar, where he took up a bottle of gin with trembling fingers. "You've aways said it can't be done."

Thistle shifted from where she was perched on the arm of Dorian's chair and fixed Hugo's back with a scowl, but Dorian rested a calming hand upon their arm as he spoke to the room at large. "My fellow practitioners of the canny arts and I have been delving into Elegy's situation, and we believe we have the craft necessary to unbind the Spirit Collection and return them to rest."

Hugo managed to pour a generous measure of gin into the cocktail shaker, followed by a splash of vermouth, and began to shake it far more vigorously than the poor liquor deserved.

"And what exactly is canny?"

Elegy worried on her bottom lip. "Perhaps I should have started with that. You see, there are those who can, with stone and earth and blood and song, do extraordinary things. The woman who summoned and bound the Collection was one such person."

The Spirit Collection of Thorne Hall

"Like witchcraft?" Sebastian squeaked, looking quite pale for someone who had only moments before claimed he did not believe in ghosts.

Thistle snorted. "We're not witches."

"You're one too?"

"Yeah," they answered, jerking their thumb at Dorian. "So's he. And so is Elegy."

Silence followed this revelation, and Elegy squirmed with guilt at the betrayal upon her friends' faces. "I only just discovered it," she said, her voice pitifully small. "Please believe that I would have told you straightaway."

"Never mind all that," said Floss firmly. "Of course you would have told us. So how exactly would it work, the banishing?"

"Our craft is strongest when performed on a sabbat, and none is stronger than Samhain," Dorian said. "It was on a Samhain night that Sparrow summoned the first of the Collection, in fact."

Thistle leaned forward and fixed Hugo with a withering stare. "Samhain is Halloween."

"But that's only three days away!"

"Which is why we must act quickly," agreed Dorian. "Elegy will need you all if she is to succeed."

"We are fortunate that, like Sparrow, my canny gift seems to stem from song," Elegy explained. "Dorian will see to the runes, and I will shed my blood as the craft requires, but the banishing circle demands those closest to me to bear the tenets."

Floss stood at once. "Yes. Whatever it is, yes."

"But I've not even told you what it entails yet."

"Doesn't matter. The answer would still be yes."

It seemed as though all gathered had worked out what came next. Their gazes slid to Hugo, who had long finished his drink and stood bent over the bar cart with his hands braced upon either side.

"Well?" Floss demanded.

"Well, what?"

"Elegy needs us. She can finally be free from this fucking hellscape of a house, and so can you. You should be bending over fucking backwards to help her."

A flush appeared upon Hugo's high cheekbones. "I'm not a monster, Floss—of course I'm happy to do my part and all that—but how do we know it's going to work? If it fails, can you imagine what Thaddeus will do?"

"Thaddeus is not long for this world," Elegy said. "Mere weeks, according to our family doctor."

"But if he did?" ventured Sebastian, "Find out, that is."

"None of us would stand a chance against him, that's what," said Hugo. "So maybe we wait until after he's dead to try."

"Wait," echoed Atticus. "You want her to continue living here alongside them?"

"You know, no one ever said anything about banishment until you came around."

"That's a shame, because they should have."

"You know nothing about it!"

"I've seen them," said Atticus upon a growl. "I've seen them put their fucking hands on her."

"And she's their mistress!" Hugo exclaimed. "What do you think they'll do to *us*?"

"For someone who claims to care about Elegy, you seem to be far more concerned with what will happen to *you*."

"You don't know anything about me, about any of us—"

"I know she can't stay here until you find wherever it is you left your courage."

Hugo's eyes went impossibly wide. "Who the fuck do you think you are, talking to me like that?"

Across the room, the clear gray of Dorian's eyes met Elegy's, and he gave her a deep, steady nod.

And Elegy said, "Enough."

The grandfather clock tolled the hour, and the fire in the great hearth went out, as did every light and every candle until the room was plunged into shadow.

Sebastian whimpered, his plate clattering to the ground as he gripped the arms of his chair with eyes gone wide and white with terror.

With a shaking hand, Hugo set his glass back on the bar, half the liquid sloshing over the rim to coat his hand. "Elegy, what are you doing?"

"You think that because you saw one of them once over a decade ago that you know what it is to live alongside them, but you don't. And perhaps if I had shown you long ago, you would not have agreed to our parents' plan."

Hugo shook his head, the plea stark and desperate in his eyes. "Not tonight."

And in anguish of it, Elegy answered: "It *must* be tonight."

The Spirit Collection of Thorne Hall

"What must be tonight?" asked Sebastian. "Will someone *please* tell me what is going on?"

"I shall not tell you," answered Elegy. "But I will show you."

Bernard came first, his arrival heralded by the sound of heavy feet dragged slowly upon the floor as his hulking form lumbered through the doorway of the dining room. Cook peered around his burly arm, keeping a safe distance, even though it was supposed to be Elegy's guests who were afraid of her and not the other way round.

Hugo staggered backward at the sight of them, colliding with the bar cart and sending a number of expensive bottles of liquor crashing to the floor.

Thistle gripped the arms of their chair and murmured under their breath, "Are you fucking kidding me?"

Elegy answered, "I am not."

One by one they slid from the shadows until the great hall was full of their gray, decaying figures, skin mottled with rot, bones protruding where time had robbed them of what little flesh their circumstances afforded.

Delphine descended the stairs, and behind her trailed Calliope with her ruined face, her delicate fingers moving absently in the gauzy folds of her wedding gown, and whatever tune she played was known only to her.

The door of the library creaked open, and Nathan Bride peered around it, pushing his spectacles futilely upon a nose that had nearly decayed to the point where it could no longer hold them. He clutched a book to his chest, eyes darting about as though one of them might snatch it from him at any moment.

The children—oh God, the children—the sight of them was worst of all, Reed leaving a trail of black water behind him as they settled upon the second-floor landing and stared through the slats the way they might've done were they rosy with life and drawn from their beds by the sounds of merriment below, a party they were forbidden from attending but were desperate to see.

And above them all, where orchestras once played on the balcony overlooking the great hall, stood Hester.

"Please allow me to introduce the Spirit Collection of Thorne Hall," Elegy said. "There are seven others, but I've locked six of them away because they either cannot be trusted or they are dangerous even while my father lives."

"And the seventh?" croaked Sebastian.

"Oh, he mostly keeps to the basement, but if you should happen to see him aboveground, *run*—he has a penchant for ripping off people's faces."

With a terrible gurgling sound, he flung his champagne coupe into the air and bolted toward the front door, only to be stopped by Calliope, for Elegy had bade her do so. Swaying upon her bare, rotting feet, she stood between him and freedom in the ruination of her wedding dress, while Sebastian stared in horror at the left side of her skull, the crushed bones there protruding through sinew and skin.

"Best gird your stomach," Elegy advised him. "I cannot know for certain, as I've never done it, but I doubt she will take kindly to being thrown up on."

"I remember her," Hugo croaked. "Sebastian, she won't hurt you."

"Actually, Sebastian, she might."

She wouldn't.

But he did not need to know that.

Hugo raked both hands through his hair as Sebastian took hold of the coatrack and thrust it before him, sending wool and cashmere flying in his attempt to remove the obstacle before him. "Tell her to stop."

"This is how it shall be once my father is gone, Hugo," Elegy said. "They shall be our companions in all things and at all times, even by day when you cannot see them. Of course, I will not only see them day or night but also feel them. They will ever be a part of me."

"But you'll keep us safe," Hugo said. "Sebastian, she'll keep us safe. She'll control them."

"She shouldn't have to. She never should have had to." Atticus had unfolded his long body from the chair and came to stand at Elegy's side, resting one of those warm, capable hands of his upon her lower back. It was that weight that steadied her enough to say that which she must, and it was to Hugo alone that she spoke.

"I've often thought of what I do not want, but never what I did want, because until now I did not believe it possible. And why would I torture myself imagining things I could not have? I know I do not want to live in this house. I do not want to wear clothing that belongs in a museum, and I do not want to command the dead," she said. "What I *do* want is to see the ocean. I want to tend a garden that is not destined to die. I want to love a man and for him to love me and to have children who will not inherit the same burden as every Thorne since Jasper."

The Spirit Collection of Thorne Hall

"Elegy—"

"I hate what your parents have done to you as much as what mine have done to me, but if we do this, we are no better than they, and it is I who will pay a price higher than you ever will."

His throat bobbed heavily. "My parents will cut me off. If I don't marry you, they said they'll make sure I don't get a cent, and I'll be left with nothing. I'll be nothing."

"Is that what you really think?"

The words came not from Elegy but from Sebastian, still clutching the coatrack so as to keep Calliope at a respectable distance, though she'd done naught but sway, humming what sounded very much like "The True Lover's Farewell."

Hugo turned to face him, his hands hanging limp at his sides. "Without them, I have nothing. My allowance, inheritance, Brightleigh . . . all of it gone. I don't even remember what degree I got in college, and I've never worked a day in my life. I have a couple of investments but nothing like the life you're used to."

"Do you honestly think I care about that?"

Hugo snorted. "Of course you do."

"I don't!" Sebastian cried. "I never have. And fuck you for thinking that I would."

"Why wouldn't you? There's not much else of me to be had. This?" He gestured to himself, to their lavish surroundings. "This is all I've ever known, and it's all I'm good for. Marrying Elegy, propping up my father's coffers . . . money, Sebastian. It's all about money; I'm all about money. Without it, I'm just . . . I'm just me."

Sebastian dropped the coatrack, the sound echoing in the terrible, suffocating silence of the hall, and Cook darted behind Bernard's stalwart bulk.

"I know you think I'm an imbecile," Sebastian said with a deprecating laugh. "And that's okay, because most days I can't believe you're still with me; *me*. Christ, when we were at school together, you called me Tubs and I loved you anyway. Still do. But if you think it's because of your money, then fuck you. And fuck you again for thinking that's all there is to you. I want to be with you if you don't have a penny to your name. And that's exactly what you'll have, and you'll do it willingly, because there is no way the man I love would inflict *this* on anyone, let alone a friend, inheritance be damned."

This was the Spirit Collection, to whom he gestured with a wide, sweeping arm.

Hugo swallowed, and when he spoke, his voice emerged as a croak. "You don't understand. I can't just say no."

"You never should have said yes." A wretched expression fell upon Sebastian's ordinarily sweet, guileless face. "This is a nightmare, and I'm sorry, Elegy. I'm so, so sorry. I thought . . . well, it doesn't matter what I thought. I wish I was as close a friend to you as Hugo and Floss, because I'd help you in a heartbeat."

Silence followed, and Elegy dared not break it, for Sebastian didn't need her to speak; he needed Hugo. And Hugo said nothing.

At last, Sebastian said, "Thank you for the dreadful evening, but I think I'd like to leave now."

"Of course," she whispered, numbness beginning to spread unpleasantly throughout her extremities at her calamitous failure.

Calliope slid away from the door, still singing, fingers still fluttering at her sides, and Sebastian threw open the front door and stalked off into the night.

Hugo stared after him, at the yawning dark where he'd disappeared, his clenched jaw working itself back and forth. Then pushed his lanky body away from the wall and followed his lover without a backward glance.

The moment the door slammed shut, the lights of Thorne Hall flickered once, twice, and then came back on, bathing the great hall in golden light.

The spirits had vanished.

"What the fuck just happened?" Thistle whispered to Dorian.

Floss let out a groan and buried her face in her hands. "I'm sorry, Elegy, but I have to go—I drove us here, and if those two idiots get lost in the woods, I'm not going in after them."

Elegy helped her collect the coats and scarves that lay in a pile beside the fallen coatrack.

"Thank you for coming."

"Hey, it's not over yet. We still have two more days, and if that fucker still hasn't come around, we'll just do it without him."

Elegy managed a weak nod as Floss hefted the bundle of wool and cashmere into her arms and walked out the door.

"I believe we need to leave as well," said Dorian. "The runes will only last a little while longer, and in light of . . . recent events, I must consider our options."

Atticus scrubbed a hand across the back of his neck. "I'll meet you at your place—help however I can."

The Spirit Collection of Thorne Hall

Dorian did not meet Elegy's gaze as he set his hand upon her shoulder and squeezed, but only briefly before he ducked his head and strode down the corridor toward the butler's pantry.

"So, that was the Spirit Collection," said Thistle.

"Only the ones who aren't occasionally given to betrayal and murder."

"You know, I thought you were okay before, but after tonight, you're my fucking hero."

"I never really had a choice," Elegy demurred upon an embarrassed flush, so unused to praise, particularly Thistle's vulgar sort.

"Yeah, you did. You didn't become your father."

It was, perhaps, one of the nicest things anyone had said about her.

Thistle jammed their hands in their pockets and, whistling jocularly, strode off down the corridor after Dorian. When they'd gone, when the only sounds in the great hall were the settling of dying embers in the hearth and the steady, swinging heart of the grandfather clock, Atticus turned and held open his arms.

Elegy fell into them, pressing her face into his chest and inhaling his scent like a filthy addict, and with a deep and ragged sigh, he rested his head upon hers. "It's going to be okay. We'll figure out how to make it work without him, I promise."

"Samhain is in three days."

"I know."

"And if we cannot make it work without him, what then?"

"We will."

A laugh that sounded more like a groan escaped her lips. "How can you be so certain of everything?"

"Remember that thing you were supposed to figure out?"

"Yes," she answered, biting back a smile.

"That's how."

The True Lover's Farewell
Circa 1719
Collected by Cecil J. Sharp in 1916

O fare you well, I must be gone
And leave you for a while
But wherever I go, I will return
If I go ten thousand mile, my dear
If I go ten thousand mile

Ten thousand miles it is so far
To leave me here alone
Whilst I may lie, lament and cry
And you will not hear my moan, my dear
And you will not hear my moan

The crow that is so black, my dear
Shall change his color white
And if ever I prove false to thee
The day shall turn to night, my dear
The day shall turn to night

O don't you see that milk-white dove a-sitting on yonder tree
Lamenting for her own true love
As I lament for thee, my dear
As I lament for thee

The river never will run dry
Nor the rocks melt with the sun
And I'll never prove false to the girl I love
Till all these things be done, my dear
Till all these things be done

CHAPTER TWENTY-EIGHT

When the runes keeping the worst of the Spirit Collection at bay had at last relinquished their hold upon them, Elegy was busying herself with a mop and a dustpan, cleaning up the mess Hugo had made of the bar cart. Bancroft leered from the shadows, having decided that her offense was worth his leaving the dining room to torment her, which was a mistake. He was a nearly mindless thing without Gideon Constant at his side to strengthen his malice and resolve. She succeeded in ignoring him most admirably until he took to flicking bits of cheese at her from the platter Atticus and Cook had so lovingly prepared, and that was that. Elegy sent him screaming through the walls into the basement. Let Amos see to him.

Cook and Bernard assisted Elegy with the rest of the cleaning before they slid back into the shadows and, at last, Elegy dragged her weary weight up the stairs of the butler's pantry and down the corridor to the main hall, where her feet turned to lead and would carry her no farther.

Standing before the great hearth with his hands clasped behind him, Gideon Constant greeted her with a smile.

"Good evening, Gideon," she said wearily. "You've not come this way in a long time."

"No, I haven't. Perhaps I shall make it more of a habit once Thaddeus is gone, which should be very soon."

"He has life in him yet."

Gideon's smile stretched wide. "You are a terrible liar, my dear, so let us dispense with such tediousness and speak frankly with one another. Tonight you invited that loathsome medium into Thorne Hall and used unfamiliar runes to lock us away; for what purpose, I wonder?"

"Wonder all you like, for I'll tell you nothing."

"Your father doesn't know," he said flatly. "Perhaps I shall have to tell him."

"What, that Dorian was here? He taught me new runes that proved quite effective. What fault is my father to find with that?"

He was no longer smiling. "Perhaps I was mistaken. Perhaps you are a far more capable liar than I believed you to be."

"It is the truth."

He prowled toward her, leaving shadow in his wake, reached out one moldering hand, and wrapped what remained of his fingers around her throat.

"Unhand me!" Elegy gasped, and when he only stared at her with his milky eyes and black lips contorted in an ugly grimace, she reached up and took hold of his arm. Nausea churned within her stomach, and as she struggled to draw breath, she sank her nails into his rotting skin.

Gideon lowered his face until it was a mere hairsbreadth away from her own. "No one denies me, least of all you."

"I am mistress of this house," she choked out.

"Not yet."

Not ever.

The wish gave her strength.

"Unhand me," Elegy commanded, and pretended it was a song. "Unhand me *now*!"

His fingers tightened for the briefest of moments, during which she was certain the Thorne line was about to come to an end, but then he released her.

She stumbled backward and fell so hard that black spots crowded the edge of her vision. She blinked, and when she opened her eyes, it was to darkness. Gideon Constant had gone and taken the light with him.

* * *

A necklace of bruises bloomed upon Elegy's throat during the night.

She covered them with the high neck of a black crepe blouse that did nothing to brighten her complexion, though it hardly mattered. The woman she'd seen in the mirror the previous evening with her lively eyes

The Spirit Collection of Thorne Hall

and color in her cheeks had vanished, even if the sliver of hope she allowed herself had not.

Hugo would come around.

It had been a mistake, the way she'd cornered him, she saw that now. And she could not possibly have anticipated that Sebastian, ordinarily so amiable, so *docile*, would react in such a way.

She simply needed to speak to Hugo alone, and away from the house.

Ambling slowly down the staircase owing to the unfortunate state of her tailbone, Elegy was shocked to find the fire in the great hall unlit.

Had she in fact woken far earlier than she supposed? There was no other possible explanation, for even if Mrs. Griswold were ill, and Mrs. Griswold was *never* ill, Lucy would have seen to the fire, or at the very least Arthur would have. And yet the hands of the grandfather clock showed the hour to be half past eight.

In the cold and quiet dark, Elegy moved upon swift steps through the dining room and descended into the kitchen, whereupon she was greeted by the astonishing sight of yet another unlit hearth and, even more puzzling, no sign of Lucy whatsoever.

"Lucy?" she called into the pantry. "Mrs. Griswold? Is anyone there?"

Dread burrowed between her ribs and lodged itself there, companion to her heart.

Grabbing one of Arthur's thick woolen jackets from the peg beside the door, she dashed outside into fog as thick as she'd ever seen it. With one hand pressed to the red brick, she walked the perimeter of the manor, calling for the groundskeeper as she went, but like the others, he was nowhere to be found.

Letting herself back in through the kitchen door, Elegy took the stairs two at a time and stumbled into her office. They were all bedridden, too sick to attend the Thornes; there could be no other explanation.

She lifted the receiver from its cradle and pressed it to her ear, but rather than the usual dial tone, she heard only silence. What little technology there was to be had at Thorne Hall was hardly reliable, but it had been three years since the last time the phone lines had gone down, and that had been on account of a snowstorm coating them in two inches of ice.

Her hands began to shake, and when she tried to set the receiver back into its cradle, she missed it entirely.

All thoughts fled Elegy's mind save one: she was no longer safe within the walls of Thorne Hall.

Cinching the belt of Arthur's coat around her middle, she fled her office and made her way down the corridor with the singular purpose of putting as much distance between herself and the house as possible, despite wearing a rather unfortunate pair of ivory Strohbeck boots she'd chosen for their pleasing silhouette and not for the purpose of a quick getaway down a muddy drive.

She broke into a sprint as she rounded the corner past The Mourning and into the great hall, then stopped short at the sight of Adelaide standing before the unlit hearth, wringing her hands.

"I'm afraid I've done something terribly naughty, Elegy," she said.

"Of that I've no doubt, but as you can see, I've rather more pressing matters to attend to."

"I did something naughty," Adelaide repeated, and her lower lip began to quiver. "Dreadfully naughty. It's only that I was so angry with you for leaving so often and forgetting to play with me, and so when he told me that if I did as he asked, he would make you play with me, I could not help myself."

Elegy stilled. "Who asked you to do what?"

"Elegy!" Fletcher's rusty bark preceded her down the stairs. She wore a celadon green dressing gown trimmed with gold lace and a thunderous expression, which only darkened when she took in the unlit hearth. "Where the hell is Griswold?"

"There's no one here. Not the Griswolds, not Lucy, no one."

"That's absurd."

Elegy shook her head. "I need to get out. I need to get to Atticus."

"What the fuck are you talking about?"

Stumbling past her stepmother, Elegy made for the door, only to find her way blocked by a most extraordinary sight.

The heavy dragging of his feet had ever preceded Bernard, for Elegy had never known him to move at anything other than a glacial pace, and yet one moment her path was clear and the next it was not, obstructed entirely by his enormous bulk.

"Bernard?" she said slowly. "What are you doing?"

He did not answer, and neither did he move, but he stared past her as though she'd not spoken at all.

"Bernard," she said again. "Please move aside and let me pass."

But he did not. Instead, he opened his rotting mouth, and a wheezing rasp emerged. "You are forbidden from leaving Thorne Hall."

The Spirit Collection of Thorne Hall

If he'd struck her face, she could not have been more shocked. "Forbidden? By whom?"

"By me."

Elegy and Fletcher lifted their heads. Clad in a pair of silk pajamas that hung from his skeletal frame and leaning heavily upon a cane, Thaddeus Thorne stood upon the landing of the grand staircase. Beside him, a sly smile upon his face, was Gideon Constant.

"Oh, Adelaide," Elegy breathed. "What have you done?"

"It is rather what *you* have done," answered her father, spitting the words as though the very taste of them had gone rancid in his mouth. "Gideon has told me everything—how you've been sneaking out, how you poisoned me so that I would not know you brought outsiders into this house, and worst of all, how you plotted with Dorian Everwood and Jeremiah's son to banish the Collection on Samhain. Deny it."

"Father—"

"Deny it!" he thundered, then hunched over the cane, the effort sending him into paroxysms of wet, racking coughs. When he had once more composed himself, he continued. "You cannot, because it is a vile truth. Were it not necessary for you to continue the Thorne line, I would call you no daughter of mine. You have disgraced me and you have disgraced this house, and for naught. Whatever craft the medium promised, whatever pretty lies the contractor's son put in your head, the Spirit Collection cannot and will never be banished."

He drew a deep, rattling breath and drove deep the final nail.

"You are henceforth forbidden to leave Thorne Hall, nor are you to have any visitors, until the day of my death, when the Collection shall pass to you."

"Do not do this," Elegy whispered. "Please do not do this."

"It is done."

A wild, guttural sound tore from Fletcher's throat. Her bare feet slapping upon the gleaming wood, she flew up the stairs until she reached Thaddeus, whereupon she reared her head back and spat at him, her chest and shoulders heaving in her rage.

Thaddeus calmly took a handkerchief from the breast pocket of his pajamas, then, with the slightest tilt of his head, set Gideon upon her. With a gleeful smile he lunged, shoving Fletcher so hard she tumbled backward down the stairs, landing in a heap at The Mourning's feet.

"Fletcher!" Elegy cried, falling to her knees beside her groaning stepmother. She'd struck her head on the way down, and blood streamed down her face and pooled in the wild tangle of her hair.

"I've given the Griswolds and the rest of the staff leave until after Samhain," Thaddeus said. "Until that time, you shall ensure the Collection serves us in their place. Now see to your stepmother. She appears to have taken quite a tumble."

Leaning heavily upon Gideon's arm, her father turned and, without a backward glance, heaved himself up the stairs.

Fletcher was not a short woman, nor was she insubstantial the way Elegy was. It took a great deal of effort to drag her to the hearth and prop her in one of the chairs, where she slumped with her fingers pressed to her bleeding temple while Elegy fetched a warm, wet cloth from the butler's pantry as well as the small first aid kit Lucy kept in the kitchen.

"Is it true?" Fletcher asked as Elegy wiped away the blood, revealing a cut that was not so very deep that it required any sort of care other than what she herself could provide.

"Is what true?"

"Were you really going to try to banish them?"

"Yes."

Fletcher winced as Elegy applied antiseptic to the wound. "You sneaky little shit, why didn't you tell me?"

"The Collection delights in your torment. I could not risk it."

"Well, now the cat's out of the bag, you might as well tell me."

She could have, particularly now that there was not the smallest hope of their plan succeeding, and yet the words simply would not come. She cast her gaze to the bloodied cloth in her lap and pressed her lips together.

"They can't guard every single door and window at once," said Fletcher softly. "There are sixteen of them, including your father, and far more ways out. You only need one."

Elegy lifted her head. "What are you suggesting?"

"I'm suggesting that once upon a time to spite your father, I took a sledgehammer to the wall separating my room and the room on the other side of it."

"Whatever for?"

Fletcher lifted her shoulder. "I was drunk, your father is an asshole, and I wanted a walk-in closet."

* * *

Two healthy doses of whiskey within her and a bandage upon her wound held in place by a silk garter, Fletcher retired to the attic to rest while Elegy instructed Delphine and Cook regarding the care of her father.

The Spirit Collection of Thorne Hall

Then she shut herself away in her office under the guise of having been properly chastised until the sky began to darken, during which time she did nothing but pace and fret and go over the plan she'd concocted with her stepmother until she was sick with fear and fraught with nerves.

Just outside the westernmost window of Fletcher's bedroom, which Elegy would access by means of the failed walk-in-closet attempt, was a ledge. And beyond it, a narrow metal ladder was built into the red brick beside the drainpipe. From there, she would walk the distance to Lenox in the pouring rain.

For the occasion, she donned trousers, a sturdy pair of Wellingtons, and Arthur Griswold's coat. If she was cunning and quick and willing to risk bodily harm, her plan just might work.

Or she'd be buried in the graveyard beside Sparrow. Really, it could go either way.

Through the shadows she stole until she reached the bedroom beside Fletcher's, where she softly rapped thrice upon the wall. As they'd planned, Fletcher burst from her room, shrieking at the top of her lungs. and although they'd agreed she should pretend at being drunk for the ruse to be convincing, Elegy suspected she'd taken a more method approach. She heard her stepmother stagger down the corridor toward the servants' rooms, stumbling into walls as she went, babbling nonsense. As predicted, Calliope was at once agitated to such a degree that she began banging her head against a nearby wall, while Reed fled into one of the moldering bathrooms.

It was not until Hester left her usual post at Fletcher's door to see what was the matter that Elegy plunged through the hole between the two rooms, pushing aside the tapestry on Fletcher's wall that had been covering the destruction, and darted toward the window.

Gripping the bottom rail, Elegy pushed upward with every ounce of strength in her woefully scrawny arms, but she managed only a few inches, the window being so unused to being opened.

Outside the door there was a great deal of commotion, and Elegy threw herself against the glass, straining and sweating, pulling and then pushing from below. She'd managed to open it just enough to fit herself through when a sick, fetid awareness washed over her, and she turned to see Gideon Constant step right through Fletcher's locked door. Although the runes there had been freshly painted, it was her father's will that prevailed above all else where the Spirit Collection was concerned. If Thaddeus had appointed them with a task, then neither rune nor any other craft might gainsay his command.

She thrust a shaking hand at him. "Go no further!"

But of course he did not heed her; her father had made certain of it.

He strode forward with a snarl upon his lips, reaching for her, reaching—

And then his body jerked and went utterly still before it was thrown violently backward. Elegy could only stand frozen, one leg upon the ground and the other out the window, and gape at her rescuer.

"Go," said Hester. "Go *now*."

Elegy did not hesitate.

Finding her footing on the ledge below, she pressed herself against the house as the rain soaked her hair and the wind whipped the wet strands across her face. She slid inch by inch away from the window and toward the ladder, but as she reached out to grip it, she felt a vicious tug upon Arthur Griswold's coat.

Gideon had thrust his arm through the open window and seized the hem of the woolen jacket, evidently having subdued Hester. It would be a bitter journey to Lenox without it, but she could not hope to pull free of his grip without slipping from the ledge to her great injury or death. Shrugging her shoulders, she pulled her arms free and lunged for the ladder just as Gideon fell back into the manor with a shriek of rage.

She was a soaking, shivering mess by the time she reached the ladder, descended gracelessly, slipped several feet above the ground, and landed in an undignified heap upon the grass. She might've stayed there, laughing and rolling about like a lunatic, had she not so very far to walk. She came to her hands and knees, then to her feet, and thus her journey began.

CHAPTER TWENTY-NINE

There were many ancient songs suited for a long walk through the countryside, and had her lips not gone numb with cold, Elegy would have sung them all to pass the time.

Instead, she staggered like a drunk through the underbrush with nothing but the moon to guide her. It was a fickle thing, swallowed by mist and the grasping branches of trees who had given up their ghosts to the last bout of heavy rain. Their corpses made a slippery carpet of the forest floor, and more than once she slipped and found herself lying facedown, dazed and with a face streaked with mud. And each time, with scraped hands, she pushed herself to her feet and carried on.

Only when the lights of Lenox finally appeared on the horizon did she allow herself to cry, great fat tears of relief that blurred the streetlamps as she staggered toward the town center. With her sodden clothing, wild hair, and muddy face, she far more resembled some sort of swamp creature from a Victorian penny dreadful than she did a young woman, and so naturally she began to gather stares the way Jasper had ghosts. Lurching onto a side street, she pressed her body close to the cars parked along the curb until she found Oak Street. Two blocks west, a turn to the right, and there was the rented Victorian sitting cheerfully behind the little picket fence.

She dashed up the walkway and up the steps, and when she could not curl her cold, stiff fingers into a fist, she banged her palm upon the door. Footsteps echoed in the foyer, the door opened, and there he stood, wreathed in soft, golden light.

"My father knows everything," she managed to croak out. "I just thought you ought to know."

His handsome face began to distort, and her legs, which had carried her so admirably from Thorne Hall, finally gave out.

"Fuck," she thought she heard him say, and then she was weightless, her soaked, trembling body lifted into his arms and into the warmth of his house.

She was dimly aware of the sound of running water, of her wet clothing being peeled from her skin, and when he uttered a harsh expletive in a voice gone low, she knew he'd seen the bruises decorating her neck. While the room grew thick with steam, he carefully cleaned the mud from her face and hands, a difficult task as she'd begun to shake quite uncontrollably.

And when the cast-iron tub was at last filled, he lowered her shivering body in.

She promptly tried to fling herself right back out of it.

He'd mistakenly filled the tub with needles instead of water; there could be no other explanation for the excruciating pain that seized her limbs, thousands of sharp pinpricks that made her howl and thrash, but there was little strength left in her to fight him, not when he climbed into the tub behind her and pulled her back against his chest.

"It hurts," she wept.

"I know, sweetheart. I'm sorry. I'm so, so sorry."

He pressed his mouth to the crown of her head and murmured into her hair until the worst of it abated, until she grew soft and quiet in his arms, the warmth of the water no longer a foe but a cherished friend. When it grew tepid, Atticus pulled the plug and allowed some of it to drain before filling it anew, fresh steam curling up around them, and Elegy's whimpers at last gave way to words.

"How can we possibly hope to succeed now that my father is aware of our plans? The moment we set foot in that house tomorrow, he'll bring the Collection down upon us."

"You're not powerless against them."

She said quietly, "You saw the marks. And tonight, when I tried to escape, he would have pulled me back inside were it not for Hester."

"She disobeyed your father's command?"

"I suppose she must have. He got out of bed today—it must have left him weak."

"You're dear to her."

A small smile bloomed upon her lips. "And she to me. I used to call her my Night Mother. She looked after me as best she could when the staff was gone home."

"Maybe that's something to do with it. You have an easier time commanding the spirits you are closest to."

"But why should that be when my father commands them equally?"

"All I can say to that is that you are not your father."

When the pads of her fingers were well and truly wrinkled and she'd nearly fallen asleep, he dried her gently with a towel and dressed her in one of his white undershirts, the fabric worn and soft and absolutely saturated with his scent. While she sat at the edge of his bed combing the tangles from her black hair, he brought her three fingers of whiskey and made her drink the whole thing. When it was done, he took the glass and helped her slide beneath the covers.

"Sleep," he murmured against her temple.

"No," she protested, but it was a very weak protestation indeed. Her eyelids had grown dreadfully heavy, and she could already feel the liquor softening her body as well as her senses. She was aware of him moving about the room, banking the fire in the little hearth across from the bed and drawing the curtains, and by the time he'd closed the door, she'd surrendered to the blessed black of sleep.

* * *

Elegy woke to the sound of male voices murmuring low.

She'd no idea of the time nor how long she'd slept; the fire was little more than a bed of shimmering coals, and outside the window was a miasma of late-afternoon fog, but she felt a great deal more herself than she had when she'd turned up on Atticus's doorstep: wretched still, but warm and better rested. Folded upon a nearby chair were a pair of sleep pants that were so comically large that she had to roll the legs up several times and knot the waist; then she set off in search of the voices.

She discovered Atticus and Dorian in the sitting room, hunched over the sketch of the runes she'd last seen at his cottage, two empty coffee mugs beside it. She cleared her throat, and they lifted their heads.

Atticus was off the couch in an instant. "You should be in bed."

"I am well," she assured him. "And how can you expect me to sleep when you are here plotting?"

Dorian had risen respectfully upon her appearance, despite the fact that she was wearing men's pajamas with nothing at all beneath them. The mistress of Thorne Hall had, it appeared, had sunk very low indeed.

"Atticus told me what he could of what befell you last night," he said. "But I would hear more, if you are able."

"I am able."

Wrapped in a blanket, she sat in her favorite chair with her knees drawn tight to her chest and told them everything from her waking to an empty house to her desperate flight in the rain. There was anguish upon their faces, and rage and guilt as well, and she was glad when it was finished and they might move forward.

"In conclusion," she said. "I believe we are well and truly fucked."

Atticus managed a huff of rueful laughter. "Look at you, cursing."

"I do endeavor to impress."

"And I do not believe all hope is lost," said Dorian.

"I appreciate your optimism, but even if I could persuade certain spirits in the Collection to act against the others, there is the matter of my father."

"The craft may yet be managed. We still have time. There is a man who mentored me upon certain aspects of death craft when I first came to Thorne Hall to instruct Tabitha. He lives an hour away in Lowood, so I should not be long."

"And what am I to do in the meantime?"

"Speak with your friend Hugo, if you can, but do not under any circumstances return to the house. It was with extraordinary luck that you were able to escape. I fear it will not happen a second time."

A shaky laugh escaped her. "In truth, I wish I never had to set foot in that house again. Watching him like that, conspiring with Gideon against me . . . that was far more terrifying than any of them have ever been before."

Dorian rose. "With luck, the next time will be the last time. Get some rest if you can—it will be a long night."

At that moment Elegy's traitorous stomach reminded her that she'd eaten nothing since Hugo's disastrous visit to Thorne Hall, grumbling loud enough to wake the dead, should there happen to be any nearby.

"Sounds like I need to feed you first," Atticus said with a grin.

Once Dorian had departed, Elegy sat perched upon the counter of Atticus's kitchen singing "The Gardener Child" while he prepared grilled cheese sandwiches. They ate on the floor of the sitting room in front of the fire, and after she'd polished off her own sandwich and half of his, she lay down with her head in his lap and his fingers combing gently through her hair until it was soft and gleaming, tendrils of ink uncorked and spilled over them both.

The Spirit Collection of Thorne Hall

Eventually she grew hungry again in an altogether different way and pulled his mouth down upon her own ravenous one.

"You should rest," he murmured.

"I'm not tired."

"I can think of a few ways to fix that."

He carried her back up the stairs as night fell outside the stained-glass window on the landing, and for the very first time in her life, Elegy did not notice. There did not come the sick plummet of her stomach, the skittering of ice across her skin; her teeth did not worry her lip and her mind did not begin to race with awareness, a catalog of the spirits' faces and intentions as they slid from the shadows in which they'd drowsed, languidly stretching as they contemplated how best to whittle away the lonely hours while the house was abed.

The Collection was far away, and she would not allow herself, allow this moment, to be tainted by them.

She kissed him, slow and languid and with nothing else upon her mind but the scent of his skin and the feel of it beneath her fingertips, the taste of it upon her tongue.

When he laid her down upon the rumpled sheets of his bed, she reached to pull him down with her, but to her very great surprise he stayed her hands. Instead, his long body stretched out beside her small, pale one, and gently guiding her hips, he pulled her over him. At first, she blinked in confusion, but he tugged his shirt over her head and tossed it to the floor before he spread his hands across her back and pressed her down, sliding his mouth over hers until she was gasping and shaking with want, rocking shamelessly against him because nothing had ever felt so wonderful nor fit her quite so perfectly as he.

If they failed tomorrow and one day many years from now she became the mad woman in the attic, she wanted to remember what it felt like to love someone to madness, to feel as precious in his hands as the firelight that bathed their skin in gold, and so she took him into her body slowly, and to her collection of him, to his scent and smile and laughter, she added the hitch in his breath as awkward fumbling gave way to the smooth rolling of her hips; the way his large, capable hands spanned her back as he knelt and brought her with him; the brush of that stupid thumb of his upon her lips before he kissed her slow and sweet.

And most of all, the way he looked at her after, awed and grateful and thoroughly undone; her mirror.

* * *

Elegy had been asleep only a few hours before Atticus pressed his mouth upon her shoulder and told her in a roughened voice to stay, that he had an early-morning meeting and that she should continue to rest.

Despite her determination to sleep only an hour more, it was far into the dull, gray Samhain afternoon when she finally woke again, the tea Atticus had prepared and left at her bedside table gone woefully cold and the fire in the hearth reduced to embers.

In the bathroom he'd set out her pink lounge set and, beside it, a toothbrush still in its package as well as an assortment of unfamiliar toiletries. She picked them up one by one, examining the labels and inhaling the scent of each before taking in after her haggard appearance. Once she was somewhat presentable, she padded barefoot down the stairs in search of Atticus.

She found him in the sitting room on a video call, half a dozen men and women staring back at him through the screen of his laptop. Terrified even to be glimpsed for a moment, she flattened herself against the wall and made her way to the kitchen, where she set the kettle to heat upon the stove.

The raven had returned, and through the thick afternoon fog she watched him prance about on the fence post, cocking his head this way and that as he contemplated her through the window. She hoped his presence was not an ill omen; when it came to the Child ballads, it was the cock's crow that heralded the departure of any visiting spirits, while ravens tended to discuss amongst themselves whether it was in bad taste to feast upon the poor remains of abandoned knights.

She supposed it was too much to hope that Atticus's temporary neighbors kept chickens.

She was still thinking upon it when Atticus slid his arms around her waist and buried his face in the hair at the nape of her neck, inhaling deep.

"I should put you back in bed," he rumbled against her skin.

"Not unless you put yourself in it as well."

Groaning softly, he turned her to face him. "If I do that, I'll miss all my meetings, and then I won't be able to buy that house on the beach I want. The one with the garden."

"You never said your house on the beach had a garden."

"It won't unless you're there."

She went still in his arms, the implication of his words pulling her taut as though she were a puppet upon a string and he the unwitting master.

The Spirit Collection of Thorne Hall

"Fuck," he said low, and shook his head. "I'm sorry, I shouldn't have just said it like that. We haven't talked about what you want to do after all this is over."

"You want me to go with you?" she asked. "To Seattle?"

"Only if that is what you want."

She scowled. "Well, that is exceedingly vague. I do not care for it."

"You've been told what to do your entire life. I won't do the same."

"I've a confession to make," she said with a guilty squirm. "The last time we were at Dorian's cottage, I overheard you say something very similar."

"Eavesdropping, were you?"

"I did not mean to, but I am very glad that I did, else I would not have also heard you say that you love me."

"I hope you know that's why I won't make the choice for you."

"I know. And I love you all the more for it."

A slow, sweet smile spread across his face. "Say it again."

"No."

"Why not?"

"Because you've not said it to me at all."

The warmth of his laughter spread through her veins like whiskey, and just as it had done on the very first day she'd heard it, her heart gamboled about in her chest. She rather hoped it always would.

"I love you, Elegy; you can't imagine how much."

"I'm possessed of rather a keen imagination."

"You are the very last thing I ever expected to find out here, but I'm so glad I did."

She looked up at him hopefully. "Ghosts and all?"

"Ghosts and all."

He framed her face and slanted his lips against hers once, twice, until she sighed and parted her own, the kiss slow and languid and entirely unhurried. It was, therefore, quite vexing when the doorbell chimed.

"Perhaps it is Dorian," she ventured.

It was not the medium who stood upon Atticus's doorstep, but Floss, and she was not alone. Beside her stood Hugo, looking as solemn and contrite as she'd ever seen him, despite his vulgar orange suit and purple brocade waistcoat.

Atticus rested a hand upon her lower back. "Take the sitting room. I'll be upstairs."

He kissed her forehead and shoed her toward her friends.

Hugo and Floss sat side by side upon the couch, and Elegy sat across from them.

Hugo cleared his throat. "We went to Thorne Hall, but no one answered the door and the phone lines are disconnected."

"How did you know where to find me?"

"Where else would you go?" he answered, and his oft-lively eyes were dulled and brimming with remorse. "Elegy, I—"

She held up one hand. "Before another word is spoken, you should know that my father discovered our plans and forbade me from leaving the house until after his death. To that end, he turned the Collection against me and sent the Griswolds as well as the rest of our staff away until after Samhain. I escaped with great difficulty."

"Well, fuck."

"Indeed."

"So, if he's so intent on having you there, why hasn't Thaddeus sent someone to bring you back?" asked Floss.

"Because he knows I will come back on my own."

"You're still going through with it, then?"

"I am."

They exchanged a look between them, and at Floss's encouraging nod, Hugo took a deep breath.

"Okay, here goes. I'm so, so sorry, Elegy."

"Hugo—"

"No, wait, let me say this." He looked as though he might be sick. "Ever since my parents, well . . . found out about me, about who I am, I've been a disappointment. My mom even told me once when she was drunk that she wished they'd been able to have another kid so they'd have someone else to leave it all to. I'd always known Brightleigh meant more to them than I did, but hearing her say it out loud . . ."

He shook his copper curls as if the action might rid him of such festering notions, but Elegy knew full well that once they'd taken root, they would stay with him always, just as they had with her.

"I was never going to mean anything to them if I couldn't continue their legacy, and neither were you to Thaddeus, so I never bothered to question whether the Collection could be banished, because I thought it would work out in my favor. But then I'd be just like them, with another kid who had to grow up with ghosts."

"It wasn't easy for either of us."

"It was for you. You refused to be your father, and the second a chance came to give up the ghost, so to speak, you didn't hesitate."

"Oh, I assure you I did."

"For the right reasons, El," he admonished gently. "Before Atticus came along, you had no choice. You've *never* had a choice. But I did, and I chose to accept my life because I'm a coward and it was easier to just go along with tradition, just another thing for our kind to inherit from our parents."

"We've inherited so much more from them than ghosts," she said.

"Haven't we just," Hugo agreed. "But we don't have to keep passing it down. I don't want to be my parents."

"Nor I." Hope unfurled within her, fresh and raw, but she would not nurture it, not when it might be snatched away as soon as it was offered. "And what of all you will lose?"

"Brightleigh? I don't care, and fuck my inheritance too, or what's left of it, anyway. Fuck all of it, because it's shit without him. Seb and I had a little chat, and it turns out the idiot never cared about my money. He really does just love me. *Me*, none of the rest of it. Can you imagine that?"

"I can," said Elegy upon a tremulous smile. "I love you the same."

Floss reached out and gripped his hand. "So do I."

"You deserve better, El," said Hugo. "And the only way you're going to get it is if we fuck up some ghosts. So let's do it."

Elegy's breath hitched. "Are you certain? Everything is different now. I cannot guarantee your safety should you set one foot in that house tonight."

"You both know I'm craven in the face of the most minor of inconveniences, so I can't promise not to shit myself if one of them comes at me, but I'll do my best."

Floss sighed. "Are you sure we can't just burn the whole thing down?"

"I'm afraid not."

"Fucking up ghosts it is."

A throat cleared at the threshold of the room, and Elegy looked to where Atticus stood with his arms folded across his chest.

"Oh, it's you," said Hugo dispassionately.

Elegy shot him a glare. "Be nice."

"How can I when he's going to take you away from us and give you a disgustingly wonderful life full of fat, green-eyed babies?"

Elegy's cheeks flamed. "You're getting rather ahead of yourself. First we must banish the Collection."

"To that end," said Atticus, "Dorian is on his way back from Lowood, so I suggest we get ready to do just that."

CHAPTER THIRTY

In Elegy's absence, Thorne Hall had succumbed to weariness and despair. Spine bowing under the weight of its terrible burden, its carcass loomed in the dark and bitter cold, no fit place now for any living thing. Red bricks once held fast by neat and tidy mortar had crumbled, covered now by ivy left to run amok, and those panes of glass still stubbornly clinging to their lead frames bore such thick layers of dust that no one could hope to see in nor out.

Within, every light had been extinguished, the shadows remained still, and the chimneys were barren of smoke.

Thorne Hall's message was clear: no one was to be welcomed nor tolerated within.

Beneath the porte cochere, Elegy stared at the front doors but could not convince her feet to carry her forward, however comfortable they were in a pair of shearling boots Floss had purchased for her at a boutique in town. In fact, every stitch upon her person was new. The black crepe set she'd worn during her sodden flight had disintegrated when Atticus attempted to clean it, to say nothing of its impracticality. When she'd come down the stairs in a pair of jeans, a thick gray turtleneck sweater, and a black wool pea coat with a flared skirt, her hair tumbling around her face and down to the small of her back, his grin was as wide and as beautiful as she'd ever seen it.

The Spirit Collection of Thorne Hall

At her side, Dorian carried in his arms a simple wooden box upon which he'd carved all manner of runes, some familiar to Elegy's eyes, far more not, and within lay the tenets of the canny arts the medium had carefully, reverently chosen to anchor the craft.

The soil had come from Sparrow's grave, newly turned, to be borne by Floss, who had always nurtured Elegy's spirit even from afar.

For bones, the twenty-seven that made up Sparrow's hand had been cleansed and placed in a pouch of softest deerskin, and although Hugo made a terrible fuss at the general unpleasantness, he and Elegy had for many years been bound by the mistakes of their forebears, men and women whose bones lay in gilded tombs, indifferent to their sins and those who must suffer the consequences of them. It was right that he should bear them now.

Rather than desecrate the stone in the graveyard carved with Sparrow's namesake, the box that had housed Willie Abner's journal was to serve as the third tenet, anchored by Atticus, whose love was new but steadfast and certain; as solid a thing as Elegy had ever known in a life spun from shadow.

When Dorian had asked permission to lift Sparrow from the ground the week before when their plans were only just beginning to take shape, she'd confessed to more than a modicum of surprise. Would it not be more effective to exhume Jasper himself, in whose name the Spirit Collection had been bound?

Even if they managed to breach the marble sepulcher that held his remains, it was Sparrow's craft that had summoned them, he had replied, and she'd thought little of it save that he could not seem to meet her gaze during the telling of it.

Elegy and Dorian would share the burden of song, and as for the final tenet . . . the knife with its hilt of bone, passed down through generations of Dorian's family, was a heavy weight in her pocket.

She'd spent many hours ruminating upon the hundreds of ancient melodies that, with her canny gift, she had used to soothe the Collection before she knew what canny was.

In the end, she knew it could be none but "The Unquiet Grave," for the Collection were not the only dead things that would be laid to rest that night should they succeed.

Their hunger, their desperate, insatiable hunger, had kept the song from her lips since that terrible night, but that same hunger had grown within her such that she could no longer deny it; they were the same, she and the Collection, and sought the same end.

If the craft served its purpose, if they banished the Spirit Collection that night, she would never have to sing it again.

"Stay close to me," she said. "Whatever you see, stay close to me."

Her fingertips had barely brushed the handle when the door swung open with a sigh, enveloping her at once in cold, fetid air thick with age and sorrow and the bitter tang of anger.

It was as if no one had set foot in the house since the day it was raised, and Delilah's estate had been left to fester and fall into ruin. Whatever craft it was that had kept the wolves of time at bay was spent at last, and now they'd come to prey.

Tentatively, Elegy took one step inside the foyer, and another, and another until she stood at the bottom of the great staircase. A dark stain marked the place where Fletcher's head had struck the floor, but there was no further sign of her stepmother nor anyone else, the house alone drawing breath and exhaling it again in gusting moans rank with the stench of discord.

"My stepmother—" she said, but Dorian's hand upon her arm prevented her from ascending the stairs.

"There is no time."

He was right, of course; the fact they'd not been set upon immediately upon entering the house was welcome if highly suspicious. Steeling her resolve, Elegy pressed on with her friends at her back, sidestepping places where the floor had succumbed to rot. They made it as far as the hearth before the stale air shifted, the hairs standing up on the back of her neck and along her arms.

One moment they were alone, and the next, in the space of a breath, the blink of an eye, they were surrounded by the Spirit Collection.

All save one, and it wasn't Amos.

The summons from the master of Thorne Hall he'd obeyed, but why had Gideon refused?

And how?

Elegy's spine went taut, for she knew all too well how fresh fear fed the Collection. It was why she had refused to allow Dorian's fellow mediums to join them that night despite their protestations; they were strangers, the Collection's reaction to them an unknown, and because she could guarantee their safety even less than that of those who walked alongside her, she had insisted.

Vehemently.

The Spirit Collection of Thorne Hall

Now she turned and, sure enough, the spirits were stealing forward from the darkest corners with what remained of their fingers greedily outstretched and blackened lips pulled back from bared teeth.

Floss looked as though she were about to be sick all over the fine Persian rug, and Hugo had taken several large steps backward. Even Atticus, who had seen them under far more unpleasant circumstances, did not look at all as resolute as he had only a moment ago.

"Look at me," she commanded them softly. "Look *only* at me."

The moment stretched impossibly thin while she pleaded with them to trust her with naught but her eyes, until at last their attention was fixed upon her, however much it sickened them to turn from imminent danger.

"Now, keep your eyes on me," she murmured. Then she turned to the Collection. "Leave them be and let us pass. I've business tonight in the ballroom, and if you cross me, I shall not be kind. Nor shall I forget it when my father has passed and I am master here."

And when, after only a moment of mulish hesitation, they retreated into the shadows once more, she gave a crisp nod of satisfaction. "Good. Let's go."

Through the great hall and down the corridor, the passage of the living was marked by the spirits' milky-white, sunken eyes, but they did not attempt to touch anyone again. A small mercy, that, for the worst was yet to come.

Sitting in a puddle of crimson taffeta with her back against the ballroom door was Fletcher. Her eyes were closed, her head tipped back, and in her lap was a rusted axe.

"Where on earth did you get that?" asked Elegy.

"Hello to you too. And I stole this from the carriage house the day your father introduced me to the Collection."

"Axes don't really work on them, I'm afraid."

Fletcher's mouth split into a grim smile. "It's not for them."

"Maiming only," Elegy said, as Fletcher rose and bundled her into a terribly awkward hug, what with the enormous sleeves of the Worth ball gown, to say nothing of the axe slung over her shoulder.

"Meeting the end in style, eh, Fletcher?" said Hugo with a pained laugh, his complexion gone quite gray beneath his freckles.

"It won't be *my* end."

"That's the spirit," murmured Elegy, as she stepped to the door and set her hands against it gently. "I cannot feel him beyond, and he was not with the others, so he must be here."

"Hold him as long as you can," said Dorian, who knew exactly of whom she spoke. "We will endeavor to be quick."

Atticus stepped to her side, brushed his lips upon her temple, then took hold of both handles and pulled the heavy doors open.

The vast room was dark, bitterly cold, and utterly empty.

"I do not understand," she spoke to the shadows. "He should be here."

"Personally, I'm thrilled he's not," said Hugo.

"But he should be here—"

"Let's not look a gift horse in the mouth, yeah?" Floss said upon a grimace.

"I am inclined to agree with your friend," Dorian said. "The more time we have before your attention will be diverted from the craft, the better."

But Elegy could not quell the unease unfurling within her and upon several occasions was forced to wipe away a smudge of white gone astray. The electrical lights appeared to be in the same sorry state as the phone lines, and so it was by candle that they painted the runes to Dorian's exact specifications, and even after they had finished and wiped their hands clean, Gideon Constant still had not come.

"Something is wrong," she murmured to Dorian as they lifted the lid of the wooden box and withdrew the gifts of Sparrow's grave.

"I feel it too," he answered. "That Thaddeus has allowed us to proceed this far does not bode well."

A wave of guilt swelled and dragged her under. "I never should have allowed any of you to come here."

"We came in full possession of our faculties," he reminded her gently.

To Floss he passed the bag of soil, to Atticus the box of stone, and, with a shudder of revulsion, Hugo took the pouch that held the bones of Sparrow's hand. They took their places with Elegy at the head of the circle. Slowly she knelt, and her eyes were drawn to the knife Dorian had given her. She would know when to use it, he'd said; she'd know when the craft would require her blood, and she must not hesitate to give it.

"Now then," said Dorian. "Shall we begin?"

The clasp of her throat was so tight it strangled the first few words of her song, for she was both the dead come to beg for rest and the one determined to give it, and the ancient melody was the means by which she might achieve both.

The wind doth blow today, my love
And a few small drops of rain

The Spirit Collection of Thorne Hall

I never had but one true love
In cold clay he was lain
I'll do as much for my true love as any young lady may
I'll sit and mourn all at his grave
For twelvemonth and a day

Dorian's voice joined hers, his rich baritone the perfect counterpoint to the clear timbre of her own, and together they wove the craft.

At first, she felt nothing but the peace that always accompanied the singing of the old songs, a mantle settling about her shoulders, warm as a tear and soft as a sigh. But as she began the second verse, a peculiar prickle began behind her breastbone and grew as she sang of lips of clay and breath putrefied by death and decay, and it swelled until her skin could not contain it. Carried by the song, it flowed from her, through the runes, through bone and earth and stone, and through those who bore them.

"Do you feel that?" hissed Hugo, and he very nearly dropped Sparrow's bones. "What *is* that?"

"I feel it, too," answered Floss. "I think it's canny."

Their voices blurred and faded as she sang until all she knew was the craft she and Dorian wove, a question asked by the dead through her song and a promise given by the canny they both shared.

It was not the first time they'd sung together. Over the last two days, Dorian had insisted upon practicing endlessly once she'd decided upon "The Unquiet Grave," testing this harmony and that and consulting seemingly endless variations upon the same ballad so as to choose that which best suited the melody, the task.

How different the act of it felt this time; how peculiar! Her bone and sinew and muscle were become staves both treble and bass, and with her canny she wrote craft upon them: notes and rests written in the ink of her blood and sung upon the breath in her lungs. And through it all, those who were to her no different than kin gave freely of their strength as her canny threaded through and bound them all together.

She'd not summoned them, but the Spirit Collection came all the same, helplessly drawn to her song, to the craft, and because they knew.

It was time.

"Hold fast," Dorian told the others, for he'd felt it too. "She needs you now."

The knife was heavier now than when she'd taken it up, and a shudder racked her body as she lay the blade against the delicate skin of her wrist.

She did not hesitate.

The cut was deep enough to yield that which was required for the craft and shallow enough that she would not bleed out all over the ballroom floor, yet she was forced to take hold of her wrist, squeezing tight until rivers of crimson spilled over her pale skin and dripped upon the runes.

Where they fell, the floor began to blacken and smoke, exactly the way Willie Abner had described it in his journals, and Elegy sang with renewed fervor, each word fairly saturated with the canny that had always flowed through her veins even when she'd not known what name to give it, nor that it was something that *could* be named.

> *You crave one kiss from my clay-cold lips*
> *But my breath is earthy strong*
> *Had you one kiss from my clay-cold lips*
> *Your time would not be long*

The rest of the verse was lost in the groan of hinges and wood as the doors of the ballroom were forced open, gutting all save the most resilient candles at the fringes of the banishing circle. And into the last of their golden light stepped the very last person Elegy expected to see.

It was her father, and yet it was not.

Something shifted beneath the sallow skin and feeble bones, moving with him—no, not with him, *for* him, compelling his legs to walk and his torso to remain upright, setting his hand upon his cane and holding it fast.

Her father had not simply allowed Gideon to touch him; no, he had allowed the first and foulest of the Collection to pour himself into the feeble remains of his body and wear him as an ill-fitting suit. It was the very deepest of blasphemes, one she would never have believed her father capable of, were it not for the promise she now knew governed his every thought and deed.

Raising the axe, Fletcher stepped between him and the banishing circle, teeth bared in a snarl. "That's close enough, *dear*."

"Get of our way," the father who was not her father rasped, and it was both his voice and Gideon's that thundered. "And we shall spare you."

Fletcher threw back her head with a bark of laughter. "You haven't spared me a day in your life."

"You cannot kill us."

"Doesn't mean I can't hurt you a little. How many limbs do you think would be payment enough for thirteen years spent in an attic?"

The Spirit Collection of Thorne Hall

Gideon lurched forward, dragging the husk of Thaddeus with him, and Fletcher's fingers tightened upon the handle of the axe.

"That's enough!" Elegy stood, blood sluicing down her hand and dripping from the tips of her fingers. "Good evening, Father. Or is it Gideon to whom I speak?"

Thaddeus was so unused to smiling that when Gideon forced his thin, unyielding mouth to stretch into some semblance of one, it was with great difficulty, the result a hideous approximation of mirth.

Then the spirit exited Thaddeus's bones and blood and sinew as though he were descending from a carriage, and once they were free of one another, Thaddeus fell upon his cane with a groan while Gideon strode forward to meet her.

"Good evening, Elegy," he said, the very soul of amiability. "Your father wished to attend your little shindig tonight, but he was far too frail to descend the stairs, and so I helped him."

"How generous of you."

"I am nothing if not generous."

Elegy looked past him at her father, diminished further still without Gideon, a puppet without a master. He was not breathing at all well, the sound wet and rasping and with laborious effort.

"Traitorous child," he gasped. "No child of mine."

"It is time to let them go, Father," she said. "Let us all go."

"The promise must be kept," he hissed, spittle flying from his lips.

She shook her head. "It was Jasper who made the promise, not you."

"The Spirit Collection must always remain at Thorne Hall. And there must always be a master to command them."

It was then that Elegy saw the gun.

The Colt revolver had belonged to Jasper himself and had been well maintained enough throughout the years to still be a danger. And Elegy, stupid, *stupid* Elegy, did not realize his intentions until it was too late.

Until Thaddeus lifted the revolver and pressed the barrel against his shriveled temple.

Until he pulled the trigger.

"*No!*"

Her horrified cry was swallowed by the explosion of gunpowder and the decimation of her father's skull.

His body plummeted to the floor, limbs twitching once, twice, then going still as the blood pooled and spread beneath him.

And thus the Spirit Collection passed to her.

CHAPTER THIRTY-ONE

The day Elegy fainted at the sight of Amos's face (or lack thereof), it was Thaddeus himself who had carried her limp little body upstairs, and when she woke, groggy and disoriented some hours later, he was still there, folded into the rickety chair at her desk.

She'd thought him a dream at first until he rose at the sight of her sluggishly blinking eyes and came to loom over her bed like some kind of gargoyle peering down in pitiless judgment from the roof of a Gothic cathedral.

"Father," she croaked, for she was forbidden from calling him anything softer.

"I think perhaps you were not yet ready to see Amos." It was the closest approximation to an apology she'd ever known him to give.

"He frightened me."

"You will become accustomed to him. With time, and with skill."

He turned toward the door, and still quite shaken from her ordeal and not wishing to be alone even if the company *was* her father, she blurted out, "What will it feel like?"

"What will what feel like?"

"When the Collection passes to me?"

His face pinched in distaste, as it so often did when he was reminded that he'd no heir but she, but he lowered himself back into the chair nonetheless. "I asked my father the very same thing when I was near your age, and I shall tell you what he told me. Before, there is awareness of them, and commands given by word or thought. After, they cease to be separate entities and become an extension of yourself. Your eyes, your ears, even your hands when needs must. You will keep no secrets from them, nor will they from you, but you'll share your lives more intimately than any friend or lover. You will be as one."

But as Elegy stood inside a circle of runes with her blood dripping sluggishly from her fingertips and looked upon the corpse of her father, she felt no different than she had before he'd pulled the trigger and could not account for it at all.

Neither could Gideon, who stared at her with his gray eyes narrowed.

"I don't understand," she said. "You're meant to be a part of me now, but you feel exactly as you always have. With his death you should have passed to me—why did it not work?"

"Because you are not a Thorne."

It was Dorian who had spoken, and Elegy turned to regard him with as much consternation as Gideon did her.

"What do you mean? Of course I'm a Thorne."

"Elegy—" he began, and the rest was lost as he crumpled to the floor.

Heedless of her father, of Gideon and the rest of the Collection, she rushed to his side, reaching him at the very same moment that Atticus did. He lifted the medium beneath his arms, and Elegy's heart lurched behind her ribs as she took in the shocking pallor of his face, his shallow, labored breathing.

"Dorian, what's happened—what's wrong?"

And then Atticus lifted his hand, and Elegy stilled at the sight of so much blood.

Blood that was not hers.

With shaking fingers, she pushed up the sleeve of Dorian's shirt. The cut he'd made was far deeper than hers, the sort he'd told her not to make; the sort that led to bleeding out, and it was not the only one. His other wrist had been similarly cut and, where the blood fell, the runes had turned black, a growing stain at the center of their banishing circle.

Hugo's gasp cut through the muffled ringing in her ears as Floss slapped both hands over her mouth, eyes impossibly wide.

"Oh, Dorian," Elegy breathed. "What have you done?"

His eyelids fluttered, and the clear gray of his gaze met her own. "You look like your mother," he said, lifting a bloodied fingertip and gently tracing the curve of her cheek. "Except for your eyes. You have my eyes. Sparrow's eyes. And Gideon's eyes, Hester's, Calliope's . . ."

Her strange gray eyes, pale and clear and too large for her face. How had she not seen it before? They were not Thaddeus's eyes, nor were they her mother's.

And the Spirit Collection had not passed to her.

"I am not a Thorne," she said.

"You are not."

"You and my mother."

"Yes."

She closed her eyes, forcing the tears that had gathered there to spill down her cheeks.

"How long have you known?"

"I thought it possible the day I came to teach you the runes, when I saw you for the first time and saw your eyes," said he. "But I knew for certain the day you visited me in the woods."

"Why did you not tell me?"

He closed his eyes, and she could not be sure whether it was the pain of her inquiry or his injuries that rippled over his features. "Forgive me. Elegy, we've not much time."

Dorian's blood-soaked fingers reached into his pocket and withdrew a sheath of papers with edges torn and pressed them into her hands. Elegy recognized them at once: the missing pages from Willie Abner's journal. "You took them that night in the forest."

"I am sorry to have kept it from you, but I needed to know for sure. And once I found out, I could not allow you to go through with it. I have failed you enough."

"I do not understand—"

"Read them," he said. "And you will."

October 31, 1910

Sparrow was dying.

At Jasper's frantic demand, Willie had sent for the village doctor, a pompous old fool who would not take kindly to being roused from his bed on such a frigid night, the coldest Lenox had seen since that fateful one eight years ago when first Willie had come to Thorne Hall.

But Willie knew there was nothing to be done. This time she'd cut her wrists far too deep and allowed far too much blood to blacken the runes.

The Spirit Collection of Thorne Hall

She lay now in Jasper's arms, watching the spreading stain with gray eyes beginning to dim, and yet there was a smile on her face, peaceful and soft.

Fourteen spirits she had summoned in this manner, fourteen spirits she had bound to Jasper and to his house and his name over and over again, but none were the one she'd sought; none were him.

"I know what I must do," she'd murmured as she'd drawn the runes upon the ballroom floor that night. "You understand, Willie, don't you? You know what I must do?"

"I wish you wouldn't," he answered.

"My thoughtlessness took his life. And now he shall have it back, surrounded by family to care for him."

There had been no discernible pattern to those summoned at first, save that one or two had shared Sparrow's peculiar gray eyes. It had not been until Bancroft clapped eyes upon the newly summoned Vivian and flew into a rage at the aunt who had denied him her fortune in favor of two dogs that there arose the first suspicion of a connection between the spirits.

With his considerable resources, Jasper had then pieced together her family tree, the gnarled branches dotted here and there with the deceased that now roamed the halls of his home.

But although Sparrow could summon her long-dead kin, she could not summon her child.

A child she had lost when she and her sister came to the nearby wood to pick mushrooms. He'd wandered off, drawn by the glimmer of the late-afternoon sun upon the surface of the lake just beyond the tree line, and by the time his absence was marked, it was too late to bring him back as anything more than a shade.

And even then, she'd failed. Again and again, she'd failed, and the Spirit Collection grew with each passing Samhain, each passing Beltane.

When it came to her at last what she must do, she kept it from Jasper, for if he'd even an inkling of what she intended, he would've forbidden the summoning of any further spirits posthaste. Although truth be told, he should have done so long ago.

The once-proud titan had withered with the years and the weight of the spirits he bore, all for love of a woman who, many years ago, he'd glimpsed standing at the shore of the lake on his newly minted property. A woman who had bewitched him at first glance and embedded herself in his heart like his namesake, twisting so deep that to remove her would cost him his life.

J. Ann Thomas

Willie wondered now and again if 'twas Sparrow's canny that had ensnared him so completely, but he always dismissed the idea the moment it entered his head, for his mother had always believed that while canny could stir desire and cause infatuation, it could not force love. And what Jasper Thorne felt for Sparrow was indeed a great love, and a terrible one.

Sparrow's breathing grew very slow, and the master of Thorne Hall, brought low his head and rested it upon hers.

"I must go very soon," she murmured. "I hope he comes before I do, I so long to see him. You will care for him, won't you, Jasper?"

"I will," he answered, his voice rough and broken. "Damn you, Sparrow. *Damn you.*"

"Don't you see? This was the only way. A life for a life; there is no craft to rival it. That is why it never worked before. I took his life, and so I must give mine in return."

"His death was not of your making."

But Sparrow did not believe that, and Willie knew all too well what came of sincere belief. He'd seen it far too often in the eight years since he had come to work for Jasper, six of them as the youngest valet any house in the Berkshires had ever known, twenty-six years of age and already the master's closest confidant on account of the Spirit Collection.

His grandmother, thankfully, had not lived to see it.

It was not as terribly great a responsibility, managing Thorne Hall; no one came to visit anymore if they could help it. Oh, Jasper still had plenty of friends willing to overlook his indiscretions with Sparrow and make the journey to the Berkshires when the streets of New York and Boston had grown ripe and sweltering—he was, after all, still fabulously wealthy—but they became fewer and fewer. One need not be aware of the Collection to feel ill at ease among them; to feel desperately the need to escape.

Willie could only be thankful that, after tonight, there would be no more spirits to collect.

"He comes now," whispered Sparrow, and Willie's attention was brought back at once to the blackened hole that her blood had wrought. "Please let him come now."

A bloated little hand appeared and then another; a dripping wet head of sandy hair; arms and shoulders that pulled the body of a small boy up from the pit and onto the ballroom floor in a soaking, trembling heap.

The Spirit Collection of Thorne Hall

"Mama?"

"Reed," she breathed upon a smile. "Oh, my love."

The boy's darkened lips turned down as he examined his hands, looked farther down at his sodden clothing, at the ink-dark water and bracken that sluiced down his legs to pool at his feet.

"I remember a lake," said he. "I went into the water, didn't I, Mama?"

"Yes, my love."

"But I didn't come out."

"It doesn't matter, because you're here now."

Sparrow's pallor was now very much like that of her son, a sickly gray, and far too much time passed between breaths that were each a battle. Her son crept forward and knelt at her side, and he reached out tentatively with his bloated little hand and touched Sparrow's own.

"The Thornes will care for you now," she whispered, eyelids fluttering closed over the gray eyes she'd bequeathed to her son. "And your ancestors."

"But I don't want them—I want *you*," he replied. "Why can you not stay?"

"I am sorry, my love. I am so very sorry," said Sparrow with a voice grown small, she who had always exuded such life that it frightened Willie now to see her so diminished in his arms.

"Promise me, Jasper. Promise me that this will ever remain their home; *his* home. That your kin will keep them after I am gone."

"I swear it," Jasper said. "Upon my life, I swear it."

She continued to draw breath for several long minutes while Reed and Jasper and Willie kept silent vigil. At last her skin grew cold and stiff and her eyes could no longer see, and with an ugly, guttural cry torn from deep within his chest, the master of Thorne Hall gathered the husk of her into his arms.

Footsteps approached and there was Hester, her hand outstretched, beckoning gently to the bloated little ghost of Sparrow's son, the last spirit Jasper Thorne would ever collect.

Reed slipped his hand in hers, and she led him gently into the shadows.

CHAPTER THIRTY-TWO

Elegy's hand fell, and the final pages of Willie Abner's journal fluttered softly to the floor, coming to rest in a pool of Dorian's blood.

"It was love," she said, giving Atticus the answer he'd sought that day in the aspen grove when he wondered why a man would want to own the dead. "He did it for love, and she . . ."

"Grief is a terrible, corrosive thing," Dorian rasped. "It wasn't her fault he went into the water that day, but her sorrow grew so large that it swallowed her whole. All she could think of was to bring him back."

It wasn't her fault, Reed had said.

All this time, she'd thought he meant the Wife of Usher's Well.

Elegy lifted her head, her gaze resting upon the unwitting cause of so much suffering.

"Sparrow's son. Her ancestors. *Your* ancestors."

"And yours. You are canny and you share their blood, and so you hold dominion over them in your own way, but you are not a Thorne. They are not bound to you, and you could never have inherited them."

"It was meant to be me," she said, her eyes falling on the mess he'd made of his wrists. "I was supposed to banish them."

"To summon her son, Sparrow gave her life. To return him to rest demands the same, and I could not bear it. I have failed you time and time again, but I will not fail you again."

Elegy shook her head. "Dorian, *no*—"

"Finish the song, Elegy," he said. "And let them be at peace."

A sob tore from her throat. "But you'll die."

"And you shall live. *Live*, Elegy. Leave this place or stay; the choice is yours. Every choice for the rest of your life is yours. If this is what I have bought with my life, it was well worth it."

"No!" came a snarl from behind them.

Elegy lifted her head to see Gideon Constant striding across the ballroom toward the banishing circle, his face twisted in rage and something else that looked very much like fear.

"You cannot do this—I forbid it!"

Atticus sprang to his feet, Hugo and Floss upon his heels. But Elegy knew they had no power over him, could not touch or hinder him in the slightest.

But two enormous arms banded around him, and these Gideon could not escape. They lifted him clear off his feet and hauled him backward. Then Elegy saw the blackened flesh and the patches of raw, pulsing red beneath, and she realized that it was Amos.

Amos—who held Gideon fast in an ironclad grip.

Elegy could only guess at where his eyes had once been before the tragedy that took his life, although she guessed now they'd been the same color as Sparrow's, as her own; but she fixed her own upon the ruination of his face nonetheless and nodded.

"You've not much time," Dorian rasped. "Sing, Elegy, before the gift of my life is spent."

She threaded her fingers through his, the once-warm skin of his hand gone papery thin and cold, then she gently rested her forehead upon the crown of her father's head and began to sing.

Tis down in yonder garden green, love
Where we used to walk
The finest flower that e'er was seen
Is withered to a stalk
The stalk is withered dry, my love
So will our hearts decay
So make yourself content, my love
Till death calls you away

His lips moved, shaping the craft even though he'd no voice left with which to harmonize with her own. And when the last verse of "The Unquiet Grave" faded away into the gloom, Dorian took up the melody of "The True Lover's Farewell," and there was neither craft to be woven nor canny in his voice as he held fast to Elegy's hand with the last of his strength and looked up into her face with his gray eyes shining and clear.

> *The river never will run dry*
> *Nor the rocks melt with the sun*
> *And I'll never prove false to the one I love*
> *Till all the things be done, my dear*
> *Till all these things be done*

With the last word, his breath left his body upon a gentle sigh, and there was a smile upon his face.

Within Elegy's chest her heart cracked open, and from the wound poured a thing far greater than sorrow, and the taste of it was bitter with regret. Elegy folded her body around Dorian's and began to weep, her quiet sobs the only sound in the hushed stillness of the room.

"Elegy?"

She lifted her tearstained face to see Reed standing just beyond the banishing circle, staring at his bloated little hands; hands that were disintegrating into ash to be borne away upon the wind.

"Elegy," he said again, his voice the soft rustling of parchment. "What's happening?" Elegy let go of Dorian's cold hand and rose.

"It worked," Hugo breathed, letting the pouch containing Sparrow's bones fall from his shaking hands. "Holy shit, it worked."

She ought to have felt relief: that the sacrifice of the man who was her father had not been in vain, that the bravery of her friends was rewarded, that her life was now her own.

But instead she felt something rather closer to panic fluttering in her chest as she stared at the little boy before her.

As he'd done so many times before, he sought her songs, her arms. And neither now might comfort him, this boy who had lived and died and lived once more, even if it was only a half-life. It was a second death he faced now, and he was afraid.

"I don't want to go," he whimpered.

"It's all right," she said through trembling lips wet with salt. "It will be all right."

"Am I going to my mother?"

"Do you believe you are?"

He was nearly gone now, dust held together in the shape of a boy by the grace of his mother's canny.

The Spirit Collection of Thorne Hall

"Yes," he sighed.

"Then you are."

They were, it seemed, to return to death in the same order they'd been dragged from it.

Delphine followed Reed, and next was Nathan, who lifted a longing hand toward his beloved library before he was taken. As in all things, Eugenia and Mabel went together, arms firmly locked and matching grins upon their faces, gloriously defiant to the end.

As Amos's arms crumbled into ash, Gideon staggered from his hold and fell to his knees beside white paint and flickering candles. Elegy braced herself for his rage, for a desperate attempt to thwart the inevitable, for a curse or cruel word, but none came. Instead, he looked about him in bewilderment, at those who had gone, at those yet to depart, and she said nothing; did nothing.

So, Elegy allowed herself to look upon Amos in his final moments, Amos whom she had misunderstood more than any of them, who, in the end, had desired the same as she: peace. He lifted one hand in farewell, and Elegy lifted her own in answer, throat tight with so many words unspoken, realized too late.

The Mourning's veils disintegrated next, and Elegy caught a glimpse before she went of sunken cheeks and gaunt gray skin stretched too thin over the protruding bones of her face.

Cook was afraid, and so Bernard held her hand until the last of her had turned to dust. Then he looked upon the place where she had disappeared with his massive shoulders slumped until he too had gone.

Fear robbed Bancroft of all decorum. He threw himself headlong against the ballroom wall, clawing at it and begging Elegy to send him away, send him to some forgotten corner of the manor where the craft could not touch him, but he met the same fate as the rest, sent off with a nasty smile courtesy of his aunt, before she followed him to her own fate.

Elegy found she could not help but pity him in the end.

"I am so sorry, Elegy," said Adelaide when her turn came. "Forgive me. Please forgive me."

"Of course," Elegy managed around a throat gone swollen. "Of course I forgive you."

"I shall miss you."

"Oh, Adelaide!"

Her tears came fast, relentless in the face of so much loss, and she wondered how it was possible for someone to lose so much and yet live.

Perhaps she was not meant to. As Adelaide's sweet, round face turned to dust and Calliope began to sing, her heart was torn asunder.

It would mend, that much she knew, but it would never be entirely whole again, for there were pieces of it that would always be missing, taken by the Collection.

Calliope's fingers at last went still, and she reached out and gently touched them to Elegy's wet face, and as she disappeared, the sweetness of her song lingered upon the air:

And it's time that the living should part from the dead
So now, my love, I must away, away
So now, my love, I must away

And then Hester stood before her, and Elegy put her hands to her face and sobbed.

"It is a good, right thing you've done," Hester rasped. "A good, right thing."

"I don't know how," Elegy wept. "I don't know how to live without you all."

"You will learn."

Elegy clung to her Night Mother until there was nothing left of her to hold, until at last only he remained: the first to have been summoned and the last to depart.

In the face of true death, Gideon was much diminished. Gone was the malicious charm with which he'd ruled over the Collection and held her father's ear. In its place was a king upon his deathbed who watched his court fall one by one and knew himself to be next, crown or no.

Death came for all, and Gideon could not cheat him a second time.

He did not sneer nor curse her; he did not belittle her, and he did not plead. There was no cruelty in the way he gazed upon her, no mischief in his eyes, no smirk curling his lips.

Her tormenter had at last been stripped and laid bare.

He'd been the cause of so much misery, taken great delight in it, and yet she could not find it within her to do the same, for she was not her father; she was not a Thorne.

"Go in peace, Gideon Constant," she bid him. "Go in peace."

He bowed his head in surrender as a gentle wind took up what remained of him, of all of them.

Through the corridors of Thorne Hall they stole, past every corner and crevice and shadow they had occupied over so many long years, the

The Spirit Collection of Thorne Hall

great halls of a house that had become their prison. Their hold upon it now relinquished, its floors gleamed anew beneath pristine white plaster ceilings, the leaded panes bore nary a speck of dust, and neither was rot to be found upon the walls nor cobwebs in any of the corners. Damask curtains hung heavy and proud, and fixtures of brass and crystal flared and settled, bathing fine furnishings in a soft, golden glow.

The midnight bell tolled, and the Collection took their leave, rushing through wood and plaster and brick and glass to vanish upon a sigh beneath the glittering firmament of a cloudless night.

And within, the mistress of Thorne Hall knelt, weeping upon floors now indelibly stained, songs of mourning upon her lips.

EPILOGUE

Six years later

The little girl was covered in viscera.

Globs of stringy orange caked in the brown wisps of her hair, seeds plastered to her face and hands; Elegy had given her a spoon with which to scrape the innards from the pumpkin, but upon discovery of the delicious squelching sound the pulp made in her bare hands, it had been promptly discarded. It was far more enjoyable to make a glorious mess of herself and her general vicinity—Dorian, at nearly two years of age, was terribly fond of making messes. In this she was the anathema to Elegy as a child, as she was in every aspect but her eyes, she who had been born squalling, red faced and indignant, eager to greet the world and heralded by laughter.

Clad in matching overalls, mother and daughter sat upon the large front porch of a ranch-style house with cedar siding and stone accents, surrounded by hollowed-out gourds with intricately whittled faces, some jovial, others grotesque. It had taken hours to carve them, but the overall effect would be quite spectacular indeed, once they'd placed little flickering candles within to illuminate the many splendid eyes and noses and mouths.

Elegy studied the tall, thin pumpkin before her, newly carved, all sly eyes and smile full of teeth; Bancroft's leering face stared back.

The Spirit Collection of Thorne Hall

"Scary," declared Dorian with an adamant shake of her head that sent brown curls and stringy bits of pumpkin flying.

Well, that simply would not do.

A few swift cuts, and soon the loathsome spirit's likeness had only two teeth and a rather beaky nose far better resembling their neighbor Mr. Poots, who often visited the nursery to complain that Elegy had sold him faulty hydrangeas when, in fact, his frugal nature led him to deprive them of the water they so desperately needed. Hydrangeas were a hearty shrub, keen to thrive even in the rugged and rainy chill of the Pacific Northwest, but they required a great deal more than rainwater. After all, their name was literally derived from the Greek for "water vessel," which she had pointed out to him gently the last time he'd brought Polaroid photos of a sadly drooping Firelight.

"There, that's better, isn't it, love?"

Dorian thrust her chubby fist into a nearby pile of pumpkin innards and set a handful solemnly atop Mr. Poot's scowling face. "Better."

If one were to look closely, a great many of the pumpkins upon Elegy's porch might appear to resemble faces decidedly more human in nature than the usual triangle-eyed, gap-toothed sort: one had spectacles perched atop a sunken, skeletal nose; one was a profile half covered in lacy veils; two squat pumpkins sat side by side bearing matching Cheshire grins. She'd not bothered carving Amos's likeness, for Dorian would hardly know what to make of a pumpkin with its face caved in.

At the sound of tires upon the gravel drive, both Elegy and Dorian looked up.

A sleek, black electric Volvo slid into the driveway beside the truck painted with the sprig of blooming aster that was the logo of Seeds of Love, and her husband emerged, as tall and beautiful as the day she'd first laid eyes upon him at the bottom of the staircase of Thorne Hall. Dorian squealed and threw her pudgy arms above her head, her little fists clenching and unclenching as she reached for her father, and Elegy's heart swelled as it always did whenever the two of them were in each other's general vicinity.

"There's my girl," said Atticus, lifting her into his arms to peals of delighted laughter. He kissed the disheveled mop of soft brown curls and settled her little body against his chest, heedless of the mess of pumpkin currently being smeared all over his coat. "Both my girls."

Elegy stood that she might receive her own kiss, and when Dorian began to wriggle with the usual impatience of a two-year-old, Atticus set her down to toddle on unsteady legs toward the grinning jack-o'-lanterns on the front porch. "Dada, look!"

"Wow," he said upon a laugh. "How many this year?"

"Twenty!" she shrieked, holding up three fingers.

"Are these all from the garden?" asked Atticus as he bent to gather the corners of the garbage bag Elegy had been using to collect the pumpkin innards, save those currently decorating their daughter.

"Most of them. There were a few left at the nursery, and I didn't want them to go to waste."

"Who closed up today?"

"Martin, of course, and River."

"You still have that feeling about him?"

Elegy smiled.

When Seeds of Love did not fold after its first year in the way most new business ventures did and rather became a resounding success, she'd hired on two new boys, Ethan and River, who attended university and spent their summers hauling and watering and trimming plants. A fledgling football player, Ethan better resembled a small mountain and consumed his weight in calories, while River, with his thatch of unruly red hair and overlarge nose, was as nimble and spry as his name suggested (and it suggested quite a bit more, though only Elegy was apt to notice). When Atticus had first met him, he'd thought it terribly amusing that she'd hired someone who could hardly lift a large ceramic pot, but River had gained some strength in his spindly arms since, and besides, Elegy had known the moment she'd met him that the plants in his care would thrive in another way.

He talked to them.

Ethan—as well as everyone else under Elegy's employment—had made enormous fun of him for it at first, but even the most wretched of plants thrived under his tender ministrations, though not a one of them could make out what he said that affected them so. They were not historical speeches of great import or sonnets written by English dramaturges or even the entrée section of a beloved local restaurant. No, he simply spoke of his day; simple observations and ponderings such as the things he'd done and the places he'd gone, the meals he'd eaten and with whom he'd eaten them.

And no matter how dreadful their state, they were soon set to rights after a few idle conversations.

"Will you ever tell him, do you think?" Atticus asked, as Elegy placed a candle inside each jack-o'-lantern and positioned them just so before she began to light their little flames.

"Someday, perhaps. I don't think he wants for knowing it."

"Dada," said Dorian, pulling on her father's hand. "*Cat*."

Atticus laughed and allowed himself to be pulled over the threshold, and once the last candle was aglow, Elegy followed and closed the door behind them.

Their home was as unlike Thorne Hall as it was possible to be, most of all because no one had ever lived in it before. Resolute that Elegy should never have to wonder and worry over what stains might've been left by those before, canny or no, Atticus had insisted on tearing down the neglected, moss-stricken split-level squatting on the piece of waterfront land he'd so desperately coveted and begun designing the sprawling ranch with its vaulted ceilings and vast banks of windows. Elegy had been determined to start afresh in her new home with its gleaming darkwood floors and neutral palate, but then she'd encountered an ornate eight-pane slag-glass lamp with a spelter base in a little antique store in Belltown, and so great was the ache behind her breastbone at the sight of it, so similar to the one that had been on the little table by the hearth in the great hall, she'd not been able to resist. A gilded mirror soon followed that, and then a white ironstone pitcher, a brass candelabra, a tapestry.

As in most things, Atticus indulged her quiet way of honoring her past, particularly when, for their first anniversary, he'd blindfolded and led her into the room off the foyer they'd fashioned into a parlor, and when he removed the cloth with a flourish, she found two yellow tufted velvet chairs standing before the gas fireplace.

The owner of the Queen Anne had charged him twice their value, to say nothing of the exorbitant cost of shipping the pair of them from Lenox to Seattle, but when she scrambled into the chair to the left, hooking her legs over the curved back and grinning upside down at him like a fool, he'd declared hoarsely that they'd been worth every penny. Then he kissed her absolutely senseless.

She was as enamored of the grounds as by the house.

An enormous set of sliding glass barn doors led to a flagstone patio strung with lights, and then to a wide lawn lined with fragrant evergreens. It sloped down, gently giving way to rock and sand and, finally, the ocean beyond, where they took walks most evenings even in poor weather, Dorian collecting sea glass and shells as she went, tiptoeing to the edge of the water, then darting back shrieking in laughter when a playful wave dared come too close.

And best of all, at least where Elegy was concerned, was the garden—her dream come to life at last. Surrounded by a handsome wrought-iron fence and not a brick wall, during the harvest season it overflowed with all manner of vegetables: beans and tomatoes trained to climb trellises; carrots and beets and onions and celery in neat, orderly rows; fountains of kale and chard; stalks of brussels sprouts and bunches of broccoli. There were even potatoes she'd learned to grow in wine barrels and, of course, canes of fruit: blackberries, raspberries, and several blueberry bushes that Dorian loved to sit underneath as she ate the sun-warmed jewels by the handful. Elegy also grew a small cut-flower garden and, beside it, a small patch for pumpkins and other such gourds.

There was a little orchard to one side of the garden and to the other a chicken coop, where their three hens had likely shut themselves away already, cooing and drowsing around the heat lamp.

And beside it, in neat and tidy rows and yielding fruit enough for several cases of truly mediocre wine, Muscadine vines flourished from the seeds Elegy had taken from her father's garden.

Elegy could most often be found there no matter how poor the weather, singing to herself and pulling weeds, gently guiding the vines and tying up the gourds when they grew too heavy for their trellises to support them, tilling and treating the soil. Sometimes she curled up on one of the benches and read a book or flipped through seed catalogs and scribbled ideas for the nursery in a worn leather journal. And other times she simply walked carefully between the rows and breathed in the heady aroma of mint and lavender and fennel, her feet bare and her overalls rolled up past the ankle, her hair loose and woven through with chamomile.

Dorian toddled into the sitting room, presumably to smear pumpkin all over the cat, who was curled up on one of the armchairs by the fire, far too rotund and lazy to bother removing herself. As Atticus hung his wool overcoat in the foyer, his eyes fell upon a parcel beside a pitcher full to bursting with the last of the rudbeckia Elegy had picked that morning. That the cheerful sprays of yellow with their black centers meant justice was apt, considering the date.

"What's this?" He took it up, turning it this way and that until he could properly read the return address. "It's from Lenox."

"Yes."

"You haven't opened it."

"Later, perhaps."

A frown appeared between Atticus's brows, and gently she took the package from his hands and set it back upon the table. He set his cheek against the crown of her head and murmured, "How are you, sweetheart?"

The Spirit Collection of Thorne Hall

He asked her every year, and upon each occasion she smoothed away his frown with her thumb and then a kiss.

"I'm fine, I promise."

She'd set a stew to simmer upon the stove earlier that afternoon, and after a vigorous stirring she added a few more pinches of this and handfuls of that, then shed her overalls in favor of a pair of leggings and a soft, oversized tunic. Piling her hair atop her head, she padded back down the hall to help her husband.

Atticus had filled the claw-foot tub and was in the process of wrangling their daughter into it. Bath time with Dorian was always a messy affair—sometimes more water and lavender-scented bubbles ending up outside the tub than in it—but Elegy had a feeling he would need to drain the water several times before their daughter was well and truly clean.

"Are you sure you don't want to come with us?" asked Atticus afterward as they dressed Dorian in the cat costume Elegy had sewn herself. "We won't be gone long, so you'll hardly miss any of them."

She wrinkled her nose in reply. "You know I don't like to miss *any* of them."

Having never received a single trick-or-treater at Thorne Hall, Elegy was quite enamored of the little ghosts and ghouls and princesses and superheroes that came begging for sweets, and she rewarded them with handfuls of candy into their little buckets.

But that evening she had another reason entirely for wanting a moment to herself, and so with kisses for each, she sent husband and daughter out into the misty evening air fragrant with the sweet tang of woodsmoke and emptied bowl after bowl into the cheerful orange buckets of the children in their neighborhood.

When the house stood still and quiet at last and she was, at least for the moment, alone, Elegy looked to the package lying quite innocuously upon the foyer table.

She poured herself a generous glass of red wine and took it and the package into the sitting room, where she curled up in her chair, drained the entire glass in one go, then tore open the brown paper.

Out fluttered a letter.

Dearest Elegy,

> *My dear, dear Mrs. Hart. I hope that you are well, that you and your husband and delicious daughter are well—give her a kiss, one for all of us!*

J. Ann Thomas

Even though I was tasked with putting these words to paper, I speak for us all—for Brio and Thistle and Winter. We miss you more than words can say or songs can impart.

The enclosed was found in the pages of one of Dorian's books only just opened the other day in search of a cantrip. (A fluffle of rabbits have quite overtaken poor Mrs. Musgrove's garden, and Dorian was always so much better at natural craft.) I think he might've placed it there and forgotten about it, or perhaps he knew one day I might come looking for just such a bit of craft and that it must be there when I did. Who can say, with canny? But I am very glad that it has come to me, so that I can pass it on to you.

With all our love,
Mavis

With shaking hands Elegy opened the parcel to reveal a black-and-white photograph within a handsome wood frame.

He was a great deal younger than the last time she'd seen him, but it was unmistakably Dorian Everwood who stared back at her from the photograph. And beside him was her mother. They were sitting together upon a blanket, and Elegy recognized at once the place with its sloping lawns and view of the Painted Grove beyond.

With one arm Dorian held the camera up and away against the late-afternoon sun, and with the other he cradled her mother; no, he cradled them both, their entwined fingers resting upon the gentle curve of Tabitha's stomach where her daughter grew. And Elegy knew at once by the joy in their eyes and their smiles that they'd known she was theirs.

For a very long time Elegy could do nothing but stare at the photograph in her hand, taking in each and every detail: her mother's dark hair braided in a coronet atop her head, a few errant strands escaping to curl around the high neck of an ivory lace afternoon dress with a wide satin sash that, even though the photograph revealed no color, Elegy knew was the color of forget-me-nots, for she had worn the dress herself upon more than one occasion when the weather was fine. Dorian's homespun shirt with a pattern of ivy embroidered upon the collar.

The little dish of strawberries upon the blanket beside them.

She set the photograph gently back inside its packaging, then fetched a hammer and nail from one of Atticus's toolboxes in the garage, poured herself another glass of wine, and stood in front of a very particular wall in the foyer.

The Spirit Collection of Thorne Hall

Dozens upon dozens of photographs of varying sizes in frames each as wildly different as the next formed a collage of their lives since they'd left Thorne Hall six years ago.

It had not happened right away; there was, after all, the matter of two men lying dead in the ballroom—an unfortunate ritualistic murder-suicide gone wrong, or so they'd told the police. It pained Elegy to paint either Thaddeus or Dorian as a murderer, for neither was responsible for the cuts upon her wrist, but to admit she'd done it to herself would've seen her sent straight to the nearest asylum for observation. Thaddeus was eventually buried in the graveyard alongside his forebears, and Dorian's remains were given into the care of Winter and Mavis. He was laid to rest in the Lenox cemetery beneath a great yew tree with the rest of his family; all save Sparrow, of course.

Her bones rested in the graveyard of Thorne Hall, covered in anemone flowers.

Once the police had gone, the lawyers descended—and after a great deal of blustering over the state of Thaddeus's last will and testament, the lot of it had gone to Elegy.

She did not want it; nor did Fletcher.

Her stepmother did, however, take with her a trunk full of silk dressing gowns, her unfinished novel, and a cache of jewels that Floss helped her sell at a private auction at Sotheby's. The proceeds purchased and restored a historic factory in downtown Portland where Fletcher opened a lounge in which local artists displayed their work and musicians took the stage and hipster mixologists experimented with scented smoke and rock candy and pickled *everything*. There were poetry readings and philosophical discussions, rallies and book signings, and Fletcher at last had the salon she'd hoped Thorne Hall might be so many years before.

Elegy smiled at a photograph of her stepmother during the renovations, in coveralls with a brightly colored scarf that barely contained her frizzy curls, straddling a beam with a cigar poking out of her mouth. Beside it was another taken the night of her grand opening. Standing between Elegy and Atticus, her stepmother was resplendent in emerald green, her smile lush and brilliant and unfettered at last, lacquered in rust.

Elegy let her eyes drift to photographs of Hugo and Sebastian on their wedding day, and several more on each European tour they'd taken since, the two of them sun kissed and endlessly fashionable, posing outrageously in this Parisian café or poolside at that Tuscan villa and so forth. Hugo's parents had, as predicted, cut him off without a cent, and when he attempted to drown his sorrows in a Sbagliato on the balcony of their suite in a posh hotel in the French Riviera, Sebastian had captured a series of photos that led to a flourishing career in travel blogging for the blissful couple.

Phineas and Lavinia Prescott had not attended their son's wedding, nor had they welcomed the happy couple to Brightleigh, and as such the happy couple rarely visited the Berkshires, particularly after Floss officially called it quits with Conrad and made Boston her permanent home, but even when they did come, when any of them came, they did not visit Thorne Hall.

Atticus had been right, in the end: Thorne Hall ought to have been a museum, and so a museum it became.

Elegy gifted the house and its contents to the Lenox Historical Society, all save the wardrobe, which went to the Metropolitan Museum of Art's Costume Institute. Selling off some of the land had yielded enough funds to repair the third floor and the roof, and the museum opened its doors two years later. A photograph of its grand opening had been sent to her as well, the staff posing awkwardly beneath the porte cochere and, inside the wide-open doors, a gleaming mahogany desk laden with brochures waiting to greet guests wishing to tour the once-shuttered house that had held darkness and death and secrets within. The tour guides put their own spin on it, mostly to do with Jasper and his infamous Samhain séance that might or might not have actually happened; but as a stipulation of Elegy's gifting the manor to the historical society, they were expressly forbidden both from discussing the events of six years ago and from speaking of Thorne Hall's recent residents whatsoever.

And as for Elegy Thorne . . .

She'd fled her ancestral home with only a few crumbling documents and the terrifying, exhilarating task of forging life anew.

Once they'd arrived in Seattle, Atticus had been beside himself at first, insisting Elegy live with his mother in a sweet but misguided attempt at avoiding a potential case of Stockholm syndrome, but it proved a tedious arrangement due to the fact that Elegy could not sleep a wink when she was alone in bed (and it would have been terribly awkward to ask Mrs. Hart to push over and let her climb under her covers with her), and so she stayed over with Atticus and he with her as often as if they'd just disregarded such nonsense and lived together the way Elegy had expected they would the moment she'd boarded the train in New York that would take her all the way across the country.

The Spirit Collection of Thorne Hall

She loved him all the more for his stubborn insistence that the choice was hers, that wholly and completely and with no strings attached he would help her to go anywhere, do anything, be anything, she had only to ask, but her answer would have been the same if they'd lived apart one night or one hundred: her choice was him, and she'd wasted enough time living a life she'd not chosen.

To that end, there was a great deal of learning involved.

Ordinary things like using a washer and dryer, cooking, and getting an actual driver's license (who on earth would have dared pull her over in Lenox, given her father's reputation, to say nothing of the fact that she fastidiously obeyed every traffic law to a fault?), as well as more monumental occasions such as flying on a plane for the first time or receiving her long-coveted college education.

Elegy approached it all with solemn and steadfast determination, and Atticus documented it all, every moment, however tedious, and especially those that were exultant, each triumph and accomplishment and dream fulfilled.

There they were on their wedding day, blissful smiles upon both of their faces and a large bouquet of fragrant summer flowers crushed between them. They'd married in their own backyard, frills and frippery be damned, with only a few dozen of their closest friends and family as witnesses. Under the stars and to the sound of the gently lapping waves, they'd danced and laughed and kissed the night away.

There were photographs of her first day of class studying horticulture at the university and of the day of her graduation, with her gold hood and honors cords draped around her neck. Of the day she opened Seeds of Love, and the day Atticus and his company received an Innovation in Sustainable Engineering award for his work in tidal energy.

Of their travels, from sun-drenched and sand-swept Egypt to the rainy highlands of Scotland, white sand beaches and turquoise waters, the ruins of great temples; galleries and museums, concert halls and cobblestone streets filled with cheerful little shops, lights twinkling beneath a fresh dusting of snow.

Of Elegy, pregnant and beaming, and of Dorian newly born, cradled in her mother's arms and against her father's chest. Photographs of the three of them as she grew.

They would continue to add their memories until the wall could no longer hold them, and then they would pick a new wall. There was, after all, such a terribly big world to see and ever so many things to do.

Atticus and Dorian returned as she was tilting the frame into place, bringing with them the chill of the autumn night and peals of sugar-soaked laughter, her daughter's rosebud mouth already smeared with chocolate.

Her husband wrapped his arms around her from behind, pulling her into the warmth and safety of his body as Dorian danced past on unsteady yet determined legs, careening into the parlor with her orange trick-or-treat bucket clutched to her chest. A series of small thumps and a delighted shout soon followed, said bucket having ostensibly been emptied over the coffee table.

"Oh, wow," breathed Atticus as he realized what it was Elegy had been staring at so intently. "They look happy."

"They do," she agreed.

"They knew."

"Yes. Yes, I think they did."

His hand slid around her waist to rest gently upon her stomach, as if he were remembering those months poised between terror and elation while they waited for Dorian to make their acquaintance, a child whose choices had not yet been made, whose life was hers to be most thoroughly and joyfully lived.

At the distant sound of the crinkling of wrappers, Atticus groaned into her neck.

"Go," Elegy said, nudging him gently. "Before she eats the lot of it."

Off he went, and then his gaze flickered to the photograph of her parents, then back to her and his eyes softened. "Are you coming?"

"Of course. Always."

Dorian's joyful shriek echoed down the hall, her husband's laughter followed, and there went Elegy's heart just as it always did; as it always would.

She took them in one last time, took *all* of them in, and she with them; the girl who had once been so much a ghost that an image of her had never before been captured stared back at her full to bursting with life such that frames could not contain it.

"Mama?" Dorian called from the sitting room. "Mama?"

"I'm coming," she answered. "I'm coming, my loves."

She pulled the delicate chains on the slag-glass lamp, dousing the foyer in darkness, and left the past be that she might dwell amongst the living.

ACKNOWLEDGMENTS

Elegy Thorne and her fifteen spirits needed a home; a grand Gilded Age mansion where time stood still, magic was real, and when the floorboards creaked in the dead of night one could almost believe the dead danced and played long games of whist within its walls.

First, I thought of the Hudson Valley. A beloved friend had married on Long Island some years before, and on a day trip to Sleepy Hollow (in which I might have broken the law by climbing over the fence of the Old Dutch Church Burying Ground to take a picture next to Washington Irving's grave), I fell in love with the lavish estates nestled within ancient woods and the tiny hamlets so steeped in folklore and mystery one could easily believe hauntings were a frequent and common occurrence.

But the moment I saw a photograph of Ventfort Hall, a Gilded Age Jacobean-style mansion in the small town of Lenox, Massachusetts, I knew that Elegy's story would take place in the Berkshires, 135.8 miles from where my mother was born in Tewksbury, a small suburb just outside of Boston.

I must emphatically state that Ventfort Hall is not haunted by fifteen ghosts, nor did a family named Thorne ever reside within its walls. In fact, the mansion was built by J.P. Morgan, famed American financier and investment banker, for his sister, Sarah and her husband,

George, in 1983. Elegy's story is entirely fictional; however, I wanted to portray her grand home and its contents as well as the nearby town and surrounding area as authentically as possible. Plenty of photographs and detailed blueprints of Ventfort Hall exist, and the wealth of information regarding the Child Ballads, perpetual pills, and the House of Worth available at my fingertips was staggering, but shortly after I began drafting the novel, I knew I needed to visit the mansion and the town of Lenox for myself.

After the Morgans' death, Ventfort Hall changed hands several times, even serving as the dormitories for the Tanglewood music students before a nursing home developer planned to demolish the building. In response, a local preservation group raised funds to purchase the property in 1997, restoring and reopening it as a Gilded Age museum, and it has been welcoming visitors and hosting events ever since.

My request to tour the property was answered by Kelly Blau, the president of the Ventfort Hall Association board. A fellow author herself, Kelly was warm and welcoming and happy to give me a tour of the mansion and share her vast knowledge, earned over twenty years of service.

I flew to Massachusetts, rented a 250-year-old Airbnb, and on a crisp, clear autumn morning, met Kelly beneath the porte cocher of Ventfort Hall.

Over the hours that followed, I was permitted to tour not only the fully restored first and second floors of the 28,000-square-foot "summer cottage," but also the basement and the third floor, off-limits to the public due to deterioration (a grant was awarded in 2023 to restore the roof and chimneys.) The house is a marvel, peerless in its beauty and craftsmanship and rich with history and lore, but even more remarkable was Kelly herself. We spoke of the Morgans, of the design and construction of the house and grounds, and of the manners and customs of the Gilded Age, as well as of the town of Lenox and the history of the Berkshires as a wealthy getaway from the sweltering heat of New York and Boston in the summer.

And toward the end of our time together, after I'd seen every plaster mold and methane lamp and stained-glass window, we sat together in the corridor outside Sarah Morgan's office and I simply listened, insatiable for Kelly's stories and the way history came alive in her thoughtful, measured way of speaking.

Places like Ventfort Hall hold more than just history within their walls; they hold memory and stories, and in the absence of ghosts it falls

The Spirit Collection of Thorne Hall

to the living to preserve and pass them on to those who would listen. When it came time to say goodbye, Kelly told me how much it meant to her to share her love for Ventfort Hall and for the Berkshires with someone as genuinely interested in the past as she was. I thanked her, not only for the boundless wealth of information I now had with which to write Thorne the way I wanted to but also for one of the most genuinely fascinating and moving experiences of my life.

Time passed, I wrote, and when I found out *The Spirit Collection of Thorne Hall* had been acquired by Holly Ingraham and the incredible team at Alcove Press, I reached out to Kelly to tell her the news. But my email was returned to me, the address no longer valid.

Kelly had passed away nearly a year to the day after I visited Lenox, and she never knew that I finished the book or that it would be published.

I wish she could have read it, could have known the impact that sharing her love of Ventfort, of the Morgans, and of history itself had on Elegy's story. Without Kelly, without her kindness and her generous spirit, Thorne Hall would not be Thorne Hall, and you, my dear readers, would be the poorer for it.

As for the living . . .

To my incredible agent, Rick Lewis, who championed this book and found it the perfect home. I am so glad you hit that *like* button all those years ago.

To my team: my editor at Alcove Press, Holly Ingraham; my copy editor, Rachel Keith; and Marisa Ware, who designed the beautiful cover. Thorne Hall could not possibly have been in safer or more trustworthy hands.

To Adam and Tomomi, who always put my books out on your coffee table when you have company, and to Maureen, who has loaned out her copies so many times they are falling apart. You are the best unofficial street team an author could ask for.

To my mother, who devoured an early draft of Thorne in a single day despite it taking me more than a year to write, then told me her only critique was that it wasn't nearly long enough. I can think of no greater compliment from the person whose opinion matters most. And no, dad, this is *not* a true story, although it does feature quite a few dark and stormy nights.

To my children, Lyn and Erin: you are my inspiration and my greatest adventure. Please stay courageous and joyful and strange forever.

J. Ann Thomas

And to Brian, the love of my life and my dearest friend . . . how do I begin to thank the person without whom this book would not exist? Through every long afternoon and late night, every moment in which you caught me staring off into space at dinner because I was plotting in my head, every tear, every smile, and every step however small, there has been you. There will always be you.

I adore you all more than I can ever express in words, though I will continue to strive for it with every book I write.